OTHER PEOPLE'S
MONEY

"We must hear what these two men are saying"

From a drawing by Victor Perard

OTHER PEOPLE'S MONEY

Translated from the French of

EMILE GABORIAU

WILDSIDE PRESS: MMIII

Published by
Wildside Press, LLC
P.O. Box 301
Holicong, PA 18928-0301 USA
www.wildsidepress.com

Wildside Press Edition: MMIII

OTHER PEOPLE'S MONEY

PART I.

I.

THERE is not, perhaps, in all Paris, a quieter street than the Rue St. Gilles in the Marais, within a step of the Place Royale. No carriages there; never a crowd. Hardly is the silence broken by the regulation drums of the Minims Barracks near by, by the chimes of the Church of St. Louis, or by the joyous clamors of the pupils of the Massin School during the hours of recreation.

At night, long before ten o'clock, and when the Boulevard Beaumarchais is still full of life, activity, and noise, every thing begins to close. One by one the lights go out, and the great windows with diminutive panes become dark. And if, after midnight, some belated citizen passes on his way home, he quickens his step, feeling lonely and uneasy, and apprehensive of the reproaches of his *concierge,* who is likely to ask him whence he may be coming at so late an hour.

In such a street, every one knows each other: houses have no mystery; families, no secrets,—a small town, where idle curiosity has always a corner of the veil slyly raised, where gossip flourishes as rankly as the grass on the street.

Thus on the afternoon of the 27th of April, 1872 (a Saturday), a fact which anywhere else might have passed unnoticed was attracting particular attention.

A man some thirty years of age, wearing the working livery of servants of the upper class,—the long striped waistcoat with sleeves, and the white linen apron,—was going from door to door.

"Who can the man be looking for?" wondered the idle neighbors, closely watching his evolutions.

He was not looking for any one. To such as he spoke to, he stated that he had been sent by a cousin of his, an excellent cook, who, before taking a place in the neighborhood, was anxious to have all possible information on the subject of her prospective masters. And then, "Do you know M. Vincent Favoral?" he would ask.

Concierges and shop-keepers knew no one better; for it was more than a quarter of a century before, that M. Vincent Favoral, the day after his wedding, had come to settle in the Rue St. Gilles; and there his two children were born,—his son M. Maxence, his daughter Mlle. Gilberte.

He occupied the second story of the house No. 38,— one of those old-fashioned dwellings, such as they build no more, since ground is sold at twelve hundred francs the square metre; in which there is no stinting of space. The stairs, with wrought iron balusters, are wide and easy, and the ceilings twelve feet high.

"Of course, we know M. Favoral," answered every one to the servant's questions; "and, if there ever was an honest man, why, he is certainly the one. There is a man whom you could trust with your funds, if you had

any, without fear of his ever running off to Belgium
with them." And it was further explained, that M.
Favoral was chief cashier, and probably, also, one of the
principal stockholders, of the Mutual Credit Society, one
of those admirable financial institutions which have
sprung up with the second empire, and which had won
at the Bourse the first installment of their capital, the
very day that the game of the *Coup d' Etat* was being
played in the street.

"I know well enough the gentleman's business," remarked the servant; "but what sort of a man is he?
That's what my cousin would like to know."

The wine-man at No. 43, the oldest shop-keeper in the
street, could best answer. A couple of *petits-verres*
politely offered soon started his tongue; and, whilst sip-
ping his Cognac:—

"M. Vincent Favoral," he began, "is a man some
fifty-two or three years old, but who looks younger, not
having yet a single gray hair. He is tall and thin, with
neatly-trimmed whiskers, thin lips, and small yellow
eyes; not talkative. It takes more ceremony to get a
word from his throat than a dollar from his pocket.
'Yes,' 'no,' 'good-morning,' 'good-evening;' that's
about the extent of his conversation. Summer and winter, he wears gray pantaloons, a long frock-coat, laced
shoes, and lisle-thread gloves. 'Pon my word, I should
say that he is still wearing the very same clothes I saw
upon his back for the first time in 1845, did I not know
that he has two full suits made every year by the *concierge* at No. 29, who is also a tailor."

"Why, he must be an old miser," muttered the servant.

"He is above all peculiar," continued the shop-keeper,
"like most men of figures, it seems. His own life is

ruled and regulated like the pages of his ledger. In the neighborhood they call him Old Punctuality; and, when he passes through the Rue Turenne, the merchants set their watches by him. Rain or shine, every morning of the year, on the stroke of nine, he appears at the door on the way to his office. When he returns, you may be sure it is between twenty and twenty-five minutes past five. At six he dines; at seven he goes to play a game of dominoes at the Café Turc; at ten he comes home and goes to bed; and, at the first stroke of eleven at the Church of St. Louis, out goes his candle."

" Hem ! " grumbled the servant with a look of contempt, " the question is, Will my cousin be willing to live with a man who is a sort of walking clock? "

" It isn't always pleasant," remarked the wine-man; " and the best evidence is, that the son, M. Maxence, got tired of it."

" He does not live with his parents any more? "

" He dines with them; but he has his own lodgings on the Boulevard du Temple. The falling-out made talk enough at the time; and some people do say that M. Maxence is a worthless scamp, who leads a very dissipated life; but I say that his father kept him too close. The boy is twenty-five, quite good looking, and has a very stylish mistress: I have seen her. . . . I would have done just as he did."

" And what about the daughter, Mlle. Gilberte? "

" She is not married yet, although she is past twenty, and pretty as a rosebud. After the war, her father tried to make her marry a stock-broker, a stylish man who always came in a two-horse carriage; but she refused him outright. I should not be a bit surprised to hear that she has some love-affair of her own. I have noticed lately a young gentleman about here who looks up quite suspiciously when he goes by No. 38." The servant did not seem to find these particulars very interesting.

"It's the lady," he said, "that my cousin would like to know most about."

"Naturally. Well, you can safely tell her that she never will have had a better mistress. Poor Madame Favoral! She must have had a sweet time of it with her maniac of a husband! But she is not young any more; and people get accustomed to every thing, you know. The days when the weather is fine, I see her going by with her daughter to the Place Royale for a walk. That's about their only amusement."

"The mischief!" said the servant, laughing. "If that is all, she won't ruin her husband, will she?"

"That is all," continued the shop-keeper, "or rather, excuse me, no: every Saturday, for many years, M. and Mme. Favoral receive a few of their friends: M. and Mme. Desclavettes, retired dealers in bronzes, Rue Turenne; M. Chapelain, the old lawyer from the Rue St. Antoine, whose daughter is Mlle. Gilberte's particular friend; M. Desormeaux, head clerk in the Department of Justice; and three or four others; and as this just happens to be Saturday "—

But here he stopped short, and pointing towards the street,—

"Quick," said he, "look! Speaking of the—you know— It is twenty minutes past five, there is M. Favoral coming home."

It was, in fact, the cashier of the Mutual Credit Society, looking very much indeed as the shop-keeper had described him. Walking with his head down, he seemed to be seeking upon the pavement the very spot upon which he had set his foot in the morning, that he might set it back again there in the evening.

With the same methodical step, he reached his house, walked up the two pairs of stairs, and, taking out his pass-key, opened the door of his apartment.

The dwelling was fit for the man; and every thing, from the very hall, betrayed his peculiarities. There, evidently, every piece of furniture must have its invaria- ble place, every object its irrevocable shelf or hook. All around were evidences, if not exactly of poverty, at least of small means, and of the artifices of a respectable econ- omy. Cleanliness was carried to its utmost limits: every thing shone. Not a detail but betrayed the industrious hand of the housekeeper, struggling to defend her furni- ture against the ravages of time. The velvet on the chairs was darned at the angles as with the needle of a fairy. Stitches of new worsted showed through the faded designs on the hearth-rugs. The curtains had been turned so as to display their least worn side.

All the guests enumerated by the shop-keeper, and a few others besides, were in the parlor when M. Favoral came in.

But, instead of returning their greeting,—

" Where is Maxence? " he inquired.

" I am expecting him, my dear," said Mme. Favoral gently.

" Always behind time," he scolded. " It is too tri- fling."

His daughter, Mlle. Gilberte, interrupted him,—

" Where is my bouquet, father? " she asked.

M. Favoral stopped short, struck his forehead, and with the accent of a man who reveals something incredi- ble, prodigious, unheard of,—

" Forgotten," he answered, scanning the syllables: " I have for-got-ten it."

It was a fact. Every Saturday, on his way home, he

was in the habit of stopping at the old woman's shop in front of the Church of St. Louis, and buying a bouquet for Mlle. Gilberte. And to-day—

"Ah! I catch you this time, father!" exclaimed the girl.

Meantime, Mme. Favoral, whispering to Mme. Desclavettes,—

"Positively," she said in a troubled voice, "something serious must have happened to my husband. He to forget! He to fail in one of his habits! It is the first time in twenty-six years."

The appearance of Maxence at this moment prevented her from going on. M. Favoral was about to administer a sound reprimand to his son, when dinner was announced.

"Come," exclaimed M. Chapelain, the old lawyer, the conciliating man *par excellence,*—"come, let us to the table."

They sat down. But Mme. Favoral had scarcely helped the soup, when the bell rang violently. Almost at the same moment the servant appeared, and announced,

"The Baron de Thaller!"

More pale than his napkin, the cashier stood up.

"The manager," he stammered, "the director of the Mutual Credit Society."

II.

CLOSE upon the heels of the servant M. de Thaller came.

Tall, thin, stiff, he had a very small head, a flat face, pointed nose, and long reddish whiskers, slightly shaded with silvery threads, falling half-way down his chest. Dressed in the latest style, he wore a loose overcoat of rough material, pantaloons that spread nearly to the tip of his boots, a wide shirt-collar turned over a light cravat, on the bow of which shone a large diamond, and a tall hat with rolled brims.

With a blinking glance, he made a rapid estimate of the dining-room, the shabby furniture, and the guests seated around the table. Then, without even condescending to touch his hat, with his large hand tightly fitted into a lavender glove, in a brief and imperious tone, and with a slight accent which he affirmed was the Alsatian accent,—

"I must speak with you, Vincent," said he to his cashier, "alone and at once."

M. Favoral made visible efforts to conceal his anxiety.

"You see," he commenced, "we are dining with a few friends, and "—

"Do you wish me to speak in presence of everybody?" interrupted harshly the manager of the Mutual Credit.

The cashier hesitated no longer. Taking up a candle from the table, he opened the door leading to the parlor, and, standing respectfully to one side,—

"Be kind enough to pass on, sir," said he: "I follow you."

And, at the moment of disappearing himself,—

"Continue to dine without me," said he to his guests, with a last effort at self-control. "I shall soon catch up with you. This will take but a moment. Do not be uneasy in the least."

They were not uneasy, but surprised, and, above all, shocked at the manners of M. de Thaller.

"What a brute!" muttered Mme. Desclavettes.

M. Desormeaux, the head clerk at the Department of Justice, was an old legitimist, much imbued with re-actionary ideas.

"Such are our masters," said he with a sneer, "the high barons of financial feudality. Ah! you are indignant at the arrogance of the old aristocracy; well, on your knees, by Jupiter! on your face, rather, before the golden crown on field of gules."

No one replied: every one was trying his best to hear.

In the parlor, between M. Favoral and M. de Thaller, a discussion of the utmost violence was evidently going on. To seize the meaning of it was not possible; and yet through the door, the upper panels of which were of glass, fragments could be heard; and from time to time such words distinctly reached the ear as dividend, stockholders, deficit, millions, etc.

"What can it all mean? great heaven!" moaned Mme. Favoral.

Doubtless the two interlocutors, the director and the cashier, had drawn nearer to the door of communication; for their voices, which rose more and more, had now become quite distinct.

"It is an infamous trap!" M. Favoral was saying. "I should have been notified "—

"Come, come," interrupted the other. "Were you not fully warned? did I ever conceal any thing from you?"

Fear, a fear vague still, and unexplained, was slowly taking possession of the guests; and they remained motionless, their forks in suspense, holding their breath.

"Never," M. Favoral was repeating, stamping his foot so violently that the partition shook,—"never, never!"

"And yet it must be," declared M. de Thaller. "It is the only, the last resource "—

"And suppose I will not!"

"Your will has nothing to do with it now. It is twenty years ago that you might have willed, or not willed. But listen to me, and let us reason a little."

Here M. de Thaller dropped his voice; and for some minutes nothing was heard in the dining-room, except confused words, and incomprehensible exclamations, until suddenly,—

"That is ruin," he resumed in a furious tone: "it is bankruptcy on the last of the month."

"Sir," the cashier was replying,—" sir!"

"You are a forger, M. Vincent Favoral; you are a thief!"

Maxence leaped from his seat.

"I shall not permit my father to be thus insulted in his own house," he exclaimed.

"Maxence," begged Mme. Favoral, "my son!"

The old lawyer, M. Chapelain, held him by the arm; but he struggled hard, and was about to burst into the parlor, when the door opened, and the director of the Mutual Credit stepped out.

With a coolness quite remarkable after such a scene, he advanced towards Mlle. Gilberte, and, in a tone of offensive protection,—

"Your father is a wretch, mademoiselle," he said; "and my duty should be to surrender him at once into the hands of justice. On account of your worthy mother, however, of your father himself, above all, on your own account, mademoiselle, I shall forbear doing so. But let him fly, let him disappear, and never more be heard from."

He drew from his pocket a roll of bank-notes, and, throwing them upon the table,—

"Hand him this," he added. "Let him leave this very night. The police may have been notified. There is a train for Brussels at five minutes past eleven."

And, having bowed, he withdrew, no one addressing him a single word, so great was the astonishment of all the guests of this house, heretofore so peaceful.

Overcome with stupor, Maxence had dropped upon his chair. Mlle. Gilberte alone retained some presence of mind.

"It is a shame," she exclaimed, "for us to give up thus! That man is an impostor, a wretch; he lies! Father, father!"

M. Favoral had not waited to be called, and was standing up against the parlor-door, pale as death, and yet calm.

"Why attempt any explanations?" he said. "The money is gone; and appearances are against me."

His wife had drawn near to him, and taken his hand.

"The misfortune is immense," she said, "but not irreparable. We will sell everything we have."

"Have you not friends? Are we not here," insisted the others,—M. Desclavettes, M. Desormeaux, and M. Chapelain.

Gently he pushed his wife aside, and coldly.

"All we had," he said, "would be as a grain of sand in an ocean. But we have no longer anything; we are ruined."

"Ruined!" exclaimed M. Desormeaux,—"ruined! And where are the forty-five thousand francs I placed into your hands?"

He made no reply.

"And our hundred and twenty thousand francs?" groaned M. and Mme. Desclavettes.

"And my sixty thousand francs?" shouted M. Chapelain, with a blasphemous oath.

The cashier shrugged his shoulders.

"Lost," he said, "irrevocably lost!"

Then their rage exceeded all bounds. Then they forgot that this unfortunate man had been their friend for twenty years, that they were his guests; and they commenced heaping upon him threats and insults without name.

He did not even deign to defend himself.

"Go on," he uttered, "go on. When a poor dog, carried away by the current, is drowning, men of heart cast stones at him from the bank. Go on!"

"You should have told us that you speculated," screamed M. Desclavettes.

On hearing these words, he straightened himself up, and with a gesture so terrible that the others stepped back frightened.

"What!" said he, in a tone of crushing irony, "it is this evening only, that you discover that I speculated? Kind friends! Where, then, and in whose pockets, did you suppose I was getting the enormous interests I have been paying you for years? Where have you ever seen honest money, the money of labor, yield twelve or fourteen per cent? The money that yields thus is the money of the gaming table, the money of the *bourse*. Why did you bring me your funds? Because you were fully satisfied that I knew how to handle the cards. Ah! If I was to tell you that I had doubled your capital, you would not ask how I did it, nor whether I had stocked the cards. You would virtuously pocket the money. But I have lost: I am a thief. Well, so be it. But, then, you

are all my accomplices. It is the avidity of the dupes
which induces the trickery of the sharpers."

Here he was interrupted by the servant coming in.
" Sir," she exclaimed excitedly, " O sir ! the courtyard
is full of police agents. They are speaking to the *concierge*. They are coming up stairs : I hear them ! "

III.

ACCORDING to the time and place where they are uttered, there are words which acquire a terrible signifi-
cance. In this disordered room, in the midst of these excited people, that word, the " police," sounded like a
thunderclap.

" Do not open," Maxence ordered ; " do not open,
however they may ring or knock. Let them burst the
door first."

The very excess of her fright restored to Mme. Favoral a portion of her energy. Throwing herself before
her husband as if to protect him, as if to defend him,—

" They are coming to arrest you, Vincent," she exclaimed. " They are coming ; don't you hear them ? "

He remained motionless, his feet seemingly riveted to
the floor.

" That is as I expected," he said.

And with the accent of the wretch who sees all hope
vanish, and who utterly gives up all struggle,—

" Be it so," he said. " Let them arrest me, and let all
be over at once. I have had enough anxiety, enough un-
bearable alternatives. I am tired always to feign, to deceive, and to lie. Let them arrest me ! Any misfortune
will be smaller in reality than the horrors of uncertainty.

I have nothing more to fear now. For the first time in many years I shall sleep to-night."

He did not notice the sinister expression of his guests.

" You think I am a thief," he added: " well, be satisfied, justice shall be done."

But he attributed to them sentiments which were no longer theirs. They had forgotten their anger, and their bitter resentment for their lost money.

The imminence of the peril awoke suddenly in their souls the memories of the past, and that strong affection which comes from long habit, and a constant exchange of services rendered. Whatever M. Favoral might have done, they only saw in him now the friend, the host whose bread they had broken together more than a hundred times, the man whose probity, up to this fatal night, had remained far above suspicion.

Pale, excited, they crowded around him.

" Have you lost your mind?" spoke M. Desormeaux. " Are you going to wait to be arrested, thrown into prison, dragged into a criminal court?"

He shook his head, and in a tone of idiotic obstinacy,—

" Have I not told you," he repeated, " that every thing is against me? Let them come; let them do what they please with me."

" And your wife," insisted M. Chapelain, the old lawyer, " and your children!"

" Will they be any the less dishonored if I am condemned by default?"

Wild with grief, Mme. Favoral was wringing her hands.

" Vincent," she murmured, " in the name of Heaven, spare us the harrowing agony to have you in prison."

Obstinately he remained silent. His daughter, Mlle.

Gilberte, dropped upon her knees before him, and, joining her hands,—

"I beseech you, father," she begged.

He shuddered all over. An unspeakable expression of ⌡ suffering and anguish contracted his features; and, speaking in a scarcely intelligible voice,—

"Ah! you are cruelly protracting my agony," he · stammered. "What do you ask of me?"

"You must fly," declared M. Desclavettes.

"Which way? How? Do you not think that every precaution has been taken, that every issue is closely watched?"

Maxence interrupted him with a gesture,—

"The windows in sister's room, father," said he, "open upon the courtyard of the adjoining house."

"Yes; but here we are up two pairs of stairs."

"No matter: I have a way."

And turning towards his sister,—

"Come, Gilberte," went on the young man, "give me a light, and let me have some sheets."

They went out hurriedly. Mme. Favoral felt a gleam of hope.

"We are saved!" she said.

"Saved!" repeated the cashier mechanically.

"Yes; for I guess Maxence's idea. But we must have an understanding. Where will you take refuge?"

"How can I tell?"

"There is a train at five minutes past eleven," remarked M. Desormeaux. "Don't let us forget that."

"But money will be required to leave by that train," interrupted the old lawyer. "Fortunately, I have some."

And, forgetting his hundred and sixty thousand francs lost, he took out his pocket-book. Mme. Favoral stopped him. "We have more than we need," said she.

She took from the table, and held out to her husband, the roll of bank-notes which the director of the Mutual Credit Society had thrown down before going.

He refused them with a gesture of rage.

" Rather starve to death ! " he exclaimed.   " 'Tis he, 'tis that wretch "—

But he interrupted himself, and more gently,—

" Put away those bank-bills," said he to his wife, " and let Maxence take them back to M. de Thaller to-morrow."

The bell rang violently.

" The police ! " groaned Mme. Desclavettes, who seemed on the point of fainting away.

" I am going to negotiate," said M. Desormeaux. " Fly, Vincent : do not lose a minute."

And he ran to the front-door, whilst Mme. Favoral was hurrying her husband towards Mlle. Gilberte's room.

Rapidly and stoutly Maxence had fastened four sheets together by the ends, which gave a more than sufficient length.   Then, opening the window, he examined carefully the courtyard of the adjoining house.

" No one," said he : " everybody is at dinner.   We'll succeed."

M. Favoral was tottering like a drunken man.   A terrible emotion convulsed his features.   Casting a long look upon his wife and children,—

" O Lord ! " he murmured, " what will become of you ? "

" Fear nothing, father," uttered Maxence.   " I am here.   Neither my mother nor my sister will want for any thing."

" My son ! " resumed the cashier, " my children ! "

Then, with a choking voice,—

"I am worthy neither of your love nor your devotion, wretch that I am! I made you lead a miserable existence, spend a joyless youth. I imposed upon you every trial of poverty, whilst I—And now I leave you nothing but ruin and a dishonored name."

"Make haste, father," interrupted Mlle. Gilberte.

It seemed as if he could not make up his mind.

"It is horrible to abandon you thus. What a parting! Ah! death would indeed be far preferable: What will you think of me? I am very guilty, certainly, but not as you think. I have been betrayed, and I must suffer for all. If at least you knew the whole truth. But will you ever know it? We will never see each other again."

Desperately his wife clung to him.

"Do not speak thus," she said. "Wherever you may find an asylum, I will join you. Death alone can separate us. What do I care what you may have done, or what the world will say? I am your wife. Our children will come with me. If necessary, we will emigrate to America; we'll change our name; we will work."

The knocks on the outer door were becoming louder and louder; and M. Desormeaux's voice could be heard, endeavoring to gain a few moments more.

"Come," said Maxence, "you cannot hesitate any longer."

And, overcoming his father's reluctance, he fastened one end of the sheets around his waist.

"I am going to let you down, father," said he; "and, as soon as you touch the ground, you must undo the knot. Take care of the first-story windows; beware of the *concierge;* and, once in the street, don't walk too fast. Make for the Boulevard, where you will be sooner lost in the crowd."

The knocks had now become violent blows; and it was evident that the door would soon be broken in, if M. Desormeaux did not make up his mind to open it.

The light was put out. With the assistance of his daughter, M. Favoral lifted himself upon the window-sill, whilst Maxence held the sheets with both hands.

" I beseech you, Vincent," repeated Mme. Favoral, " write to us. We shall be in mortal anxiety until we hear of your safety."

Maxence let the sheets slip slowly: in two seconds M. Favoral stood on the pavement below.

" All right," he said.

The young man drew the sheets back rapidly, and threw them under the bed. But Mlle. Gilberte remained long enough at the window to recognize her father's voice asking the *concierge* to open the door, and to hear the heavy gate of the adjoining house closing behind him.

" Saved ! " she said.

It was none too soon. M. Desormeaux had just been compelled to yield; and the commissary of police was walking in.

IV.

THE commissaries of police of Paris, as a general thing, are no simpletons; and, if they are ever taken in, it is because it has suited them to be taken in.

Their modest title covers the most important, perhaps, of magistracies, almost the only one known to the lower classes; an enormous power, and an influence so decisive, that the most sensible statesman of the reign of

Louis Philippe ventured once to say, " Give me twenty good commissaries of police in Paris, and I'll undertake to suppress any government: net profit, one hundred millions."

Parisian above all, the commissary has had ample time to study his ground when he was yet only a peace-officer. The dark side of the most brilliant lives has no mysteries for him. He has received the strangest confidences: he has listened to the most astounding confessions. He knows how low humanity can stoop, and what aberrations there are in brains apparently the soundest. The workwoman whom her husband beats, and the great lady whom her husband cheats, have both come to him. He has been sent for by the shop-keeper whom his wife deceives, and by the millionaire who has been blackmailed. To his office, as to a lay confessional, all passions fatally lead. In his presence the dirty linen of two millions of people is washed *en famille*.

A Paris commissary of police, who after ten years' practice, could retain an illusion, believe in something, or be astonished at any thing in the world, would be but a fool. If he is still capable of some emotion, he is a good man.

The one who had just walked into M. Favoral's apartment was already past middle age, colder than ice, and yet kindly, but of that commonplace kindliness which frightens like the executioner's politeness at the scaffold.

He required but a single glance of his small but clear eyes to decipher the physiognomies of all these worthy people standing around the disordered table.

And beckoning to the agents who accompanied him to stop at the door,—

" Monsieur Vincent Favoral? " he inquired.

The cashier's guests, M. Desormeaux excepted,

seemed stricken with stupor. Each one felt as if he had a share of the disgrace of this police invasion. The dupes who are sometimes caught in clandestine " hells " have the same humiliated attitudes.

At last, and not without an effort,—

" M. Favoral is no longer here," replied M. Chapelain, the old lawyer.

The commissary of police started.

Whilst they were discussing with him through the door, he had perfectly well understood that they were only trying to gain time; and, if he had not at once burst in the door, it was solely owing to his respect for M. Desormeaux himself, whom he knew personally, and still more for his title of head clerk at the Department of Justice. But his suspicions did not extend beyond the destruction of a few compromising papers. Whereas, in fact,—

" You have helped M. Favoral to escape, gentlemen ? " said he.

No one replied.

" Silence means assent," he added. " Very well: which way did he get off ? "

Still no answer. M. Desclavettes would have been glad to add something to the forty-five thousand francs he had just lost, to be, together with Mme. Desclavettes, a hundred miles away.

" Where is Mme. Favoral ? " resumed the commissary, evidently well informed. " Where are Mlle. Gilberte and M. Maxence Favoral ? "

They continued silent. No one in the dining-room knew what might have taken place in the other room; and a single word might be treason.

The commissary then became impatient.

" Take up a light," said he to one of the agents who

had remained at the door, "and follow me. We shall see."

And without a shadow of hesitation, for it seems to be the privilege of police-agents to be at home everywhere, he crossed the parlor, and reached Mlle. Gilberte's room just as she was withdrawing from the window.

"Ah, it is that way he escaped!" he exclaimed.

He rushed to the window, and remained long enough leaning on his elbows to thoroughly examine the ground, and understand the situation of the apartment.

"It's evident," he said at last, "this window opens on the courtyard of the next house."

This was said to one of his agents, who bore an unmistakable resemblance to the servant who had been asking so many questions in the afternoon.

"Instead of gathering so much useless information," he added, "why did you not post yourself as to the outlets of the house?"

He was "sold;" and yet he manifested neither spite nor anger. He seemed in no wise anxious to run after the fugitive. Upon the features of Maxence and of Mlle. Gilberte, and more still in Mme. Favoral's eyes, he had read that it would be useless for the present.

"Let us examine the papers, then," said he.

"My husband's papers are all in his study," replied Mme. Favoral.

"Please lead me to it, madame."

The room which M. Favoral called loftily his study was a small room with a tile floor, white-washed walls, and meanly lighted through a narrow transom.

It was furnished with an old desk, a small wardrobe with grated door, a few shelves upon which were piled some bandboxes and bundles of old newspapers, and two or three deal chairs.

"Where are the keys?" inquired the commissary of police.

"My father always carries them in his pocket, sir," replied Maxence.

"Then let some one go for a locksmith."

Stronger than fear, curiosity had drawn all the guests of the cashier of the Mutual Credit Society, M. Desormeaux, M. Chapelain, M. Desclavettes himself; and, standing within the door-frame, they followed eagerly every motion of the commissary, who, pending the arrival of the locksmith, was making a flying examination of the bundles of papers left exposed upon the desk.

After a while, and unable to hold in any longer,—

"Would it be indiscreet," timidly inquired the old bronze-merchant, "to ask the nature of the charges against that poor Favoral?"

"Embezzlement, sir."

"And is the amount large?"

"Had it been small, I should have said theft. Embezzling commences only when the sum has reached a round figure."

Annoyed at the sardonic tone of the commissary,—

"The fact is," resumed M. Chapelain, "Favoral was our friend; and, if we could get him out of the scrape, we would all willingly contribute."

"It's a matter of ten or twelve millions, gentlemen."

Was it possible? Was it even likely? Could any one imagine so many millions slipping through the fingers of M. de Thaller's methodic cashier?

"Ah, sir!" exclaimed Mme. Favoral, "if any thing could relieve my feelings, the enormity of that sum would. My husband was a man of simple and modest tastes."

The commissary shook his head.

" There are certain passions," he interrupted, " which nothing betrays externally. Gambling is more terrible than fire. After a fire, some charred remnants are found. What is there left after a lost game? Fortunes may be thrown into the vortex of the *bourse*, without a trace of them being left."

The unfortunate woman was not convinced.

" I could swear, sir," she protested, " that I knew how my husband spent every hour of his life."

" Do not swear, madame."

" All our friends will tell you how parsimonious my husband was."

" Here, madame, towards yourself and your children, I have no doubt; for seeing is believing: but elsewhere "—

He was interrupted by the arrival of the locksmith, who, in less than five minutes, had picked all the locks of the old desk.

But in vain did the commissary search all the drawers. He found only those useless papers which are made relics of by people who have made order their religious faith,— uninteresting letters, grocers' and butchers' bills running back twenty years.

" It is a waste of time to look for any thing here," he growled.

And in fact he was about to give up his perquisitions, when a bundle thinner than the rest attracted his attention. He cut the thread that bound it; and almost at once,—

" I knew I was right," he said. And holding out a paper to Mme. Favoral,—

" Read, madame, if you please."

It was a bill. She read thus:—

" Sold to M. Favoral an India Cashmere, fr. 8,500.
Received payment, FORBE & TOWLER."

" Is it for you, madame," asked the commissary, " that this magnificent shawl was bought? "

Stupefied with astonishment, the poor woman still refused to admit the evidence.

" Madame de Thaller spends a great deal," she stammered. " My husband often made important purchases for her account."

" Often, indeed! " interrupted the commissary of police; " for here are many other receipted bills,—earrings, sixteen thousand francs; a bracelet, three thousand francs; a parlor set, a horse, two velvet dresses. Here is a part, at least, if not the whole, of the ten millions."

V.

HAD the commissary received any information in advance? or was he guided only by the scent peculiar to men of his profession, and the habit of suspecting every thing, even that which seems most unlikely?

At any rate he expressed himself in a tone of absolute certainty.

The agents who had accompanied and assisted him in his researches were winking at each other, and giggling stupidly. The situation struck them as rather pleasant.

The others, M. Desclavettes, M. Chapelain, and the worthy M. Desormeaux himself, could have racked their brains in vain to find terms wherein to express the immensity of their astonishments. Vincent Favoral, their old friend, paying for cashmeres, diamonds, and parlor sets! Such an idea could not enter in their mind. For whom could such princely gifts be intended? For a mistress, for one of those redoubtable creatures whom fancy represents crouching in the depths of love, like monsters at the bottom of their caves!

But how could any one imagine the methodic cashier of the Mutual Credit Society carried away by one of those insane passions which knew no reason? Ruined by gambling, perhaps, but by a woman!

Could any one picture him, so homely and so plain here, Rue St. Gilles, at the head of another establishment, and leading elsewhere, in one of the brilliant quarters of Paris, a reckless life, such as strike terror in the bosom of quiet families?

Could any one understand the same man at once miserly-economical and madly-prodigal, storming when his wife spent a few cents, and robbing to supply the expenses of an adventuress, and collecting in the same drawer the jeweler's accounts and the butcher's bills?

"It is the climax of absurdity," murmured good M. Desormeaux.

Maxence fairly shook with wrath. Mlle. Gilberte was weeping.

Mme. Favoral alone, usually so timid, boldly defended, and with her utmost energy, the man whose name she bore. That he might have embezzled millions, she admitted: that he had deceived and betrayed her so shamefully, that he had made a wretched dupe of her for so many years, seemed to her insensate, monstrous, impossible.

And purple with shame,—

"Your suspicions would vanish at once, sir," she

said to the commissary, " if I could but explain to you
our mode of life."

Encouraged by his first discovery, he was proceeding
more minutely with his perquisitions, undoing the
strings of every bundle.

"It is useless, madame," he answered in that brief tone
which made so much impression upon M. Desclavettes.
" You can only tell me what you know; and you know
nothing."

" Never, sir, did a man lead a more regular life than
M. Favoral."

" In appearance, you are right. Besides, to regulate
one's disorder is one of the peculiarities of our time. We
open credits to our passions, and we keep account of
our infamies by double entry. We operate with method.
We embezzle millions that we may hang diamonds to
the ears of an adventuress; but we are careful, and we
keep the receipted bills."

" But, sir, I have already told you that I never lost
sight of my husband."

" Of course."

" Every morning, precisely at nine o'clock, he left
home to go to M. de Thaller's office."

" The whole neighborhood knows that, madame."

" At half-past five he came home."

" That, also, is a well-known fact."

" After dinner he went out to play a game, but it was
his only amusement; and at eleven o'clock he was always
in bed."

" Perfectly correct."

" Well, then, sir, where could M. Favoral have found
time to abandon himself to the excesses of which you
accuse him? "

Imperceptibly the commissary of police shrugged his shoulders.

"Far from me, madame," he uttered, "to doubt your good faith. What matters it, moreover, whether your husband spent in this way or in that way the sums which he is charged with having appropriated? But what do your objections prove? Simply that M. Favoral was very skilful, and very much self-possessed. Had he breakfasted when he left you at nine? No. Pray, then, where did he breakfast? In a restaurant? Which? Why did he come home only at half-past five, when his office actually closed at three o'clock? Are you quite sure that it was to the Café Turc that he went every evening. Finally, why do not you say any thing of the extra work which he always had to attend to, as he pretended, once or twice a month? Sometimes it was a loan, sometimes a liquidation, or a settlement of dividends, which devolved upon him. Did he come home then? No. He told you that he would dine out, and that it would be more convenient for him to have a cot put up in his office; and thus you were twenty-four or forty-eight hours without seeing him. Surely this double existence must have weighed heavily upon him; but he was forbidden from breaking off with you, under penalty of being caught the very next day with his hand in the till. It is the respectability of his official life here which made the other possible,—that which has absorbed such enormous sums. The harsher and the closer he were here, the more magnificent he could show himself elsewhere. His household in the Rue St. Gilles was for him a certificate of impunity. Seeing him so economical, every one thought him rich. People who seem to spend nothing are always trusted. Every privation which he imposed upon you increased his reputation of austere probity, and raised him farther above suspicion."

Big tears were rolling down Mme. Favoral's cheeks.

" Why not tell me the whole truth? " she stammered.

" Because I do not know it," replied the commissary; " because these are all mere presumptions. I have seen so many instances of similar calculations! "

Then regretting, perhaps, to have said so much,—

" But I may be mistaken," he added: " I do not pretend to be infallible." He was just then completing a brief inventory of all the papers found in the old desk. There was nothing left but to examine the drawer which was used for a cash drawer. He found in it in gold, notes, and small change, seven hundred and eighteen francs.

Having counted this sum, the commissary offered it to Mme. Favoral, saying,—

" This belongs to you madame."

But instinctively she withdrew her hand.

" Never! " she said.

The commissary went on with a gesture of kindness,—

" I understand your scruples, madame, and yet I must insist. You may believe me when I tell you that this little sum is fairly and legitimately yours. You have no personal fortune."

The efforts of the poor woman to keep from bursting into loud sobs were but too visible.

" I possess nothing in the world, sir," she said in a broken voice. " My husband alone attended to our business-affairs. He never spoke to me about them; and I would not have dared to question him. Alone he disposed of our money. Every Sunday he handed me the amount which he thought necessary for the expenses of the week, and I rendered him an account of it. When my children or myself were in need of any thing, I told him so, and he gave me what he thought proper. This is Saturday: of what I received last Sunday I have five francs left: that is our whole fortune."

Positively the commissary was moved.

"You see, then, madame," he said, "that you cannot hesitate: you must live."

Maxence stepped forward.

"Am I not here, sir?" he said.

The commissary looked at him keenly, and in a grave tone,—

"I believe indeed, sir," he replied, "that you will not suffer your mother and sister to want for any thing. But resources are not created in a day. Yours, if I have not been deceived, are more than limited just now."

And as the young man blushed, and did not answer, he handed the seven hundred francs to Mlle. Gilberte, saying,—

"Take this, mademoiselle: your mother permits it."

His work was done. To place his seals upon M. Favoral's study was the work of a moment.

Beckoning, then, to his agents to withdraw, and being ready to leave himself,—

"Let not the seals cause you any uneasiness, madame," said the commissary of police to Mme. Favoral. "Before forty-eight hours, some one will come to remove these papers, and restore to you the free use of that room."

He went out; and, as soon as the door had closed behind him,—

"Well?" exclaimed M. Desormeaux.

But no one had any thing to say. The guests of that house where misfortune had just entered were making haste to leave. The catastrophe was certainly terrible and unforeseen; but did it not reach them too? Did they not lose among them more than three hundred thousand francs?

Thus, after a few commonplace protestations, and some of those promises which mean nothing, they withdrew; and, as they were going down the stairs,—

"The commissary took Vincent's escape too easy," remarked M. Desormeaux. "He must know some way to catch him again."

VI.

At last Mme. Favoral found herself alone with her children and free to give herself up to the most frightful despair.

She dropped heavily upon a seat; and, drawing to her bosom Maxence and Gilberte,—

"O my children!" she sobbed, covering them with her kisses and her tears,—"my children, we are most unfortunate."

Not less distressed than herself, they strove, nevertheless, to mitigate her anguish, to inspire her with sufficient courage to bear this crushing trial; and kneeling at her feet, and kissing her hands,—

"Are we not with you still, mother?" they kept repeating.

But she seemed not to hear them.

"It is not for myself that I weep," she went on. "I! what had I still to wait or hope for in life? Whilst you, Maxence, you, my poor Gilberte!—If, at least, I could feel myself free from blame! But no. It is my weakness and my want of courage that have brought on this catastrophe. I shrank from the struggle. I purchased my domestic peace at the cost of your future in the world. I forgot that a mother has sacred duties towards her children."

Mme. Favoral was at this time a woman of some forty-three years, with delicate and mild features, a countenance overflowing with kindness, and whose whole being exhaled, as it were, an exquisite perfume of noblesse and distinction.

Happy, she might have been beautiful still,—of that autumnal beauty whose maturity has the splendors of the luscious fruits of the later season.

But she had suffered so much! The livid paleness of her complexion, the rigid fold of her lips, the nervous shudders that shook her frame, revealed a whole existence of bitter deceptions, of exhausting struggles, and of proudly concealed humiliations.

And yet every thing seemed to smile upon her at the outset of life.

She was an only daughter; and her parents, wealthy silk-merchants, had brought her up like the daughter of an archduchess destined to marry some sovereign prince.

But at fifteen she had lost her mother. Her father, soon tired of his lonely fireside, commenced to seek away from home some diversion from his sorrow.

He was a man of weak mind,—one of those marked in advance to play the part of eternal dupes. Having money, he found many friends. Having once tasted the cup of facile pleasures, he yielded readily to its intoxication. Suppers, cards, amusements, absorbed his time, to the utter detriment of his business. And, eighteen months after his wife's death, he had already spent a large portion of his fortune, when he fell into the hands of an adventuress, whom, without regard for his daughter, he audaciously brought beneath his own roof.

In provincial cities, where everybody knows everybody

else, such infamies are almost impossible. They are not quite so rare in Paris, where one is, so to speak, lost in the crowd, and where the restraining power of the neighbor's opinion is lacking.

For two years the poor girl, condemned to bear this illegitimate stepmother, endured nameless sufferings.

She had just completed her eighteenth year, when, one evening, her father took her aside.

" I have made up my mind to marry again," he said; " but I wish first to provide you with a husband. I have looked for one, and found him. He is not very brilliant perhaps; but he is, it seems, a good, hard-working, economical fellow, who'll make his way in the world. I had dreamed of something better for you; but times are hard, trade is dull: in short, having only a dowry of twenty thousand francs to give you, I have no right to be very particular. To-morrow I'll bring you my candidate."

And, sure enough, the next day that excellent father introduced M. Vincent Favoral to his daughter.

She was not pleased with him; but she could hardly have said that she was displeased.

He was, at the age of twenty-five, which he had just reached, a man so utterly lacking in individuality, that he could scarcely have excited any feeling either of sympathy or affection.

Suitably dressed, he seemed timid and awkward, reserved, quite diffident, and of mediocre intelligence. He confessed to have received a most imperfect education, and declared himself quite ignorant of life. He had scarcely any means outside his profession. He was at this time chief accountant in a large factory of the Faubourg St. Antoine, with a salary of four thousand francs a year.

The young girl did not hesitate a moment. Any thing appeared to her preferable to the contact of a woman whom she abhorred and despised.

She gave her consent; and, twenty days after the first interview, she had become Mme. Favoral.

Alas! six weeks had not elapsed, before she knew that she had but exchanged her wretched fate for a more wretched one still.

Not that her husband was in any way unkind to her (he dared not, as yet); but he had revealed himself enough to enable her to judge him. He was one of those formidably selfish men who wither every thing around them, like those trees within the shadow of which nothing can grow. His coldness concealed a stupid obstinacy; his mildness, an iron will.

If he had married, 'twas because he thought a wife a necessary adjunct, because he desired a home wherein to command, because, above all, he had been seduced by the dowry of twenty thousand francs.

For the man had one passion,—money. Under his placid countenance revolved thoughts of the most burning covetousness. He wished to be rich.

Now, as he had no illusion whatever upon his own merits, as he knew himself to be perfectly incapable of any of those daring conceptions which lead to rapid fortune, as he was in no wise enterprising, he conceived but one means to achieve wealth, that is, to save, to economize, to stint himself, to pile penny upon penny.

His profession of accountant had furnished him with a number of instances of the financial power of the penny daily saved, and invested so as to yield its maximum of interest.

If ever his blue eye became animated, it was when he calculated what would be at the present time the capital

produced by a simple penny placed at five per cent interest the year of the birth of our Saviour.

For him this was sublime. He conceived nothing beyond. One penny! He wished, he said, he could have
lived eighteen hundred years, to follow the evolutions
of that penny, to see it grow tenfold, a hundred-fold,
produce, swell, enlarge, and become, after centuries, millions and hundreds of millions.

In spite of all, he had, during the early months of his
marriage, allowed his wife to have a young servant. He
gave her from time to time, a five-franc-piece, and took
her to the country on Sundays.

This was the honeymoon; and, as he declared himself,
this life of prodigalities could not last.

Under a futile pretext, the little servant was dismissed. He tightened the strings of his purse. The
Sunday excursions were suppressed.

To mere economy succeeded the niggardly parsimony
which counts the grains of salt in the *pot-au-feu*, which
weighs the soap for the washing, and measures the evening's allowance of candle.

Gradually the accountant took the habit of treating his
young wife like a servant, whose honesty is suspected;
or like a child, whose thoughtlessness is to be feared.
Every morning he handed her the money for the expenses of the day; and every evening he expressed his
surprise that she had not made better use of it. He accused her of allowing herself to be grossly cheated, or
even to be in collusion with the dealers. He charged
her with being foolishly extravagant; which fact, however, he added, did not surprise him much on the part of
the daughter of a man who had dissipated a large fortune.

To cap the climax, Vincent Favoral was on the worst

possible terms with his father-in-law. Of the twenty thousand francs of his wife's dowry, twelve thousand only had been paid, and it was in vain that he clamored for the balance. The silk-merchant's business had become unprofitable; he was on the verge of bankruptcy. The eight thousand francs seemed in imminent danger.

His wife alone he held responsible for this deception. He repeated to her constantly that she had connived with her father to " take him in," to fleece him, to ruin him.

What an existence! Certainly, had the unhappy woman known where to find a refuge, she would have fled from that home where each of her days was but a protracted torture. But where could she go? Of whom could she beg a shelter?

She had terrible temptations at this time, when she was not yet twenty, and they called her the beautiful Mme. Favoral.

Perhaps she would have succumbed, when she discovered that she was about to become a mother. One year, day for day, after her marriage, she gave birth to a son, who received the name of Maxence.

The accountant was but indifferently pleased at the coming of this son: It was, above all, a cause of expense. He had been compelled to give some thirty francs to a nurse, and almost twice as much for the baby's clothes. Then a child breaks up the regularity of one's habits; and he, as he affirmed, was attached to his as much as to life itself. And now he saw his household disturbed, the hours of his meals altered, his own importance reduced, his authority, even ignored.

But what mattered now to his young wife the ill-humor which he no longer took the trouble to conceal? Mother, she defied her tyrant.

Now, at least, she had in this world a being upon whom she could lavish all her caresses so brutally repelled. There existed a soul within which she reigned supreme. What troubles would not a smile of her son have made her forget?

With the admirable instinct of an egotist, M. Favoral understood so well what passed in the mind of his wife, that he dared not complain too much of what the little fellow cost. He made up his mind bravely; and when four years later, his daughter Gilberte was born, instead of lamenting,—

"Bash!" said he: "God blesses large families."

VII.

BUT already, at this time, M. Vincent Favoral's situation had been singularly modified.

The revolution of 1848 had just taken place. The factory in the Faubourg St. Antoine, where he was employed, had been compelled to close its doors.

One evening, as he came home at the usual hour, he announced that he had been discharged.

Mme. Favoral shuddered at the thought of what her husband might be, without work, and deprived of his salary.

"What is to become of us?" she murmured.

He shrugged his shoulders. Visibly he was much excited. His cheeks were flushed; his eyes sparkled.

"Bash!" he said: "we shan't starve for all that."

And, as his wife was gazing at him in astonishment,—

"Well," he went on, "what are you looking at? It

is so: I know many a one who affects to live on his income, and who are not as well off as we are."

It was, for over six years since he was married, the first time that he spoke of his business otherwise than to groan and complain, to accuse fate, and curse the high price of living. The very day before, he had declared himself ruined by the purchase of a pair of shoes for Maxence. The change was so sudden and so great, that she hardly knew what to think, and wondered if grief at the loss of his situation had not somewhat disturbed his mind.

"Such are women," he went on with a giggle. "Results astonish them, because they know nothing of the means used to bring them about. Am I a fool, then? Would I impose upon myself privations of all sorts, if it were to accomplish nothing? Parbleu! I love fine living too, I do, and good dinners at the restaurant, and the theatre, and the nice little excursions in the country. But I want to be rich. At the price of all the comforts which I have not had, I have saved a capital, the income of which will support us all. Eh, eh! That's the power of the little penny put out to fatten!"

As she went to bed that night, Mme. Favoral felt more happy than she had done since her mother's death. She almost forgave her husband his sordid parsimony, and the humiliations he had heaped upon her.

"Well, be it so," she thought. "I shall have lived miserably, I shall have endured nameless sufferings; but my children shall be rich, their life shall be easy and pleasant."

The next day M. Favoral's excitement had completely abated. Manifestly he regretted his confidences.

"You must not think on that account that you can

waste and pillage every thing," he declared rudely. " Besides, I have greatly exaggerated."

And he started in search of a situation.

To find one was likely to be difficult. Times of revolution are not exactly propitious to industry. Whilst the
parties discussed in the Chamber, there were on the street
twenty thousand clerks, who, every morning as they
rose, wondered where they would dine that day.

For want of any thing better, Vincent Favoral undertook to keep books in various places,—an hour here, an
hour there, twice a week in one house, four times in another.

In this way he earned as much and more than he did
at the factory; but the business did not suit him.

What he liked was the office from which one does not
stir, the stove-heated atmosphere, the elbow-worn desk,
the leather-cushioned chair, the black alpaca sleeves over
the coat. The idea that he should on one and the same
day have to do with five or six different houses, and be
compelled to walk an hour, to go and work another hour
at the other end of Paris, fairly irritated him. He found
himself out of his reckoning, like a horse who has turned
a mill for ten years, if he is made to trot straight before
him.

So, one morning, he gave up the whole thing, swearing that he would rather remain idle until he could find
a place suited to his taste and his convenience; and, in
the mean time, all they would have to do would be to put
a little less butter in the soup, and a little more water
in the wine.

He went out, nevertheless, and remained until dinner-
time. And he did the same the next and the following
days.

He started off the moment he had swallowed the last

mouthful of his breakfast, came home at six o'clock, dined in haste, and disappeared again, not to return until about midnight. He had hours of delirious joy, and moments of frightful discouragement. Sometimes he seemed horribly uneasy.

" What can he be doing? " thought Mme. Favoral.

She ventured to ask him the question one morning, when he was in fine humor.

" Well," he answered, " am I not the master? I am operating at the *bourse*, that's all! "

He could hardly have owned to any thing that would have frightened the poor woman as much.

" Are you not afraid," she objected, " to lose all we have so painfully accumulated? We have children "—

He did not allow her to proceed.

" Do you take me for a child? " he exclaimed; " or do I look to you like a man so easy to be duped? Mind to economize in your household expenses, and don't meddle with my business."

And he continued. And he must have been lucky in his operations; for he had never been so pleasant at home. All his ways had changed. He had had clothes made at a first-class tailor's, and was evidently trying to look elegant. He gave up his pipe, and smoked only cigars. He got tired of giving every morning the money for the house, and took the habit of handing it to his wife every week, on Sunday. A mark of vast confidence, as he observed to her. And so, the first time,—

" Be careful," he said, " that you don't find yourself penniless before Thursday."

He became also more communicative. Often during the dinner, he would tell what he had heard during the day, anecdotes, gossip. He enumerated the persons with whom he had spoken. He named a number of people whom he called his friends, and whose names Mme. Favoral carefully stored away in her memory.

There was one especially, who seemed to inspire him with a profound respect, a boundless admiration, and of whom he never tired of talking. He was, said he, a man of his age,—M. de Thaller, the Baron de Thaller.

" This one," he kept repeating, " is really mad: he is rich, he has ideas, he'll go far. It would be a great piece of luck if I could get him to do something for me!"

Until at last one day,—

" Your parents were very rich once? " he asked his wife.

" I have heard it said," she answered.

" They spent a good deal of money, did they not? They had friends: they gave dinner-parties."

" Yes, they received a good deal of company."

" You remember that time? "

" Surely I do."

" So that if I should take a fancy to receive some one here, some one of note, you would know how to do things properly? "

" I think so."

He remained silent for a moment, like a man who thinks before taking an important decision, and then,—

" I wish to invite a few persons to dinner," he said.

She could scarcely believe her ears. He had never received at his table any one but a fellow-clerk at the factory, named Desclavettes, who had just married the daughter of a dealer in bronzes, and succeeded to his business.

" Is it possible? " exclaimed Mme. Favoral.

" So it is. The question is now, How much would a first-class dinner cost, the best of every thing? "

" That depends upon the number of guests."

" Say three or four persons."

The poor woman set herself to figuring diligently for some time; and then timidly, for the sum seemed formidable to her,—

" I think," she began, " that with a hundred francs "—

Her husband commenced whistling.

" You'll need that for the wines alone," he interrupted. " Do you take me for a fool? But here, don't let us go into figures. Do as your parents did when they did their best; and, if it's well, I shall not complain of the expense. Take a good cook, hire a waiter who understands his business well."

She was utterly confounded; and yet she was not at the end of her surprises.

Soon M. Favoral declared that their table-ware was not suitable, and that he must buy a new set. He discovered a hundred purchases to be made, and swore that he would make them. He even hesitated a moment about renewing the parlor furniture, although it was in tolerably good condition still, and was a present from his father-in-law.

And, having finished his inventory,—

" And you," he asked his wife: " what dress will you wear?"

" I have my black silk dress "—

He stopped her.

" Which means that you have none at all," he said. " Very well. You must go this very day and get yourself one,—a very handsome, a magnificent one; and you'll send it to be made to a fashionable dressmaker. And at the same time you had better get some little suits for Maxence and Gilberte. Here are a thousand francs."

Completely bewildered.—

"Who in the world are you going to invite, then?" she asked.

"The Baron and the Baroness de Thaller," he replied with an emphasis full of conviction. "So try and distinguish yourself. Our fortune is at stake."

That this dinner was a matter of considerable import, Mme. Favoral could not doubt when she saw her husband's fabulous liberality continue without flinching for a number of days.

Ten times of an afternoon he would come home to tell his wife the name of some dish that had been mentioned before him, or to consult her on the subject of some exotic viand he had just noticed in some shop-window. Daily he brought home wines of the most fantastic vintages,—those wines which dealers manufacture for the special use of verdant fools, and which they sell in odd-shaped bottles previously overlaid with secular dust and cobwebs.

He subjected to a protracted cross-examination the cook whom Mme. Favoral had engaged, and demanded that she should enumerate the houses where she had cooked. He absolutely required the man who was to wait at the table to exhibit the dress-coat he was to wear.

The great day having come, he did not stir from the house, going and coming from the kitchen to the dining-room, uneasy, agitated, unable to stay in one place. He breathed only when he had seen the table set and loaded with the new china he had purchased and the magnificent silver he had gone to hire in person.

And when his young wife made her appearance, looking lovely in her new dress, and leading by the hands the two children, Maxence and Gilberte, in their new suits,—

"That's perfect," he exclaimed, highly delighted.

" Nothing could be better. Now, let our four guests come ! "

They arrived a few minutes before seven, in two carriages, the magnificence of which astonished the Rue St. Gilles.

And, the presentations over, Vincent Favoral had at last the ineffable satisfaction to see seated at his table the Baron and Baroness de Thaller, M. Saint Pavin, who called himself a financial editor, and M. Jules Jottras, of the house of Jottras & Brother.

It was with an eager curiosity that Mme. Favoral observed these people whom her husband called his friends, and whom she saw herself for the first time.

M. de Thaller, who could not then have been much over thirty, was already a man without any particular age.

Cold, stiff, aping evidently the English style, he expressed himself in brief sentences, and with a strong foreign accent. Nothing to surprise on his countenance. He had the forehead prominent, the eyes of a dull blue, and the nose very thin. His scanty hair was spread over the top of his head with labored symmetry ; and his red, thick, and carefully-trimmed whiskers seemed to engross much of his attention.

M. Saint Pavin had not the same stiff manner. Careless in his dress, he lacked breeding. He was a robust fellow, dark and bearded, with thick lips, the eye bright and prominent, spreading upon the table-cloth broad hands ornamented at the joints with small tufts of hair, speaking loud, laughing noisily, eating much and drinking more.

By the side of him, M. Jules Jottras, although looking like a fashion-plate, did not show to much advantage. Delicate, blonde, sallow, almost beardless, M. Jottras dis-

tinguished himself only by a sort of unconscious impudence, a harmless cynicism, and a sort of spasmodic
giggle, that shook the eye-glasses which he wore stuck
over his nose.

But it was above all Mme. de Thaller who excited
Mme. Favoral's apprehensions.

Dressed with a magnificence of at least questionable
taste, very much *décolletée,* wearing large diamonds at
her ears, and rings on all her fingers, the young baroness
was insolently handsome, of a beauty sensuous even to
coarseness. With hair of a bluish black, twisted over the
neck in heavy ringlets, she had skin of a pearly whiteness, lips redder than blood, and great eyes that threw
flames from beneath their long, curved lashes. It was
the poetry of flesh ; and one could not help admiring.
Did she speak, however, or make a gesture, all admiration vanished. The voice was vulgar, the motion common. Did M. Jouras venture upon a *double-entendre,*
she would throw herself back upon her chair to laugh,
stretching her neck, and thrusting her throat forward.

Wholly absorbed in the care of his guests, M. Favoral
remarked nothing. He only thought of loading the
plates, and filling the glasses, complaining that they ate
and drank nothing, asking anxiously if the cooking was
not good, if the wines were bad, and almost driving
the waiter out of his wits with questions and sugges-
tions.

It is a fact, that neither M. de Thaller nor M. Jottras
had much appetite. But M. Saint Pavin officiated for
all ; and the sole task of keeping up with him caused M.
Favoral to become visibly animated.

His cheeks were much flushed, when, having passed
the champagne all around, he raised his froth-tipped
glass, exclaiming,—

" I drink to the success of the business."

" To the success of the business," echoed the others,
touching his glass.

And a few moments later they passed into the parlor
to take coffee.

This toast had caused Mme. Favoral no little uneasiness. But she found it impossible to ask a single question; Mme de Thaller dragging her almost by force to a
seat by her side on the sofa, pretending that two women
always have secrets to exchange, even when they see
each other for the first time.

The young baroness was fully *au fait* in matters of
bonnets and dresses; and it was with giddy volubility
that she asked Mme. Favoral the names of her milliner
and her dressmaker, and to what jeweller she intrusted
her diamonds to be reset.

This looked so much like a joke, that the poor housekeeper of the Rue St. Gilles could not help smiling whilst
answering that she had no dressmaker, and that, having
no diamonds, she had no possible use for the services of
a jeweller.

The other declared she could not get over it. No diamonds! That was a misfortune exceeding all. And
quick she seized the opportunity charitably to enumerate
the *parures* in her jewel-case, and laces in her drawers,
and the dresses in her wardrobes. In the first place, it
would have been impossible for her, she swore, to live
with a husband either miserly or poor. Hers had just
presented her with a lovely *coupé*, lined with yellow
satin, a perfect *bijou*. And she made good use of it too;
for she loved to go about. She spent her days shopping,
or riding in the Bois. Every evening she had the choice
of the theatre or a ball, often both. The *genre* theatres
were those she preferred. To be sure, the opera and the

Italiens were more stylish; but she could not help gaping there.

Then she wished to kiss the children; and Gilberte and Maxence had to be brought in. She adored children, she vowed: it was her weakness, her passion. She had herself a little girl, eighteen months old, called Césarine, to whom she was devoted; and certainly she would have brought her, had she not feared she would have been in the way.

All this verbiage sounded like a confused murmur to Mme. Favoral's ears. "Yes, no," she answered, hardly knowing to what she did answer.

Her head heavy with a vague apprehension, it required her utmost attention to observe her husband and his guests.

Standing by the mantel-piece, smoking their cigars, they conversed with considerable animation, but not loud enough to enable her to hear all they said. It was only when M. Saint Pavin spoke that she understood that they were still discussing the "business;" for he spoke of articles to publish, stocks to sell, dividends to distribute, sure profits to reap.

They all, at any rate, seemed to agree perfectly; and at a certain moment she saw her husband and M. de Thaller strike each other's hand, as people do who exchange a pledge.

Eleven o'clock struck.

M. Favoral was insisting to make his guests accept a cup of tea or a glass of punch; but M. de Thaller declared that he had some work to do, and that, his carriage having come, he must go.

And go he did, taking with him the baroness, followed by M. Saint Pavin and M. Jottras.

And when, the door having closed upon them, M. Favoral found himself alone with his wife,—

" Well," he exclaimed, swelling with gratified vanity, " what do you think of our friends? "

" They surprised me," she answered.

He fairly jumped at that word.

" I should like to know why? "

Then, timidly, and with infinite precautions, she commenced explaining that M. de Thaller's face inspired her with no confidence; that M. Jottras had seemed to her a very impudent personage; that M. Saint Pavin appeared low and vulgar; and that, finally, the young baroness had given her of herself the most singular idea.

M. Favoral refused to hear more.

" It's because you have never seen people of the best society," he exclaimed.

" Excuse me. Formerly, during my mother's life "—

" Eh! Your mother never received but shop-keepers."

The poor woman dropped her head.

" I beg of you, Vincent," she insisted, " before doing any thing with these new friends, think well, consult "—·

He burst out laughing.

" Are you not afraid that they will cheat me? " he said,—" people ten times as rich as we are. Here, don't let us speak of it any more, and let us go to bed. You'll see what this dinner will bring us, and whether I ever have reason to regret the money we have spent."

VIII.

WHEN, on the morning after this dinner, which was to form an era in her life, Mme. Favoral woke up, her husband was already up, pencil in hand, and busy figuring.

The charm had vanished with the fumes of the champagne; and the clouds of the worst days were gathering upon his brow.

Noticing that his wife was looking at him,—

" It's expensive work," he said in a bluff tone, " to set a business going; and it wouldn't do to commence over again every day."

To hear him speak, one would have thought that Mme. Favoral alone, by dint of hard begging, had persuaded him, into that expense which he now seemed to regret so much. She quietly called his attention to the fact, reminding him that, far from urging, she had endeavored to hold him back; repeating that she augured ill of that business over which he was so enthusiastic, and that, if he would believe her, he would not venture.

" Do you even know what the project is? " he interrupted rudely.

" You have not told me."

" Very well, then: leave me in peace with your presentiments. You dislike my friends; and I saw very well how you treated Mme. de Thaller. But I am the master; and what I have decided shall be. Besides, I have signed. Once for all, I forbid you ever speaking to me again on that subject."

Whereupon, having dressed himself with much care, he started off, saying that he was expected at breakfast by Saint Pavin, the financial editor, and by M. Jottras, of the house of Jottras & Brother.

A shrewd woman would not have given it up so easy, and, in the end, would probably have mastered the despot, whose intellect was far from brilliant. But Mme. Favoral was too proud to be shrewd; and besides, the springs of her will had been broken by the successive oppression of an odious stepmother and a brutal master. Her abdication of all was complete. Wounded, she kept the secret of her wound, hung her head, and said nothing.

She did not, therefore, venture a single allusion; and nearly a week elapsed, during which the names of her late guests were not once mentioned.

It was through a newspaper, which M. Favoral had forgotten in the parlor, that she learned that the Baron de Thaller had just founded a new stock company, the Mutual Credit Society, with a capital of several millions.

Below the advertisement, which was printed in enormous letters, came a long article, in which it was demonstrated that the new company was, at the same time, a patriotic undertaking and an institution of credit of the first class; that it supplied a great public want; that it would be of inestimable benefit to industry; that its profits were assured; and that to subscribe to its stock was simply to draw short bills upon fortune.

Already somewhat re-assured by the reading of this article, Mme. Favoral became quite so when she read the names of the board of directors. Nearly all were titled, and decorated with many foreign orders; and the remainder were bankers, office-holders, and even some ex-ministers.

" I must have been mistaken," she thought, yielding unconsciously to the influence of printed evidence.

And no objection occurred to her, when, a few days later, her husband told her,—

" I have the situation I wanted. I am head cashier of the company of which M. de Thaller is manager."

That was all. Of the nature of this society, of the advantages which it offered him, not one word.

Only by the way in which he expressed himself did Mme. Favoral judge that he must have been well treated; and he further confirmed her in that opinion by granting her, of his own accord, a few additional francs for the daily expenses of the house.

" We must," he declared on this memorable occasion, " do honor to our social position, whatever it may cost."

For the first time in his life, he seemed heedful of public opinion. He recommended his wife to be careful of her dress and of that of the children, and re-engaged a servant. He expressed the wish of enlarging their circle of acquaintances, and inaugurated his Saturday dinners, to which came assiduously, M. and Mme. Desclavettes, M. Chapelain the attorney, the old man Desormeaux, and a few others.

As to himself he gradually settled down into those habits from which he was nevermore to depart, and the chronometric regularity of which had secured him the nickname of Old Punctuality, of which he was proud.

In all other respects never did a man, to such a degree, become so utterly indifferent to his wife and children. His house was for him but a mere hotel, where he slept, and took his evening meal. He never thought of questioning his wife as to the use of her time, and what she did in his absence. Provided she did not ask him for money, and was there when he came home, he was satisfied.

Many women, at Mme. Favoral's age, might have

made a strange use of that insulting indifference and of that absolute freedom.

If she did avail herself of it, it was solely to follow one of those inspirations which can only spring in a mother's heart.

The increase in the budget of the household was relatively large, but so nicely calculated, that she had not one cent more that she could call her own.

With the most intense sorrow, she thought that her children might have to endure the humiliating privations which had made her own life wretched. They were too young yet to suffer from the paternal parsimony; but they would grow; their desires would develop; and it would be impossible for her to grant them the most innocent satisfactions.

Whilst turning over and over in her mind this distressing thought, she remembered a friend of her mother's, who kept, in the Rue St. Denis, a large establishment for the sale of hosiery and woollen goods. There, perhaps, lay the solution of the problem. She called to see the worthy woman, and, without even needing to confess the whole truth to her, she obtained sundry pieces of work, ill paid as a matter of course, but which, by dint of close application, might be made to yield from eight to twelve francs a week.

From this time she never lost a minute, concealing her work as if it were an evil act.

She knew her husband well enough to feel certain that he would break out, and swear that he spent money enough to enable his wife to live without being reduced to making a workwoman of herself.

But what joy, the day when she hid way down at the bottom of a drawer the first twenty-franc-piece she had earned, a beautiful gold-piece, which belonged to her

without contest, and which she might spend as she
pleased, without having to render any account to any
one!

And with what pride, from week to week, she saw her
little treasure swell, despite the drafts she made upon it,
sometimes to buy a toy for Maxence, sometimes to add a
few ribbons or trinkets to Gilberte's toilet!

This was the happiest time of her life, a halt in that
painful journey through which she had been dragging
herself for so many years.   Between her two children,
the hours flew light and rapid as so many seconds.   If
all the hopes of the young girl and of the woman had
withered before they had blossomed, the mother's joys,
at least should not fail her.   Because, whilst the present
sufficed to her modest ambition, the future had ceased to
cause her any uneasiness.

No reference had ever been made, between herself and
her husband, to that famous dinner-party: he never
spoke to her of the Mutual Credit Society; but now and
then he allowed some words or exclamations to escape,
which she carefully recorded, and which betrayed a prosperous state of affairs.

" That Thaller is a tough fellow! " he would exclaim,
" and he has the most infernal luck! "

And at other times,—

" Two or three more operations like the one we
have just successfully wound up, and we can shut up
shop! "

From all this, what could she conclude, if not that he
was marching with rapid strides towards that fortune,
the object of all his ambition?

Already in the neighborhood he had that reputation
to be very rich, which is the beginning of riches itself.
He was admired for keeping his house with such rigid

economy; for a man is always esteemed who has money, and does not spend it.

" He is not the man ever to squander what he has," the neighbors repeated.

The persons whom he received on Saturdays believed him more than comfortably off. When M. Desclavettes and M. Chapelain had complained to their hearts' contents, the one of the shop, the other of his office, they never failed to add,—

" You laugh at us, because you are engaged in large operations, where people make as much money as they like."

They seemed to hold his financial capacities in high estimation. They consulted him, and followed his advice.

M. Desormeaux was wont to say,—

" Oh! he knows what he is about."

And Mme. Favoral tried to persuade herself, that, in this respect at least, her husband was a remarkable man. She attributed his silence and his distractions to the grave cares that filled his mind. In the same manner that he had once announced to her that they had enough to live on, she expected him, some fine morning, to tell her that he was a millionaire.

IX.

BUT the respite granted by fate to Mme. Favoral was drawing to an end: her trials were about to return more poignant than ever, occasioned, this time, by her children, hitherto her whole happiness and her only consolation.

Maxence was nearly twelve. He was a good little

fellow, intelligent, studious at times, but thoughtless in the extreme, and of a turbulence which nothing could tame.

At the Massin School, where he had been sent, he made his teachers' hair turn white; and not a week went by that he did not signalize himself by some fresh misdeed.

A father like any other would have paid but slight attention to the pranks of a schoolboy, who, after all, ranked among the first of his class, and of whom the teachers themselves, whilst complaining, said,—

" Bash ! What matters it, since the heart is sound and the mind sane ? "

But M. Favoral took every thing tragically. If Maxence was kept in, or otherwise punished, he pretended that it reflected upon himself, and that his son was disgracing him.

If a report came home with this remark, " execrable conduct," he fell into the most violent passion, and seemed to lose all control of himself.

" At your age," he would shout to the terrified boy, " I was working in a factory, and earning my livelihood. Do you suppose that I will not tire of making sacrifices to procure you the advantages of an education which I lacked myself? Beware. Havre is not far off; and cabin-boys are always in demand there."

If, at least, he had confined himself to these admonitions, which, by their very exaggeration, failed in their object ! But he favored mechanical appliances as a necessary means of sufficiently impressing reprimands upon the minds of young people; and therefore, seizing his cane, he would beat poor Maxence most unmercifully, the more so that the boy, filled with pride, would have allowed himself to be chopped to pieces rather than utter a cry, or shed a tear.

The first time that Mme. Favoral saw her son struck, she was seized with one of those wild fits of anger which do not reason, and never forgive. To be beaten herself would have seemed to her less atrocious, less humiliating. Hitherto she had found it impossible to love a husband such as hers: henceforth, she took him in utter aversion: he inspired her with horror. She looked upon her son as a martyr for whom she could hardly ever do enough.

And so, after these harrowing scenes, she would press him to her heart in the most passionate embrace; she would cover with her kisses the traces of the blows; and she would strive, by the most delirious caresses, to make him forget the paternal brutalities. With him she sobbed. Like him, she would shake her clinched fists in the vacant space, exclaiming, " Coward, tyrant, assassin!" The little Gilberte mingled her tears with theirs; and, pressed against each other, they deplored their destiny, cursing the common enemy, the head of the family.

Thus did Maxence spend his boyhood between equally fatal exaggerations, between the revolting brutalities of his father, and the dangerous caresses of his mother; the one depriving him of every thing, the other refusing him nothing.

For Mme. Favoral had now found a use for her humble savings.

If the idea had never come to the cashier of the Mutual Credit Society to put a few sous in his son's pocket, the too weak mother would have suggested to him the want of money in order to have the pleasure of gratifying it.

She who had suffered so many humiliations in her life, she could not bear the idea of her son having his pride wounded, and being unable to indulge in those little trifling expenses which are the vanity of school-boys.

" Here, take this," she would tell him on holidays, slipping a few francs into his hands.

Unfortunately, to her present she joined the recommendation not to allow his father to know any thing about it; forgetting that she was thus training Maxence to dissimulate, warping his natural sense of right, and perverting his instincts.

No, she gave; and, to repair the gaps thus made in her treasure, she worked to the point of ruining her sight, with such eager zeal, that the worthy shop-keeper of the Rue St. Denis asked her if she did not employ working girls. In truth, the only help she received was from Gilberte, who, at the age of eight, already knew how to make herself useful.

And this is not all. For this son, in anticipation of growing expenses, she stooped to expedients which formerly would have seemed to her unworthy and disgraceful. She robbed the household, cheating on her own marketing. She went so far as to confide to her servant, and to make of the girl the accomplice of her operations. She applied all her ingenuity to serve to M. Favoral dinners in which the excellence of the dressing concealed the want of solid substance. And on Sunday, when she rendered her weekly accounts, it was without a blush that she increased by a few centimes the price of each object, rejoicing when she had thus scraped a dozen francs, and finding, to justify herself to her own eyes, those sophisms which passion never lacks.

At first Maxence was too young to wonder from what

sources his mother drew the money she lavished upon his schoolboy fancies. She recommended him to hide from his father: he did so, and thought it perfectly natural.

As he grew older, he learned to discern.

The moment came when he opened his eyes upon the system under which the paternal household was managed. He noticed there that anxious economy which seems to betray want, and the acrimonious discussions which arose upon the inconsiderate use of a twenty-franc-piece. He saw his mother realize miracles of industry to conceal the shabbiness of her toilets, and resort to the most skilful diplomacy when she wished to purchase a dress for Gilberte.

And, despite all this, he had at his disposition as much money as those of his comrades whose parents had the reputation to be the most opulent and the most generous.

Anxious, he questioned his mother.

" Eh what does it matter? " she answered, blushing and confused. " Is that any thing to worry you? "

And, as he insisted,—

" Go ahead," she said: " we are rich enough."

But he could hardly believe her, accustomed as he was to hear every one talk of poverty; and, as he fixed upon her his great astonished eyes,—

" Yes," she resumed, with an imprudence which fatally was to bear its fruits, " we are rich; and, if we live as you see, it is because it suits your father, who wishes to amass a still greater fortune."

This was hardly an answer; and yet Maxence asked no further question. But he inquired here and there, with that patient shrewdness of young people possessed with a fixed idea.

Already, at this time, M. Favoral had in the neighborhood, and even among his friends, the reputation to be worth at least a million. The Mutual Credit Society had considerably developed itself: he must, they thought, have benefited largely by the circumstance; and the profits must have swelled rapidly in the hands of so able a man, and one so noted for his rigid economy.

Such is the substance of what Maxence heard; and people did not fail to add ironically, that he need not rely upon the paternal fortune to amuse himself.

M. Desormeaux himself, whom he had "pumped" rather cleverly, had told him, whilst patting him amicably on the shoulder,—

"If you ever need money for your frolics, young man, try and earn it; for I'll be hanged if it's the old man who'll ever supply it."

Such answers complicated, instead of explaining, the problem which occupied Maxence.

He observed, he watched; and at last he acquired the certainty that the money he spent was the fruit of the joint labor of his mother and sister.

"Ah! why not have told me so?" he exclaimed, throwing his arms around his mother's neck. "Why have exposed me to the bitter regrets which I feel at this moment?"

By this sole word the poor woman found herself amply repaid. She admired the *noblesse* of her son's feelings and the kindness of his heart.

"Do you not understand," she told him, shedding tears of joy, "do you not see, that the labor which can promote her son's pleasure is a happiness for his mother?"

But he was dismayed at his discovery.

"No matter!" he said. "I swear that I shall no longer scatter to the winds, as I have been doing, the money that you give me."

For a few weeks, indeed, he was faithful to his pledge. But at fifteen resolutions are not very stanch. The impressions he had felt wore off. He became tired of the small privations which he had to impose upon himself.

He soon came to take to the letter what his mother had told him, and to prove to his own satisfaction that to deprive himself of a pleasure was to deprive her. He asked for ten francs one day, then ten francs another, and gradually resumed his old habits.

He was at this time about leaving school.

"The moment has come," said M. Favoral, "for him to select a career, and support himself."

X.

To think of a profession, Maxence Favoral had not waited for the paternal warnings.

Modern schoolboys are precocious: they know the strong and the weak side of life; and, when they take their degree, they already have but few illusions left.

And how could it be otherwise? In the interior of the colleges is fatally found the echo of the thoughts, and the reflex of the manners, of the time. Neither walls nor keepers can avail. At the same time, as the city mud that stains their boots, the scholars bring back on their return from holidays their stock of observations and of facts.

And what have they seen during the day in their families, or among their friends?

Ardent cravings, insatiable appetites for luxuries, comforts, enjoyments, pleasures, contempt for patient labor, scorn for austere convictions, eager longing for money, the will to become rich at any cost, and the fi. resolution to ravish fortune on the first favorable occasion.

To be sure, they have dissembled in their presence; but their perceptions are keen.

True, their father has told them in a grave tone, that there is nothing respectable in this world except labor and honesty; but they have caught that same father scarcely noticing a poor devil of an honest man, and bowing to the earth before some clever rascal bearing the stigma of three judgments, but worth six millions.

Conclusion? Oh! they know very well how to conclude; for there are none such as young people to be logical, and to deduce the utmost consequences of a fact.

They know, the most of them, that they will have to do something or other; but what? And it is then, that, during the recreations, their imagination strives to find that hitherto unknown profession which is to give them fortune without work, and freedom at the same time as a brilliant situation.

They discuss and criticise freely all the careers which are open to youthful ambition. And how they laugh, if some simple fellow ventures upon suggesting some of those modest situations where they earn one hundred and fifty francs a month at the start! One hundred and fifty francs!—why, it's hardly as much as many a boy spends for his cigars, and his cab-fares when he is late.

Maxence was neither better nor worse than the rest. Like the rest he strove to discover the ideal profession which makes a man rich, and amuses him at the same time.

Under the pretext that he drew nicely, he spoke of becoming a painter, calculating coolly what painting may yield, and reckoning, according to some newspaper, the earnings of Corot or Gérome, Ziem, Bouguereau, and some others, who are reaping at last the fruits of unceasing efforts and crushing labors.

But, in the way of pictures, M. Vincent Favoral appreciated only the blue vignettes of the Bank of France.

"I wish no artists in my family," he said, in a tone that admitted of no reply.

Maxence would willingly have become an engineer, for it's rather the style to be an engineer now-a-days; but the examinations for the Polytechnic School are rather steep. Or else a cavalry officer; but the two years at Saint Cyr are not very gay. Or chief clerk, like M. Desormeaux; but he would have to begin by being supernumerary.

Finally after hesitating for a long time between law and medicine, he made up his mind to become a lawyer, influenced above all, by the joyous legends of the Latin quarter.

That was not exactly M. Vincent Favoral's dream.

"That's going to cost money again," he growled.

The fact is, he had indulged in the fallacious hope that his son, as soon as he left college, would enter at once some business-house, where he would earn enough to take care of himself.

He yielded at last, however, to the persistent entreaties of his wife, and the solicitations of his friends.

"Be it so," he said to Maxence: " you will study law. Only, as it cannot suit me that you should waste your days lounging in the billiard-rooms of the left bank, you shall at the same time work in an attorney's office. Next Saturday I shall arrange with my friend Chapelain."

Maxence had not bargained for such an arrangement; and he came near backing out at the prospect of a discipline which he foresaw must be as exacting as that of the college.

Still, as he could think of nothing better, he persevered. And, vacations over, he was duly entered at the law-school, and settled at a desk in M. Chapelain's office, which was then in the Rue St. Antoine.

The first year every thing went on tolerably. He enjoyed as much freedom as he cared to. His father did not allow him one centime for his pocket-money; but the attorney, in his capacity of an old friend of the family, did for him what he had never done before for an amateur clerk, and allowed him twenty francs a month. Mme. Favoral adding to this a few five-franc pieces, Maxence declared himself entirely satisfied.

Unfortunately, with his lively imagination and his impetuous temper, no one was less fit than himself for that peaceful existence, that steady toil, the same each day, without the stimulus of difficulties to overcome, or the satisfaction of results obtained.

Before long he became tired of it.

He had found at the law-school a number of his old schoolmates whose parents resided in the provinces, and who, consequently, lived as they pleased in the Latin quarter, less assiduous to the lectures than to the Spring Brewery and the Closerie des Lilas.*

He envied them their joyous life, their freedom without control, their facile pleasures, their furnished rooms,

---

* A noted dancing-garden

and even the low eating-house where they took their meals. And, as much as possible, he lived with them and like them.

But it is not with M. Chapelain's twenty francs that it would have been possible for him to keep up with fellows, who, with superb recklessness, took on credit every thing they could get, reserving the amount of their allowance for those amusements which had to be paid for in cash.

But was not Mme. Favoral here?

She had worked so much, the poor woman, especially since Mlle. Gilberte had become almost a young lady; she had so much saved, so much stinted, that her reserve, notwithstanding repeated drafts, amounted to a good round sum.

When Maxence wanted two or three napoleons, he had but a word to say; and he said it often. Thus, after a while, he became an excellent billiard-player; he kept his colored meerschaum in the rack of a popular brewery; he took absinthe before dinner, and spent his evenings in the laudable effort to ascertain how many mugs of beer he could "put away." Gaining in audacity, he danced at Bullier's, dined at Foyd's, and at last had a mistress.

So much so, that one afternoon, M. Favoral having to visit on business the other side of the water, found himself face to face with his son, who was coming along, a cigar in his mouth, and having on his arm a young lady, painted in superior style, and harnessed with a toilet calculated to make the cab-horses rear.

He returned to the Rue St. Gilles in a state of indescribable rage.

"A woman!" he exclaimed in a tone of offended modesty. "A woman!—he, my son!"

And when that son made his appearance, looking quite sheepish, his first impulse was to resort to his former mode of correction.

But Maxence was now over nineteen years of age.

At the sight of the uplifted cane, he became whiter than his shirt; and, wrenching it from his father's hands, he broke it across his knees, threw the pieces violently upon the floor, and sprang out of the house.

" He shall never again set his foot here!" screamed the cashier of the Mutual Credit, thrown beside himself by an act of resistance which seemed to him unheard of. " I banish him. Let his clothes be packed up, and taken to some hotel: I never want to see him again."

For a long time Mme. Favoral and Gilberte fairly dragged themselves at his feet, before he consented to recall his determination.

" He will disgrace us all!" he kept repeating, seeming unable to understand that it was himself who had, as it were, driven Maxence on to the fatal road which he was pursuing, forgetting that the absurd severities of the father prepared the way for the perilous indulgence of the mother, unwilling to own that the head of a family has other duties besides providing food and shelter for his wife and children, and that a father has but little right to complain who has not known how to make himself the friend and the adviser of his son.

At last, after the most violent recriminations, he forgave, in appearance at least.

But the scales had dropped from his eyes. He started in quest of information, and discovered startling enormities.

He heard from M. Chapelain that Maxence remained whole weeks at a time without appearing at the office. If he had not complained before, it was because he had yielded to the urgent entreaties of Mme. Favoral; and he was now glad, he added, of an opportunity to relieve his conscience by a full confession.

Thus the cashier discovered, one by one, all his son's tricks. He heard that he was almost unknown at the law-school, that he spent his days in the *cafés*, and that, in the evening, when he believed him in bed and asleep, he was in fact running out to theatres and to balls.

" Ah! that's the way, is it? " he thought. " Ah, my wife and children are in league against me,—me, the master. Very well, we'll see."

XI.

FROM that morning war was declared.

From that day commenced in the Rue St. Gilles one of those domestic dramas which are still awaiting their Molière,—a drama of distressing vulgarity and sickening realism, but poignant, nevertheless; for it brought into action tears, blood, and a savage energy.

M. Favoral thought himself sure to win; for did he not have the key of the cash, and is not the key of the cash the most formidable weapon in an age where every thing begins and ends with money?

Nevertheless, he was filled with irritating anxieties.

He who had just discovered so many things which he did not even suspect a few days before, he could not discover the source whence his son drew the money which flowed like water from his prodigal hands.

He had made sure that Maxence had no debts; and yet it could not be with M. Chapelain's monthly twenty francs that he fed his frolics.

Mme. Favoral and Gilberte, subjected separately to

a skilful interrogatory, had managed to keep inviolate the secret of their mercenary labor. The servant, shrewdly questioned, had said nothing that could in any way cause the truth to be suspected.

Here was, then, a mystery; and M. Favoral's constant anxiety could be read upon his knitted brows during his brief visits to the house; that is, during dinner.

From the manner in which he tasted his soup, it was easy to see that he was asking himself whether that was real soup, and whether he was not being imposed upon. From the expression of his eyes, it was easy to guess this question constantly present to his mind :—

" They are robbing me evidently; but how do they do it? "

And he became distrustful, fussy, and suspicious, to an extent that he had never been before. It was with the most insulting precautions that he examined every Sunday his wife's accounts. He took a book at the grocer's, and settled it himself every month: he had the butcher's bills sent to him in duplicate. He would inquire the price of an apple as he peeled it over his plate, and never failed to stop at the fruiterer's and ascertain that he had not been deceived.

But it was all in vain.

And yet he knew that Maxence always had in his pocket two or three five-franc pieces.

" Where do you steal them? " he asked him one day.

" I save them out of my salary," boldly answered the young man.

Exasperated, M. Favoral wished to make the whole world take an interest in his investigations. And one Saturday evening, as he was talking with his friends, M. Chapelain, the worthy Desclavettes, and old man Desormeaux, pointing to his wife and daughter,—

" Those d—d women rob me," he said, " for the benefit of my son ; and they do it so cleverly that I can't find
out how. They have an understanding with the shop-
keepers, who are but licensed thieves ; and nothing is
eaten here that they don't make me pay double its
value."

M. Chapelain made an ill-concealed grimace; whilst
M. Desclavettes sincerely admired a man who had courage enough to confess his meanness.

But M. Desormeaux never minced things.

" Do you know, friend Vincent," he said, " that it
requires a strong stomach to take dinner with a man
who spends his time calculating the cost of every mouthful that his guests swallow ? "

M. Favoral turned red in the face.

" It is not the expense that I deplore," he replied,
" but the duplicity. I am rich enough, thank Heaven !
not to begrudge a few francs ; and I would gladly give
to my wife twice as much as she takes, if she would only
ask it frankly."

But that was a lesson.

Hereafter he was careful to dissimulate, and seemed
exclusively occupied in subjecting his son to a system of
his invention, the excessive rigor of which would have
upset a steadier one than he.

He demanded of him daily written attestations of his
attendance both at the law-school and at the lawyer's
office. He marked out the itinerary of his walks for him,
and measured the time they required, within a few minutes. Immediately after dinner he shut him up in his
room, under lock and key, and never failed, when he
came home at ten o'clock to make sure of his presence.

He could not have taken steps better calculated to ex-
alt still more Mme. Favoral's blind tenderness.

When she heard that Maxence had a mistress, she had been rudely shocked in her most cherished feelings. It is never without a secret jealousy that a mother discovers that a woman has robbed her of her son's heart. She had retained a certain amount of spite against him on account of disorders, which, in her candor, she had never suspected. She forgave him every thing when she saw of what treatment he was the object.

She took sides with him, believing him to be the victim of a most unjust persecution. In the evening, after her husband had gone out, Gilberte and herself would take their sewing, sit in the hall outside his room, and converse with him through the door. Never had they worked so hard for the shop-keeper in the Rue St. Denis. Some weeks they earned as much as twenty-five or thirty francs.

But Maxence's patience was exhausted; and one morning he declared resolutely that he would no longer attend the law-school, that he had been mistaken in his vocation, and that there was no human power capable to make him return to M. Chapelain's.

" And where will you go ? " exclaimed his father. " Do you expect me eternally to supply your wants ? "

He answered that it was precisely in order to support himself, and conquer his independence, that he had resolved to abandon a profession, which, after two years, yielded him twenty francs a month.

" I want some business where I have a chance to get rich," he replied. " I would like to enter a banking-house, or some great financial establishment."

Mme. Favoral jumped at the idea.

" That's a fact," she said to her husband. " Why couldn't you find a place for our son at the Mutual Credit? There he would be under your own eyes. Intelligent as he is, backed by M. de Thaller and yourself, he would soon earn a good salary."

M. Favoral knit his brows.

" That I shall never do," he uttered. " I have not sufficient confidence in my son. I cannot expose myself to have him compromise the consideration which I have acquired for myself."

And, revealing to a certain extent the secret of his conduct,—

" A cashier," he added, " who like me handles immense sums cannot be too careful of his reputation. Confidence is a delicate thing in these times, when there are so many cashiers constantly on the road to Belgium. Who knows what would be thought of me, if I was known to have such a son as mine? "

Mme. Favoral was insisting, nevertheless, when he seemed to make up his mind suddenly.

" Enough," he said. " Maxence is free. I allow him two years to establish himself in some position. That delay over, good-by: he can find board and lodging where he please. That's all. I don't want to hear any thing more about it."

It was with a sort of frenzy that Maxence abused that freedom; and in less than two weeks he had dissipated three months' earnings of his mother and sister.

That time over, he succeeded, thanks to M. Chapelain, in finding a place with an architect.

This was not a very brilliant opening; and the chances were, that he might remain a clerk all his life. But the future did not trouble him much. For the present, he was delighted with this inferior position, which assured him each month one hundred and seventy-five francs.

One hundred and seventy-five francs! A fortune.

And so he rushed into that life of questionable pleasures, where so many wretches have left not only the money which they had, which is nothing, but the money which they had not, which leads straight to the police-court.

He made friends with those shabby fellows who walk up and down in front of the Café Riche, with an empty stomach, and a tooth-pick between their teeth. He became a regular customer at those low *cafés* of the Boulevards, where plastered girls smile to the men. He frequented those suspicious *table d'hôtes* where they play baccarat after dinner on a wine-stained table-cloth, and where the police make periodical raids. He ate suppers in those night restaurants where people throw the bottles at each other's heads after drinking their contents.

Often he remained twenty-four hours without coming to the Rue St. Gilles; and then Mme. Favoral spent the night in the most fearful anxiety. Then, suddenly, at some hour when he knew his father to be absent, he would appear, and, taking his mother to one side,—

" I very much want a few louis," he would say in a sheepish tone.

She gave them to him; and she kept giving them so long as she had any, not, however, without observing timidly to him that Gilberte and herself could not earn very much.

Until finally one evening, and to a last demand,—

" Alas ! " she answered sorrowfully, " I have nothing left, and it is only on Monday that we are to take our work back. Couldn't you wait until then ? "

He could not wait : he was expected for a game. Blind devotion begets ferocious egotism. He wanted his mother to go out and borrow the money from the grocer or the butcher. She was hesitating. He spoke louder.

Then Mlle. Gilberte appeared.

" Have you, then, really no heart? " she said. " It seems to me, that, if I were a man, I would not ask my mother and sister to work for me."

XII.

GILBERTE FAVORAL had just completed her eighteenth year. Rather tall, slender, her every motion betrayed the admirable proportions of her figure, and had that grace which results from the harmonious blending of litheness and strength. She did not strike at first sight; but soon a penetrating and indefinable charm arose from her whole person; and one knew not which to admire most,—the exquisite perfections of her figure, the divine roundness of her neck, her aerial carriage, or the placid ingenuousness of her attitudes. She could not be called beautiful, inasmuch as her features lacked regularity; but the extreme mobility of her countenance, upon which could be read all the emotions of her soul, had an irresistible seduction. Her large eyes, of velvety blue, had untold depths and an incredible intensity of expression; the imperceptible quiver of her rosy nostrils revealed an untamable pride; and the smile that played upon her lips told her immense contempt for every thing mean and small. But her real beauty was her hair,—of a blonde so luminous that it seemed powdered with diamond-dust; so thick and so long, that to be able to twist and confine it, she had to cut off heavy locks of it to the very root.

Alone, in the house, she did not tremble at her father's voice. The studied despotism which had subdued Mme.

Favoral had revolted her, and her energy had become tempered under the same system of oppression which had unnerved Maxence.

Whilst her mother and her brother lied with that quiet impudence of the slave, whose sole weapon is duplicity, Gilberte preserved a sullen silence. And if complicity was imposed upon her by circumstances, if she had to maintain a falsehood, each word cost her such a painful effort, that her features became visibly altered.

Never, when her own interests were alone at stake, had she stooped to an untruth. Fearlessly, and whatever might be the result,—

" That is the fact," she would say.

Accordingly, M. Favoral could not help respecting her to a degree; and, when he was in fine humor, he called her the Empress Gilberte. For her alone he had some deference and some attentions. He moderated, when she looked at him, the brutality of his language. He brought her a few flowers every Saturday.

He had even allowed her a professor of music; though he was wont to declare that a woman needs but two accomplishments,—to cook and to sew. But she had insisted so much, that he had at last discovered for her, in an attic of the Rue du Pas-de-la-Mule, an old Italian master, the Signor Gismondo Pulei, a sort of unknown genius, for whom thirty francs a month were a fortune, and who conceived a sort of religious fanaticism for his pupil.

Though he had always refused to write a note, he consented, for her sake, to fix the melodies that buzzed in his cracked brain; and some of them proved to be admirable. He dreamed to compose for her an opera that would transmit to the most remote generations the name of Gismondo Pulei.

" The Signora Gilberte is the very goddess of music,"
he said to M. Favoral, with transports of enthusiasm,
which intensified still his frightful accent.

The cashier of the Mutual Credit Society shrugged
his shoulders, answering that there is no harmony for a
man who spends his days listening to the exciting music
of golden coins. In spite of which his vanity seemed
highly gratified, when on Saturday evenings, after dinner, Mlle. Gilberte sat at the piano, and Mme. Desclavettes, suppressing a yawn, would exclaim,—

" What remarkable talent the dear child has ! "

The young girl had, then, a positive influence ; and it
was to her entreaties alone, and not to those of his wife,
that he had several times forgiven Maxence. He would
have done much more for her, had she wished it ; but
she would have been compelled to ask, to insist, to beg.

" And it's humiliating," she used to say.

Sometimes Mme. Favoral scolded her gently, saying
that her father would certainly not refuse her one of
those pretty toilets which are the ambition and the joy
of young girls.

But she,—

" It is much less mortification to me to wear these
rags than to meet with a refusal," she replied. " I am
satisfied with my dresses."

With such a character, surrounded, however, by a
meek resignation, and an unalterable *sang-froid*, she
inspired a certain respect to both her mother and her
brother, who admired in her an energy of which they
felt themselves incapable.

And when she appeared, and commenced reproaching
him in an indignant tone of voice, with the baseness
of his conduct, and his insatiate demands, Maxence was
almost stunned.

" I did not know," he commenced, turning as red as
fire.

She crushed him with a look of mingled contempt and
pity; and, in an accent of haughty irony,—

" Indeed," she said, " you do not know whence the
money comes that you extort from our mother ! "

And holding up her hand, still remarkably handsome,
though slightly deformed by the constant handling of
the needle; the fourth finger of the right hand bent by
the thread, and the fore-finger of the left tattooed and
lacerated by the needle,—

" Indeed," she repeated, " you do not know that my
mother and myself, we spend all our days, and the
greater part of our nights, working ? "

Hanging his head, he said nothing.

" If it were for myself alone," she continued, " I
would not speak to you thus. But look at our mother !
See her poor eyes, red and weak from her ceaseless
labor ! If I have said nothing until now, it is because I did not as yet despair of your heart; because I hoped that you would recover some feeling of
decency. But no, nothing. With time, your last scruples
seem to have vanished. Once you begged humbly; now
you demand rudely. How soon will you resort to
blows ? "

" Gilberte ! " stammered the poor fellow, " Gilberte ! "

She interrupted him,—

" Money ! " she went on, " always, and without time,
you must have money; no matter whence it comes, nor
what it costs. If, at least, you had, to justify your expenses, the excuse of some great passion, or of some
object, were it absurd, ardently pursued ! But I defy
you to confess upon what degrading pleasures you lavish our humble economies. I defy you to tell us what

you mean to do with the sum that you demand to-night,
—that sum for which you would have our mother stoop
to beg the assistance of a shop-keeper, to whom we
would be compelled to reveal the secret of our shame."

Touched by the frightful humiliation of her son,—

" He is so unhappy ! " stammered Mme. Favoral.

" He unhappy ! " she exclaimed. " What, then, shall
we say of us ? and, above all, what shall you say of yourself, mother ?   Unhappy !—he, a man, who has liberty
and strength, who may undertake every thing, attempt
any thing, dare any thing.   Ah, I wish I were a man !
I !   I would be a man as there are some, as I know some ;
and I would have avenged you, O beloved mother ! long,
long ago, from father ; and I would have begun to repay
you all the good you have done me."

Mme. Favoral was sobbing.

" I beg of you," she murmured, " spare him."

" Be it so," said the young girl.   " But you must allow me to tell him that it is not for his sake that I devote
my youth to a mercenary labor.   It is for you, adored
mother, that you may have the joy to give him what
he asks, since it is your only joy."

Maxence shuddered under the breath of that superb
indignation.   That frightful humiliation, he felt that he
deserved it only too much.   He understood the justice of
these cruel reproaches.   And, as his heart had not yet
spoiled with the contact of his boon companions, as he
was weak, rather than wicked, as the sentiments which
are the honor and pride of a man were not dead within
him,—

" Ah ! you are a brave sister, Gilberte," he exclaimed ;
" and what you have just done is well.   You have been
harsh, but not as much as I deserve.   Thanks for your
courage, which will give me back mine.   Yes, it is a

shame for me to have thus cowardly abused you both."

And, raising his mother's hand to his lips,—

"Forgive, mother," he continued, his eyes overflowing with tears, "forgive him who swears to you to redeem his past, and to become your support, instead of being a crushing burden "—

He was interrupted by the noise of steps on the stairs, and the shrill sound of a whistle.

"My husband!" exclaimed Mme. Favoral,—"your father, my children!"

"Well," said Mlle. Gilberte coldly.

"Don't you hear that he is whistling? and do you forget that it is a proof that he is furious? What new trial threatens us again?"

XIII.

Mme. Favoral spoke from experience. She had learned, to her cost, that the whistle of her husband, more surely than the shriek of the stormy petrel, announces the storm. And she had that evening more reasons than usual to fear. Breaking from all his habits, M. Favoral had not come home to dinner, and had sent one of the clerks of the Mutual Credit Society to say that they should not wait for him.

Soon his latch-key grated in the lock; the door swung open; he came in; and, seeing his son,—

"Well, I am glad to find you here," he exclaimed with a giggle, which with him was the utmost expression of anger.

Mme. Favoral shuddered. Still under the impression of the scene which had just taken place, his heart heavy, and his eyes full of tears, Maxence did not answer.

"It is doubtless a wager," resumed the father, "and you wish to know how far my patience may go."

"I do not understand you," stammered the young man.

"The money that you used to get, I know not where, doubtless fails you now, or at least is no longer sufficient, and you go on making debts right and left,—at the tailor's, the shirt maker's, the jeweller's. Of course, it's simple enough. We earn nothing; but we wish to dress in the latest style, to wear a gold chain across our vest, and then we make dupes."

"I have never made any dupes, father."

"Bah! And what, then, do you call all these people who came this very day to present me their bills? For they did dare to come to my office! They had agreed to come together, expecting thus to intimidate me more easily. I told them that you were of age, and that your business was none of mine. Hearing this, they became insolent, and commenced speaking so loud, that their voices could be heard in the adjoining rooms. At that very moment, the manager, M. de Thaller, happened to be passing through the hall. Hearing the noise of a discussion, he thought that I was having some difficulty with some of our stockholders, and he came in, as he had a right to. Then I was compelled to confess every thing."

He became excited at the sound of his words, like a horse at the jingle of his bells. And, more and more beside himself,—

"That is just what your creditors wished," he pursued. "They thought I would be afraid of a row, and that I would 'come down.' It is a system of blackmailing, like any other. An account is opened to some young rascal; and, when the amount is reasonably large, they

take it to the family, saying, ' Money, or I make row.'
Do you think it is to you, who are penniless, that they
give credit? It's on my pocket that they were drawing,
—on my pocket, because they believed me rich. They
sold you at exorbitant prices every thing they wished;
and they relied on me to pay for trousers at ninety
francs, shirts at forty francs, and watches at six hundred
francs."

Contrary to his habit, Maxence did not offer any denial.

" I expect to pay all I owe," he said.

" You! "

" I give my word I will! "

" And with what, pray? "

" With my salary."

" You have a salary, then? "

Maxence blushed.

" I have what I earn at my employer's."

" What employer? "

" The architect in whose office M. Chapelain helped
me to find a place."

With a threatening gesture, M. Favoral interrupted
him.

" Spare me your lies," he uttered. " I am better
posted than you suppose. I know, that, over a month
ago, your employer, tired of your idleness, dismissed
you in disgrace."

Disgrace was superfluous. The fact was, that Maxence, returning to work after an absence of five days,
had found another in his place.

" I shall find another place," he said.

M. Favoral shrugged his shoulders with a movement
of rage.

" And in the mean time," he said, " I shall have to
pay. Do you know what your creditors threaten to do?
—to commence a suit against me. They would lose it, of
course, they know it; but they hope that I would yield
before a scandal. And this is not all: they talk of entering a criminal complaint. They pretend that you
have audaciously swindled them; that the articles you
purchased of them were not at all for your own use, but
that you sold them as fast as you got them, at any price
you could obtain, to raise ready money. The jeweller has
proofs, he says, that you went straight from his shop
to the pawnbroker's, and pledged a watch and chain
which he had just sold you. It is a police matter. They
said all that in presence of my superior officer,—in presence of M. de Thaller. I had to get the janitor to put
them out. But, after they had left, M. de Thaller gave
me to understand that he wished me very much to settle
every thing. And he is right. My consideration could
not resist another such scene. What confidence can be
placed in a cashier whose son behaves in this manner?
How can a key of a safe containing millions be left
with a man whose son would have been dragged
into the police-courts? In a word, I am at your mercy.
In a word, my honor, my position, my fortune, rest upon
you. As often as it may please you to make
debts, you can make them, and I shall be compelled
to pay."

Gathering all his courage,—

" You have been sometimes very harsh with me,
father," commenced Maxence; " and yet I will not try
to justify my conduct. I swear to you, that hereafter
you shall have nothing to fear from me."

" I fear nothing," uttered M. Favoral with a sinister

smile. " I know the means of placing myself beyond
the reach of your follies; and I shall use them."

" I assure you, father, that I have taken a firm resolution."

" Oh! you may dispense with your periodical repentance."

Mlle. Gilberte stepped forward.

" I'll stand warrant," she said, " for Maxence's resolutions."

Her father did not permit her to proceed.

" Enough," he interrupted somewhat harshly. " Mind
your own business, Gilberte! I have to speak to you
too."

" To me, father."

" Yes."

He walked up and down three or four times through
the parlor, as if to calm his irritation. Then planting
himself straight before his daughter, his arms folded
across his breast,—

" You are eighteen years of age," he said; " that is to
say, it is time to think of your marriage. An excellent
match offers itself."

She shuddered, stepped back, and, redder than a
peony,—

" A match!" she repeated in a tone of immense surprise.

" Yes, and which suits me."

" But I do not wish to marry, father."

" All young girls say the same thing; and, as soon as
a pretender offers himself, they are delighted. Mine
is a fellow of twenty-six, quite good looking, amiable,
witty, and who has had the greatest success in society."

" Father, I assure you that I do not wish to leave
mother."

"Of course not. He is an intelligent, hard-working man, destined, everybody says, to make an immense fortune. Although he is rich already, for he holds a controlling interest in a stock-broker's firm, he works as hard as any poor devil. I would not be surprised to hear that he makes half a million of francs a year. His wife will have her carriage, her box at the opera, diamonds, and dresses as handsome as Mme. de Thaller's."

"Eh! What do I care for such things?"

"It's understood. I'll present him to you on Saturday."

But Mlle. Gilberte was not one of those young girls who allow themselves, through weakness or timidity, to become engaged, and so far engaged, that later, they can no longer withdraw. A discussion being unavoidable, she preferred to have it out at once.

"A presentation is absolutely useless, father," she declared resolutely.

"Because?"

"I have told you that I did not wish to marry."

"But if it is my will?"

"I am ready to obey you in every thing except that."

"In that as in every thing else," interrupted the cashier of the Mutual Credit in a thundering voice.

And, casting upon his wife and children a glance full of defiance and threats,—

"In that, as in every thing else," he repeated, "because I am the master; and I shall prove it. Yes, I will prove it; for I am tired to see my family leagued against my authority."

And out he went, slamming the door so violently, that the partitions shook.

"You are wrong to resist your father thus," murmured the weak Mme. Favoral.

The fact is, that the poor woman could not under-stand why her daughter refused the only means at her command to break off with her miserable existence.

" Let him present you this young man," she said. " You might like him."

" I am sure I shall not like him."

She said this in such a tone, that the light suddenly flashed upon Mme. Favoral's mind.

" Heavens ! " she murmured. " Gilberte, my darling child, have you then a secret which your mother does not know ? "

XIV.

YES, Mlle. Gilberte had her secret,—a very simple one, though, chaste, like herself, and one of those which, as the old women say, must cause the angels to rejoice.

The spring of that year having been unusually mild, Mme. Favoral and her daughter had taken the habit of going daily to breathe the fresh air in the Place Royale. They took their work with them, crotchet or knitting; so that this salutary exercise did not in any way diminish the earnings of the week. It was during these walks that Mlle. Gilberte had at last noticed a young man, unknown to her, whom she met every day at the same place.

Tall and robust, he had a grand look, notwithstanding his modest clothes, the exquisite neatness of which betrayed a sort of respectable poverty. He wore his full beard; and his proud and intelligent features were lighted up by a pair of large black eyes, of those eyes whose straight and clear look disconcerts hypocrites **and** knaves.

He never failed, as he passed by Mlle. Gilberte, to

look down, or turn his head slightly away; and in spite
of this, in spite of the expression of respect which she
had detected upon his face, she could not help blushing.

"Which is absurd," she thought; "for after all, what
on earth do I care for that young man?"

The infallible instinct, which is the experience of in-
experienced young girls, told her that it was not chance
alone that brought this stranger in her way. But she
wished to make sure of it. She managed so well, that
each day of the following week, the hour of their walk
was changed. Sometimes they went out at noon, sometimes after four o'clock.

But, whatever the hour, Mlle. Gilberte, as she turned
the corner of the Rue des Minimes, noticed her unknown admirer under the arcades, looking in some shop-
window, and watching out of the corner of his eye. As
soon as she appeared, he left his post, and hurried fast
enough to meet her at the gate of the Place.

"It is a persecution," thought Mlle. Gilberte.

How, then, had she not spoken of it to her mother?
Why had she not said any thing to her the day, when,
happening, to look out of the window, she saw her
"persecutor" passing before the house, or evidently
looking in her direction?

"Am I losing my mind?" she thought, seriously irritated against herself. "I will not think of him any
more."

And yet she was thinking of him, when one afternoon, as her mother and herself were working, sitting
upon a bench, she saw the stranger come and sit down
not far from them. He was accompanied by an elderly
man with long white mustaches, and wearing the rosette
of the Legion of Honor.

"This is an insolence," thought the young girl, whilst

seeking a pretext to ask her mother to change their seats.

But already had the young man and his elderly friend seated themselves, and so arranged their chairs, that Mlle. Gilberte could not miss a word of what they were about to say. It was the young man who spoke first.

"You know me as well as I know myself, my dear count," he commenced,—"you who were my poor father's best friend, you who dandled me upon your knees when I was a child, and who has never lost sight of me."

"Which is to say, my boy, that I answer for you as for myself," put in the old man. "But go on."

"I am twenty-six years old. My name is Yves-Marius-Genost de Trégars. My family, which is one of the oldest of Brittany, is allied to all the great families."

"Perfectly exact," remarked the old gentleman.

"Unfortunately, my fortune is not on a par with my nobility. When my mother died, in 1856, my father, who worshipped her, could no longer bear, in the intensity of his grief, to remain at the Château de Trégars where he had spent his whole life. He came to Paris, which he could well afford, since we were rich then, but unfortunately, made acquaintances who soon inoculated him with the fever of the age. They proved to him that he was mad to keep lands which barely yielded him forty thousand francs a year, and which he could easily sell for two millions; which amount, invested merely at five per cent, would yield him an income of one hundred thousand francs. He therefore sold every thing, except our patrimonial homestead on the road from Quimper to Audierne, and rushed into speculations. He was rather lucky at first. But he was too honest and too loyal to be lucky long. An operation in which he be-

came interested early in 1869 turned out badly. His as-
sociates became rich; but he, I know not how, was
ruined, and came near being compromised. He died of
grief a month later."

The old soldier was nodding his assent.

"Very well, my boy," he said. "But you are too
modest; and there's a circumstance which you neglect.
You had a right, when your father became involved in
these troubles, to claim and retain your mother's fortune; that is, some thirty thousand francs a year. Not
only you did not do so; but you gave up every thing to
his creditors. You sold the domain of Trégars, except
the old castle and its park, and paid over the proceeds
to them; so that, if your father did die ruined, at least
he did not owe a cent. And yet you knew, as well as
myself, that your father had been deceived and swindled
by a lot of scoundrels who drive their carriages now,
and who, perhaps, if the courts were applied to, might
still be made to disgorge their ill-gotten plunder."

Her head bent upon her tapestry, Mlle. Gilberte
seemed to be working with incomparable zeal. The truth
is, she knew not how to conceal the blushes on her
cheeks, and the trembling of her hands. She had something like a cloud before her eyes; and she drove her
needle at random. She scarcely preserved enough presence of mind to reply to Mme. Favoral, who, not noticing any thing, spoke to her from time to time.

Indeed, the meaning of this scene was too clear to
escape her.

"They have had an understanding," she thought,
"and it is for me alone that they are speaking."

Meantime, Marius de Trégars was going on,—

"I should lie, my old friend, were I to say that I was
indifferent to our ruin. Philosopher though one may

be, it is not without some pangs that one passes from a sumptuous hotel to a gloomy garret. But what grieved me most of all was that I saw myself compelled to give up the labors which had been the joy of my life, and upon which I had founded the most magnificent hopes. A positive vocation, stimulated further by the accidents of my education, had led me to the study of physical sciences. For several years, I had applied all I have of intelligence and energy to certain investigations in electricity. To convert electricity into an incomparable motive-power which would supersede steam, —such was the object I pursued without pause. Already, as you know, although quite young, I had obtained results which had attracted some attention in the scientific world. I thought I could see the last of a problem, the solution of which would change the face of the globe. Ruin was the death of my hopes, the total loss of the fruits of my labors; for my experiments were costly, and it required money, much money, to purchase the products which were indispensable to me, and to construct the machines which I contrived.

" And I was about being compelled to earn my daily bread.

" I was on the verge of despair, when I met a man whom I had formerly seen at my father's, and who had seemed to take some interest in my researches, a speculator named Marcolet. But it is not at the *bourse* that he operates. Industry is the field of his labors. Ever on the lookout for those obstinate inventors who are starving to death in their garrets, he appears to them at the hour of supreme crisis: he pities them, encourages them, consoles them, helps them, and almost always succeeds in becoming the owner of their discovery. Some-

times he makes a mistake; and then all he has to do is to
put a few thousand francs to the debit of profit or loss.
But, if he has judged right, then he counts his profits
by hundreds of thousands; and how many patents does
he work thus! Of how many inventions does he reap
the results which are a fortune, and the inventors of
which have no shoes to wear! Every thing is good to
him; and he defends with the same avidity a cough-
sirup, the formula of which he has purchased of some
poor devil of a druggist, and an improvement to the
steam-engine, the patent for which has been sold to him
by an engineer of genius. And yet Marcolet is not
a bad man. Seeing my situation, he offered me a certain yearly sum to undertake some studies of indus-
trial chemistry which he indicated to me. I accepted;
and the very next day I hired a small basement in the
Rue des Tournelles, where I set up my laboratory, and
went to work at once. That was a year ago. Marcolet
must be satisfied. I have already found for him a new
shade for dyeing silk, the cost price of which is almost
nothing. As to me, I have lived with the strictest economy, devoting all my surplus earnings to the prosecution
of the problem, the solution of which would give me
both glory and fortune."

Palpitating with inexpressible emotion, Mlle. Gilberte
was listening to this young man, unknown to her a few
moments since, and whose whole history she now knew
as well as if she had always lived near him; for it never
occurred to her to suspect his sincerity.

No voice had ever vibrated to her ear like this voice,
whose grave sonorousness stirred within her strange
sensations, and legions of thoughts which she had never
suspected. She was surprised at the accent of sim-

plicity with which he spoke of the illustriousness of his
family, of his past opulence, of his obscure labors, and
of his exalted hopes.

She admired the superb disregard for money which
beamed forth in his every word. Here was then one
man, at least, who despised that money before which
she had hitherto seen all the people she knew prostrated
in abject worship.

After a pause of a few moments, Marius de Trégars,
still addressing himself apparently to his aged companion, went on,—

"I repeat it, because it is the truth, my old friend,
this life of labor and privation, so new to me, was not
a burden. Calm, silence, the constant exercise of all the
faculties of the intellect, have charms which the vulgar
can never suspect. I was happy to think, that, if I was
ruined, it was through an act of my own will. I found
a positive pleasure in the fact that I, the Marquis de
Trégars, who had had a hundred thousand a year,—I
must the next moment go out in person to the baker's
and the green-grocer's to purchase my supplies for the
day. I was proud to think that it was to my labor alone,
to the work for which I was paid by Marcolet, that I
owed the means of prosecuting my task. And, from the
summits where I was carried on the wings of science,
I took pity on your modern existence, on that ridiculous
and tragical medley of passions, interests, and cravings,
that struggle without truce or mercy, whose law is, woe
to the weak, in which whosoever falls is trampled under
feet.

"Sometimes, however, like a fire that has been smoul-
dering under the ashes, the flame of youthful passions
blazed up within me. I had hours of madness, of discouragement, of distress, during which solitude was

loathsome to me. But I had the faith which raises mountains,—faith in myself and my work. And soon, tranquilized, I would go to sleep in the purple of hope, beholding in the vista of the distant future the triumphal arches erected to my success.

" Such was my situation, when, one afternoon in the month of February last, after an experiment upon which I had founded great hopes, and which had just miserably failed, I came here to breathe a little fresh air.

" It was a beautiful spring day, warm and sunny. The sparrows were chirping on the branches, swelled with sap: bands of children were running along the alleys, filling the air with their joyous screams.

" I was sitting upon a bench, ruminating over the causes of my failure, when two ladies passed by me; one somewhat aged, the other quite young. They were walking so rapidly, that I hardly had time to see them.

" But the young lady's step, the noble simplicity of her carriage, had struck me so much, that I rose to follow her with the intention of passing her, and then walking back to have a good view of her face. I did so; and I was fairly dazzled. At the moment when my eyes met hers, a voice rose within me, crying that it was all over now, and that my destiny was fixed."

" I remember, my dear boy," remarked the old soldier in a tone of friendly raillery; " for you came to see me that night, and I had not seen you for months before."

Marius proceeded without heeding the remark.

" And yet you know that I am not the man to yield to a first impression. I struggled: with determined energy I strove to drive off that radiant image which I carried within my soul, which left me no more, which haunted me in the midst of my studies.

"Vain efforts. My thoughts obeyed me no longer: my will escaped my control. It was indeed one of those passions that fill the whole being, overpower all, and which make of life an ineffable felicity or a nameless torture, according that they are reciprocated, or not. How many days I spent there, waiting and watching for her of whom I had thus had a glimpse, and who ignored my very existence! And what insane palpitations, when, after hours of consuming anxiety, I saw at the corner of the street the undulating folds of her dress! I saw her thus often, and always with the same elderly person, her mother. They had adopted in this square a particular bench, where they sat daily, working at their sewing with an assiduity and zeal which made me think that they lived upon the product of their labor."

Here he was suddenly interrupted by his companion. The old gentleman feared that Mme. Favoral's attention might at last be attracted by too direct allusions.

"Take care, boy!" he whispered, not so low, however, but what Gilberte overheard him.

But it would have required much more than this to draw Mme. Favoral from her sad thoughts. She had just finished her band of tapestry; and, grieving to lose a moment,—

"It is perhaps time to go home," she said to her daughter. "I have nothing more to do."

Mlle. Gilberte drew from her basket a piece of canvas, and, handing it to her mother,—

"Here is enough to go on with, mamma," she said in a troubled voice. "Let us stay a little while longer."

And, Mme. Favoral having resumed her work, Marius proceeded,—

"The thought that she whom I loved was poor delighted me. Was not this similarity of positions a link between us? I felt a childish joy to think that I would work for her and for her mother, and that they would be indebted to me for their ease and comfort in life.

"But I am not one of those dreamers who confide their destiny to the wings of a chimera. Before undertaking any thing, I resolved to inform myself. Alas! at the first words that I heard, all my fine dreams took wings. I heard that she was rich, very rich. I was told that her father was one of those men whose rigid probity surrounds itself with austere and harsh forms. He owed his fortune, I was assured, to his sole labor, but also to prodigies of economy and the most severe privations. He professed a worship, they said, for that gold that had cost him so much; and he would never give the hand of his daughter to a man who had no money. This last comment was useless. Above my actions, my thoughts, my hopes, higher than all, soars my pride. Instantly I saw an abyss opening between me and her whom I love more than my life, but less than my dignity. When a man's name is Genost de Trégars, he must support his wife, were it by breaking stones. And the thought that I owed my fortune to the woman I married would make me execrate her.

"You must remember, my old friend, that I told you all this at the time. You thought, too, that it was singularly impertinent, on my part, thus to flare up in advance, because certainly a millionaire does not give his daughter to a ruined nobleman in the pay of Marcolet, the patent-broker, to a poor devil of an inventor, who is building the castles of his future upon the solution of a problem which has been given up by the most brilliant minds.

"It was then that I determined upon an extreme resolution, a foolish one, no doubt, and yet to which you, the Count de Villegré, my father's old friend, you have consented to lend yourself.

" I thought that I would address myself to her, to her alone, and that she would at least know what great, what immense love she had inspired. I thought I would go to her and tell her, ' This is who I am, and what I am. For mercy's sake, grant me a respite of three years. To a love such as mine there is nothing impossible. In three years I shall be dead, or rich enough to ask your hand. From this day forth, I give up my task for work of more immediate profit. The arts of industry have treasures for successful inventors. If you could only read in my soul, you would not refuse me the delay I am asking. Forgive me! One word, for mercy's sake, only one! It is my sentence that I am awaiting.' "

Mlle. Gilberte's thoughts were in too great a state of confusion to permit her to think of being offended at this extraordinary proceeding.

She rose, quivering, and addressing herself to Mme. Favoral,—

" Come, mother," she said, " come: I feel that I have taken cold. I must go home and think. To-morrow, yes, to-morrow, we will come again."

Deep as Mme. Favoral was plunged in her meditations, and a thousand miles as she was from the actual situation, it was impossible that she should not notice the intense excitement under which her daughter labored, the alteration of her features, and the incoherence of her words.

" What is the matter? " she asked, somewhat alarmed. " What are you saying? "

" I feel unwell," answered her daughter in a scarcely audible voice, " quite unwell. Come, let us go home."

As soon as they reached home, Mlle. Gilberte took

refuge in her own room. She was in haste to be alone, to recover her self-possession, to collect her thoughts, more scattered than dry leaves by a storm wind.

It was a momentous event which had just suddenly fallen in her life so monotonous and so calm,—an inconceivable, startling event, the consequences of which were to weigh heavily upon her entire future.

Staggering still, she was asking herself if she was not the victim of an hallucination, and if really there was a man who had dared to conceive and execute the audacious project of coming thus under the eyes of her mother, of declaring his love, and of asking her in return a solemn engagement. But what stupefied her more still, what confused her, was that she had actually endured such an attempt.

Under what despotic influence had she, then, fallen? To what undefinable sentiments had she obeyed? And if she had only tolerated! But she had done more: she had actually encouraged. By detaining her mother when she wished to go home (and she had detained her), had she not said to this unknown?—

" Go on, I allow it: I am listening."

And he had gone on. And she, at the moment of returning home, she had engaged herself formally to reflect, and to return the next day at a stated hour to give an answer. In a word, she had made an appointment with him.

It was enough to make her die of shame. And, as if she had needed the sound of her own words to convince herself of the reality of the fact, she kept repeating loud,—

" I have made an appointment,—I, Gilberte, with a man whom my parents do not know, and of whose name I was still ignorant yesterday."

And yet she could not take upon herself to be indignant at the imprudent boldness of her conduct. The bitterness of the reproaches which she was addressing to herself was not sincere. She felt it so well, that at last,—

" Such hypocrisy is unworthy of me." she exclaimed, " since now, still, and without the excuse of being taken by surprise, I would not act otherwise."

The fact is, the more she pondered, the less she could succeed in discovering even the shadow of any offensive intention in all that Marius de Trégars had said. By the choice of his confidant, an old man, a friend of his family, a man of the highest respectability, he had done all in his power to make his step excusable. It was impossible to doubt his sincerity, to suspect the fairness of his intentions.

Mlle. Gilberte, better than almost any other young girl, could understand the extreme measure resorted to by M. de Trégars. By her own pride she could understand his. No more than he, in his place, would she have been willing to expose herself to a certain refusal. What was there, then, so extraordinary in the fact of his coming directly to her, in his exposing to her frankly and loyally his situation, his projects, and his hopes?

" Good heavens!" she thought, horrified at the sentiments which she discovered in the deep recesses of her soul, " good heavens! I hardly know myself any more. Here I am actually approving what he has done!"

Well, yes, she did approve him, attracted, fascinated, by the very strangeness of the situation. Nothing seemed to her more admirable than the conduct of Marius de Trégars sacrificing his fortune and his most legitimate aspirations to the honor of his name, and condemning himself to work for his living.

" That one," she thought, " is a man; and his wife will have just cause to be proud of him."

Involuntarily she compared him to the only men she knew,—to M. Favoral, whose miserly parsimony had made his whole family wretched; to Maxence, who did not blush to feed his disorders with the fruits of his mother's and his sister's labor.

How different was Marius! If he was poor, it was of his own will. Had she not seen what confidence he had in himself. She shared it fully. She felt certain, that, within the required delay, he would conquer that indispensable fortune. Then he might present himself boldly. He would take her away from the miserable surroundings among which she seemed fated to live: she would become the Marchioness de Trégars.

" Why, then, not answer, Yes! " thought she, with the harrowing emotions of the gambler who is about to stake his all upon one card. And what a game for Mlle. Gilberte, and what a stake!

Suppose she had been mistaken. Suppose that Marius should be one of those villains who make of seduction a science. Would she still be her own mistress, after answering? Did she know to what hazards such an engagement would expose her? Was she not about rushing blindfolded towards those deceiving perils where a young girl leaves her reputation, even when she saves her honor?

She thought, for a moment, of consulting her mother. But she knew Mme. Favoral's shrinking timidity, and that she was as incapable of giving any advice as to make her will prevail. She would be frightened; she would approve all; and, at the first alarm, she would confess all.

" Am I, then, so weak and so foolish," she thought,

"that I cannot take a determination which affects me personally?"

She could not close her eyes all night; but in the morning her resolution was settled.

And toward one o'clock,—

"Are we not going out mother?" she said.

Mme. Favoral was hesitating.

"These early spring days are treacherous," she objected: "you caught cold yesterday."

"My dress was too thin. To-day I have taken my precautions."

They started, taking their work with them, and came to occupy their accustomed seats.

Before they had even passed the gates, Mlle. Gilberte had recognized Marius de Trégars and the Count de Villegré, walking in one of the side alleys. Soon, as on the day before, they took two chairs, and settled themselves within hearing.

Never had the young girl's heart beat with such violence. It is easy enough to take a resolution; but it is not always quite so easy to execute it, and she was asking herself if she would have strength enough to articulate a word. At last, gathering her whole courage,—

"You don't believe in dreams, do you mother?" she asked.

Upon this subject, as well as upon many others, Mme. Favoral had no particular opinion.

"Why do you ask the question?" said she.

"Because I have had such a strange one."

"Oh!"

"It seemed to me that suddenly a young man, whom I did not know, stood before me. He would have been most happy, said he to me, to ask my hand, but he dared not, being very poor. And he begged me to wait three years, during which he would make his fortune."

Mme. Favoral smiled.

"Why it's quite a romance," said she.

"But it wasn't a romance in my dream," interrupted Mlle. Gilberte. "This young man spoke in a tone of such profound conviction, that it was impossible for me, as it were, to doubt him. I thought to myself that he would be incapable of such an odious villainy as to abuse the confiding credulity of a poor girl."

"And what did you answer him?"

Moving her seat almost imperceptibly, Mlle. Gilberte could, from the corner of her eye, have a glimpse of M. de Trégars. Evidently he was not missing a single one of the words which she was addressing to her mother. He was whiter than a sheet; and his face betrayed the most intense anxiety.

This gave her the energy to curb the last revolts of her conscience.

"To answer was painful," she uttered; "and yet I dared to answer him. I said to him, 'I believe you, and I have faith in you. Loyally and faithfully I shall await your success; but until then we must be strangers to one another. To resort to ruse, deceit, and falsehood would be unworthy of us. You surely would not expose to a suspicion her who is to be your wife.'"

"Very well," approved Mme. Favoral; "only I did not know you were so romantic."

She was laughing, the good lady, but not loud enough to prevent Gilberte from hearing M. de Trégar's answer.

"Count de Villegré," said he, "my old friend, receive the oath which I take to devote my life to her who has not doubted me. It is to-day the 4th of May, 1870:

on the 4th of May, 1873, I shall have succeeded: I feel
it, I will it, it must be!"

XV.

It was done: Gilberte Favoral had just irrevocably
disposed of herself. Prosperous or wretched, her destiny henceforth was linked with another. She had set
the wheel in motion; and she could no longer hope to
control its direction, any more than the will can pretend
to alter the course of the ivory ball upon the surface
of the roulette-table. At the outset of this great storm
of passion which had suddenly surrounded her, she felt
an immense surprise, mingled with unexplained apprehensions and vague terrors.

Around her, apparently, nothing was changed.
Father, mother, brother, friends, gravitated mechanically in their accustomed orbits. The same daily facts
repeated themselves monotonous and regular as the tick-
tack of the clock.

And yet an event had occurred more prodigious for
her than the moving of a mountain.

Often during the weeks that followed, she would repeat to herself, " Is it true, is it possible even?"

Or else she would run to a mirror to make sure once
more that nothing upon her face or in her eyes betrayed
the secret that palpitated within her.

The singularity of the situation was, moreover, well
calculated to trouble and confound her mind.

Mastered by circumstances, she had in utter disregard
of all accepted ideas, and of the commonest propriety,
listened to the passionate promises of a stranger, and

pledged her life to him. And, the pact concluded and solemnly sworn, they had parted without knowing when propitious circumstances might bring them together again.

"Certainly," thought she, "before God, M. de Trégars is my betrothed husband; and yet we have never exchanged a word. Were we to meet in society, we should be compelled to meet as strangers: if he passes by me in the street, he has no right to bow to me. I know not where he is, what becomes of him, nor what he is doing."

And in fact she had not seen him again: he had given no sign of life, so faithfully did he conform to her expressed wish. And perhaps secretly, and without acknowledging it to herself, had she wished him less scrupulous. Perhaps she would not have been very angry to see him sometimes gliding along at her passage under the old Arcades of the Rue des Vosges.

But, whilst suffering from this separation, she conceived for the character of Marius the highest esteem; for she felt sure that he must suffer as much and more than she from the restraint which he imposed upon himself.

Thus he was ever present to her thoughts. She never tired of turning over in her mind all he had said of his past life: she tried to remember his words, and the very tone of his voice.

And by living constantly thus with the memory of Marius de Trégars, she made herself familiar with him, deceived to that extent, by the illusion of absence, that she actually persuaded herself that she knew him better and better every day.

Already nearly a month had elapsed, when one afternoon, as she arrived on the Place Royale, she recognized him, standing near that same bench where they had so strangely exchanged their pledges.

He saw her coming too: she knew it by his looks. But, when she had arrived within a few steps of him, he walked off rapidly, leaving on the bench a folded news-paper.

Mme. Favoral wished to call him back and return it; but Mlle. Gilberte persuaded her not to.

"Never mind, mother," said she, "it isn't worth while; and, besides, the gentleman is too far now."

But while getting out her embroidery, with that dexterity which never fails even the most *naive* girls, she slipped the newspaper in her work-basket.

Was she not certain that it had been left there for her?

As soon as she had returned home, she locked herself up in her own room, and, after searching for some time through the columns, she read at last,—

"One of the richest and most intelligent manufacturers in Paris, M. Marcolet, has just purchased in Grenelle the vast grounds belonging to the Lacoche estate. He proposes to build upon them a manufacture of chemical products, the management of which is to be placed in the hands of M. de T——.

"Although still quite young, M. de T—— is already well known in connection with his remarkable studies on electricity. He was, perhaps, on the eve of solving the much controverted problem of electricity as a mo-tive-power, when his father's ruin compelled him to suspend his labors. He now seeks to earn by his personal industry the means of prosecuting his costly experiments.

"He is not the first to tread this path. Is it not to the invention of the machine bearing his name, that the engineer Giffard owes the fortune which enables him to continue to seek the means of steering balloons? Why should not M. de T——, who has as much skill and energy, have as much luck?"

"Ah! he does not forget me," thought Mlle. Gilberte, moved to tears by this article, which, after all, was but a mere puff, written by Marcolet himself, without the knowledge of M. de Trégars.

She was still under that impression, thinking that Marius was already at work, when her father announced to her that he had discovered a husband, and enjoined her to find him to her liking, as he, the master, thought it proper that she should.

Hence the energy of her refusal.

But hence also, the imprudent vivacity which had enlightened Mme. Favoral, and which made her say,—

"You hide something from me, Gilberte?"

Never had the young girl been so cruelly embarrassed as she was at this moment by this sudden and unforeseen perspicacity.

Would she confide to her mother?

She felt, indeed, no repugnance to do so, certain as she was, in advance, of the inexhaustible indulgence of the poor woman; and, besides, she would have been delighted to have some one at last with whom she could speak of Marius.

But she knew that her father was not the man to give up a project conceived by himself. She knew that he would return to the charge obstinately, without peace, and without truce. Now, as she was determined to resist with a no less implacable obstinacy, she foresaw terrible struggles, all sorts of violence and persecutions.

Informed of the truth, would Mme. Favoral have strength enough to resist these daily storms? Would not a time come, when, called upon by her husband to explain the refusals of her daughter, threatened, terrified, she would confess all?

At one glance Mlle. Gilberte estimated the danger; and, drawing from necessity an audacity which was very foreign to her nature,—

" You are mistaken, dear mother," said she, " I have concealed nothing from you."

Not quite convinced, Mme. Favoral shook her head.

" Then," said she, " you will yield."

" Never! "

" Then there must be some reason you do not tell me."

" None, except that I do not wish to leave you. Have you ever thought what would be your existence if I were no longer here? Have you ever asked yourself what would become of you, between my father, whose despotism will grow heavier with age, and my brother? "

Always prompt to defend her son,—

" Maxence is not bad," she interrupted: " he will know how to compensate me for the sorrows he has inflicted upon me."

The young girl made a gesture of doubt,—

" I wish it, dear mother," said she, " with all my heart; but I dare not hope for it. His repentance to-night was great and sincere; but will he remember it to-morrow? Besides, don't you know that father has fully resolved to separate himself from Maxence? Think of yourself alone here with father."

Mme. Favoral shuddered at the mere idea.

" I would not suffer very long," she murmured.

Mlle. Gilberte kissed her.

" It is because I wish you to live to be happy that I refuse to marry," she exclaimed. " Must you not have your share of happiness in this world? Let me manage.

Who knows what compensations the future may have in store for you? Besides, this person whom father has selected for me does not suit me. A stock-jobber, who would think of nothing but money, who would examine my house-accounts as papa does yours, or else who would load me with cashmeres and diamonds, like Mme. de Thaller, to make of me a sign for his shop? No, no! I want no such man. So, mother dear, be brave, take sides boldly with your daughter, and we shall soon be rid of this would-be husband."

"Your father will bring him to you: he said he would."

"Well, he is a man of courage, if he returns three times."

At this moment the parlor-door opened suddenly.

"What are you plotting here again?" cried the irritated voice of the master. "And you, Mme. Favoral, why don't you go to bed?"

The poor slave obeyed, without saying a word. And, whilst making her way to her room,—

"There is trouble ahead," thought Mlle. Gilberte. "But bash! If I do have to suffer some, it won't be great harm, after all. Surely Marius does not complain, though he gives up for me his dearest hopes, becomes the salaried employé of M. Marcolet, and thinks of nothing but making money,—he so proud and so disinterested!"

Mlle. Gilberte's anticipations were but too soon realized. When M. Favoral made his appearance the next morning, he had the sombre brow and contracted lips of a man who has spent the night ruminating a plan from which he does not mean to swerve.

Instead of going to his office, as usual, without saying a word to any one, he called his wife and children to the parlor; and, after having carefully bolted all the doors, he turned to Maxence.

"I want you," he commenced, "to give me a list of your creditors. See that you forget none; and let it be ready as soon as possible."

But Maxence was no longer the same man. After the terrible and well-deserved reproaches of his sister, a salutary revolution had taken place in him. During the preceding night, he had reflected over his conduct for the past four years; and he had been dismayed and terrified. His impression was like that of the drunkard, who, having become sober, remembers the ridiculous or degrading acts which he has committed under the influence of alcohol, and, confused and humiliated, swears never more to drink.

Thus Maxence had sworn to himself to change his mode of life, promising that it would be no drunkard's oath, either. And his attitude and his looks showed the pride of great resolutions.

Instead of lowering his eyes before the irritated glance of M. Favoral, and stammering excuses and vague promises,—

"It is useless, father," he replied, "to give you the list you ask for. I am old enough to bear the responsibility of my acts. I shall repair my follies: what I owe, I shall pay. This very day I shall see my creditors, and make arrangements with them."

"Very well, Maxence," exclaimed Mme. Favoral, delighted.

But there was no pacifying the cashier of the Mutual Credit.

"Those are fine-sounding words," he said with a sneer; "but I doubt if the tailors and the shirt-makers will take them in payment. That's why I want that list."

" Still "—

" It's I who shall pay. I do not mean to have another such scene as that of yesterday in my office. It must not be said that my son is a sharper and a cheat at the very moment when I find for my daughter a most unhoped-for match."

And, turning to Mlle. Gilberte,—

" For I suppose you have got over your foolish ideas," he uttered.

The young girl shook her head.

" My ideas are the same as they were last night."

" Ah, ah ! "

" And so, father, I beg of you, do not insist. Why wrangle and quarrel? You must know me well enough to know, that, whatever may happen, I shall never yield."

Indeed, M. Favoral was well aware of his daughter's firmness; for he had already been compelled on several occasions, as he expressed it himself, " to strike his flag " before her. But he could not believe that she would resist when he took certain means of enforcing his will.

" I have pledged my word," he said.

" But I have not pledged mine, father."

He was becoming excited: his cheeks were flushed; and his little eyes sparkled.

" And suppose I were to tell you," he resumed, doing at least to his daughter the honor of controlling his anger,—" suppose I were to tell you that I would derive from this marriage immense, positive, and immediate advantages ? "

" Oh ! " she interrupted with a look of disgust, " oh, for mercy's sake ! "

" Suppose I were to tell you that I have a powerful

interest in it; that it is indispensable to the success of
vast combinations? "

Mlle. Gilberte looked straight at him.

" I would answer you," she exclaimed, " that it does
not suit me to be made use of as an earnest to your combinations. Ah! it's an operation, is it? an enterprise, a
big speculation? and you throw in your daughter in the
bargain as a bonus. Well, no! You can tell your partner that the thing has fallen through."

M. Favoral's anger was growing with each word.

" I'll see if I can't make you yield," he said.

" You may crush me, perhaps. Make me yield,
never! "

" Well, we shall see. You will see—Maxence and you
—whether there are no means by which a father can
compel his rebellious children to submit to his authority."

And, feeling that he was no longer master of himself,
he left, swearing loud enough to shake the plaster from
the stair-walls.

Maxence shook with indignation.

" Never," he uttered, " never until now, had I understood the infamy of my conduct. With a father such as
ours, Gilberte, I should be your protector. And now I
am debarred even of the right to interfere. But never
mind, I have the will; and all will soon be repaired."

Left alone, a few moments after, Mlle. Gilberte was
congratulating herself upon her firmness.

" I am sure," she thought, " Marius would approve,
if he knew."

She had not long to wait for her reward. The bell
rang: it was her old professor, the Signor Gismondo
Pulei, who came to give her his daily lesson.

The liveliest joy beamed upon his face, more shrivelled than an apple at Easter; and the most magnificent anticipations sparkled in his eyes.

"I knew it, signora!" he exclaimed from the threshold: "I knew that angels bring good luck. As every thing succeeds to you, so must every thing succeed to those who come near you."

She could not help smiling at the appropriateness of the compliment.

"Something fortunate has happened to you, dear master?" she asked.

"That is to say, I am on the high-road to fortune and glory," he replied. "My fame is extending; pupils dispute the privilege of my lesson."

Mlle. Gilberte knew too well the thoroughly Italian exaggeration of the worthy *maëstro* to be surprised.

"This morning," he went on, "visited by inspiration, I had risen early, and I was working with marvellous facility, when there was a knock at my door. I do not remember such an occurrence since the blessed day when your worthy father called for me. Surprised, I nevertheless said, 'Come in;' when there appeared a tall and robust young man, proud and intelligent-looking."

The young girl started.

"Marius!" cried a voice within her."

"This young man," continued the old Italian, "had heard me spoken of, and came to apply for lessons. I questioned him; and from the first words I discovered that his education had been frightfully neglected, that he was ignorant of the most vulgar notions of the divine art, and that he scarcely knew the difference between a sharp and a quaver. It was really the A, B, C, which he wished me to teach him. Laborious task, ungrateful labor! But he manifested so much shame at his ignorance, and so much desire to be instructed, that I felt moved in his favor. Then his countenance was most winning, his voice of a superior tone; and finally he offered me sixty francs a month. In short, he is now my pupil."

As well as she could, Mlle. Gilberte was hiding her blushes behind a music-book.

" We remained over two hours talking," said the good and simple *maëstro*, " and I believe that he has excellent dispositions. Unfortunately, he can only take two lessons a week. Although a nobleman, he works; and, when he took off his glove to hand me a month in advance, I noticed that one of his hands was blackened, as if burnt by some acid. But never mind, signora, sixty francs, together with what your father gives me, it's a fortune. The end of my career will be spared the privations of its beginning. This young man will help making me known. The morning has been dark; but the sunset will be glorious."

The young girl could no longer have any doubts: M. de Trégars had found the means of hearing from her, and letting her hear from him.

The impression she felt contributed no little to give her the patience to endure the obstinate persecution of her father, who, twice a day, never failed to repeat to her,—

" Get ready to properly receive my *protégé* on Saturday. I have not invited him to dinner: he will only spend the evening with us."

And he mistook for a disposition to yield the cold tone in which she answered,—

" I beg you to believe that this introduction is wholly unnecessary."

Thus, the famous day having come, he told his usual

Saturday guests, M. and Mme. Desclavettes, M. Chapelain, and old man Desormeaux,—

"Eh, eh! I guess you are going to see a future son-in-law!"

At nine o'clock, just as they had passed into the parlor, the sound of carriage-wheels startled the Rue St. Gilles.

"There he is!" exclaimed the cashier of the Mutual Credit.

And, throwing open a window,—

"Come, Gilberte," he added, "come and see his carriage and horses."

She never stirred; but M. Desclavettes and M. Chapelain ran. It was night, unfortunately; and of the whole equipage nothing was visible but the two lanterns that shone like stars. Almost at the same time the parlor-door flew open; and the servant, who had been properly trained in advance, announced,—

"Monsieur Costeclar."

Leaning toward Mme. Favoral, who was seated by her side on the sofa,—

"A nice-looking man, isn't he? a really nice-looking man," whispered Mme. Desclavettes.

And indeed he really thought so himself. Gesture, attitude, smile, every thing in M. Costeclar, betrayed the satisfaction of self, and the assurance of a man accustomed to success. His head, which was very small, had but little hair left; but it was artistically drawn towards the temples, parted in the middle, and cut short around the forehead. His leaden complexion, his pale lips, and his dull eye, did not certainly betray a very rich blood; but he had a great long nose, sharp and curved like a sickle; and his beard, of undecided color, trimmed in

the Victor Emmanuel style, did the greatest honor to
the barber who cultivated it. Even when seen for the
first time, one might fancy that he recognized him, so
exactly was he like three or four hundred others who
are seen daily in the neighborhood of the Café Riche,
who are met everywhere where people run who pretend
to amuse themselves,—at the *bourse* or in the *bois;* at
the first representations, where they are just enough hidden to be perfectly well seen at the back of boxes filled
with young ladies with astonishing chignons; at the
races; in carriages, where they drink champagne to the
health of the winner.

He had on this occasion *hoisted* his best looks, and
the full dress *de rigueur,*—dress-coat with wide sleeves,
shirt cut low in the neck, and open vest, fastened below
the waist by a single button.

" Quite the man of the world," again remarked Mme.
Desclavettes.

M. Favoral rushed toward him ; and the latter, hastening, met him half way, and, taking both his hands into
his,—

" I cannot tell you, dear friend," he commenced, " how
deeply I feel the honor you do me in receiving me in the
midst of your charming family and your respectable
friends."

And he bowed all around during this speech, which
he delivered in the condescending tone of a lord visiting
his inferiors.

" Let me introduce you to my wife," interrupted the
cashier. And, leading him towards Mme. Favoral,—

" Monsieur Costeclar, my dear," said he,—" the
friend of whom we have spoken so often."

M. Costeclar bowed, rounding his shoulders, bending

his lean form in a half-circle, and letting his arms hang forward.

"I am too much the friend of our dear Favoral, madame," he uttered, "not to have heard of you long since, nor to know your merits, and the fact that he owes to you that peaceful happiness which he enjoys, and which we all envy him."

Standing by the mantel-piece, the usual Saturday-evening guests followed with the liveliest interest the evolutions of the pretender. Two of them, M. Chapelain and old Desormeaux, were perfectly able to appreciate him at his just value; but, in affirming that he made half a million a year, M. Favoral had, as it were, thrown over his shoulders that famous ducal cloak which concealed all deformities.

Without waiting for his wife's answer, M. Favoral brought his *protégé* in front of Mlle. Gilberte.

"Dear daughter,"said he, "Monsieur Costeclar, the friend of whom I have spoken."

M. Costeclar bowed still lower, and rounded off his shoulders again; but the young lady looked at him from head to foot with such a freezing glance, that his tongue remained as if paralyzed in his mouth, and he could only stammer out,—

"Mademoiselle! the honor, the humblest of your admirers."

Fortunately Maxence was standing three steps off: he fell back in good order upon him, and seizing his hand, which he shook vigorously,—

"I hope, my dear sir, that we shall soon be quite intimate friends. Your excellent father, whose special concern you are, has often spoken to me of you. Events, so he has confided to me, have not hitherto responded to your expectations. At your age, this is not a very grave matter. People, now-a-days, do not always find at the first attempt the road that leads to fortune. You will find yours. From this time forth I place at your command my influence and my experience; and, if you will consent to take me for your guide "—

Maxence had withdrawn his hand.

" I am very much obliged to you, sir," he answered coldly; " but I am content with my lot, and I believe myself old enough to walk alone."

Almost any one would have lost countenance. But M. Costeclar was so little put out, that it seemed as though he had expected just such a reception. He turned upon his heels, and advanced towards M. Favoral's friends with a smile so engaging as to make it evident that he was anxious to conquer their suffrages.

This was at the beginning of the month of June, 1870. No one as yet could foresee the frightful disasters which were to mark the end of that fatal year. And yet there was everywhere in France that indefinable anxiety which precedes great social convulsions. The plebiscitum had not succeeded in restoring confidence. Every day the most alarming rumors were put in circulation; and it was with a sort of passion that people went in quest of news.

Now, M. Costeclar was a wonderfully well-posted man. He had, doubtless, on his way, stopped on the Boulevard des Italiens, that blessed ground where nightly the street-brokers labor for the financial prosperity of the country. He had gone through the Passage de l'Opéra, which is, as is well known, the best market for the most correct and the most reliable news. Therefore he might safely be believed.

Placing his back to the chimney, he had taken the lead

in the conversation; and he was talking, talking, talking. Being a " bull," he took a favorable view of every
thing. He believed in the eternity of the second empire.
He sang the praise of the new cabinet: he was ready to
pour out his blood for Émile Ollivier. True, some people
complained that business was dull and slow; but those
people, he thought, were merely " bears." Business had
never been so brilliant. At no time had prosperity been
greater. Capital was abundant. The institutions of
credit were flourishing. Securities were rising. Everybody's pockets were full to bursting. And the others
listened in astonishment to this inexhaustible prattle,
this " gab," more filled with gold spangles than Dantzig
cordial, with which the commercial travellers of the
bourse catch their customers.

Suddenly,—

" But you must excuse me," he said, rushing towards
the other end of the parlor.

Mme. Favoral had just left the room to order tea to
be brought in; and, the seat by Mlle. Gilberte being vacant, M. Costeclar occupied it promptly.

" He understands his business," growled M. Desormeaux.

" Surely," said M. Desclavettes, " If I had some
funds to dispose of just now."

" I would be most happy to have him for my son-in-
law," declared M. Favoral.

He was doing his best. Somewhat intimidated by
Mlle. Gilberte's first look, he had now fully recovered
his wits.

He commenced by sketching his own portrait.

He had just turned thirty, and had experienced the
strong and the weak side of life. He had had " successes," but had tired of them. Having gauged the emp-

tiness of what is called pleasure, he only wished now to find a partner for life, whose graces and virtues would secure his domestic happiness.

He could not help noticing the absent look of the young girl; but he had, thought he, other means of compelling her attention. And he went on, saying that he felt himself cast of the metal of which model husbands are made. His plans were all made in advance. His wife would be free to do as she pleased. She would have her own carriage and horses, her box at the Italiens and at the Opera, and an open account at Worth's and Van Klopen's. As to diamonds, he would take care of that. He meant that his wife's display of wealth should be noticed, and even spoken of in the newspapers.

Was this the terms of a bargain that he was offering?

If so, it was so coarsely, that Mlle. Gilberte, ignorant of life as she was, wondered in what world it might be that he had met with so many " successes."

And, somewhat indignantly,—

" Unfortunately," she said, " the *bourse* is perfidious ; and the man who drives his own carriage to-day, to-morrow may have no shoes to wear."

M. Costeclar nodded with a smile.

" Exactly so," said he. " A marriage protects one against such reverses."

" Ah ! "

" Every man in active business, when he marries, settles upon his wife a reasonable fortune. I expect to settle six hundred thousand francs upon mine."

" So that, if you were to meet with an—accident ? "

" We should enjoy our thirty thousand a year under the very nose of the creditors."

Blushing with shame, Mlle. Gilberte rose.

"But then," said she, "it isn't a wife that you are looking for: it is an accomplice."

He was spared the embarrassment of an answer, by the servant, who came in, bringing in tea. He accepted a cup; and after two or three anecdotes, judging that he had done enough for a first visit, he withdrew, and a moment later they heard his carriage driving off at full gallop.

XVI.

It was not without mature thought that M. Costeclar had determined to withdraw, despite M. Favoral's pressing overtures. However infatuated he might be with his own merits, he had been compelled to surrender to evidence, and to acknowledge that he had not exactly succeeded with Mlle. Gilberte. But he also knew that he had the head of the house on his side; and he flattered himself that he had produced an excellent impression upon the guests of the house.

"Therefore," had he said to himself, "if I leave first, they will sing my praise, lecture the young person, and make her listen to reason."

He was not far from being right. Mme. Desclavettes had been completely subjugated by the grand manners of this pretender; and M. Desclavettes did not hesitate to affirm that he had rarely met any one who pleased him more.

The others, M. Chapelain and old Desormeaux, did not, doubtless, share this optimism; but M. Costeclar's annual half-million obscured singularly their clear-sightedness.

They thought, perhaps, they had discovered in him

some alarming features; but they had full and entire confidence in their friend Favoral's prudent sagacity.

The particular and methodic cashier of the Mutual Credit was not apt to be enthusiastic; and, if he opened the doors of his house to a young man, if he was so anxious to have him for his son-in-law, he must evidently have taken ample information.

Finally there are certain family matters from which sensible people keep away as they would from the plague; and, on the question of marriage especially, he is a bold man who would take side for or against.

Thus Mme. Desclavettes was the only one to raise her voice. Taking Mlle. Gilberte's hands within hers,—

" Let me scold you, my dear," said she, " for having received thus a poor young man who was only trying to please you."

Excepting her mother, too weak to take her defence, and her brother, who was debarred from interfering, the young girl understood readily, that, in that parlor, every one, overtly or tacitly, was against her. The idea came to her mind to repeat there boldly what she had already told her father,—that she was resolved not to marry, and that she would not marry, not being one of those weak girls, without energy, whom they dress in white, and drag to church against their will.

Such a bold declaration would be in keeping with her character. But she feared a terrible, and perhaps degrading scene. The most intimate friends of the family were ignorant of its most painful sores. In presence of his friends, M. Favoral dissembled, speaking in a mild voice, and assuming a kindly smile. Should she suddenly reveal the truth?

" It is childish of you to run the risk of discouraging

a clever fellow who makes half a million a year," continued the wife of the old bronze-merchant, to whom such conduct seemed an abominable crime of lese-money.

Mlle. Gilberte had withdrawn her hands.

" You did not hear what he said, madame."

" I beg your pardon : I was quite near, and involuntarily "—

" You have heard his—propositions ? "

" Perfectly. He was promising you a carriage, a box at the opera, diamonds, freedom. Isn't that the dream of all young ladies ? "

" It is not mine, madame ! "

" Dear me ! What better can you wish ? You must not expect more from a husband than he can possibly give."

" That is not what I shall expect of him."

In a tone of paternal indulgence, which his looks belied,—

" She is mad," suggested M. Favoral.

Tears of indignation filled Mlle. Gilberte's eyes.

" Mme. Desclavettes," she exclaimed, " forgets something. She forgets that this gentleman dared to tell me that he proposed to settle upon the woman he marries a large fortune, of which his creditors would thus be cheated in case of his failure in business."

She thought, in her simplicity, that a cry of indignation would rise at these words. Instead of which,—

" Well, isn't it perfectly natural ? " said M. Desclavettes.

" It seems to me more than natural," insisted Mme. Desclavettes, " that a man should be anxious to preserve from ruin his wife and children."

" Of course," put in M. Favoral.

Stepping resolutely toward her father,—

"Have you, then, taken such precautions yourself?" demanded Mlle. Gilberte.

"No," answered the cashier of the Mutual Credit.

And, after a moment of hesitation,—

"But I am running no risks," he added. "In business, and when a man may be ruined by a mere rise or fall in stocks, he would be insane indeed who did not secure bread for his family, and, above all, means for himself, wherewith to commence again. The Baron de Thaller did not act otherwise; and, should he meet with a disaster, Mme. de Thaller would still have a handsome fortune."

M. Desormeaux was, perhaps, the only one not to admit freely that theory, and not to accept that ever-decisive reason, "Others do it."

But he was a philosopher, and thought it silly not to be of his time. He therefore contented himself with saying,—

"Hum! M. de Thaller's creditors might not think that mode of proceeding entirely regular."

"Then they might sue," said M. Chapelain, laughing. "People can always sue; only when the papers are well drawn"—

Mlle. Gilberte stood dismayed. She thought of Marius de Trégars giving up his mother's fortune to pay his father's debts.

"What would he say," thought she, "should he hear such opinions!"

The cashier of the Mutual Credit resumed,—

"Surely I blame every species of fraud. But I pretend, and I maintain, that a man who has worked twenty years to give a handsome dowry to his daughter has the right to demand of his son-in-law certain conservative measures to guarantee the money, which, after all, is his own, and which is to benefit no one but his own family."

This declaration closed the evening. It was getting late. The Saturday guests put on their overcoats; and, as they were walking home,—

" Can you understand that little Gilberte ? " said Mme. Desclavettes. " I'd like to see a daughter of mine have such fancies ! But her poor mother is so weak ! "

" Yes; but friend Favoral is firm enough for both," interrupted M. Desormeaux; " and it is more than probable that at this very moment he is correcting his daughter of the sin of sloth."

Well, not at all. Extremely angry as M. Favoral must have been, neither that evening, nor the next day, did he make the remotest allusion to what had taken place.

The following Monday only, before leaving for his office, casting upon his wife and daughter one of his ugliest looks,—

" M. Costeclar owes us a visit," said he; " and it is possible that he may call in my absence. I wish him to be admitted; and I forbid you to go out, so that you can have no pretext to refuse him the door. I presume there will not be found in my house any one bold enough to ill receive a man whom I like, and whom I have selected for my son-in law."

But was it probable, was it even possible, that M. Costeclar could venture upon such a step after Mlle. Gilberte's treatment of him on the previous Saturday evening ?

" No, a thousand times no ! " affirmed Maxence to his mother and sister. " So you may rest easy."

Indeed they tried to be, until that very afternoon the sound of rapidly-rolling wheels attracted Mme. Favoral to the window. A *coupé,* drawn by two gray horses, had just stopped at the door.

"It must be he," she said to her daughter.

Mlle. Gilberte had turned slightly pale.

"There is no help for it, mother," she said: "You must receive him."

"And you?"

"I shall remain in my room."

"Do you suppose he won't ask for you?"

"You will answer that I am unwell. He will understand."

"But your father, unhappy child, your father?"

"I do not acknowledge to my father the right of disposing of my person against my wishes. I detest that man to whom he wishes to marry me. Would you like to see me his wife, to know me given up to the most intolerable torture? No, there is no violence in the world that will ever wring my consent from me. So, mother dear, do what I ask you. My father can say what he pleases: I take the whole responsibility upon myself."

There was no time to argue: the bell rang. Mlle. Gilberte had barely time to escape through one of the doors of the parlor, whilst M. Costeclar was entering at the other.

If he did have enough perspicacity to guess what had just taken place, he did not in any way show it. He sat down; and it was only after conversing for a few moments upon indifferent subjects, that he asked how Mlle Gilberte was.

"She is somewhat—unwell," stammered Mme. Favoral.

He did not appear surprised; only,—

"Our dear Favoral," he said, "will be still more pained than I am when he hears of this mishap."

Better than any other mother, Mme. Favoral must have understood and approved Mlle. Gilberte's invincible repugnance. To her also, when she was young, her father had come one day, and said, " I have discovered a husband for you." She had accepted him blindly. Bruised and wounded by daily outrages, she had sought refuge in marriage as in a haven of safety.

And since, hardly a day had elapsed that she had not thought it would have been better for her to have died rather then to have riveted to her neck those fetters that death alone can remove. She thought, therefore, that her daughter was perfectly right. And yet twenty years of slavery had so weakened the springs of her energy, that under the glance of Costeclar, threatening her with her husband's name, she felt embarrassed, and could scarcely stammer some timid excuses. And she allowed him to prolong his visit, and consequently her torment, for over an half an hour ; then, when he had gone,—

" He and your father understand each other," said she to her daughter, " that is but too evident. What is the use of struggling? "

A fugitive blush colored the pale cheeks of Mlle. Gilberte. For the past forty-eight hours she had been exhausting herself, seeking an issue to an impossible situation ; and she had accustomed her mind to the worst eventualities.

" Do you wish me, then, to desert the paternal roof? " she exclaimed.

Mme. Favoral almost dropped on the floor.

" You would run away," she stammered, " you ! "—

" Rather than become that man's wife, yes ! "

" And where would you go, unfortunate child? what would you do? "

" I can earn my living."

Mme. Favoral shook her head sadly. The same suspicions were reviving within her that she had felt once
before.

" Gilberte," she said in a beseeching tone, " am I, then,
no longer your best friend? and will you not tell me
from what sources you draw your courage and your
resolution? "

And, as her daughter said nothing,—

" God alone knows what may happen! " sighed the
poor woman.

Nothing happened, but what could have been easily
foreseen. When M. Favoral came home to dinner, he
was whistling a perfect storm on the stairs. He abstained
at first from all recrimination; but towards the end of
the meal, with the most sarcastic look he could assume,—

" It seems," he said to his daughter, " that you were
unwell this afternoon? "

Bravely, and without flinching, she sustained his look;
and, in a firm voice,—

" I shall always be indisposed," she replied, " when M.
Costeclar calls. You hear me, don't you, father,—always! "

But the cashier of the Credit Mutual was not one of
those men whose wrath finds vent in mere sarcasms.
Rising suddenly to his feet,—

" By the holy heavens! " he screamed forth, " you
are wrong to trifle thus with my will; for, all of you
here, I shall crush you as I do this glass."

And, with a frenzied gesture, he dashed the glass he
held in his hand against the wall, where it broke in a
thousand pieces. Trembling like a leaf, Mme. Favoral
staggered upon her chair.

XVII.

" BETTER kill her at once," said Mlle. Gilberte coldly.
" She would suffer less."

It was by a torrent of invective that M. Favoral replied. His rage, dammed up for the past four days, finding at last an outlet, flowed in gross insults and insane
threats. He spoke of throwing out in the street his wife
and children, or starving them out, or shutting up his
daughter in a house of correction; until at last, language
failing his fury, beside himself, he left, swearing that he
would bring M. Costeclar home himself, and then they
would see.

" Very well, we shall see," said Mlle. Gilberte.

Motionless in his place, and white as a plaster cast,
Maxence had witnessed this lamentable scene. A gleam
of common-sense had enabled him to control his indignation, and to remain silent. He had understood, that, at
the first word, his father's fury would have turned
against him; and then what might have happened? The
most frightful dramas of the criminal courts have often
had no other origin.

" No, this is no longer bearable! " he exclaimed.

Even at the time of his greatest follies, Maxence had
always had for his sister a fraternal affection. He admired her from the day she had stood up before him to
reproach him for his misconduct. He envied her her
quiet determination, her patient tenacity, and that calm
energy that never failed her.

" Have patience, my poor Gilberte," he added: " the
day is not far, I hope, when I may commence to repay
you all you have done for me. I have not lost my time
since you restored me my reason. I have arranged with

my creditors. I have found a situation, which, if not brilliant, is at least sufficiently lucrative to enable me before long to offer you, as well as to our mother, a peaceful retreat."

"But it is to-morrow," interrupted Mme. Favoral, "to-morrow that your father is to bring M. Costeclar. He has said so, and he will do it."

And so he did. About two o'clock in the afternoon M. Favoral and his *protégé* arrived in the Rue St. Gilles, in that famous *coupé* with the two horses, which excited the wonder of the neighbors.

But Mlle. Gilberte had her plan ready. She was on the lookout; and, as soon as she heard the carriage stop, she ran to her room, undressed in a twinkling, and went to bed.

When her father came for her, and saw her in bed, he remained surprised and puzzled on the threshold of the door.

"And yet I'll make you come into the parlor!" he said in a hoarse voice.

"Then you must carry me there as I am," she said in a tone of defiance; "for I shall certainly not get up."

For the first time since his marriage, M. Favoral met in his own house a more inflexible will than his own, and a more unyielding obstinacy. He was baffled. He threatened his daughter with his clinched fists, but could discover no means of making her obey. He was compelled to surrender, to yield.

"This will be settled with the rest," he growled, as he went out.

"I fear nothing in the world, father," said the girl.

It was almost true, so much did the thought of Marius de Trégars inflame her courage. Twice already she had heard from him through the Signor Gismondo Pulei,

who never tired talking of this new pupil, to whom he
had already given two lessons.

"He is the most gallant man in the world," he said,
his eye sparkling with enthusiasm, "and the bravest,
and the most generous, and the best; and no quality that
can adorn one of God's creatures shall be wanting in
him when I have taught him the divine art. It is not
with a little contemptible gold that he means to reward
my zeal. To him I am as a second father; and it is with
the confidence of a son that he explains to me his labors
and his hopes."

Thus Mlle. Gilberte learned through the old *maëstro,*
that the newspaper article she had read was almost exactly true, and that M. de Trégars and M. Marcolet had
become associated for the purpose of working, in joint
account, certain recent discoveries, which bid fair to
yield large profits in a near future.

"And yet it is for my sake alone that he has thus
thrown himself into the turmoil of business, and has
become as eager for gain as that M. Marcolet himself."

And, at the height of her father's persecutions, she
felt glad of what she had done, and of her boldness in
placing her destiny in the hands of a stranger. The
memory of Marius had become her refuge, the element
of all her dreams and of all her hopes; in a word, her
life.

It was of Marius she was thinking, when her mother,
surprising her gazing into vacancy, would ask her,
"What are you thinking of?" And, at every new vexa-
tion she had to endure, her imagination decked him with
a new quality, and she clung to him with a more desperate grasp.

"How much he would grieve," thought she, "if he
knew of what persecution I am the object!"

And very careful was she not to allow the Signor Gismondo Pulei to suspect any thing of it, affecting, on the
contrary, in his presence, the most cheerful serenity.

And yet she was a prey to the most cruel anxiety,
since she observed a new and most incredible transfor-
mation in her father.

That man so violent and so harsh, who flattered himself never to have been bent, who boasted never to have
forgotten or forgiven any thing, that domestic tyrant,
had become quite a *debonair* personage. He had referred
to the expedient imagined by Mlle. Gilberte only to
laugh at it, saying that it was a good trick, and he deserved it; for he repented bitterly, he protested, his past
brutalities.

He owned that he had at heart his daughter's marriage with M. Costeclar; but he acknowledged that he
had made use of the surest means for making it fail.
He should, he humbly confessed, have expected every
thing of time and circumstances, of M. Costeclar's excellent qualities, and of his beautiful, darling daughter's
good sense.

More than of all his violence, Mme. Favoral was terrified at this affected good nature.

" Dear me ! " she sighed, " what does it all mean ? "

But the cashier of the Mutual Credit was not preparing any new surprise to his family. If the means were
different, it was still the same object that he was pursuing with the tenacity of an insect. When severity had
failed, he hoped to succeed by gentleness, that's all. Only
this assumption of hypocritical meekness was too new
to him to deceive any one. At every moment the mask
fell off, the claws showed, and his voice trembled with
ill-suppressed rage in the midst of his most honeyed
phrases.

Moreover, he entertained the strangest illusions.

Because for forty-eight hours he had acted the part of a good-natured man, because one Sunday he had taken his wife and daughter out riding in the Bois de Vincennes, because he had given Maxence a hundred-franc note, he imagined that it was all over, that the past was obliterated, forgotten, and forgiven.

And, drawing Gilberte upon his knees,—

" Well, daughter," he said, " you see that I don't importune you any more, and I leave you quite free. I am more reasonable than you are."

But on the other hand, and according to an expression which escaped him later, he tried to turn the enemy.

He did every thing in his power to spread in the neighborhood the rumor of Mlle. Gilberte's marriage with a financier of colossal wealth,—that elegant young man who came in a *coupé* with two horses. Mme. Favoral could not enter a shop without being covertly complimented upon having found such a magnificent establishment for her daughter.

Loud, indeed, must have been the gossip; for its echo reached even the inattentive ears of the Signor Gismondo Pulei.

One day, suddenly interrupting his lesson,—

" You are going to be married, signora? " he inquired.

Mlle. Gilberte started.

What the old Italian had heard, he would surely ere long repeat to Marius. It was therefore urgent to undeceive him.

" It is true," she replied, " that something has been said about a marriage, dear *maëstro*."

" Ah, ah ! "

" Only my father had not consulted me. That marriage will never take place: I swear it."

She expressed herself in a tone of such ardent conviction, that the old gentleman was quite astonished, little dreaming that it was not to him that this energetic denial was addressed.

" My destiny is irrevocably fixed," added Mlle. Gilberte. " When I marry, I will consult the inspirations of my heart only."

In the mean time, it was a veritable conspiracy against her. M. Favoral had succeeded in interesting in the success of his designs his habitual guests, not M. and Mme. Desclavettes, who had been seduced from the first, but M. Chapelain and old Desormeaux himself. So that they all vied with each other in their efforts to bring the " dear child " to reason, and to enlighten her with their counsels.

" Father must have a still more considerable interest in this alliance than he has allowed us to think," she remarked to her brother. Maxence was also absolutely of the same opinion.

" And then," he added, " our father must be terribly rich ; for, do not deceive yourself, it isn't solely for your pretty blue eyes that this Costeclar persists in coming here twice a week to pocket a new mortification. What enormous dowry can he be hoping for? I am going to speak to him myself, and try to find out what he is after."

But Mlle. Gilberte had but slight confidence in her brother's diplomacy.

" I beg of you," she said, " don't meddle with that business ! "

" Yes, yes, I will ! Fear nothing, I'll be prudent."

Having taken his resolution, Maxence placed himself

on the lookout; and the very next day, as M. Costeclar was stepping out of his carriage at the door, he walked straight up to him.

"I wish to speak to you, sir," he said.

Self-possessed as he was, the brilliant financier succeeded but poorly in concealing a surprise that looked very much like fright.

"I am going in to call on your parents, sir," he replied; "and whilst waiting for your father, with whom I have an appointment, I shall be at your command."

"No, no!" interrupted Maxence. "What I have to say must be heard by you alone. Come along this way, and we shall not be interrupted."

And he led M. Costeclar away as far as the Place Royal. Once there,—

"You are very anxious to marry my sister, sir," he commenced.

During their short walk M. Costeclar had recovered himself. He had resumed all his impertinent assurance. Looking at Maxence from head to foot with any thing but a friendly look,—

"It is my dearest and my most ardent wish, sir," he replied.

"Very well. But you must have noticed the very slight success, to use no harsher word, of your assiduities."

"Alas!"

"And, perhaps, you will judge, like myself, that it would be the act of a gentleman to withdraw in presence of such positive—repugnance?"

An ugly smile was wandering upon M. Costeclar's pale lips.

"Is it at the request of your sister, sir, that you make me this communication?"

" No, sir."

" Are you aware whether your sister has some in‑clination that may be an obstacle to the realization of m; hopes ? "

" Sir ! "

" Excuse me ! What I say has nothing to offend. It might very well be that your sister, before I had the honor of being introduced to her, had already fixed her choice."

He spoke so loud, that Maxence looked sharply around to see whether there was not some one within hearing. He saw no one but a young man, who seemed quite absorbed reading a newspaper.

" But, sir," he resumed, " what would you answer, if I, the brother of the young lady whom you wish to marry against her wishes,—I called upon you to cease your assiduities ? "

M. Costeclar bowed ceremoniously,—

" I would answer you, sir," he uttered, " that your father's assent is sufficient for me. My suit has nothing but is honorable. Your sister may not like me : that is a misfortune ; but it is not irreparable. When she knows me better, I venture to hope that she will overcome her unjust prejudices. Therefore I shall persist."

Maxence insisted no more. He was irritated at M. Costeclar's coolness ; but it was not his intention to push things further.

" There will always be time," he thought, " to resort to violent measures."

But when he reported this conversation to his sister,—

" It is clear," he said, " that, between our father and tnat man, there is a community of interests which I am unable to discover. What business have they together. In what respect can your marriage either help or injure them. I must see, try and find out exactly who is this Costeclar: the deuse take him!"

He started out the same day, and had not far to go.

M. Costeclar was one of those personalities which only bloom in Paris, and are only met in Paris,—the same as cab-horses, and young ladies with yellow chignons.

He knew everybody, and everybody knew him.

He was well known at the *bourse*, in all the principal restaurants, where he called the waiters by their first names, at the box-office of the theatres, at all the pool-rooms, and at the European Club, otherwise called the Nomadic Club, of which he was a member.

He operated at the *bourse:* that was sure. He was said to own a third interest in a stock-broker's office. He had a good deal of business with M. Jottras, of the house of Jottras and Brother, and M. Saint Pavin, the manager of a very popular journal, " The Financial Pilot."

It was further known that he had, Rue Vivienne, a magnificent apartment, and that he had successively honored with his liberal protection Mlle. Sidney of the *Varieties*, and Mme. Jenny Fancy, a lady of a certain age already, but so situated as to return to her lovers in notoriety what they gave her in good money.

So much did Maxence learn without difficulty. As to any more precise details, it was impossible to obtain them. To his pressing questions upon M. Costeclar's antecedents,—

" He is a perfectly honest man," answered some.

" He is simply a speculator," affirmed others.

But all agreed that he was a " sharp one," who would surely make his fortune, and without passing through the police-courts, either.

"How can our father and such a man be so intimately connected?" wondered Maxence and his sister.

And they were lost in conjectures, when suddenly, at an hour when he never set his foot in the house, M. Favoral appeared.

Throwing a letter upon his daughter's lap,—

"See what I have just received from Costeclar," he said in a hoarse voice. "Read."

She read, "Allow me, dear friend, to release you from your engagement. Owing to circumstances absolutely beyond my control, I find myself compelled to give up the honor of becoming a member of your family."

What could have happened?

Standing in the middle of the parlor, the cashier of the Mutual Credit held, bowed down beneath his glance, his wife and children, Mme. Favoral trembling, Maxence starting in mute surprise, and Mlle. Gilberte, who needed all the strength of her will to control the explosion of her immense joy.

Every thing in M. Favoral betrayed, nevertheless, much more the excitement of a disaster than the rage of a deception.

Never had his family seen him thus,—livid, his cravat undone, his hair wet with perspiration, and clinging to his temples.

"Will you please explain this letter?" he asked at last.

And, as no one answered him, he took up that letter again from the table where Mlle. Gilberte had laid it, and commenced reading it again, scanning each syllable, as if in hopes of discovering in each word some hidden meaning.

"What did you say to Costeclar?" he resumed, "what did you do to him to make him take such a determination?"

" Nothing," answered Maxence and Mlle. Gilberte.

The hope of being at last rid of that man inspired Mme. Favoral with something like courage.

" He has doubtless understood," she meekly suggested, " that he could not triumph over our daughter's repugnance."

But her husband interrupted her,—

" No," he uttered, " Costeclar is not the man to trouble himself about the ridiculous caprices of a little girl. There is something else. But what is it? Come, if you know it, any of you, if you suspect it even, speak, say it. You must see that I am in a state of fearful anxiety."

It was the first time that he thus allowed something to appear of what was passing within him, the first time that he ever complained.

" M. Costeclar alone, father, can give you the explanation you ask of us," said Mlle. Gilberte.

The cashier of the Mutual Credit shook his head.

" Do you suppose, then, that I have not questioned him? I found his letter this morning at the office. At once I ran to his apartments, Rue Vivienne. He had just gone out; and it is in vain that I called for him at Jottras', and at the office of ' The Financial Pilot.' I found him at last at the *bourse,* after running three hours. But I could only get from him evasive answers and vague explanations. Of course he did not fail to say, that, if he does withdraw, it is because he despairs of ever succeeding in pleasing Gilberte. But it isn't so: I know it; I am sure of it; I read it in his eyes. Twice his lips moved as if he were about to confess all; and then he said nothing. And the more I insisted, the more he seemed ill at ease, embarrassed, uneasy, troubled, the more he appeared to me like a man who has been threatened, and dares not brave the threat."

He directed upon his children one of those obstinate looks which search the inmost depths of the conscience.

" If you have done any thing to drive him off," he resumed, " confess it frankly, and I swear I will not reproach you."

" We did not."

" You did not threaten him? "

" No! "

M. Favoral seemed appalled.

" Doubtless you deceive me," he said, " and I hope you do. Unhappy children! you do not know what this rupture may cost you."

And, instead of returning to his office, he shut himself up in that little room which he called his study, and only came out of it at about five o'clock, holding under his arm an enormous bundle of papers, and saying that it was useless to wait for him for dinner, as he would not come home until late in the night, if he came home at all, being compelled to make up for his lost day.

" What is the matter with your father, my poor children? " exclaimed Mme. Favoral. " I have never seen him in such a state."

" Doubtless," replied Maxence, " the rupture with Costeclar is going to break up some combination."

But that explanation did not satisfy him any more than it did his mother. He, too, felt a vague apprehension of some impending misfortune. But what? He had nothing upon which to base his conjectures. He knew nothing, any more than his mother, of his father's affairs, of his relations, of his interests, or even of his life, outside the house.

And mother and son lost themselves in suppositions as

vain as if they had tried to find the solution of a problem, without possessing its terms.

With a single word Mlle. Gilberte thought she might have enlightened them.

In the unerring certainty of the blow, in the crushing promptness of the result, she thought she could recognize the hand of Marius de Trégars.

She recognized the hand of the man who acts, and does not talk. And the girl's pride felt flattered by this victory, by this proof of the powerful energy of the man whom, unknown to all, she had selected. She liked to imagine Marius de Trégars and M. Costeclar in presence of each other,—the one as imperious and haughty as she had seen him meek and trembling; the other more humble still than he was arrogant with her.

" One thing is certain," she repeated to herself, " and that is, I am saved."

And she wished the morrow to come, that she might announce her happiness to the very involuntary and very unconscious accomplice of Marius, the worthy Maëstro Gismondo Pulei.

The next day M. Favoral seemed to have resigned himself to the failure of his projects; and, the following Saturday, he told as a pleasant joke, how Mlle. Gilberte had carried the day, and had managed to dismiss her lover.

But a close observer could discover in him symptoms of devouring cares. Deep wrinkles showed along his temples; his eyes were sunken; a continued tension of mind contracted his features. Often during the dinner he would remain motionless for several minutes, his fork aloft; and then he would murmur, " How is it all going to end? "

Sometimes in the morning, before his departure for

his office, M. Jottras, of the house of Jottras and Brother, and M. Saint Pavin, the manager of " The Financial Pilot," came to see him. They closeted themselves together, and remained for hours in conference, speaking so low, that not even a vague murmur could be heard outside the door.

" Your father has grave subjects of anxiety, my children," said Mme. Favoral: " you may believe me,—me, who for twenty years have been trying to guess our fate upon his countenance."

But the political events were sufficient to explain any amount of anxiety. It was the second week of July, 1870; and the destinies of France trembled, as upon a cast of the dice, in the hands of a few presumptuous incapables. Was it war with Prussia, or was it peace, that was to issue from the complications of a childishly astute policy?

The most contradictory rumors caused daily at the *bourse* the most violent oscillations, which endangered the safest fortunes. A few words uttered in a corridor by Émile Ollivier had made a dozen heavy operators rich, but had ruined five hundred small ones. On all hands, credit was trembling.

Until one evening when he came home,—

" War is declared," said M. Favoral.

It was but too true; and no one then had any fears of the result for France. They had so much exalted the French army, they had so often said that it was invincible, that every one among the public expected a series of crushing victories.

Alas! the first telegram announced a defeat. People refused to believe it at first. But there was the evidence. The soldiers had died bravely; but the chiefs had been incapable of leading them.

From that time, and with a vertiginous rapidity, from day to day, from hour to hour, the fatal news came crowding on. Like a river that overflows its banks, Prussia was overrunning France. Bazaine was surrounded at Metz; and the capitulation of Sedan capped the climax of so many disasters.

At last, on the 4th of September, the republic was proclaimed.

On the 5th, when the Signor Gismondo Pulei presented himself at Rue St. Gilles, his face bore such an expression of anguish, that Mlle. Gilberte could not help asking what was the matter.

He rose on that question, and, threatening heaven with his clinched fist,—

"Implacable fate does not tire to persecute me," he replied. " I had overcome all obstacles: I was happy: I was looking forward to a future of fortune and glory. No, the dreadful war must break out."

For the worthy *maëstro,* this terrible catastrophe was but a new caprice of his own destiny.

"What has happened to you?" inquired the young girl, repressing a smile.

" It happens to me, signora, that I am about to lose my beloved pupil. He leaves me; he forsakes me. In vain have I thrown myself at his feet. My tears have not been able to detain him. He is going to fight; he leaves; he is a soldier! "

Then it was given to Mlle. Gilberte to see clearly within her soul. Then she understood how absolutely she had given herself up, and to what extent she had ceased to belong to herself.

Her sensation was terrible, such as if her whole blood had suddenly escaped through her open arteries. She turned pale, her teeth chattered; and she seemed so near fainting, that the Signor Gismondo sprang to the door, crying, "Help, help! she is dying."

Mme. Favoral, frightened, came running in.

But already, thanks to an all-powerful projection of will, Mlle. Gilberte had recovered, and, smiling a pale smile,—

"It's nothing, mamma," she said. "A sudden pain in the head; but it's gone already."

The worthy *maëstro* was in perfect agony. Taking Mme. Favoral aside,—

"It is my fault," he said. "It is the story of my unheard-of misfortunes that has upset her thus. Monstrous egotist that I am! I should have been careful of her exquisite sensibility."

She insisted, nevertheless, upon taking her lesson as usual, and recovered enough presence of mind to extract from the Signor Gismondo everything that his muchregretted pupil had confided to him.

That was not much. He knew that his pupil had gone, like anyone else, to Rue de Cherche Midi; that he had signed an engagement, and had been ordered to join a regiment in process of formation near Tours.

And, as he went out,—

"That is nothing," said the kind *maëstro* to Mme. Favoral. "The signora has quite recovered, and is as gay as a lark."

The signora, shut up in her room, was shedding bitter tears. She tried to reason with herself, and could not succeed. Never had the strangeness of her situation so clearly appeared to her. She repeated to herself that she must be mad to have thus become attached to a stranger. She wondered how she could have allowed that love, which was now her very life, to take posses-

sion of her soul. But to what end? It no longer rested
with her to undo what had been done.

When she thought that Marius de Trégars was about
to leave Paris to become a soldier, to fight, to die perhaps, she felt her head whirl; she saw nothing around
her but despair and chaos.

And, the more she thought, the more certain she felt
that Marius could not have trusted solely to the chance
gossip of the Signor Pulei to communicate to her his
determination.

'It is perfectly inadmissible," she thought. "It is impossible that he will not make an effort to see me before
going."

Thoroughly imbued with the idea, she wiped her eyes,
took a seat by an open window; and, whilst apparently
busy with her work, she concentrated her whole attention upon the street.

There were more people out than usual. The recent
events had stirred Paris to its lowest depths, and, as
from the crater of a volcano in labor, all the social *scoriæ*
rose to the surface. Men of sinister appearance left their
haunts, and wandered through the city. The work-
shops were all deserted; and people strolled at random,
stupor or terror painted on their countenance.

But in vain did Mlle. Gilberte seek in all this crowd
the one she hoped to see. The hours went by, and
she was getting discouraged, when suddenly, towards
dusk, at the corner of the Rue Turenne,—

" 'Tis he," cried a voice within her.

It was, in fact, M. de Trégars. He was walking
towards the Boulevard, slowly, and his eyes raised.

Palpitating, the girl rose to her feet. She was in one
of those moments of crisis when the blood, rushing

to the brain, smothers all judgment. Unconscious, as it were, of her acts, she leaned over the window, and made a sign to Marius, which he understood very well, and which meant, " Wait, I am coming down."

" Where are you going, dear ? " asked Mme. Favoral, seeing Gilberte putting on her bonnet.

" To the shop, mamma, to get a shade of worsted I need."

Mlle. Gilberte was not in the habit of going out alone; but it happened quite often that she would go down in the neighborhood on some little errand.

" Do you wish the girl to go out with you ? " asked Mme. Favoral.

" Oh, it isn't worth while ! "

She ran down the stairs; and once out, regardless of the looks that might be watching her, she walked straight to M. de Trégars, who was waiting on the corner of the Rue des Minimes.

" You are going away ? " she said, too much agitated to notice his own emotion, which was, however, quite evident.

" I must," he answered.

" Oh ! "

" When France is invaded, the place for a man who bears my name is where the fighting is."

"But there will be fighting in Paris too."

" Paris has four times as many defenders as it needs. It is outside that soldiers will be wanted."

They walked slowly, as they spoke thus, along the Rue des Minimes, one of the least frequented in Paris; and there were only to be seen at this hour five or six soldiers talking in front of the barracks gate.

" Suppose I were to beg you not to go," resumed Mlle. Gilberte. " Suppose I beseeched you, Marius ! "

"I should remain then," he answered in a troubled voice; "but I would be betraying my duty, and failing to my honor; and remorse would weigh upon our whole life. Command now, and I will obey."

They had stopped; and no one seeing them standing there side by side affectionate and familiar could have believed that they were speaking to each other for the first time. They themselves did not notice it, so much had they come, with the help of all-powerful imagination, and in spite of separation, to the understanding of intimacy.

After a moment of painful reflection,—

"I do not ask you any longer to stay," uttered the young girl.

He took her hand, and raised it to his lips.

"I expected no less of your courage," he said, his voice vibrating with love.

But he controlled himself, and, in a more quiet tone,—

"Thanks to the indiscretion of Pulei," he added, "I was in hopes of seeing you, but not to have the happiness of speaking to you. I had written "—

He drew from his pocket a large envelope, and, handing it to Mlle. Gilberte,—

"Here is the letter," he continued, "which I intended for you. It contains another, which I beg you to preserve carefully, and not to open unless I do not return. I leave you in Paris a devoted friend, the Count de Villegré. Whatever may happen to you, apply to him with all confidence, as you would to myself."

Mlle. Gilberte, staggering, leaned against the wall.

"When do you expect to leave?" she inquired.

"This very night. Communications may be cut off at any moment."

Admirable in her sorrow, but also full of energy,

the poor girl looked up, and held out her hand to him.

"Go then," she said, "O my only friend! go, since honor commands. But do not forget that it is not your life alone that you are going to risk."

And, fearing to burst into sobs, she fled, and reached the Rue St. Gilles a few moments before her father, who had gone out in quest of news.

Those he brought home were of the most sinister kind.

Like the rising tide, the Prussians spread and advanced, slowly, but steadily. Their marches were numbered; and the day and hour could be named when their flood would come and strike the walls of Paris.

And so, at all the railroad stations, there was a prodigious rush of people who wished to leave at any cost, in any way, in the baggage-car if needs be, and who certainly were not, like Marius, rushing to meet the enemy.

One after another, M. Favoral had seen nearly every one he knew take flight.

The Baron and Baroness de Thaller and their daughter had gone to Switzerland; M. Costeclar was travelling in Belgium; the elder Jottras was in England, buying guns and cartridges; and if the younger Jottras, with M. Saint Pavin of "The Financial Pilot," remained in Paris, it was because, through the gallant influence of a lady whose name was not mentioned, they had obtained some valuable contracts from the government.

The perplexities of the cashier of the Mutual Credit were great. The day that the Baron and the Baroness de Thaller had left, —

"Pack up our trunks," he ordered his wife. "The

bourse is going to close; and the Mutual Credit can very well get along without me."

But the next day he became undecided again. What Mlle. Gilberte thought she could guess, was, that he was dying to start alone, and leave his family, but dared not do it. He hesitated so long, that at last, one evening,—

" You may unpack the trunks," he said to his wife. " Paris is invested; and no one can now leave."

XVIII.

In fact, the news had just come, that the Western Railroad, the last one that had remained open, was now cut off.

Paris was invested; and so rapid had been the investment, that it could hardly be believed.

People went in crowds on all the culminating points, the hills of Montmartre, and the heights of the Trocadero. Telescopes had been erected there; and every one was anxious to scan the horizon, and look for the Prussians.

But nothing could be discovered. The distant fields retained their quiet and smiling aspect under the mild rays of the autumn sun.

So that it really required quite an effort of imagination to realize the sinister fact, to understand that Paris, with its two millions of inhabitants, was indeed cut off from the world and separated from the rest of France, by an insurmountable circle of steel.

Doubt, and something like a vague hope, could be traced in the tone of the people who met on the streets, saying,—

" Well, it's all over: we can't leave any more. Letters, even, cannot pass. No more news, eh? "

But the next day, which was the 19th of September, the most incredulous were convinced.

For the first time Paris shuddered at the hoarse voice of the cannon, thundering on the heights of Chatillon. The siege of Paris, that siege without example in history, had commenced.

The life of the Favorals during these interminable days of anguish and suffering, was that of a hundred thousand other families.

Incorporated in the battalion of his ward, the cashier of the Mutual Credit went off two or three times a week, as well as all his neighbors, to mount guard on the ramparts,—a useless service perhaps, but which those that performed it did not look upon as such,—a very arduous service, at any rate, for poor merchants, accustomed to the comforts of their shops, or the quiet of their offices.

To be sure, there was nothing heroic in tramping through the mud, in receiving the rain or the snow upon the back, in sleeping on the ground or on dirty straw, in remaining on guard with the thermometer twenty degrees below the freezing-point. But people die of pleurisy quite as certainly as of a Prussian bullet; and many died of it.

Maxence showed himself but rarely at Rue St. Gilles: enlisted in a battalion of sharpshooters, he did duty at the advanced posts. And, as to Mme. Favoral and Mlle. Gilberte, they spent the day trying to get something to live on. Rising before daylight, through rain or snow, they took their stand before the butcher's stall, and, after waiting for hours, received a small slice of horse-meat.

Alone in the evening, by the side of the hearth where a few pieces of green wood smoked without burning, they started at each of the distant reports of the cannon. At each detonation that shook the window-panes, Mme. Favoral thought that it was, perhaps, the one that had killed her son.

And Mlle. Gilberte was thinking of Marius de Trégars. The accursed days of November and December had come. There were constant rumors of bloody battles around Orleans. She imagined Marius, mortally wounded, expiring on the snow, alone, without help, and without a friend to receive his supreme will and his last breath.

One evening the vision was so clear, and the impression so strong, that she started up with a loud cry.

"What is it?" asked Mme. Favoral, alarmed. "What is the matter?"

With a little perspicacity, the worthy woman could easily have obtained her daughter's secret; for Mlle. Gilberte was not in condition to deny anything. But she contented herself with an explanation which meant nothing, and had not a suspicion, when the girl answered with a forced smile,—

"It's nothing, dear mother, nothing but an absurd idea that crossed my mind."

Strange to say, never had the cashier of the Mutual Credit been for his family what he was during these months of trials.

During the first weeks of the siege he had been anxious, agitated, nervous; he wandered through the house like a soul in trouble; he had moments of inconceivable prostration, during which tears could be seen rolling down upon his cheeks, and then fits of anger without motive.

But each day that elapsed had seemed to bring calm to his soul. Little by little, he had become to his wife so indulgent and so affectionate, that the poor helot felt her heart touched. He had for his daughter attentions which caused her to wonder.

Often, when the weather was fine, he took them out walking, leading them along the quays towards a part of the walls occupied by the battalion of their ward. Twice he took them to St. Onen, where the sharp-shooters were encamped to which Maxence belonged.

Another day he wished to take them to visit M. de Thaller's house, of which he had charge. They refused, and instead of getting angry, as he certainly would have done formerly, he commenced describing to them the splendors of the apartments, the magnificent furniture, the carpets and the hangings, the paintings by the great masters, the objects of arts, the bronzes, in a word, all that dazzling luxury of which financiers make use, somewhat as hunters do of the mirror with which larks are caught.

Of business, nothing was ever said.

He went every morning as far as the office of the Mutual Credit; but, as he said, it was solely as a matter of form. Once in a long while, M. Saint Pavin and the younger Jottras paid a visit to the Rue St. Gilles. They had suspended,—the one the payments of his banking house; the other, the publication of "The Financial Pilot."

But they were not idle for all that; and, in the midst of the public distress, they still managed to speculate upon something, no one knew what, and to realize profits.

They rallied pleasantly the fools who had faith in the defence, and imitated in the most laughable manner the appearance, under their soldier's coat, of three or four of their friends who had joined the marching battalions. They boasted that they had no privations to endure, and always knew where to find the fresh butter wherewith to dress the large slices of beef which they possessed the art of finding. Mme. Favoral heard them laugh; and M. Saint Pavin, the manager of " The Financial Pilot," exclaimed,—

" Come, come! we would be fools to complain. It is a general liquidation, without risks and without costs."

Their mirth had something revolting in it; for it was now the last and most acute period of the siege.

At the beginning the greatest optimists hardly thought that Paris could hold out longer than six weeks. And now the investment had lasted over four months. The population was reduced to nameless articles of food. The supply of bread had failed; the wounded, for lack of a little soup, died in the ambulances; old people and children perished by the hundred; on the left bank the shells came down thick and fast, the weather was intensely cold, and there was no more fuel.

And yet no one complained. From the midst of that population of two millions of inhabitants, not one voice rose to beg for their comfort, their health, their life even, at the cost of a capitulation.

Clear-sighted men had never hoped that Paris alone could compel the raising of the siege; but they thought, that by holding out, and keeping the Prussians under its walls, Paris would give to France time to rise, to organize armies, and to rush upon the enemy. There was the duty of Paris; and Paris was toiling to fulfil it to the utmost limits of possibility, reckoning as a victory each day that it gained.

Unfortunately, all this suffering was to be in vain.

The fatal hour struck, when, supplies being exhausted, it became necessary to surrender.

During three days the Prussians camped in the Champs Elysées, gazing with longing eyes upon that city, object of their most eager desires,—that Paris within which, victorious though they were, they had not dared to venture. Then, soon after, communications were reopened; and one morning, as he received a letter from Switzerland,—

"It is from the Baron de Thaller!" exclaimed M. Favoral.

Exactly so. The manager of the Mutual Credit was a prudent man. Pleasantly situated in Switzerland, he was in nowise anxious to return to Paris before being quite certain that he had no risks to run.

Upon receiving M. Favoral's assurances to that effect, he started; and, almost at the same time the elder Jottras and M. Costeclar made their appearance.

XIX.

IT was a curious spectacle, the return of those braves for whom Parisian slang had invented the new and significant expression of *franc-fileur*.

They were not so proud then as they have been since. Feeling rather embarrassed in the midst of a population still quivering with the emotions of the siege, they had at least the good taste to try and find pretexts for their absence.

"I was cut off," affirmed the Baron de Thaller. "I had gone to Switzerland to place my wife and daughter in safety. When I came back, good-by! the Prussians had closed the doors. For more than a week, I

wandered around Paris, trying to find an opening. I
became suspected of being a spy. I was arrested. A
little more, and I was shot dead!"

"As to myself," declared M. Costeclar, " I foresaw
exactly what has happened. I knew that it was outside,
to organize armies of relief, that men would be wanted.
I went to offer my services to the government of defence; and everybody in Bordeaux saw me booted and
spurred, and ready to leave."

He was consequently soliciting the Cross of the Legion of Honor, and was not without hopes of obtaining
it through the all-powerful influence of his financial
connections.

" Didn't So-and-so get it?" he replied to objections.
And he named this or that individual whose feats of
arms consisted principally in having exhibited themselves in uniforms covered with gold lace to the very
shoulders.

" But I am the man who deserves it most, that cross,"
insisted the younger M. Jottras; " for I, at least, have
rendered valuable services."

And he went on telling how, after searching for arms
all over England, he had sailed for New York, where he
had purchased any number of guns and cartridges, and
even some batteries of artillery.

This last journey had been very wearisome to him, he
added and yet he did not regret it; for it had furnished
him an opportunity to study on the spot the financial
morals of America; and he had returned with ideas
enough to make the fortune of three or four stock companies with twenty millions of capital.

" Ah, those Americans!" he exclaimed. " They are
the men who understand business! We are but children by the side of them."

It was through M. Chapelain, the Desclavettes, and old Desormeaux, that these news reached the Rue St. Gilles.

It was also through Maxence, whose battalion had been dissolved, and who, whilst waiting for something better, had accepted a clerkship in the office of the Orleans Railway, where he earned two hundred francs a month. For M. Favoral saw and heard nothing that was going on around him. He was wholly absorbed in his business: he left earlier, came home later, and hardly allowed himself time to eat and drink.

He told all his friends that business was looking up again in the most unexpected manner; that there were fortunes to be made by those who could command ready cash; and that it was necessary to make up for lost time.

He pretended that the enormous indemnity to be paid to the Prussians would necessitate an enormous movement of capital, financial combinations, a loan, and that so many millions could not be handled without allowing a few little millions to fall into intelligent pockets.

Dazzled by the mere enumeration of those fabulous sums, " I should not be a bit surprised," said the others, " to see Favoral double and treble his fortune. What a famous match his daughter will be!"

Alas! never had Mlle. Gilberte felt in her heart so much hatred and disgust for that money, the only thought, the sole subject of conversation, of those around her,—for that cursed money which had risen like an insurmountable obstacle between Marius and herself.

For two weeks past, the communications had been completely restored; and there was as yet no sign of M. de Trégars. It was with the most violent palpita-

tions of her heart that she awaited each day the hour
of the Signor Gismondo Pulei's lesson: and more painful each time became her anguish when she heard him
exclaim,—

"Nothing, not a line, not a word.   The pupil has forgotten his old master!"

But Mlle. Gilberte knew well that Marius did not
forget.   Her blood froze in her veins when she read in
the papers the interminable list of those poor soldiers
who had succumbed during the invasion,—the more fortunate ones under Prussian bullets; the others along the
roads, in the mud or in the snow, of cold, of fatigue,
of suffering and of want.

She could not drive from her mind the memory of
that lugubrious vision which had so much frightened
her; and she was asking herself whether it was not one
of those inexplicable presentiments, of which there are
examples, which announce the death of a beloved
person.

Alone at night in her little room, Mlle. Gilberte withdrew from the hiding-place, where she kept it preciously,
that package which Marius had confided to her, recommending her not to open it until she was sure that he
would not return.   It was very voluminous, enclosed
in an envelope of thick paper, sealed with red wax, bearing the arms of Trégars; and she had often wondered
what it could possibly contain.   And now she shuddered at the thought that she had perhaps the right to
open it.

And she had no one of whom she could ask for a
word of hope.   She was compelled to hide her tears,
and to put on a smile.   She was compelled to invent
pretexts for those who expressed their wonder at seeing her exquisite beauty withering in the bud,—for her

mother, whose anxiety was without limit, when she saw her thus pale, her eyes inflamed, and undermined by a continuous fever.

True, Marius, on leaving, had left her a friend, the Count de Villegré; and, if any one knew any thing, he certainly did. But she could see no way of hearing from him without risking her secret. Write to him? Nothing was easier, since she had his address,—Rue Turenne. But where could she ask him to direct his answer? Rue St. Gilles? Impossible! True, she might go to him, or make an appointment in the neighborhood. But how could she escape, even for an hour, without exciting Mme. Favoral's suspicions?

Sometimes it occurred to her to confide in Maxence, who was laboring with admirable constancy to redeem his past.

But what! must she, then, confess the truth,—confess that she, Gilberte, had lent her ears to the words of a stranger, met by chance in the street, and that she looked forward to no happiness in life save through him? She dared not. She could not take upon herself to overcome the shame of such a situation.

She was on the verge of despair, the day when the Signor Pulei arrived radiant, exclaiming from the very threshold, " I have news! "

And at once, without surprise at the awful emotion of the girl, which he attributed solely to the interest she felt for him,—him Gismondo Pulei, he went on,—

" I did not get them direct, but through a respectable signor with long mustaches, and a red ribbon at his buttonhole, who, having received a letter from my dear pupil, has deigned to come to my room, and read it to me."

The worthy *maëstro* had not forgotten a single word

of that letter; and it was almost literally that he repeated it.

Six weeks after having enlisted, his pupil had been
promoted corporal, then sergeant, then lieutenant. He
had fought in all the battles of the army of the Loire
without receiving a scratch. But at the battle of the
Maus, whilst leading back his men, who were giving
way, he had been shot twice, full in the breast. Carried
dying into an ambulance, he had lingered three weeks
between life and death, having lost all consciousness of
self. Twenty-four hours after, he had recovered his
senses; and he took the first opportunity to recall himself to the affection of his friends. All danger was over,
he suffered scarcely any more; and they promised him,
that, within a month, he would be up, and able to return to Paris.

For the first time in many weeks Mlle. Gilberte
breathed freely. But she would have been greatly
surprised, had she been told that a day was drawing
near when she would bless those wounds which detained
Marius upon a hospital cot. And yet it was so.

Mme. Favoral and her daughter were alone, one
evening, at the house, when loud clamors arose from the
street, in the midst of which could be heard drunken
voices yelling the refrains of revolutionary songs, accompanied by continuous rumbling sounds. They ran
to the window. The National Guards had just taken
possession of the cannon deposited in the Place Royale.
The reign of the Commune was commencing.

In less than forty-eight hours, people came to regret
the worst days of the siege. Without leaders, without
direction, the honest men had lost their heads. All the
braves who had returned at the time of the armistice
had again taken flight. Soon people had to hide or to

fly to avoid being incorporated in the battalions of the Commune. Night and day, around the walls, the fusillade rattled, and the artillery thundered.

Again M. Favoral had given up going to his office. What's the use? Sometimes, with a singular look, he would say to his wife and children,—

" This time it is indeed a liquidation. Paris is lost! "

And indeed they thought so, when at the hour of the supreme struggle, among the detonations of the cannon and the explosion of the shells; they felt their house shaking to its very foundations; when in the midst of the night they saw their apartment as brilliantly lighted as at mid-day by the flames which were consuming the Hôtel de Ville and the houses around the Place de la Bastille. And, in fact, the rapid action of the troops alone saved Paris from destruction.

But towards the end of the following week, matters had commenced to quiet down; and Gilberte learned the return of Marius.

XX.

" At last it has been given to my eyes to contemplate him, and to my arms to press him against my heart! "

It was in these terms that the old Italian master, all vibrating with enthusiasm, and with his most terrible accent, announced to Mlle. Gilberte that he had just seen that famous pupil from whom he expected both glory and fortune.

" But how weak he is still! " he added, " and suffering from his wounds. I hardly recognized him, he has grown so pale and so thin."

But the girl was listening to him no more. A flood of

life filled her heart. This moment made her forget all her troubles and all her anguish.

" And I too," thought she, " shall see him again to-day."

And, with the unerring instinct of the woman who loves, she calculated the moment when Marius would appear in Rue St. Gilles. It would probably be about nightfall, like the first time, before leaving; that is, about eight o'clock, for the days just then were about the longest in the year. Now it so happened, that, on that very day and hour, Mlle. Gilberte expected to be alone at home. It was understood that her mother would, after dinner, call on Mme. Desclavettes, who was in bed, half dead of the fright she had had during the last convulsions of the Commune. She would therefore be free, and would not need to invent a pretext to go out for a few moments. She could not help, however, but feel that this was a bold and most venturesome step for her to take; and, when her mother went out, she had not yet fully decided what to do. But her bonnet was within reach, and Marius' letter was in her pocket. She went to sit at the window. The street was solitary and silent as of old. Night was coming; and heavy black clouds floated over Paris. The heat was overpowering: there was not a breath of air.

One by one, as the hour was approaching when she expected to see Marius, the hesitations of the young girl vanished like smoke. She feared but one thing,— that he would not come, or that he may already have come and left, without succeeding in seeing her.

Already did the objects become less distinct; and the gas was being lit in the back-shops, when she recognized him on the other side of the street. He looked up as he went by; and, without stopping, he addressed her a rapid gesture, which she alone could understand, and which meant, "Come, I beseech you!"

Her heart beating loud enough to be heard, Mlle. Gilberte ran down the stairs. But it was only when she found herself in the street that she could appreciate the magnitude of the risk she was running. *Concierges* and shopkeepers were all sitting in front of their doors, taking the fresh air. All knew her. Would they not be surprised to see her out alone at such an hour? Twenty steps in front of her she could see Marius. But he had understood the danger; for, instead of turning the corner of the Rue des Minimes, he followed the Rue St. Gilles straight, and only stopped on the other side of the Boulevard.

Then only did Mlle. Gilberte join him; and she could not withhold an exclamation, when she saw that he was as pale as death, and scarcely able to stand and to walk.

"How imprudent of you to have returned so soon!" she said.

A little blood came to M. de Trégars' cheeks. His face brightened up, and, in a voice quivering with suppressed passion,—

"It would have been more imprudent still to stay away," he uttered. "Far from you, I felt myself dying."

They were both leaning against the door of a closed shop; and they were as alone in the midst of the throng that circulated on the Boulevards, busy looking at the fearful wrecks of the Commune.

"And besides," added Marius, "have I, then, a minute to lose? I asked you for three years. Fifteen months have gone, and I am no better off than on the first day. When this accursed war broke out, all my arrangements were made. I was certain to rapidly accumulate a sufficient fortune to enable me to ask for your hand without being refused. Whereas now "—

" Well? "

" Now every thing is changed. The future is so uncertain, that no one wishes to venture their capital. Marcolet himself, who certainly does not lack boldness, and who believes firmly in the success of our enterprise, was telling me yesterday, ' There is nothing to be done just now: we must wait.' "

There was in his voice such an intensity of grief, that the girl felt the tears coming to her eyes.

" We will wait then," she said, attempting to smile.

But M. de Trégars shook his head.

" Is it possible ? " he said. " Do you, then, think that I do not know what a life you lead? "

Mlle. Gilberte looked up.

" Have I ever complained? " she asked proudly?

" No. Your mother and yourself, you have always religiously kept the secret of your tortures; and it was only a providential accident that revealed them to me. But I learned every thing at last. I know that she whom I love exclusively and with all the power of my soul is subjected to the most odious despotism, insulted, and condemned to the most humiliating privations. And I, who would give my life for her a thousand times over,— I can do nothing for her. Money raises between us such an insuperable obstacle, that my love is actually an offence. To hear from her, I am driven to accept accomplices. If I obtain from her a few moments of conversation, I run the risk of compromising her maidenly repu⁹ tation."

Deeply affected by his emotion—

" At least," said Mlle. Gilberte, " you succeeded in delivering me from M. Costeclar."

" Yes, I was fortunately able to find weapons against that scoundrel. But can I find some against all others that may offer? Your father is very rich; and the men are numerous for whom marriage is but a speculation like any other."

" Would you doubt me? "

" Ah, rather would I doubt myself! But I know what cruel trials your refusal to marry M. Costeclar imposed upon you: I know what a merciless struggle you had to sustain. Another pretender may come, and then— No, no, you see that we cannot wait."

" What would you do? "

" I know not. I have not yet decided upon my future course. And yet Heaven knows what have been the labors of my mind during that long month I have just spent upon an ambulance-bed,—that month during which you were my only thought. Ah! when I think of it, I cannot find words to curse the recklessness with which I disposed of my fortune."

As if she had heard a blasphemy, the young girl drew back a step.

" It is impossible," she exclaimed, " that you should regret having paid what your father owed."

A bitter smile contracted M. de Trégars' lips.

" And suppose I were to tell you," he replied, " that my father in reality owed nothing? "

" Oh! "

" Suppose I told you they took from him his entire fortune, over two millions, as audaciously as a pickpocket robs a man of his handkerchief? Suppose I told you, that, in his loyal simplicity, he was but a man of straw in the hands of skilful knaves? Have you forgotten what you once heard the Count de Villegré say? "

Mlle. Gilberte had forgotten nothing.

" The Count de Villgré," she replied, " pretended that it was time enough still to compel the men who had robbed your father to disgorge."

" Exactly ! " exclaimed Marius. " And now I am determined to make them disgorge."

In the mean time night had quite come. Lights appeared in the shop-windows; and along the line of the Boulevard the gas-lamps were being lit. Alarmed by this sudden illumination, M. de Trégars drew off Mlle. Gilberte to a more obscure spot, by the stairs that lead to the Rue Amelot; and there, leaning against the iron railing, he went on,—

" Already, at the time of my father's death, I suspected the abominable tricks of which he was the victim. I thought it unworthy of me to verify my suspicions. I was alone in the world: my wants were few. I was fully convinced that my researches would give me, within a brief time, a much larger fortune than the one I gave up. I found something noble and grand, and which flattered my vanity, in thus abandoning every thing, without discussion, without litigation, and consummating my ruin with a single dash of my pen. Among my friends the Count de Villegré alone had the courage to tell me that this was a guilty piece of folly; that the silence of the dupes is the strength of the knaves ; that my indifference, which made the rascals rich, would make them laugh too. I replied that I did not wish to see the name of Trégars dragged into court in a scandalous law-suit, and that to preserve a dignified silence was to honor my father's memory. Treble fool that I was ! The only way to honor my father's memory was to avenge him, to wrest his spoils from the scoundrels who had caused his death. I see it clearly to-day. But, before undertaking any thing, I wished to consult you."

Mlle. Gilberte was listening with the most intense attention. She had come to mingle so completely in her thoughts her future life and that of M. de Trégars, that she saw nothing unusual in the fact of his consulting her upon matters affecting their prospects, and of seeing herself standing there deliberating with him.

" You will require proofs," she suggested.

" I have none, unfortunately," replied M. de Trégars ; " at least, none sufficiently positive, and such as are required by courts of justice. But I think I may find them. My former suspicions have become a certainty. The same good luck that enabled me to deliver you of M. Costeclar's persecutions, also placed in my hands the most valuable information."

" Then you must act," uttered Mlle. Gilberte resolutely.

Marius hesitated for a moment, as if seeking expression to convey what he had still to say. Then,—

" It is my duty," he proceeded, " to conceal nothing from you. The task is a heavy one. The obscure schemers of ten years ago have become big financiers, intrenched behind their money-bags as behind an impregnable fort. Formerly isolated, they have managed to gather around them powerful interests, accomplices high in office, and friends whose commanding situation protects them. Having succeeded, they are absolved. They have in their favor what is called public consideration,—that idiotic thing which is made up of the admiration of the fools, the approbation of the knaves, and the concert of all interested vanities. When they pass, their horses at full trot, their carriage raising a cloud of dust, insolent, impudent, swelled with the vulgar fatuity of wealth, people bow to the ground, and say, ' Those are smart fellows ! ' And in fact, yes, skill or luck, they have hitherto avoided the police-courts where so many others have come to grief. Those who despise them fear them, and shake hands with them. Moreover, they are rich enough not to steal any more themselves. They have employés to do that. I take Heaven to witness that never until lately had the idea come to me to disturb in their possession the men who robbed my father. Alone, what need had I of money? Later, O my friend! I thought I could succeed in conquering the fortune I needed to obtain your hand. You had promised to wait; and I was happy to think that I should owe you to my sole exertions. Events have crushed my hopes. I am to-day compelled to acknowledge that all my efforts would be in vain. To wait would be to run the risk of losing you. Therefore I hesitate no longer. I want what's mine: I wish to recover that of which I have been robbed. Whatever I may do,—for, alas! I know not to what I may be driven, what *rôle* I may have to play,—remember that of all my acts, of all my thoughts, there will not be a single one that does not aim to bring nearer the blessed day when you shall become my wife."

There was in his voice so much unspeakable affection, that the young girl could hardly restrain her tears.

" Never, whatever may happen, shall I doubt you, Marius," she uttered.

He took her hands, and, pressing them passionately within his,—

" And I," he exclaimed, " I swear, that, sustained by the thought of you, there is no disgust that I will not overcome, no obstacle that I will not overthrow."

He spoke so loud, that two or three persons stopped. He noticed it, and was brought suddenly from sentiment to the reality,—

"Wretches that we are," he said in a low voice, and very fast, "we forget what this interview may cost us!"

And he led Mlle. Gilberte across the Boulevard; and, whilst making their way to the Rue St. Gilles, through the deserted streets,—

"It is a dreadful imprudence we have just committed," resumed M. de Trégars. "But it was indispensable that we should see each other; and we had not the choice of means. Now, and for a long time, we shall be separated. Every thing you wish me to know, say it to that worthy Gismondo, who repeats faithfully to me every word you utter. Through him, also, you shall hear from me. Twice a week, on Tuesdays and Fridays, about nightfall, I shall pass by your house; and, if I am lucky enough to have a glimpse of you, I shall return home fired with fresh energy. Should any thing extraordinary happen, beckon to me, and I'll wait for you in the Rue des Minimes. But this is an expedient to which we must only resort in the last extremity. I should never forgive myself, were I to compromise your fair name."

They had reached the Rue St. Gilles. Marius stopped.

"We must part," he began.

But then only Mlle. Gilberte remembered M. de Trégars' letter, which she had in her pocket. Taking it out, and handing it to him,—

"Here," she said, "is the package you deposited with me."

"No," he answered, repelling her gently, "keep that letter: it must never be opened now, except by the Marquise de Trégars."

And raising her hand to his lips, and in a deeply agitated voice,—

"Farewell!" he murmured. "Have courage, and have hope."

XXI.

MLLE. GILBERTE was soon far away; and Marius de Trégars remained motionless at the corner of the street, following her with his eyes through the darkness.

She was walking fast, staggering over the rough pavement. Leaving Marius, she fell back upon the earth from the height of her dreams. The deceiving illusion had vanished, and, returned to the world of sad reality, she was seized with anxiety.

How long had she been out? She knew not, and found it impossible to reckon. But it was evidently getting late; for some of the shops were already closing.

Meantime, she had reached the house. Stepping back, and looking up, she saw that there was light in the parlor.

"Mother has returned," she thought, trembling with apprehension.

She hurried up, nevertheless; and, just as she reached the landing, Mme. Favoral opened the door, preparing to go down.

"At last you are restored to me!" exclaimed the poor mother, whose sinister apprehensions were revealed by that single exclamation. "I was going out to look for you at random,—in the streets, anywhere."

And, drawing her daughter within the parlor, she clasped her in her arms with convulsive tenderness, exclaiming,—

"Where were you? Where do you come from? Do you know that it is after nine o'clock?"

Such had been Mlle. Gilberte's state of mind during
the whole of that evening, that she had not even thought
of finding a pretext to justify her absence. Now it was
too late. Besides, what explanation would have been
plausible? Instead, therefore, of answering,—

"Why, dear mother," she said with a forced smile,
"has it not happened to me twenty times to go out in the
neighborhood?"

But Mme. Favoral's confiding credulity existed no
longer.

"I have been blind, Gilberte," she interrupted; "but
this time my eyes must open to evidence. There is in
your life a mystery, something extraordinary, which I
dare not try to guess."

Mlle. Gilberte drew herself up, and, looking her
mother straight in the eyes, with her beautiful, clear
glance,—

"Would you suspect me of something wrong, then?"
she exclaimed.

Mme. Favoral stopped her with a gesture.

"A young girl who conceals something from her
mother always does wrong," she uttered. "It is a long
while since I have had for the first time the presentiment
that you were hiding something from me. But, when I
questioned you, you succeeded in quieting my suspicions. You have abused my confidence and my weakness."

This reproach was the most cruel that could be addressed to Mlle. Gilberte. The blood rushed to her
face, and, in a firm voice,—

"Well, yes," said she: "I have a secret."

"Dear me!"

"And, if I did not confide it to you, it is because it is
also the secret of another. Yes, I confess it, I have been

imprudent in the extreme; I have stepped beyond all the limits of propriety and social custom; I have exposed myself to the worst calumnies. But never,—I swear it,—never have I done any thing of which my conscience can reproach me, nothing that I have to blush for, nothing that I regret, nothing that I am not ready to do again to-morrow."

" Gilberte ! "

" I said nothing, 'tis true; but it was my duty. Alone I had to suffer the responsibility of my acts. Having alone freely engaged my future, I wished to bear alone the weight of my anxiety. I should never have forgiven myself for having added this new care to all your other sorrows."

Mme. Favoral stood dismayed. Big tears rolled down her withered cheeks.

" Don't you see, then," she stammered, " that all my past suffering is as nothing compared to what I endure to-day? Good heavens! what have I ever done to deserve so many trials? Am I to be spared none of the troubles of this world? And it is through my own daughter that I am the most cruelly stricken ! "

This was more than Mlle. Gilberte could bear. Her heart was breaking at the sight of her mother's tears,— that angel of meekness and resignation. Throwing her arms around her neck, and kissing her on the eyes,—

" Mother," she murmured, " adored mother, I beg of you do not weep thus! Speak to me! What do you wish me to do?"

Gently the poor woman drew back.

" Tell me the truth," she answered.

Was it not certain that this was the very thing she would ask; in fact, the only thing she could ask? Ah! how much would the young girl have preferred one of her father's violent scenes, and brutalities which would have exalted her energy, instead of crushing it!

Attempting to gain time,—

"Well, yes," she answered, "I'll tell you every thing, mother, but not now, to-morrow, later."

She was about to yield, however, when her father's arrival cut short their conversation.

The cashier of the Mutual Credit was quite lively that night. He was humming a tune, a thing which did not happen to him four times a year, and which was indicative of the most extreme satisfaction. But he stopped short at the sight of the disturbed countenance of his wife and daughter.

"What is the matter?" he inquired.

"Nothing," hastily answered Mlle. Gilberte,—"nothing at all, father."

"Then you are crying for your amusement," he said. "Come, be candid for once, and confess that Maxence has been at his tricks again!"

"You are mistaken, father: I swear it!"

He asked no further questions, being in his nature not very curious, whether because family matters were of so little consequence to him, or because he had a vague idea that his general behavior deprived him of all right to their confidence.

"Very well, then," he said in a gruff tone, "let us all go to bed. I have worked so hard to-day, that I am quite exhausted. People who pretend that business is dull make me laugh. Never has M. de Thaller been in the way of making so much money as now."

When he spoke, they obeyed. So that Mlle. Gilberte was thus going to have the whole night before her to resume possession of herself, to pass over in her mind the events of the evening, and deliberate coolly upon the decision she must come to; for, she could not doubt it, Mme. Favoral would, the very next day, renew her questions.

What should she say? All? Mlle. Gilberte felt disposed to do so by all the aspirations of her heart, by the certainty of indulgent complicity, by the thought of finding in a sympathetic soul the echo of her joys, of her troubles, and of her hopes.

Yes. But Mme. Favoral was still the same woman, whose firmest resolutions vanished under the gaze of her husband. Let a pretender come; let a struggle begin, as in the case of M. Costeclar,—would she have strength enough to remain silent? No!

Then it would be a fearful scene with M. Favoral. He might, perhaps, even go to M. de Trégars. What scandal! For he was a man who spared no one; and then a new obstacle would rise between them, more insurmountable still than the others.

Mlle. Gilberte was thinking, too, of Marius's projects; of that terrible game he was about to play, the issue of which was to decide their fate. He had said enough to make her understand all its perils, and that a single indiscretion might suffice to set at nought the result of many months' labor and patience. Besides, to speak, was it not to abuse Marius's confidence. How could she expect another to keep a secret she had been unable to keep herself?

At last, after protracted and painful hesitation, she decided that she was bound to silence, and that she would only vouchsafe the vaguest explanations.

It was in vain, then, that, on the next and the following days, Mme. Favoral tried to obtain that confession which she had seen, as it were, rise to her daughter's lips. To her passionate adjurations, to her tears, to her ruses even, Mlle. Gilberte invariably opposed equivocal answers, a story through which nothing could be guessed, save one of those childish romances which stop at the preface,—a schoolgirl love for a chimerical hero.

There was nothing in this very re-assuring to a mother; but Mme. Favoral knew her daughter too well to hope to conquer her invincible obstinacy. She insisted no more, appeared convinced, but resolved to exercise the utmost vigilance. In vain, however, did she display all the penetration of which she was capable. The severest attention did not reveal to her a single suspicious fact, not a circumstance from which she could draw an induction, until, at last, she thought that she must have been mistaken.

The fact is, that Mlle. Gilberte had not been long in feeling herself watched; and she observed herself with a tenacious circumspection that could hardly have been expected of her resolute and impatient nature. She had trained herself to a sort of cheerful carelessness, to which she strictly adhered, watching every expression of her countenance, and avoiding carefully those hours of vague revery in which she formerly indulged.

For two successive weeks, fearing to be betrayed by her looks, she had the courage not to show herself at the window at the hour when she knew Marius would pass. Moreover, she was very minutely informed of the alternatives of the campaign undertaken by M. de Trégars.

More enthusiastic than ever about his pupil, the Signor Gismondo Pulei never tired of singing his praise, and with such pomp of expression, and so curious an exuberance of gesticulation, that Mme. Favoral was much amused; and, on the days when she was present at her daughter's lesson, she was the first to inquire,—

" Well, how is that famous pupil? "

And, according to what Marius had told him,—

" He is swimming in the purest satisfaction," answered the candid *maëstro.* " Every thing succeeds miraculously well, and much beyond his hopes."

Or else, knitting his brows,—

" He was sad yesterday," he said, " owing to an unexpected disappointment; but he does not lose courage. We shall succeed."

The young girl could not help smiling to see her mother assisting thus the unconscious complicity of the Signor Gismondo. Then she reproached herself for having smiled, and for having thus come, through a gradual and fatal descent, to laugh at a duplicity at which she would have blushed in former times. In spite of herself, however, she took a passionate interest in the game that was being played between her mother and herself, and of which her secret was the stake. It was an ever-palpitating interest in her hitherto monotonous life, and a source of constantly-renewed emotions.

The days became weeks, and the weeks months; and Mme. Favoral relaxed her useless surveillance, and, little by little, gave it up almost entirely. She still thought, that, at a certain moment, something unusual had occurred to her daughter; but she felt persuaded, that whatever that was, it had been forgotten.

So that, on the stated days, Mlle. Gilberte could go and lean upon the window, without fear of being called to account for the emotion which she felt when M. de Trégars appeared. At the expected hour, invariably, and with a punctuality to shame M. Favoral himself, he turned the corner of the Rue Turenne, exchanged a rapid glance with the young girl, and passed on.

His health was completely restored; and with it he

had recovered that graceful virility which results from the perfect blending of suppleness and strength. But he no longer wore the plain garments of former days. He was dressed now with that elegant simplicity which reveals at first sight that rarest of objects,—a " perfect gentleman." And, whilst she accompanied him with her eyes as he walked towards the Boulevard, she felt thoughts of joy and pride rising from the bottom of her soul.

" Who would ever imagine," thought she, " that this young gentleman walking away yonder is my affianced husband, and that the day is perhaps not far, when, having become his wife, I shall lean upon his arm? Who would think that all my thoughts belong to him, that it is for my sake that he has given up the ambition of his life, and is now prosecuting another object? Who would suspect that it is for Gilberte Favoral's sake that the Marquis de Trégars is walking in the Rue St. Gilles?"

And, indeed, Marius did deserve some credit for these walks; for winter had come, spreading a thick coat of mud over the pavement of all those little streets which are always forgotten by the street-cleaners.

The cashier's home had resumed its habits of before the war, its drowsy monotony scarcely disturbed by the Saturday dinner, by M. Desclavette's *naïvetés* or old Desormeaux's puns.

Maxence, in the mean time, had ceased to live with his parents. He had returned to Paris immediately after the Commune; and, feeling no longer in the humor to submit to the paternal despotism, he had taken a small apartment on the Boulevard du Temple; but, at the pressing instance, of his mother, he had consented to come every night to dine at the Rue St. Gilles.

Faithful to his oath, he was working hard, though

without getting on very fast. The moment was far
from propitious; and the occasion, which he had so often
allowed to escape, did not offer itself again. For lack
of any thing better, he had kept his clerkship at the railway; and, as two hundred francs a month were not quite
sufficient for his wants, he spent a portion of his nights
copying documents for M. Chapelain's successor.

" What do you need so much money for? " his mother
said to him when she noticed his eyes a little red.

" Every thing is so dear! " he answered with a smile,
which was equivalent to a confidence, and yet which
Mme. Favoral did not understand.

He had, nevertheless, managed to pay all his debts,
little by little. The day when, at last, he held in his
hand the last receipted bill, he showed it proudly to his
father, begging him to find him a place at the Mutual
Credit, where, with infinitely less trouble, he could earn
so much more.

M. Favoral commenced to giggle.

" Do you take me for a fool, like your mother? " he
exclaimed. " And do you think I don't know what life
you lead? "

" My life is that of a poor devil who works as hard
as he can."

" Indeed! How is it, then, that women are constantly seen at your house, whose dresses and manners
are a scandal in the neighborhood? "

" You have been deceived, father."

" I have seen."

" It is impossible. Let me explain."

" No, you would have your trouble for nothing. You
are, and you will ever remain, the same; and it would be
folly on my part to introduce into an office where I enjoy the esteem of all, a fellow, who, some day or other,

will be fatally dragged into the mud by some lost creature."

Such discussions were not calculated to make the relations between father and son more cordial. Several times M. Favoral had insinuated, that, since Maxence lodged away from home, he might as well dine away too. And he would evidently have notified him to do so, had he not been prevented by a remnant of human respect, and the fear of gossip.

On the other hand, the bitter regret of having, perhaps, spoiled his life, the uncertainty of the future, the penury of the moment, all the unsatisfied desires of youth, kept Maxence in a state of perpetual irritation.

The excellent Mme. Favoral exhausted all her arguments to quiet him.

"Your father is harsh for us," she said; "but is he less harsh for himself? He forgives nothing; but he has never needed to be forgiven himself. He does not understand youth, but he has never been young himself; and at twenty he was as grave and as cold as you see him now. How could he know what pleasure is?—he to whom the idea has never come to take an hour's enjoyment."

"Have I, then, been guilty of any crimes, to be thus treated by my father?" exclaimed Maxence, flushed with anger. "Our existence here is an unheard-of thing. You, poor, dear mother!—you have never had the free disposition of a five-franc-piece. Gilberte spends her days turning her dresses, after having had them dyed. I am driven to a petty clerkship. And my father has fifty thousand francs a year!"

Such, indeed, was the figure at which the most moderate estimated M. Favoral's fortune. M. Chapelain, who was supposed to be well informed, insinuated freely

that his friend Vincent, besides being the cashier of the
Mutual Credit, must also be one of its principal stockholders. Now, judging from the dividend which had
just been paid, the Mutual Credit must, since the war,
have realized enormous profits. All its enterprises were
successful; and it was on the point of negotiating a foreign loan which would infallibly fill its exchequer to
overflowing.

M. Favoral, moreover, defended himself feebly from
these accusations of concealed opulence. When M. Desormeaux told him, " Come, now, between us, candidly,
how many millions have you?" he had such a strange
way of affirming that people were very much mistaken,
that his friends' convictions became only the more settled. And, as soon as they had a few thousand francs
of savings, they promptly brought them to him, imitated
in this by a goodly number of the small capitalists of the
neighborhood, who were wont to remark among themselves,—

" That man is safer than the bank! "

Millionaire or otherwise, the cashier of the Mutual
Credit became daily more difficult to live with. If
strangers, those who had with him but a superficial intercourse, if the Saturday guests themselves, discovered
in him no appreciable change, his wife and his children
followed with anxious surprise the modifications of his
humor.

If outwardly he still appeared the same impassible,
precise, and grave man, he showed himself at home more
fretful than an old maid,—nervous, agitated, and subject to the oddest whims.

After remaining three or four days without opening
his lips, he would begin to speak upon all sorts of subjects with amazing volubility. Instead of watering his

wine freely, as formerly, he had begun to drink it pure; and he often took two bottles at his meal, excusing himself upon the necessity that he felt the need of stimulating himself a little after his excessive labors.

Then he would be taken with fits of coarse gayety; and he related singular anecdotes, intermingled with slang expressions, which Maxence alone could understand.

On the morning of the first day of January, 1872, as he sat down to breakfast, he threw upon the table a roll of fifty napoleons, saying to his children,—

"Here is your New Year's gift! Divide, and buy any thing you like."

And as they were looking at him, staring, stupid with astonishment,—

"Well, what of it?" he added with an oath. "Isn't it well, once in a while, to scatter the coins a little?"

Those unexpected thousand francs Maxence and Mlle. Gilberte applied to the purchase of a shawl, which their mother had wished for for ten years.

She laughed and she cried with pleasure and emotion, the poor woman; and, whilst draping it over her shoulders,—

"Well, well, my dear children," she said: "your father, after all, is not such a bad man."

Of which they did not seem very well convinced.

"One thing is sure," remarked Mlle. Gilberte: "to permit himself such liberality, papa must be awfully rich."

M. Favoral was not present at this scene. The yearly accounts kept him so closely confined to his office, that he remained forty-eight hours without coming home. A journey which he was compelled to undertake for M. de Thaller consumed the balance of the week.

But on his return he seemed satisfied and quiet. Without giving up his situation at the Mutual Credit, he was about, he stated, to associate himself with the Messrs. Jottras, M. Saint Pavin of "The Financial Pilot," and M. Costeclar, to undertake the construction of a foreign railway.

M. Costeclar was at the head of this enterprise, the enormous profits of which were so certain and so clear, that they could be figured in advance.

And whilst on this same subject,—

"You were very wrong," he said to Mlle. Gilberte, "not to make haste and marry Costeclar when he was willing to have you. You will never find another such match,—a man who, before ten years, will be a financial power."

The very name of M. Costeclar had the effect of irritating the young girl.

"I thought you had fallen out?" she said to her father.

"So we had," he replied with some embarrassment, "because he has never been willing to tell me why he had withdrawn; but people always make up again when they have interests in common."

Formerly, before the war, M. Favoral would certainly never have condescended to enter into all these details. But he was becoming almost communicative. Mlle. Gilberte, who was observing him with interested attention, fancied she could see that he was yielding to that necessity of expansion, more powerful than the will itself, which besets the man who carries within him a weighty secret.

Whilst for twenty years he had, so to speak, never breathed a word on the subject of the Thaller family, now he was continually speaking of them. He told his

Saturday friends all about the princely style of the baron, the number of his servants and horses, the color of his liveries, the parties that he gave, what he spent for pictures and objects of art, and even the very names of his mistresses; for the baron had too much respect for himself not to lay every year a few thousand napoleons at the feet of some young lady sufficiently conspicuous to be mentioned in the society newspapers.

M. Favoral confessed that he did not approve the baron; but it was with a sort of bitter hatred that he spoke of the baroness. It was impossible, he affirmed to his guests, to estimate even approximately the fabulous sums squandered by her, scattered, thrown to the four winds. For she was not prodigal, she was prodigality itself,—that idiotic, absurd, unconscious prodigality which melts a fortune in a turn of the hand; which cannot even obtain from money the satisfaction of a want, a wish, or a fancy.

He said incredible things of her,—things which made Mme. Desclavettes jump upon her seat, explaining that he learned all these details from M. de Thaller, who had often commissioned him to pay his wife's debts, and also from the baroness herself, who did not hesitate to call sometimes at the office for twenty francs; for such was her want of order, that, after borrowing all the savings of her servants, she frequently had not two cents to throw to a beggar.

Neither did the cashier of the Mutual Credit seem to have a very good opinion of Mademoiselle de Thaller.

Brought up at hap-hazard, in the kitchen much more than in the parlor, until she was twelve, and, later, dragged by her mother anywhere,—to the races, to the first representations, to the watering-places, always escorted by a squadron of the young men of the *bourse,*

Mlle. de Thaller had adopted a style which would have been deemed detestable in a man. As soon as some questionable fashion appeared, she appropriated it at once, never finding any thing eccentric enough to make herself conspicuous. She rode on horseback, fenced, frequented pigeon-shooting matches, spoke slang, sang Theresa's songs, emptied neatly her glass of champagne, and smoked her cigarette.

The guests were struck dumb with astonishment.

" But those people must spend millions ! " interrupted M. Chapelain.

M. Favoral started as if he had been slapped on the back.

" Bash ! " he answered. " They are so rich, so awfully rich ! "

He changed the conversation that evening; but on the following Saturday, from the very beginning of the dinner,—

" I believe," he said, " that M. de Thaller has just discovered a husband for his daughter."

" My compliments ! " exclaimed M. Desormeaux. " And who may this bold fellow be ? "

" A nobleman, of course," he replied. " Isn't that the tradition ? As soon as a financier has made his little million, he starts in quest of a nobleman to give him his daughter."

One of those painful presentiments, such as arise in the inmost recesses of the soul, made Mlle. Gilberte turn pale. This presentiment suggested to her an absurd, ridiculous, unlikely thing; and yet she was sure that it would not deceive her,—so sure, indeed, that she rose under the pretext of looking for something in the sideboard, but in reality to conceal the terrible emotion which she anticipated.

"And this gentleman?" inquired M. Chapelain.

"Is a marquis, if you please,—the Marquis de Tré-gars."

Well, yes, it was this very name that Mlle. Gilberte was expecting, and well that she did; for she was thus able to command enough control over herself to check the cry that rose to her throat.

"But this marriage is not made yet," pursued M. Favoral. "This marquis is not yet so completely ruined, that he can be made to do any thing they please. Sure, the baroness has set her heart upon it, oh! but with all her might!"

A discussion which now arose prevented Gilberte from learning any more; and as soon as the dinner, which seemed eternal to her, was over, she complained of a violent headache, and withdrew to her room.

She shook with fever; her teeth chattered. And yet she could not believe that Marius was betraying her, nor that he could have the thought of marrying such a girl as M. Favoral had described, and for money too! Poor, ah! No, that was not admissible. Although she remembered well that Marius had made her swear to believe nothing that might be said of him, she spent a horrible Sunday, and she felt like throwing herself in the Signor Gismondo's arms, when, in giving her his lesson the following Monday,—

"My poor pupil," he said, "feels miserable. A marriage has been spoken of for him, for which he has a perfect horror; and he trembles lest the rumor may reach his intended, whom he loves exclusively."

Mlle. Gilberte felt re-assured after that. And yet there remained in her heart an invincible sadness. She could hardly doubt that this matrimonial scheme was a part of the plan planned by Marius to recover his fortune. But why, then, had he applied to M. de Thaller? Who could be the man who had despoiled the Marquis de Trégars?

Such were the thoughts which occupied her mind on that Saturday evening when the commissary of police presented himself in the Rue St. Gilles to arrest M. Favoral, charged with embezzling ten or twelve millions.

* * *

XXII.

THE hour had now come for the *dénouement* of that home tragedy which was being enacted in the Rue St. Gilles.

The reader will remember the incidents narrated at the beginning of this story,—M. de Thaller's visit and angry words with M. Favoral, his departure after leaving a package of bank-notes in Mlle. Gilberte's hands, the advent of the commissary of police, M. Favoral's escape, and finally the departure of the Saturday evening guests.

The disaster which struck Mme. Favoral and her children had been so sudden and so crushing, that they had been, on the moment, too stupefied to realize it. What had happened went so far beyond the limits of the probable, of the possible even, that they could not believe it. The too cruel scenes which had just taken place were to them like the absurd incidents of a horrible nightmare.

But when their guests had retired after a few commonplace protestations, when they found themselves alone, all three, in that house whose master had just fled, tracked by the police,—then only, as the disturbed equilibrium of their minds became somewhat restored, did they fully realize the extent of the disaster, and the horror of the situation.

Whilst Mme. Favoral lay apparently lifeless on an arm-chair, Gilberte kneeling at her feet, Maxence was walking up and down the parlor with furious steps. He was whiter than the plaster on the walls; and a cold perspiration glued his tangled hair to his temples.

His eyes glistening, and his fists clinched,—

"Our father a thief!" he kept repeating in a hoarse voice, "a forger!"

And in fact never had the slightest suspicion arisen in his mind. In these days of doubtful reputations, he had been proud indeed of M. Favoral's reputation of austere integrity. And he had endured many a cruel reproach, saying to himself that his father had, by his own spotless conduct, acquired the right to be harsh and exacting.

"And he has stolen twelve millions!" he exclaimed.

And he went on, trying to calculatae all the luxury and splendor which such a sum represents, all the cravings gratified, all the dreams realized, all it can procure of things that may be bought. And what things are not for sale for twelve millions!

Then he examined the gloomy home in the Rue St. Gilles,—the contracted dwelling, the faded furniture. the prodigies of a parsimonious industry, his mother's privations, his sister's penury, and his own distress. And he exclaimed again,—

"It is a monstrous infamy!"

The words of the commissary of police had opened his eyes; and he now fancied the most wonderful things. M. Favoral, in his mind, assumed fabulous proportions. By what miracles of hypocrisy and dissimulation had he succeeded in making himself ubiquitous as it were, and, without awaking a suspicion, living two lives so distinct and so different,—here, in the midst of his family, parsimonious, methodic, and severe; elsewhere, in some illicit household, doubtless facile, smiling, and generous, like a successful thief.

For Maxence considered the bills found in the secretary as a flagrant, irrefutable and material proof.

Upon the brink of that abyss of shame into which his father had just tumbled, he thought he could see, not the inevitable woman, that incentive of all human actions, but the entire legion of those bewitching courtesans who possess unknown crucibles wherein to swell fortunes, and who have secret filters to stupefy their dupes, and strip them of their honor, after robbing them of their last cent.

" And I," said Maxence,—" I, because at twenty I was fond of pleasure, I was called a bad son! Because I had made some three hundred francs of debts, I was deemed a swindler! Because I love a poor girl who has for me the most disinterested affection, I am one of those rascals whom their family disown, and from whom nothing can be expected but shame and disgrace! "

He filled the parlor with the sound of his voice, which rose like his wrath.

And at the thought of all the bitter reproaches which had been addressed to him by his father, and of all the humiliations that had been heaped upon him,—

" Ah, the wretch! " he fairly shrieked, " the coward! "

As pale as her brother, her face bathed in tears, and her beautiful hair hanging undone, Mlle. Gilberte drew herself up.

" He is our father, Maxence," she said gently.

But he interrupted her with a wild burst of laughter.

" True," he answered ; " and, by virtue of the law which is written in the code, we owe him affection and respect."

" Maxence ! " murmured the girl in a beseeching tone.

But he went on, nevertheless,—

" Yes, he is our father, unfortunately. But I should like to know his titles to our respect and our affection. After making our mother the most miserable of creatures, he has imbittered our existence, withered our youth, ruined my future, and done his best to spoil yours by compelling you to marry Costeclar. And, to crown all these deeds of kindness, he runs away now, after stealing twelve millions, leaving us nothing but misery and a disgraced name.

" And yet," he added, " is it possible that a cashier should take twelve millions, and his employer know nothing of it ? And is our father really the only man who benefited by these millions ? "

Then came back to the mind of Maxence and Mlle. Gilberte the last words of their father at the moment of his flight,—

" I have been betrayed; and I must suffer for all ! "

And his sincerity could hardly be called in question; for he was then in one of those moments of decisive crisis in which the truth forces itself out in spite of all calculation.

" He must have accomplices then," murmured Maxence.

Although he had spoken very low, Mme. Favoral overheard him. To defend her husband, she found a remnant of energy, and, straightening herself on her seat,—

"Ah! do not doubt it," she stammered out. "Of his own inspiration, Vincent could never have committed an evil act. He has been circumvented, led away, duped!"

"Very well; but by whom?"

"By Costeclar," affirmed Mlle. Gilberte.

"By the Messrs. Jottras, the bankers," said Mme. Favoral, "and also by M. Saint Pavin, the editor of 'the Financial Pilot.'"

"By all of them, evidently," interrupted Maxence, "even by his manager, M. de Thaller."

When a man is at the bottom of a precipice, what is the use of finding out how he has got there,—whether by stumbling over a stone, or slipping on a tuft of grass! And yet it is always our foremost thought. It was with an eager obstinacy that Mme. Favoral and her children ascended the course of their existence, seeking in the past the incidents and the merest words which might throw some light upon their disaster; for it was quite manifest that it was not in one day and at the same time that twelve millions had been subtracted from the Mutual Credit. This enormous deficit must have been, as usual, made gradually, with infinite caution at first, whilst there was a desire, and some hope, to make it good again, then with mad recklessness towards the end when the catastrophe had become inevitable.

"Alas!" murmured Mme. Favoral, "why did not Vincent listen to my presentiments on that ever fatal day when he brought M. de Thaller, M. Jottras, and M. Saint Pavin to dine here? They promised him a fortune."

Maxence and Mlle. Gilberte were too young at the time of that dinner to have preserved any remembrance of it; but they remembered many other circumstances, which, at the time they had taken place, had not struck them. They understood now the temper of their father, his perpetual irritation, and the spasms of his humor. When his friends were heaping insults upon him, he had exclaimed,—

" Be it so! let them arrest me; and to-night, for the first time in many years, I shall sleep in peace."

There were years, then, that he lived, as it were upon burning coals, trembling at the fear of discovery, and wondering, as he went to sleep each night, whether he would not be awakened by the rude hand of the police tapping him on the shoulder. No one better than Mme. Favoral could affirm it.

" Your father, my children," she said, " had long since lost his sleep. There was hardly ever a night that he did not get up and walk the room for hours."

They understood, now, his efforts to compel Mlle. Gilberte to marry M. Costeclar.

" He thought that Costeclar would help him out of the scrape," suggested Maxence to his sister.

The poor girl shuddered at the thought, and she could not help feeling thankful to her father for not having told her his situation; for would she have had the sublime courage to refuse the sacrifice, if her father had told her? —

" I have stolen! I am lost! Costeclar alone can save me; and he will save me if you become his wife."

M. Favoral's pleasant behavior during the siege was quite natural. Then he had no fears; and one could understand how in the most critical hours of the Commune, when Paris was in flames, he could have exclaimed almost cheerfully,—

" Ah! this time it is indeed the final liquidation."

Doubtless, in the bottom of his heart, he wished

that Paris might be destroyed, and, with it, the evidences of his crime. And perhaps he was not the only one to form that impious wish.

"That's why, then," exclaimed Maxence,—"that's why my father treated me so rudely: that's why he so obstinately persisted in closing the offices of the Mutual Credit against me."

He was interrupted by a violent ringing of the door-bell. He looked at the clock: ten o'clock was about to strike.

"Who can call so late?" said Mme. Favoral.

Something like a discussion was heard in the hall,—a voice hoarse with anger, and the servant's voice.

"Go and see who's there," said Gilberte to her brother.

It was useless; the servant appeared.

"It's M. Bertan," she commenced, "the baker "—

He had followed her, and, pushing her aside with his robust arm, he appeared himself. He was a man about forty years of age, tall, thin, already bald, and wearing his beard trimmed close.

"M. Favoral?" he inquired.

"My father is not at home," replied Maxence.

"It's true, then, what I have just been told?"

"What?"

"That the police came to arrest him, and he escaped through a window."

"It's true," replied Maxence gently.

The baker seemed prostrated.

"And my money?" he asked.

"What money?"

"Why, my ten thousand francs! Ten thousand francs which I brought to M. Favoral, in gold, you hear? in ten rolls, which I placed there, on that very ta-

ble, and for which he gave me a receipt.   Here it is,—
his receipt."

He held out a paper; but Maxence did not take it.

" I do not doubt your word, sir," he replied; " but
my father's business is not ours."

" You refuse to give me back my money? "

" Neither my mother, my sister, nor myself, have any
thing."

The blood rushed to the man's face, and, with a
tongue made thick by anger,—

" And you think you are going to pay me off in that
way? " he exclaimed.   " You have nothing! Poor little
fellow ! And will you tell me, then, what has become
of the twenty millions your father has stolen? for he
has stolen twenty millions. I know it: I have been told
so. Where are they? "

" The police, sir, has placed the seals over my father's
papers."

" The police? " interrupted the baker, " the seals?
What do I care for that? It's my money I want: do
you hear? Justice is going to take a hand in it, is
it? Arrest your father, try him? What good will that
do me? He will be condemned to two or three years'
imprisonment. Will that give me a cent? He will
serve out his time quietly; and, when he gets out of
prison, he'll get hold of the pile that he's got hidden
somewhere; and while I starve, he'll spend my money
under my very nose. No, no! Things won't suit me
that way. It's at once that I want to be paid."

And throwing himself upon a chair his head back,
and his legs stretched forward,—

" And what's more," he declared, " I am not going
out of here until I am paid."

It was not without the greatest efforts that Maxence managed to keep his temper.

"Your insults are useless, sir," he commenced.

The man jumped up from his seat.

"Insults!" he cried in a voice that could have been heard all through the house. "Do you call it an insult when a man claims his own? If you think you can make me hush, you are mistaken in your man, M. Favoral, jun. I am not rich myself: my father has not stolen to leave me an income. It is not in gambling at the *bourse* that I made these ten thousand francs. It is by the sweat of my body, by working hard night and day for years, by depriving myself of a glass of wine when I was thirsty. And I am to lose them? By the holy name of heaven, we'll have to see about that! If everybody was like me, there would not be so many scoundrels going about, their pockets filled with other people's money, and from the top of their carriage laughing at the poor fools they have ruined. Come, my ten thousand francs, canaille, or I take my pay on your back."

Maxence, enraged, was about to throw himself upon the man, and a disgusting struggle was about to begin, when Mlle. Gilberte stepped between them.

"Your threats are as cowardly as your insults, Monsieur Bertan," she uttered in a quivering voice. "You have known us long enough to be aware that we know nothing of our father's business, and that we have nothing ourselves. All we can do is to give up to our creditors our very last crumb. Thus it shall be done. And now, sir, please retire."

There was so much dignity in her sorrow, and so imposing was her attitude, that the baker stood abashed.

"Ah! if that's the way," he stammered awkwardly; "and since you meddle with it, mademoiselle "—

And he retreated precipitately, growling at the same time threats and excuses, and slamming the doors after him hard enough to break the partitions.

"What a disgrace!" murmured Mme. Favoral.

Crushed by this last scene, she was choking; and her children had to carry her to the open window. She recovered almost at once; but thus, through the darkness, bleak and cold, she had like a vision of her husband; and, throwing herself back,—

"O great heavens!" she uttered, "where did he go when he left us? Where is he now? What is he doing? What has become of him?"

Her married life had been for Mme. Favoral but a slow torture. It was in vain that she would have looked back through her past life for some of those happy days which leave their luminous track in life, and towards which the mind turns in the hours of grief. Vincent Favoral had never been aught but a brutal despot, abusing the resignation of his victim. And yet, had he died, she would have wept bitterly over him in all the sincerity of her honest and simple soul. Habit! Prisoners have been known to shed tears over the grave of their jailer. Then he was her husband, after all, the father of her children, the only man who existed for her. For twenty-six years they had never been separated: they had sat at the same table: they had slept side by side.

Yes, she would have wept over him. But how much less poignant would her grief have been than at this moment, when it was complicated by all the torments of uncertainty, and by the most frightful apprehensions!

Fearing lest she might take cold, her children had removed her to the sofa, and there, all shivering,—

" Isn't it horrible," she said, " not to know any thing of your father?—to think that at this very moment, perhaps, pursued by the police, he is wandering in despair through the streets, without daring to ask anywhere for shelter."

Her children had no time to answer and comfort her; for at this moment the door-bell rang again.

" Who can it be now?" said Mme. Favoral with a start.

This time there was no discussion in the hall. Steps sounded on the floor of the dining-room; the door opened; and M. Desclavettes, the old bronze-merchant, walked, or rather slipped into the parlor.

Hope, fear, anger, all the sentiments which agitated his soul, could be read on his pale and cat-like face.

" It is I," he commenced.

Maxence stepped forward.

" Have you heard any thing from my father, sir? '

" No," answered the old merchant, " I confess I have not; and I was just coming to see if you had yourselves. Oh, I know very well that this is not exactly the hour to call at a house; but I thought, that, after what took place this evening, you would not be in bed yet. I could not sleep myself. You understand a friendship of twenty years' standing! So I took Mme. Desclavettes home, and here I am."

" We feel very thankful for your kindness," murmured Mme. Favoral.

" I am glad you do. The fact is, you see, I take a good deal of interest in the misfortune that strikes you, —a greater interest than any one else. For, after all, I, too, am a victim. I had intrusted one hundred and twenty thousand francs to our dear Vincent."

" Alas, sir!" said Mlle. Gilberte.

But the worthy man did not allow her to proceed.

"I have no fault to find with him," he went on,—
"absolutely none. Why, dear me! haven't I been in
business myself? and don't I know what it is? First,
we borrow a thousand francs or so from the cash account, then ten thousand, then a hundred thousand.
Oh! without any bad intention, to be sure, and with
the firm resolution to return them. But we don't always do what we wish to do. Circumstances sometimes work against us, if we operate at the *bourse* to
make up the deficit we lose. Then we must borrow
again, draw from Peter to pay Paul. We are afraid of
being caught: we are compelled, reluctantly of course,
to alter the books. At last a day comes when we find
that millions are gone, and the bomb-shell bursts. Does
it follow from this that a man is dishonest? Not the
least in the world: he is simply unlucky."

He stopped, as if awaiting an answer; but, as none
came, he resumed,—

"I repeat, I have no fault to find with Favoral. Only
then, now, between us, to lose these hundred and twenty
thousand francs would simply be a disaster for me. I
know very well that both Chapelain and Desormeaux
had also deposited funds with Favoral. But they are
rich: one of them owns three houses in Paris, and the
other has a good situation; whereas I, these hundred
and twenty thousand francs gone, I'd have nothing left
but my eyes to weep with. My wife is dying about it.
I assure you our position is a terrible one."

To M. Desclavettes, as to the baker a few moments
before,—

"We have nothing," said Maxence.

"I know it," exclaimed the old merchant. "I know
it as well as you do yourself. And so I have come to

beg a little favor of you, which will cost you nothing.
When you see Favoral, remember me to him, explain
my situation to him, and try to make him give me back
my money. He is a hard one to fetch, that's a fact.
But if you go right about it, above all, if our dear Gilberte will take the matter in hand "—

" Sir ! "

" Oh ! I swear I sha'n't say a word about it, either
to Desormeaux or Chapelain, nor to any one else. Although reimbursed, I'll make as much noise as the rest,
—more noise, even. Come, now, my dear friends, what
do you say ? "

He was almost crying.

" And where the deuse," exclaimed Maxence, " do
you expect my father to take a hundred and twenty
thousand francs ? Didn't you see him go without even
taking the money that M. de Thaller had brought ? "

A smile appeared upon M. Desclavettes' pale lips.

" That will do very well to say, my dear Maxence ; "
he said, " and some people may believe it. But don't
say it to your old friend, who knows too much about
business for that. When a man puts off, after borrowing twelve millions from his employers, he would be a
great fool if he had not put away two or three in safety.
Now, Favoral is not a fool."

Tears of shame and anger started from Mlle. Gilberte's eyes.

" What you are saying is abominable, sir ! " she exclaimed.

He seemed much surprised at this outburst of violence.

" Why so ? " he answered. " In Vincent's place, I
should not have hesitated to do what he has certainly
done. And I am an honest man too. I was in business

for twenty years; and I dare any one to prove that a
note signed Desclavettes ever went to protest. And
so, my dear friends, I beseech you, consent to serve your
old friend, and, when you see your father "——

The old man's tone of voice exasperated even Mme.
Favoral herself.

"We never expect to see my husband again," she
uttered.

He shrugged his shoulders, and, in a tone of paternal reproach,——

"You just give up all such ugly ideas," he said.
"You will see him again, that dear Vincent; for he is
much too sharp to allow himself to be caught. Of
course, he'll stay away as long as it may be necessary;
but, as soon as he can return without danger, he will
do so. The Statute of Limitations has not been invented for the Grand Turk. Why, the Boulevard is
crowded with people who have all had their little difficulty, and who have spent five or ten years abroad for
their health. Does any one think any thing of it? Not
in the least; and no one hesitates to shake hands with
them. Besides, those things are so soon forgotten."

He kept on as if he never intended to stop; and it was
not without trouble that Maxence and Gilberte succeeded in sending him off, very much dissatisfied to see
his request so ill received. It was after twelve o'clock.
Maxence was anxious to return to his own home; but,
at the pressing instances of his mother, he consented to
remain, and threw himself, without undressing, on the
bed in his old room.

"What will the morrow bring forth?" he thought.

XXIII.

AFTER a few. hours of that leaden sleep which follows great catastrophes, Mme. Favoral and her children were awakened on the morning of the next day,
which was Sunday, by the furious clamors of an exasperated crowd. Each one, from his own room, understood that the apartment had just been invaded. Loud
blows upon the door were mingled with the noise of
feet, the oaths of men, and the screams of women.
And, above this confused and continuous tumult, such
vociferations as these could be heard:—

" I tell you they must be at home ! "

" Canailles, swindlers, thieves ! "

" We want to go in: we will go in ! "

" Let the woman come, then: we want to see her, to
speak to her ! "

Occasionally there were moments of silence, during
which the plaintive voice of the servant could be heard;
but almost at once the cries and the threats commenced
again, louder than ever. Maxence, being ready first,
ran to the parlor, where his mother and sister joined
him directly, their eyes swollen by sleep and by tears.
Mme. Favoral was trembling so much that she could
not succeed in fastening her dress.

" Do you hear ? " she said in a choking voice.

From the parlor, which was divided from the dining-
room by folding-doors, they did not miss a single insult.

" Well," said Mlle. Gilberte coldly, " what else could
we expect ? If Bertan came alone last night, it is because he alone had been notified. Here are the others
now."

And, turning to her brother,—

"You must see them," she added, "speak to them."

But Maxence did not stir. The idea of facing the insults and the curses of these enraged creditors was too repugnant to him.

"Would you rather let them break in the door?" said Mlle. Gilberte. "That won't take long."

He hesitated no more. Gathering all his courage, he stepped into the dining-room. The disorder was beyond limits. The table had been pushed towards one of the corners, the chairs were upset. They were there some thirty men and women,—*concierges,* shop-keepers, and retired *bourgeois* of the neighborhood, their cheeks flushed, their eyes staring, gesticulating as if they had a fit, shaking their clinched fists at the ceiling.

"Gentlemen," commenced Maxence.

But his voice was drowned by the most frightful shouts. He had hardly got in, when he was so closely surrounded, that he had been unable to close the parlor-door after him, and had been driven and backed against the embrasure of a window.

"My father, gentlemen," he resumed.

Again he was interrupted. There were three or four before him, who were endeavoring before all to establish their own claims clearly.

They were speaking all at once, each one raising his own voice so as to drown that of the others. And yet, through their confused explanations, it was easy to understand the way in which the cashier of the Mutual Credit had managed things.

Formerly it was only with great reluctance that he consented to take charge of the funds which were offered to him; and then he never accepted sums less than ten thousand francs, being always careful to say, that, not being a prophet, he could not answer for any thing, and might be mistaken, like any one else. Since the Commune, on the contrary, and with a duplicity, that could never have been suspected, he had used all his ingenuity to attract deposits. Under some pretext or other, he would call among the neighbors, the shop-keepers; and, after lamenting with them about the hard times and the difficulty of making money, he always ended by holding up to them the dazzling profits which are yielded by certain investments unknown to the public.

If these very proceedings had not betrayed him, it is because he recommended to each the most inviolable secrecy, saying, that, at the slightest indiscretion, he would be assailed with demands, and that it would be impossible for him to do for all what he did for one.

At any rate, he took every thing that was offered, even the most insignificant sums, affirming, with the most imperturbable assurance, that he could double or treble them without the slightest risk.

The catastrophe having come, the smaller creditors showed themselves, as usual, the most angry and the most intractable. The less money one has, the more anxious one is to keep it. There was there an old news-paper-vender, who had placed in M. Favoral's hands all she had in the world, the savings of her entire life,— five hundred francs. Clinging desperately to Maxence's garments, she begged him to give them back to her, swearing, that, if he did not, there was nothing left for her to do, except to throw herself in the river. Her groans and her cries of distress exasperated the other creditors.

That the cashier of the Mutual Credit should have embezzled millions, they could well understand, they

said. But that he could have robbed this poor woman
of her five hundred francs,—nothing more low, more
cowardly, and more vile could be imagined; and the law
had no chastisement severe enough for such a crime.

"Give her back her five hundred francs;" they cried.

For there was not one of them but would have
wagered his head that M. Favoral had lots of money put
away; and some went even so far as to say that he
must have hid it in the house, and, if they looked well,
they would find it.

Maxence, bewildered, was at a loss what to do, when,
in the midst of this hostile crowd, he perceived M.
Chapelain's friendly face.

Driven from his bed at daylight by the bitter regrets
at the heavy loss he had just sustained, the old lawyer
had arrived in the Rue St. Gilles at the very moment
when the creditors invaded M. Favoral's apartment.
Standing behind the crowd, he had seen and heard every
thing without breathing a word; and, if he interfered
now, it was because he thought things were about to
take an ugly turn. He was well known; and, as soon
as he showed himself,—

"He is a friend of the rascal!" they shouted on all
sides.

But he was not the man to be so easily frightened.
He had seen many a worse case during twenty years
that he had practised law, and had witnessed all the
sinister comedies and all the grotesque dramas of money.
He knew how to speak to infuriated creditors, how to
handle them, and what strings can be made to vibrate
within them. In the most quiet tone,—

"Certainly," he answered, "I was Favoral's intimate
friend; and the proof of it is, that he has treated me

more friendly than the rest. I am in for a hundred and sixty thousand francs."

By this mere declaration he conquered the sympathies of the crowd. He was a brother in misfortune; they respected him: he was a skilful business-man; they stopped to listen to him.

At once, and in a short and trenchant tone, he asked these invaders what they were doing there, and what they wanted. Did they not know to what they exposed themselves in violating a domicile? What would have happened, if, instead of stopping to parley, Maxence had sent for the commissary of police? Was it to Mme. Favoral and her children that they had intrusted their funds? No! What did they want with them then? Was there by chance among them some of those shrewd fellows who always try to get themselves paid in full, to the detriment of the others?

This last insinuation proved sufficient to break up the perfect accord that had hitherto existed among all the creditors. Distrust arose; suspicious glances were exchanged; and, as the old newspaper woman was keeping up her groans,—

"I should like to know why you should be paid before us." two women told her roughly. "Our rights are just as good as yours!"

Prompt to avail himself of the dispositions of the crowd,—

"And, moreover," resumed the old lawyer, "in whom did we place our confidence? Was it in Favoral the private individual? To a certain extent, yes; but it was much more to the cashier of the Mutual Credit. Therefore that establishment owes us, at least, some explanations. And this is not all. Are we really so badly burned, that we should scream so loud? What do we know about it? That Favoral is charged with embezzlement, that they came to arrest him, and that he has run away. Is that any reason why our money should be lost? I hope not. And so what should we do? Act prudently, and wait patiently for the work of justice."

Already, by this time, the creditors had slipped out one by one; and soon the servant closed the door on the last of them.

Then Mme. Favoral, Maxence, and Mlle. Gilberte surrounded M. Chapelain, and, pressing his hands,—

" How thankful we feel, sir, for the service you have just rendered us! "

But the old lawyer seemed in no wise proud of his victory.

" Do not thank me," he said. " I have only done my duty,—what any honest man would have done in my place."

And yet, under the appearance of impassible coldness, which he owed to the long practice of a profession which leaves no illusions, he evidently felt a real emotion.

" It is you whom I pity," he added, " and with all my soul,—you, madame, you, my dear Gilberte, and you, too, Maxence. Never had I so well understood to what degree is guilty the head of a family who leaves his wife and children exposed to the consequences of his crimes."

He stopped. The servant was trying her best to put the dining-room in some sort of order wheeling the table to the centre of the room, and lifting up the chairs from the floor.

" What pillage! " she grumbled. " Neighbors too,— people from whom we bought our things! But they were worse than savages; impossible to do any thing with them."

"Don't trouble yourself, my good girl," said M. Chapelain: "they won't come back any more!"

Mme. Favoral looked as if she wished to drop on her knees before the old lawyer.

"How, very kind you are!" she murmured: "you are not too angry with my poor Vincent!"

With the look of a man who has made up his mind to make the best of a disaster that he cannot help, M. Chapelain shrugged his shoulders.

"I am angry with no one but myself," he uttered in a bluff tone. "An old bird like me should not have allowed himself to be caught in a pigeon-trap. I am inexcusable. But we want to get rich. It's slow work getting rich by working, and it's so much easier to get the money already made out of our neighbor's pockets! I have been unable to resist the temptation myself. It's my own fault; and I should say it was a good lesson, if it did not cost so dear."

XXIV.

So much philosophy could hardly have been expected of him.

"All my father's friends are not as indulgent as you are," said Maxence,—"M. Desclavettes, for instance."

"Have you seen him?"

"Yes, last night, about twelve o'clock. He came to ask us to get father to pay him back, if we should ever see him again."

"That might be an idea!"

Mlle. Gilberte started.

" What! " said she, " you, too, sir, can imagine that
my father has run away with millions? "

The old lawyer shook his head.

" I believe nothing," he answered.   " Favoral has
taken me in so completely,—me, who had the pretension of being a judge of men,—that nothing from him,
either for good or for evil, could surprise me hereafter."

Mme. Favoral was about to offer some objection;
but he stopped her with a gesture.

" And yet," he went on, " I'd bet that he has gone
off with empty pockets. His recent operations reveal
a frightful distress. Had he had a few thousand francs
at his command, would he have extorted five hundred
francs from a poor old woman, a newspaper-vender?
What did he want with the money? Try his luck once
more, no doubt."

He was seated, his elbow upon the arm of the chair,
his head resting upon his hands, thinking; and the contraction of his features indicated an extraordinary tension of mind.

Suddenly he drew himself up.

" But why," he exclaimed, " why wander in idle conjectures? What do we know about Favoral? Nothing. One entire side of his existence escapes us,—that
fantastic side, of which the insane prodigalities and inconceivable disorders have been revealed to us by the
bills found in his desk. He is certainly guilty; but is he
as guilty as we think? and, above all, is he alone guilty?
Was it for himself alone that he drew all this money?
Are the missing millions really lost? and wouldn't it be
possible to find the biggest share of them in the pockets
of some accomplice? Skilful men do not expose themselves. They have at their command poor wretches,

sacrificed in advance, and who, in exchange for a few crumbs that are thrown to them, risk the criminal court, are condemned, and go to prison."

" That's just what I was telling my mother and sister, sir," interrupted Maxence.

" And that's what I am telling myself," continued the old lawyer. " I have been thinking over and over again of last evening's scene; and strange doubts have occurred to my mind. For a man who has been robbed of a dozen millions, M. de Thaller was remarkably quiet and self-possessed. Favoral appeared to me singularly calm for a man charged with embezzlement and forgery. M. de Thaller, as manager of the Mutual Credit, is really responsible for the stolen funds, and, as such, should have been anxious to secure the guilty party, and to produce him. Instead of that, he wished him to go, and actually brought him the money to enable him to leave. Was he in hopes of hushing up the affair? Evidently not, since the police had been notified. On the other hand, Favoral seemed much more angry than surprised by the occurrence. It was only on the appearance of the commissary of police that he seems to have lost his head; and then some very strange things escaped him, which I cannot understand."

He was walking at random through the parlor, apparently rather answering the objections of his own mind than addressing himself to his interlocutors, who were listening, nevertheless, with all the attention of which they were capable.

" I don't know." he went on. " An old traveller like me to be taken in thus! Evidently there is under all this one of those diabolical combinations which time even fails to unravel. We ought to see, to inquire "—

And then, suddenly stopping in front of Maxence,—
" How much did M. de Thaller bring to your father
last evening? " he asked.

" Fifteen thousand francs."

" Where are they? "

" Put away in mother's room."

" When do you expect to take them back to M. de
Thaller? "

" To-morrow."

" Why not to-day? "

" This is Sunday. The offices of the Mutual Credit
must be closed."

" After the occurrences of yesterday, M. de Thaller
must be at his office. Besides, haven't you his private
address? "

" I beg your pardon, I have."

The old lawyer's small eyes were shining with unusual brilliancy. He certainly felt deeply the loss of his
money; but the idea that he had been swindled for the
benefit of some clever rascal was absolutely insupport-
able to him.

" If we were wise," he said again, " we'd do this.
Mme. Favoral would take these fifteen thousand francs,
and we would go together, she and I, to see M. de
Thaller."

It was an unexpected good-fortune for Mme. Favoral, that M. Chapelain should consent to assist her.
So, without hesitating,—

" The time to dress, sir," she said, " and I am ready."

She left the parlor; but as she reached her room, her
son joined her.

" I am obliged to go out, dear mother," he said; " and
I shall probably not be home to breakfast."

She looked at him with an air of painful surprise.

"What," she said, "at such a moment!"

"I am expected home."

"By whom? A woman?" she murmured.

"Well, yes."

"And it is for that woman's sake that you want to leave your sister alone at home?"

"I must, mother, I assure you; and, if you only knew "—

"I do not wish to know any thing."

But his resolution had been taken. He went off; and a few moments later Mme. Favoral and M. Chapelain entered a cab which had been sent for, and drove to M. de Thaller's.

Left alone, Mlle. Gilberte had but one thought,—to notify M. de Trégars, and obtain word from him. Any thing seemed preferable to the horrible anxiety which oppressed her. She had just commenced a letter, which she intended to have taken to the Count de Villegré, when a violent ring of the bell made her start; and almost immediately the servant came in, saying,—

"It is a gentleman who wishes to see you, a friend of monsieur's,—M. Costeclar, you know."

Mlle. Gilberte started to her feet, trembling with excitement.

"That's too much impudence!" she exclaimed.

She was hesitating whether to refuse him the door, or to see him, and dismiss him shamefully herself, when she had a sudden inspiration. "What does he want?" she thought. "Why not see him, and try and find out what he knows? For he certainly must know the truth."

But it was no longer time to deliberate. Above the servant's shoulder M. Costeclar's pale and impudent face showed itself.

The girl having stepped to one side, he appeared, hat in hand. Although it was not yet nine o'clock, his morning toilet was irreproachably correct. He had already passed through the hair-dresser's hands; and his scanty hair was brought forward over his low forehead with the usual elaborate care.

He wore a pair of those ridiculous trousers which grow wide from the knee down, and which were invented by Prussian tailors to hide their customers' ugly feet. Under his light-colored overcoat could be seen a velvet-faced jacket, with a rose in its buttonhole.

Meantime, he remained motionless on the threshold of the door, trying to smile, and muttering one of those sentences which are never intended to be finished.

"I beg you to believe, mademoiselle—your mother's absence—my most respectful admiration"—

In fact, he was taken aback by the disorder of the girl's toilet,—disorder, which she had had no time to repair since the clamors of the creditors had started her from her bed.

She wore a long brown cashmere wrapper, fitting quite close over the hips, setting off the vigorous elegance of her figure, the maidenly perfections of her waist, and the exquisite contour of her neck. Gathered up in haste, her thick blonde hair escaped from beneath the pins, and spread over her shoulders in luminous cascades. Never had she appeared to M. Costeclar as lovely as at this moment, when her whole frame was vibrating with suppressed indignation, her cheeks flushed, her eyes flashing.

"Please come in, sir," she uttered.

He stepped forward, no longer bowing humbly as formerly, but with legs outstretched, chest thrown out, with an ill-concealed look of gratified vanity.

" I did not expect the honor of your visit, sir," said the young girl.

Passing rapidly his hat and his cane from the right hand into the left, and then the right hand upon his heart, his eyes raised to the ceiling, and with all the depth of expression of which he was capable,—

" It is in times of adversity that we know our real friends, mademoiselle," he uttered. " Those upon whom we thought we could rely the most, often, at the first reverse, take flight forever ! "

She felt a shiver pass over her. Was this an allusion to Marius?

The other, changing his tone, went on,—

" It's only last night that I heard of poor Favoral's discomfiture, at the *bourse* where I had gone for news. It was the general topic of conversation. Twelve millions ! That's pretty hard. The Mutual Credit Society might not be able to stand it. From 580, at which it was selling before the news, it dropped at once to 300. At nine o'clock, there were no takers at 180. And yet, if there is nothing beyond what they say, at 180, I am in."

Was he forgetting himself, or pretending to?

" But please excuse me, mademoiselle," he resumed: " that's not what I came to tell you."

" Ah ! "

" I came to ask if you had any news of our poor Favoral."

" We have none, sir."

" Then it is true: he succeeded in getting away through this window? "

" Yes."

" And he did not tell you where he meant to take refuge? "

" No."

Observing M. Costeclar with all her power of penetration, Mlle. Gilberte fancied she discovered in him
something like a certain surprise mingled with joy.

" Then Favoral must have left without a sou! "

" They accuse him of having carried away millions,
sir; but I would swear that it is not so."

M. Costeclar approved with a nod.

" I am of the same opinion," he declared, " unless—
but no, he was not the man to try such a game. And
yet—but again no, he was too closely watched. Besides,
he was carrying a very heavy load, a load that exhausted all his resources."

Mlle. Gilberte, hoping that she was going to learn
something, made an effort to preserve her indifference.

" What do you mean? " she inquired.

He looked at her, smiled, and, in a light tone,—

" Nothing," he answered, " only some conjectures of
my own."

And throwing himself upon a chair, his head leaning
upon its back,—

" That is not the object of my visit either," he uttered.
" Favoral is overboard: don't let us say any thing more
about him. Whether he has got ' the bag ' or not, you'll
never see him again: he is as good as dead. Let us,
therefore, talk of the living, of yourself. What's going to become of you? "

" I do not understand your question, sir."

" It is perfectly limpid, nevertheless. I am asking
myself how you are going to live, your mother and
yourself? "

" Providence will not abandon us, sir? "

M. Costeclar had crossed his legs, and with the end

of his cane he was negligently tapping his immaculate boot.

" Providence ! " he giggled : " that's very good on the stage, in a play, with low music in the orchestra. I can just see it. In real life, unfortunately, the life which we both live, you and I, it is not with words, were they a yard long, that the baker, the grocer, and those rascally landlords, can be paid, or that dresses and shoes can be bought."

She made no answer.

" Now, then," he went on, " here you are without a penny. Is it Maxence who will supply you with money ? Poor fellow ! Where would he get it ? He has hardly enough for himself. Therefore, what are you going to do ? "

" I shall work, sir."

He got up, bowed low, and, resuming his seat,—

" My sincere compliments," he said. " There is but one obstacle to that fine resolution : it is impossible for a woman to live by her labor alone. Servants are about the only ones who ever get their full to eat."

" I'll be a servant, if necessary."

For two or three seconds he remained taken aback, but, recovering himself,—

" How different things would be," he resumed in an insinuating tone, " if you had not rejected me when I wanted to become your husband ! But you couldn't bear the sight of me. And yet, 'pon my word, I was in love with you, oh, but for good and earnest ! You see, I am a judge of women ; and I saw very well how you would look, handsomely dressed and got up, leaning back in a fine carriage in the Bois "—

Stronger than her will, disgust rose to her lips.

" Ah, sir ! " she said.

He mistook her meaning.

" You are regretting all that," he continued. " I see it. Formerly, eh, you would never have consented to receive me thus, alone with you, which proves that girls should not be headstrong, my dear child."

He, Costeclar, he dared to call her, " My dear child." Indignant and insulted, " Oh ! " she exclaimed.

But he had started, and kept on,—

" Well, such as I was, I am still. To be sure, there probably would be nothing further said about marriage between us; but, frankly, what would you care if the conditions were the same,—a fine house, carriages, horses, servants "—

Up to this moment, she had not fully understood him. Drawing herself up to her fullest height, and pointing to the door,—

" Leave this moment," she ordered.

But he seemed in no wise disposed to do so: on the contrary, paler than usual, his eyes bloodshot, his lips trembling, and smiling a strange smile, he advanced towards Mlle. Gilberte.

" What ! " said he. " You are in trouble, I kindly come to offer my services, and this is the way you receive me ! You prefer to work, do you ? Go ahead then, my lovely one, prick your pretty fingers, and redden your eyes. My time will come. Fatigue and want, cold in the winter, hunger in all seasons, will speak to your little heart of that kind Costeclar who adores you, like a big fool that he is, who is a serious man and who has money,—much money."

Beside herself,—

" Wretch ! " cried the girl, " leave, leave at once ! "

" One moment," said a strong voice.

M. Costeclar looked around.

Marius de Trégars stood within the frame of the open door.

" Marius ! " murmured Mlle. Gilberte, rooted to the spot by a surprise hardly less immense than her joy.

To behold him thus suddenly, when she was wondering whether she would ever see him again; to see him appear at the very moment when she found herself alone, and exposed to the basest outrages,—it was one of those fortunate occurrences which one can scarcely realize; and from the depth of her soul rose something like a hymn of thanks.

Nevertheless, she was confounded at M. Costeclar's attitude. According to her, and from what she thought she knew, he should have been petrified at the sight of M. de Trégars.

And he did not even seem to know him. He seemed shocked, annoyed at being interrupted, slightly surprised, but in no wise moved or frightened.

Knitting his brows,—

" What do you wish? " he inquired in his most impertinent tone.

M. de Trégars stepped forward. He was somewhat pale, but unnaturally calm, cool, and collected. Bowing to Mlle. Gilberte,—

" If I have thus ventured to enter your apartment, mademoiselle," he uttered gently, " it is because, as I was going by the door, I thought I recognized this gentleman's carriage."

And, with his finger over his shoulder, he was pointing to M. Costeclar.

" Now," he went on, " I had reason to be somewhat astonished at this, after the positive orders I had given him never to set his feet, not only in this house, but in this part of the city. I wished to find out exactly. I came up: I heard "—

All this was said in a tone of such crushing contempt, that a slap on the face would have been less cruel. All the blood in M. Costeclar's veins rushed to his face.

" You ! " he interrupted insolently : " I do not know you."

Imperturbable, M. de Trégars was drawing off his gloves.

" Are you quite certain of that ? " he replied. " Come, you certainly know my old friend, M. de Villegré ? "

An evident feeling of anxiety appeared on M. Costeclar's countenance.

" I do," he stammered.

" Did not M. Villegré call upon you before the war ? "

" He did."

" Well, 'twas I who sent him to you ; and the commands which he delivered to you were mine."

" Yours ? "

" Mine. I am Marius de Trégars."

A nervous shudder shook M. Costeclar's lean frame. Instinctively his eye turned towards the door.

" You see," Marius went on with the same gentleness, " we are, you and I, old acquaintances. For you quite remember me now, don't you ? I am the son of that poor Marquis de Trégars who came to Paris, all the way from his old Brittany with his whole fortune,— two millions."

" I remember," said the stock-broker : " I remember perfectly well."

" On the advice of certain clever people, the Marquis de Trégars ventured into business. Poor old man ! He was not very sharp. He was firmly persuaded that he had already more than doubled his capital, when his honorable partners demonstrated to him that he was ruined, and, besides, compromised by certain signatures imprudently given."

Mlle. Gilberte was listening, her mouth open, and wondering what Marius was aiming at, and how he could remain so calm.

"That disaster," he went on, "was at the time the subject of an enormous number of very witty jokes. The people of the *bourse* could hardly admire enough these bold financiers who had so deftly relieved that candid marquis of his money. That was well done for him: what was he meddling with? As to myself, to stop the prosecutions with which my father was threatened, I gave up all I had. I was quite young, and, as you see, quite what you call, I believe, 'green.' I am no longer so now. Were such a thing to happen to me to-day, I should want to know at once what had become of the millions: I would feel all the pockets around me. I would say, 'Stop thief!'"

At every word, as it were, M. Costeclar's uneasiness became more manifest.

"It was not I," he said, "who received the benefit of M. de Trégars' fortune."

Marius nodded approvingly.

"I know now," he replied, "among whom the spoils were divided. You, M. Costeclar, you took what you could get, timidly, and according to your means. Sharks are always accompanied by small fishes, to which they abandon the crumbs they disdain. You were but a small fish then: you accommodated yourself with what your patrons, the sharks, did not care about. But, when you tried to operate alone, you were not shrewd enough: you left proofs of your excessive appetite for other people's money. Those proofs I have in my possession."

M. Costeclar was now undergoing perfect torture.

"I am caught," he said, "I know it: I told M. de Villegré so."

"Why are you here, then?"

"How did I know that the count had been sent by you?"

"That's a poor reason, sir."

"Besides, after what has occurred, after Favoral's flight, I thought myself relieved of my engagement."

"Indeed!"

"Well, if you insist upon it, I am wrong, I suppose."

"Not only you are wrong," uttered Marius still perfectly cool, "but you have committed a great imprudence. By failing to keep your engagements, you have relieved me of mine. The pact is broken. According to the agreement, I have the right, as I leave here, to go straight to the police."

M. Costeclar's dull eye was vacillating.

"I did not think I was doing wrong," he muttered. "Favoral was my friend."

"And that's the reason why you were coming to propose to Mlle. Favoral to become your mistress? There she is, you thought, without resources, literally without bread, without relatives, without friends to protect her: this is the time to come forward. And thinking you could be cowardly, vile, and infamous with impunity, you came."

To be thus treated, he, the successful man, in presence of this young girl, whom, a moment before, he was crushing with his impudent opulence, no M. Costeclar could not stand it. Losing completely his head,—

"You should have let me know, then," he exclaimed, "that she was your mistress."

Something like a flame passed over M. de Trégars' face. His eyes flashed. Rising in all the height of his wrath, which broke out terrible at last,—

"Ah, you scoundrel!" he exclaimed.

M. Costeclar threw himself suddenly to one side.

"Sir!"

But at one bound M. de Trégars had caught him.

"On your knees!" he cried.

And, seizing him by the collar with an iron grip, he lifted him clear off the floor, and then threw him down violently upon both knees.

"Speak!" he commanded. "Repeat,—'Mademoiselle'"—

M. Costeclar had expected worse from M. de Trégars' look. A horrible fear had instantly crushed within him all idea of resistance.

"Mademoiselle," he stuttered in a choking voice.

"I am the vilest of wretches," continued Marius.

M. Costeclar's livid face was oscillating like an inert object.

"I am," he repeated, "the vilest of wretches."

"And I beg of you"—

But Mlle. Gilberte was sick of the sight.

"Enough," she interrupted, "enough!"

Feeling no longer upon his shoulders the heavy hand of M. de Trégars, the stock-broker rose with difficulty to his feet. So livid was his face, that one might have thought that his whole blood had turned to gall.

Dusting with the end of his glove the knees of his trousers, and restoring as best he could the harmony of his toilet, which had been seriously disturbed,—

" Is it showing any courage," he grumbled, " to abuse one's physical strength ? "

M. de Trégars had already recovered his self-possession; and Mlle. Gilberte thought she could read upon his face regret for his violence.

" Would it be better to make use of what you know ? "

M. Costeclar joined his hands.

" You would not do that," he said. " What good would it do you to ruin me ? "

" None," answered M. de Trégars: " you are right. But yourself ? "

And, looking straight into M. Costeclar's eyes,—

" If you could be of service to me," he inquired, " would you be willing ? "

" Perhaps. That I might recover possession of the papers you have."

M. de Trégars was thinking.

" After what has just taken place," he said at last, "an explanation is necessary between us. I will be at your house in an hour. Wait for me."

M. Costeclar had become more pliable than his own lavender kid gloves: in fact, alarmingly pliable.

" I am at your command, sir," he replied to M. de Trégars.

And, bowing to the ground before Mlle. Gilberte, he left the parlor; and, a few moments after, the street-door was heard to close upon him.

" Ah, what a wretch ! " exclaimed the girl, dreadfully agitated.

" Marius, did you see what a look he gave us as he went out ? "

" I saw it," replied M. de Trégars.

" That man hates us : he will not hesitate to commit

a crime to avenge the atrocious humiliation you have just inflicted upon him."

" I believe it too."

Mlle. Gilberte made a gesture of distress.

" Why did you treat him so harshly?" she murmured.

" I had intended to remain calm, and it would have been politic to have done so.   But there are some insults which a man of heart cannot endure.   I do not regret what I have done."

A long pause followed; and they remained standing, facing each other, somewhat embarrassed.   Mlle. Gilberte felt ashamed of the disorder of her dress.   M. de Trégars wondered how he could have been bold enough to enter this house.

" You have heard of our misfortune," said the young girl at last.

" I read about it this morning, in the papers."

" What! the papers know already?"

" Every thing."

" And our name is printed in them?"

" Yes."

She covered her face with her two hands.

" What disgrace!" she said.

" At first," went on M. de Trégars, " I could hardly believe what I read.   I hastened to come; and the first shopkeeper I questioned confirmed only too well what I had seen in the papers.   From that moment, I had but one wish,—to see and speak to you.   When I reached the door, I recognized M. Costeclar's equipage, and I had a presentiment of the truth.   I inquired from the *concierge* for your mother or your brother, and heard that Maxence had gone out a few moments before, and that Mme. Favoral had just left in a carriage with M. Chapelain, the old lawyer. At the idea that you were alone with Costeclar, I hesitated no longer. I ran up stairs, and, finding the door open, had no occasion to ring."

Mlle. Gilberte could hardly repress the sobs that rose to her throat.

"I never hoped to see you again," she stammered; "and you'll find there on the table the letter I had just commenced for you when M. Costeclar interrupted me."

M. de Trégars took it up quickly. Two lines only were written. He read: "I release you from your engagement, Marius. Henceforth you are free."

He became whiter than his shirt.

"You wish to release me from my engagement!" he exclaimed. "You "—

"Is it not my duty? Ah! if it had only been our fortune, I should perhaps have rejoiced to lose it. I know your heart. Poverty would have brought us nearer together. But it's honor, Marius, honor that is lost too! The name I bear is forever stained. Whether my father is caught, or whether he escapes, he will be tried all the same, condemned, and sentenced to a degrading penalty for embezzlement and forgery."

If M. de Trégars was allowing her to proceed thus, it was because he felt all his thoughts whirling in his brain; because she looked so beautiful thus, all in tears, and her hair loose; because there arose from her person so subtle a charm, that words failed him to express the sensations that agitated him.

"Can you," she went on, "take for your wife the daughter of a dishonored man? No, you cannot. Forgive me, then, for having for a moment turned away your life from its object; forgive the sorrow which I have caused you; leave me to the misery of my fate; forget me! "

She was suffocating.

"Ah, you have never loved me!" exclaimed Marius.

Raising her hands to heaven,—

"Thou hearest him, great God!" she uttered, as if shocked by a blasphemy.

"Would it be easy for you to forget me then? Were I to be struck by misfortune, would you break our engagement, cease to love me?"

She ventured to take his hands, and, pressing them between hers,—

"To cease loving you no longer depends on my will," she murmured with quivering lips. "Poor, abandoned of all, disgraced, criminal even, I should love you still and always."

With a passionate gesture, Marius threw his arm around her waist, and, drawing her to his breast, covered her blonde hair with burning kisses.

"Well, 'tis thus that I love you too!" he exclaimed, "and with all my soul, exclusively, and for life! What do I care for your parents? Do I know them? Your father—does he exist? Your name—it is mine, the spotless name of the Trégars. You are my wife! mine, mine!"

She was struggling feebly: an almost invincible stupor was creeping over her. She felt her reason disturbed, her energy giving way, a film before her eyes, the air failing to her heaving chest.

A great effort of her will restored her to consciousness. She withdrew gently, and sank upon a chair, less strong against joy than she had been against sorrow.

" Pardon me," she stammered, " pardon me for having doubted you ! "

M. de Trégars was not much less agitated than Mlle. Gilberte: but he was a man; and the springs of his energy were of a superior temper. In less than a minute he had fully recovered his self-possession, and imposed upon his features their accustomed expression. Drawing a chair by the side of Mlle. Gilberte,—

" Permit me, my friend," he said, " to remind you that our moments are numbered, and that there are many details which it is urgent that I should know."

" What details ? " she asked, raising her head.

" About your father."

She looked at him with an air of profound surprise.

" Do you not know more about it than I do ? " she replied, " more than my mother, more than any of us ? Did you not, whilst following up the people who robbed your father, strike mine unwittingly ? And 'tis I, wretch that I am, who inspired you to that fatal resolution ; and I have not the heart to regret it."

M. de Trégars had blushed imperceptibly.

" How did you know ? " he began.

" Was it not said that you were about to marry Mlle. de Thaller ? "

He drew up suddenly.

" Never," he exclaimed, " has this marriage existed, except in the brain of M. de Thaller, and, more still, of the Baroness de Thaller. That ridiculous idea occurred to her because she likes my name, and would be delighted to see her daughter Marquise de Trégars. She has never breathed a word of it to me ; but she has spoken of it everywhere, with just enough secrecy to give rise to a good piece of parlor gossip. She went so

far as to confide to several persons of my acquaintance
the amount of the dowry, thinking thus to encourage
me.   As far as I could, I warned you against this false
news through the Signor Gismondo."

"The Signor Gismondo relieved me of cruel anxieties," she replied; "but I had suspected the truth from
the first.   Was I not the confidante of your hopes?   Did
I not know your projects?   I had taken for granted
that all this talk about a marriage was but a means to
advance yourself in M. de Thaller's intimacy without
awaking his suspicions."

M. de Trégars was not the man to deny a true fact.

"Perhaps, indeed, I have not been wholly foreign to
M. Favoral's disaster.   At least I may have hastened it
a few months, a few days only, perhaps; for it was inevitable, fatal.   Nevertheless, had I suspected the real
facts, I would have given up my designs—Gilberte, I
swear it—rather than risk injuring your father.   There
is no undoing what is done; but the evil may, perhaps,
be somewhat lessened."

Mlle. Gilberte started.

"Great heavens!" she exclaimed, "do you, then,
believe my father innocent?"

Better than any one else, Mlle. Gilberte must have
been convinced of her father's guilt.   Had she not seen
him humiliated and trembling before M. de Thaller?
Had she not heard him, as it were, acknowledge the
truth of the charge that was brought against him?   But
at twenty hope never forsakes us, even in presence of
facts.

And when she understood by M. de Trégars' silence
that she was mistaken,—

"It's madness," she murmured, dropping her head:

"I feel it but too well. But the heart speaks louder than reason. It is so cruel to be driven to despise one's father!"

She wiped the tears which filled her eyes, and, in a firmer voice,—

"What happens is so incomprehensible!" she went on. "How can I help imagining some one of those mysteries which time alone unravels. For twenty-four hours we have been losing ourselves in idle conjectures, and, always and fatally, we come to this conclusion,— that my father must be the victim of some mysterious intrigue.

"M. Chapelain, whom a loss of a hundred and sixty thousand francs has not made particularly indulgent, is of that opinion."

"And so am I," exclaimed Marius.

"You see, then"—

But without allowing her to proceed and taking gently her hand,—

"Let me tell you all," he interrupted, "and try with you to find an issue to this horrible situation. Strange rumors are afloat about M. Favoral. It is said that his austerity was but a mask, his sordid economy a means of gaining confidence. It is affirmed that in fact he abandoned himself to all sorts of disorders; that he had, somewhere in Paris, an establishment, where he lavished the money of which he was so sparing here. Is it so? The same thing is said of all those in whose hands large fortunes have melted."

The young girl had become quite red.

"I believe that is true," she replied. "The commissary of police stated so to us. He found among my father's papers receipted bills for a number of costly articles, which could only have been intended for a woman."

M. de Trégars looked perplexed.

"And does any one know who this woman is?" he asked.

"No."

"Whoever she may be, I admit that she may have cost M. Favoral considerable sums. But can she have cost him twelve millions?"

"Precisely the remark which M. Chapelain made."

"And which every sensible man must also make. I know very well that to conceal for years a considerable deficit is a costly operation, requiring purchases and sales, the handling and shifting of funds, all of which is ruinous in the extreme. But, on the other hand, M. Favoral was making money, a great deal of money. He was rich: he was supposed to be worth millions. Otherwise, Costeclar would never have asked your hand."

"M. Chapelain pretends that at a certain time my father had at least fifty thousand francs a year."

"It's bewildering."

For two or three minutes M. de Trégars remained silent, reviewing in his mind every imaginable eventuality, and then,—

"But no matter," he resumed. "As soon as I heard this morning the amount of the deficit, doubts came to my mind. And it is for that reason, dear friend, that I was so anxious to see you and speak to you. It would be necessary for me to know exactly what occurred here last night."

Rapidly, but without omitting a single useful detail, Mlle. Gilberte narrated the scenes of the previous night,—the sudden appearance of M. de Thaller, the arrival of the commissary of police, M. Favoral's escape, thanks to Maxence's presence of mind. Every one of her father's words had remained present to her mind; and it was almost literally that she repeated his strange speeches to his indignant friends, and his incoherent remarks at the moment of flight, when, whilst acknowledging his fault, he said that he was not as guilty as they thought; that, at any rate, he was not alone guilty; and that he had been shamefully sacrificed. When she had finished,—

" That's exactly what I thought," said M. de Trégars.

" What? "

" M. Favoral accepted a *rôle* in one of those terrible financial dramas which ruin a thousand poor dupes to the benefit of two or three clever rascals. Your father wanted to be rich: he needed money to carry on his intrigues. He allowed himself to be tempted. But whilst he believed himself one of the managers, called upon to divide the receipts, he was but a scene-shifter with a stated salary. The moment of this *dénouement* having come, his so-called partners disappeared through a trap-door with the cash, leaving him alone, as they say, to face the music."

" If that's the case," replied the young girl, " why didn't my father speak? "

" What was he to say? "

" Name his accomplices."

" And suppose he had no proofs of their complicity to offer? He was the cashier of the Mutual Credit; and it is from his cash that the millions are gone."

Mlle. Gilberte's conjectures had run far ahead of that sentence. Looking straight at Marius,—

" Then," she said, " you believe, as M. Chapelain does, that M. de Thaller "—

"Ah! M. Chapelain thinks"—

"That the manager of the Mutual Credit must have known the fact of the frauds."

"And that he had his share of them?"

"A larger share than his cashier, yes."

A singular smile curled M. de Trégars' lips.

"Quite possible," he replied: "that's quite possible."

For the past few moments Mlle. Gilberte's embarrassment was quite evident in her look. At last, overcoming her hesitation,—

"Pardon me," said she, "I had imagined that M. de Thaller was one of those men whom you wished to strike; and I had indulged in the hope, that, whilst having justice done to your father, you were thinking, perhaps, of avenging mine."

M. de Trégars stood up, as if moved by a spring.

"Well, yes!" he exclaimed. "Yes, you have correctly guessed. But how can we obtain this double result? A single misstep at this moment might lose all. Ah, if I only knew your father's real situation; if I could only see him and speak to him! In one word he might, perhaps, place in my hands a sure weapon,—the weapon that I have as yet been unable to find."

"Unfortunately," replied Mlle. Gilberte with a gesture of despair, "we are without news of my father; and he even refused to tell us where he expected to take refuge."

"But he will write, perhaps. Besides, we might look for him, quietly, so as not to excite the suspicions of the police; and if your brother Maxence was only willing to help me"—

"Alas! I fear that Maxence may have other cares. He insisted upon going out this morning, in spite of mother's request to the contrary."

But Marius stopped her, and, in the tone of a man who knows much more than he is willing to say,—

"Do not calumniate Maxence," he said: "it is through him, perhaps, that we will receive the help that we need."

Eleven o'clock struck. Mlle. Gilberte started.

"Dear me!" she exclaimed, "mother will be home directly."

M. de Trégars might as well have waited for her. Henceforth he had nothing to conceal. Yet, after duly deliberating with the young girl, they decided that he should withdraw, and that he would send M. de Villegré to declare his intentions. He then left, and, five minutes later, Mme. Favoral and M. Chapelain appeared.

The ex-attorney was furious; and he threw the package of bank-notes upon the table with a movement of rage.

"In order to return them to M. de Thaller," he exclaimed, "it was at least necessary to see him. But the gentleman is invisible; keeps himself under lock and key, guarded by a perfect cloud of servants in livery."

Meantime, Mme. Favoral had approached her daughter.

"Your brother?" she asked in a whisper.

"He has not yet come home."

"Dear me!" sighed the poor mother: "at such a time he forsakes us, and for whose sake?"

XXV.

MME. FAVORAL, usually so indulgent, was too severe this time; and it was very unjustly that she accused her son. She forgot, and what mother does not forget, that he was twenty-five years of age, that he was a man, and that, outside of the family and of herself, he must have his own interests and his passions, his affections and his duties. Because he happened to leave the house for a few hours, Maxence was surely not forsaking either his mother or his sister. It was not without a severe internal struggle that he had made up his mind to go out, and, as he was going down the steps,—

"Poor mother," he thought. "I am sure I am making her very unhappy; but how can I help it?"

This was the first time that he had been in the street since his father's disaster had been known; and the impression produced upon him was painful in the extreme. Formerly, when he walked through the Rue St. Gilles, that street where he was born, and where he used to play as a boy, every one met him with a friendly nod or a familiar smile. True he was then the son of a man rich and highly esteemed; whereas this morning not a hand was extended, not a hat raised, on his passage. People whispered among themselves, and pointed him out with looks of hatred and irony. That was because he was now the son of the dishonest cashier tracked by the police, of the man whose crime brought disaster upon so many innocent parties.

Mortified and ashamed, Maxence was hurrying on, his head down, his cheek burning, his throat parched, when, in front of a wine-shop,—

"Halloo!" said a man; "that's the son. What cheek!"

And farther on, in front of the grocer's.

"I tell you what," said a woman in the midst of a group, "they still have more than we have."

Then, for the first time, he understood with what

crushing weight his father's crime would weigh upon his whole life; and, whilst going up the Rue Turenne,—

"It's all over," he thought: "I can never get over it."

And he was thinking of changing his name, of emigrating to America, and hiding himself in the deserts of the Far West, when, a little farther on, he noticed a group of some thirty persons in front of a newspaper-stand. The vender, a fat little man with a red face and an impudent look, was crying in a hoarse voice,—

"Here are the morning papers! The last editions! All about the robbery of twelve millions by a poor cashier. Buy the morning papers!"

And, to stimulate the sale of his wares, he added all sorts of jokes of his own invention, saying that the thief belonged to the neighborhood; that it was quite flattering, etc.

The crowd laughed; and he went on,—

"The cashier Favoral's robbery! twelve millions! Buy the paper, and see how it's done."

And so the scandal was public, irreparable. Maxence was listening a few steps off. He felt like going; but an imperative feeling, stronger than his will, made him anxious to see what the papers said.

Suddenly he made up his mind, and, stepping up briskly, he threw down three sous, seized a paper, and ran as if they had all known him.

"Not very polite, the gentleman," remarked two idlers whom he had pushed a little roughly.

Quick as he had been, a shopkeeper of the Rue Turenne had had time to recognize him.

"Why, that's the cashier's son!" he exclaimed.

"Is it possible?"

"Why don't they arrest him?"

Half a dozen curious fellows, more eager than the

rest, ran after him to try and see his face.   But he was already far off.

Leaning against a gas-lamp on the Boulevard, he un-folded the paper he had just bought.   He had no trouble looking for the article.   In the middle of the first page, in the most prominent position, he read in large letters,—

"ANOTHER FINANCIAL DISASTER.

" At the moment of going to press, the greatest agita-tion prevails among the stock-brokers and operators at the *bourse* generally, owing to the news that one of our great banking establishments has just been the victim of a theft of unusual magnitude.

" At about five o'clock in the afternoon, the manager of the Mutual Credit Society, having need of some documents, went to look for them in the office of the head cashier, who was then absent.   A memorandum forgotten on the table excited his suspicions.   Sending at once for a locksmith, he had all the drawers broken open, and soon acquired the irrefutable evidence that the Mutual Credit had been defrauded of sums, which, as far as now known, amount to upwards of twelve millions.

" At once the police was notified; and M. Brosse, commissary of police, duly provided with a warrant, called at the guilty cashier's house.

" That cashier, named Favoral,—we do not hesitate to name him, since his name has already been made pub-lic,—had just sat down to dinner with some friends. Warned, no one knows how, he succeeded in escaping through a window into the yard of the adjoining house, and up to this hour has succeeded in eluding all search.

" It seems that these embezzlements had been going on for years, but had been skilfully concealed by false entries.

" M. Favoral had managed to secure the esteem of all who knew him.   He led at home a more than modest existence.   But that was only, as it were, his official life.   Elsewhere, and under another name, he indulged in the most reckless expenses for the benefit of a woman with whom he was madly in love.

" Who this woman is, is not yet exactly known.

" Some mention a very fascinating young actress, who performs at a theatre not a hundred miles from the Rue Vivienne; others, a lady of the financial high life, whose equipages, diamonds, and dresses are justly famed.

" We might easily, in this respect, give particulars which would astonish many people; for *we know all;* but, at the risk of seeming less well informed than some others of our morning contemporaries, we will observe a silence which our readers will surely appreciate. We do not wish to add, by a premature indiscretion, any thing to the grief of a family already so cruelly stricken; for M. Favoral leaves behind him in the deepest sorrow a wife and two children,—a son of twenty-five, employed in a railroad office, and a daughter of twenty, remarkably handsome, who, a few months ago, came very near marrying M. C.—

" Next "—

Tears of rage obscured Maxence's sight whilst reading the last few lines of this terrible article. To find himself thus held up to public curiosity, though innocent, was more than he could bear.

And yet he was, perhaps, still more surprised than indignant. He had just learned in that paper more than his father's most intimate friends knew, more than he knew himself. Where had it got its information? And what could be these other details which the writer pretended to know, but did not wish to publish as yet? Maxence felt like running to the office of the paper, fancying that they could tell him there exactly where and under what name M. Favoral led that existence of pleasure and luxury, and who the woman was to whom the article alluded.

But in the mean time he had reached his hotel,—the Hôtel des Folies. After a moment of hesitation,—

" Bash ! " he thought, " I have the whole day to call at the office of the paper."

And he started in the corridor of the hotel, a corridor that was so long, so dark, and so narrow, that it gave an idea of the shaft of a mine, and that it was prudent, before entering it, to make sure that no one was coming in the opposite direction. It was from the neighboring theatre, *des Folies-Nouvelles* (now the Theatre Déjazet), that the hotel had taken its name.

It consists of the rear building of a large old house, and has no frontage on the Boulevard, where nothing betrays its existence, except a lantern hung over a low and narrow door, between a *café* and a confectionery-shop. It is one of those hotels, as there are a good many in Paris, somewhat mysterious and suspicious, ill-kept, and whose profits remain a mystery for simple-minded folks. Who occupy the apartments of the first and second story? No one knows. Never have the most curious of the neighbors discovered the face of a tenant. And yet they are occupied; for often, in the afternoon, a curtain is drawn aside, and a shadow is seen to move. In the evening, lights are noticed within; and sometimes the sound of a cracked old piano is heard.

Above the second story, the mystery ceases. All the upper rooms, the price of which is relatively modest, are occupied by tenants who may be seen and heard,—clerks like Maxence, shop-girls from the neighborhood, a few restaurant-waiters, and sometimes some poor devil of an actor or chorus-singer from the Theatre Déjazet, the Circus, or the Château d'Eau. One of the great advantages of the Hôtel des Folies—and Mme.

Fortin, the landlady, never failed to point it out to the new tenants, an inestimable advantage, she declared—was a back entrance on the Rue Béranger.

"And everybody knows," she concluded, "that there is no chance of being caught, when one has the good luck of living in a house that has two outlets."

When Maxence entered the office, a small, dark, and dirty room, the proprietors, M. and Mme. Fortin were just finishing their breakfast with an immense bowl of coffee of doubtful color, of which an enormous red cat was taking a share.

"Ah, here is M. Favoral!" they exclaimed.

There was no mistaking their tone. They knew the catastrophe; and the newspaper lying on the table showed how they had heard it.

"Some one called to see you last night," said Mme. Fortin, a large fat woman, whose nose was always besmeared with snuff, and whose honeyed voice made a marked contrast with her bird-of-prey look.

"Who?"

"A gentleman of about fifty, tall and thin, with a long overcoat, coming down to his heels."

Maxence imagined, from this description, that he rec‧ognized his own father. And yet it seemed impossible, after what had happened, that he should dare to show himself on the Boulevard du Temple, where everybody knew him, within a step of the Café Turc, of which he was one of the oldest customers.

"At what o'clock was he here?" he inquired.

"I really can't tell," answered the landlady. "I was half asleep at the time; but Fortin can tell us."

M. Fortin, who looked about twenty years younger than his wife, was one of those small men, blonde, with scanty beard, a suspicious glance, and uneasy smile,

such as the Madame Fortins know how to find, Heaven
knows where.

" The confectioner had just put up his shutters," he
replied: " consequently, it must have been between
eleven and a quarter-past eleven."

" And didn't he leave any word? " said Maxence.

" Nothing, except that he was very sorry not to find
you in. And, in fact, he did look quite annoyed. We
asked him to leave his name; but he said it wasn't worth
while, and that he would call again."

At the glance which the landlady was throwing
toward him from the corner of her eyes, Maxence understood that she had on the subject of that late visitor
the same suspicion as himself.

And, as if she had intended to make it more apparent
still,—

" I ought, perhaps, to have given him your key," she
said.

" And why so, pray? "

" Oh! I don't know, an idea of mine, that's all. Besides, Mlle. Lucienne can probably tell you more about
it; for she was there when the gentleman came, and I
even think that they exchanged a few words in the
yard."

Maxence, seeing that they were only seeking a pretext to question him, took his key, and inquired,—

" Is Mlle. Lucienne at home? "

" Can't tell. She has been going and coming all the
morning, and I don't know whether she finally staid in
or out. One thing is sure, she waited for you last
night until after twelve; and she didn't like it much, I
can tell you."

Maxence started up the steep stairs; and, as he
reached the upper stories, a woman's voice, fresh and

beautifully toned, reached his ears more and more distinctly.

She was singing a popular tune,—one of those songs
which are monthly put in circulation by the singing
cafés:—

> " To hope! O charming word,
>   Which, during all life,
>   Husband and children and **wife**
>   Repeat in common accord!
>   When the moment of success
>   From us ever further slips,
>   'Tis Hope from its rosy lips
>   Whispers, To-morrow you will **bless.**
>   'Tis very nice to run,
>   But to have is better fun."

" She is in," murmured Maxence, breathing more
freely.

Reaching the fourth story, he stopped before the door
which faced the stairs, and knocked lightly.

At once, the voice, which had just commenced another verse stopped short, and inquired, " Who's
there? "

" I, Maxence! "

" At this hour! " replied the voice with an ironical
laugh. " That's lucky. You have probably forgotten
that we were to go to the theatre last night, and start
for St. Germain at seven o'clock this morning."

" Don't you know then? " Maxence began, as soon as
he could put in a word.

" I know that you did not come home last night."

" Quite true. But when I have told you "—

" What? the lie you have imagined? Save yourself
the trouble."

" Lucienne, I beg of you, open the door."

"Impossible, I am dressing. Go to your own room: as soon as I am dressed, I'll join you."

And, to cut short all these explanations, she took up her song again :—

> "Hope, I've waited but too long
> For thy manna divine!
> I've drunk enough of thy wine,
> And I know thy siren song:
> Waiting for a lucky turn,
> I have wasted my best days:
> Take up thy magic-lantern
> And elsewhere display its rays.
> 'Tis very nice to run,
> But to have is better fun!"

XXVI.

IT was on the opposite side of the landing that what Mme. Fortin pompously called " Maxence's apartment " was situated.

It consisted of a sort of antechamber, almost as large as a handkerchief (decorated by the Fortins with the name of dining-room), a bedroom, and a closet called a dressing-room in the lease. Nothing could be more gloomy than this lodging, in which the ragged paper and soiled paint retained the traces of all the wanderers who had occupied it since the opening of the Hôtel des Folies. The dislocated ceiling was scaling off in large pieces; the floor seemed affected with the dry-rot; and the doors and windows were so much warped and sprung, that it required an effort to close them. The furniture was on a par with the rest.

"How everything does wear out!" sighed Mme.

Fortin. " It isn't ten years since I bought that furniture."

In point of fact it was over fifteen, and even then she
had bought it secondhanded, and almost unfit for use.
The curtains retained but a vague shade of their original color. The veneer was almost entirely off the bedstead. Not a single lock was in order, whether in the
bureau or the secretary. The rug had become a nameless rag; and the broken springs of the sofa, cutting
through the threadbare stuff, stood up threateningly
like knife-blades.

The most sumptuous object was an enormous China
stove, which occupied almost one-half of the hall-dining-
room. It could not be used to make a fire; for it had
no pipe. Nevertheless, Mme. Fortin refused obstinately to take it out, under the pretext that it gave
such a comfortable appearance to the apartment. All
this elegance cost Maxence forty-five francs a month,
and five francs for the service; the whole payable
in advance from the 1st to the 3d of the month. If,
on the 4th, a tenant came in without money, Mme. Fortin squarely refused him his key, and invited him to
seek shelter elsewhere.

" I have been caught too often," she replied to those
who tried to obtain twenty-four hours' grace from her.
" I wouldn't trust my own father till the 5th, he who
was a superior officer in Napoleon's armies, and the
very soul of honor."

It was chance alone which had brought Maxence,
after the Commune, to the Hôtel des Folies; and he had
not been there a week, before he had fully made up his
mind not to wear out Mme. Fortin's furniture very long.
He had even already found another and more suitable
lodging, when, about a year ago, a certain meeting on

the stairs had modified all his views, and lent a charm
to his apartment which he did not suspect.

As he was going out one morning to his office, he met
on the very landing a rather tall and very dark girl, who
had just come running up stairs. She passed before
him like a flash, opened the opposite door, and disappeared. But, rapid as the apparition had been, it had
left in Maxence's mind one of those impressions which
are never obliterated. He could not think of any thing
else the whole day; and after business-hours, instead
of going to dine in Rue St. Gilles, as usual, he sent a
despatch to his mother to tell her not to wait for him,
and bravely went home.

But it was in vain, that, during the whole evening,
he kept watch behind his door, left slyly ajar: he did
not get a glimpse of the neighbor. Neither did she
show herself on the next or the three following days;
and Maxence was beginning to despair, when at last,
on Sunday, as he was going down stairs, he met her
again face to face. He had thought her quite pretty at
the first glance: this time he was dazzled to that extent, that he remained for over a minute, standing like
a statue against the wall.

And certainly it was not her dress that helped setting
off her beauty. She wore a poor dress of black merino,
a narrow collar, and plain cuffs, and a bonnet of the
utmost simplicity. She had nevertheless an air of incomparable dignity, a grace that charmed, and yet inspired respect, and the carriage of a queen. This was
on the 30th of July. As he was handing in his key,
before leaving,—

" My apartment suits me well enough," said Maxence
to Mme. Fortin: " I shall keep it. And here are fifty
francs for the month of August."

And, while the landlady was making out a receipt,—
" You never told me," he began with his most indifferent look, " that I had a neighbor."

Mme. Fortin straightened herself up like an old war-
horse that hears the sound of the bugle.

" Yes, yes ! " she said,—" Mademoiselle Lucienne."

" Lucienne," repeated Maxence: " that's a pretty
name."

" Have you seen her ? "

" I have just seen her.   She's rather good looking."

The worthy landlady jumped on her chair.

" Rather good looking ! " she interrupted.   " You
must be hard to please, my dear sir ; for I, who am a
judge, I affirm that you might hunt Paris over for four
whole days without finding such a handsome girl.
Rather good looking !   A girl who has hair that comes
down to her knees, a dazzling complexion, eyes as big
as this, and teeth whiter than that cat's.   All right, my
friend.   You'll wear out more than one pair of boots
running after women before you catch one like her."

That was exactly Maxence's opinion ; and yet with his
coldest look,—

" Has she been long your tenant, dear Mme. Fortin ? "
he asked.

" A little over a year.   She was here during the
siege ; and just then, as she could not pay her rent, I
was, of course, going to send her off ; but she went
straight to the commissary of police, who came here,
and forbade me to turn out either her or anybody else.
As if people were not masters in their own house ! "

" That was perfectly absurd ! " objected Maxence,
who was determined to gain the good graces of the
landlady.

" Never heard of such a thing ! " she went on.

" Compel you to lodge people free! Why not feed them too? In short, she remained so long, that, after the Commune, she owed me a hundred and eighty francs. Then she said, that, if I would let her stay, she would pay me each month in advance, besides the rent, ten francs on the old account. I agreed, and she has already paid up twenty francs."

" Poor girl! " said Maxence.

But Mme. Fortin shrugged her shoulders.

" Really," she replied, " I don't pity her much; for, if she only wanted, in forty-eight hours I should be paid, and she would have something else on her back besides that old black rag. I tell her every day, ' In these days, my child, there is but one reliable friend, which is better than all others, and which must be taken as it comes, without making any faces if it is a little dirty: that's money.' But all my preaching goes for nothing. I might as well sing."

Maxence was listening with intense delight.

" In short, what does she do? " he asked.

" That's more than I know," replied Mme. Fortin. " The young lady has not much to say. All I know is, that she leaves every morning bright and early, and rarely gets home before eleven. On Sunday she stays home, reading; and sometimes, in the evening, she goes out, always alone, to some theatre or ball. Ah! she is an odd one, I tell you! "

A lodger who came in interrupted the landlady; and Maxence walked off, dreaming how he could manage to make the acquaintance of his pretty and eccentric neighbor.

Because he had once spent some hundreds of napoleons in the company of young ladies with yellow chignons, Maxence fancied himself a man of experience.

and had but little faith in the virtue of a girl of twenty,
living alone in a hotel, and left sole mistress of her own
fancy. He began to watch for every occasion of meeting her; and, towards the last of the month, he had got
so far as to bow to her, and to inquire after her health.
But, the first time he ventured to make love to her, she
looked at him head to foot, and turned her back upon
him with so much contempt, that he remained, his
mouth wide open, perfectly stupefied.

" I am losing my time like a fool," he thought.

Great, then, was his surprise, when the following
week, on a fine afternoon, he saw Mlle. Lucienne leave
her room, no longer clad in her eternal black dress, but
wearing a brilliant and extremely rich toilet. With a
beating heart he followed her.

In front of the Hôtel des Folies stood a handsome
carriage and horses.

As soon as Mlle. Lucienne appeared, a footman
opened respectfully the carriage-door. She went in;
and the horses started at a full trot.

Maxence watched the carriage disappear in the distance, like a child who sees the bird fly upon which he
hoped to lay hands.

" Gone," he muttered, " gone! "

But, when he turned around, he found himself face to
face with the Fortins, man and wife, who were laughing
a sinister laugh.

" What did I tell you? " exclaimed Mme Fortin.
" There she is, started at last. Get up, horse! She'll
do well, the child."

The magnificent equipage and elegant dress had already produced quite an effect among the neighbors.
The customers sitting in front of the *café* were laughing
among themselves. The confectioner and his wife were

casting indignant glances at the proprietors of the Hôtel des Folies.

" You see, M. Favoral," replied Mme. Fortin, " such a girl as that was not made for our neighborhood. You must make up your mind to it; you won't see much more of her on the Boulevard du Temple."

Without saying a word, Maxence ran to his room, the hot tears streaming from his eyes. He felt ashamed of himself; for, after all, what was this girl to him? " She is gone! " he repeated to himself. " Well, good-by, let her go! "

But, despite all his efforts at philosophy, he felt an immense sadness invading his heart: ill-defined regrets and spasms of anger agitated him. He was thinking what a fool he had been to believe in the grand airs of the young lady, and that, if he had had dresses and horses to give her, she might not have received him so harshly. At last he made up his mind to think no more of her,—one of those fine resolutions which are always taken, and never kept; and in the evening he left his room to go and dine in the Rue St. Gilles.

But, as was often his custom, he stopped at the *café* next door, and called for a drink. He was mixing his absinthe when he saw the carriage that had carried off Mlle. Lucienne in the morning returning at a rapid gait, and stopping short in front of the hotel. Mlle. Lucienne got out slowly, crossed the sidewalk, and entered the narrow corridor. Almost immediately, the carriage turned around, and drove off.

" What does it mean? " thought Maxence, who was actually forgetting to swallow his absinthe.

He was losing himself in absurd conjectures, when, some fifteen minutes later, he saw the girl coming out again. Already she had taken off her elegant clothes, and resumed her cheap black dress. She had a basket on her arm, and was going towards the Rue Charlot. Without further reflections, Maxence rose suddenly, and started to follow her, being very careful that she should not see him. After walking for five or six minutes, she entered a shop, half-eating house, and half wine-shop, in the window of which a large sign could be read: *"Ordinary at all hours for forty centimes. Hard boiled eggs, and salad of the season."*

Maxence, having crept up as close as he could, saw Mlle. Lucienne take a tin box out of her basket, and have what is called an " ordinaire " poured into it; that is, half a pint of soup, a piece of beef as large as the fist, and a few vegetables. She then had a small bottle half-filled with wine, paid, and walked out with that same look of grave dignity which she always wore.

" Funny dinner," murmured Maxence, " for a woman who was spreading herself just now in a ten-thousand-franc carriage."

From that moment she became the sole and only object of his thoughts. A passion, which he no longer attempted to resist, was penetrating like a subtle poison to the innermost depths of his being. He thought himself happy, when, after watching for hours, he caught a glimpse of this singular creature, who, after that extraordinary expedition, seemed to have resumed her usual mode of life. Mme. Fortin was dumfounded.

" She has been too exacting," she said to Maxence, " and the thing has fallen through."

He made no answer. He felt a perfect horror for the honorable landlady's insinuations; and yet he never ceased to repeat to himself that he must be a great simpleton to have faith for a moment in that young lady's virtue. What would he not have given to be able to

question her? But he dared not. Often he would
gather up his courage, and wait for her on the stairs;
but, as soon as she fixed upon him her great black eye,
all the phrases he had prepared took flight from his
brain, his tongue clove to his mouth, and he could
barely succeed in stammering out a timid,—

"Good-morning, mademoiselle."

He felt so angry with himself, that he was almost on
the point of leaving the Hôtel des Folies, when one
evening:—

"Well," said Mme. Fortin to him, "all is made up
again, it seems. The beautiful carriage called again to-
day."

Maxence could have beaten her.

"What good would it do you," he replied, "if Lucienne were to turn out badly?"

"It's always a pleasure," she grumbled, "to have one
more woman to torment the men. Those are the girls,
you see, who avenge us poor honest women!"

The sequel seemed at first to justify her worst pre-
visions. Three times during that week, Mlle. Lucienne
rode out in grand style; but as she always returned, and
always resumed her eternal black woolen dress,—

"I can't make head or tail of it," thought Maxence.
"But, never mind, I'll clear the matter up yet."

He applied, and obtained leave of absence; and from
the very next day he took up a position behind the
window of the adjoining *café*. On the first day he lost
his time; but on the second day, at about three o'clock,
the famous equipage made its appearance; and, a few
moments later, Mlle. Lucienne took a seat in it. Her
toilet was richer, and more showy still, than the first
time. Maxence jumped into a cab.

"You see that carriage," he said to the coachman.

" Wherever it goes, you must follow it. I give ten francs extra pay."

" All right!" replied the driver, whipping up his horses.

And much need he had, too, of whipping them; for the carriage that carried off Mlle. Lucienne started at full trot down the Boulevards, to the Madeleine, then along the Rue Royale, and through the Place de la Concorde, to the Avenue des Champs-Elysées, where the horses were brought down to a walk. It was the end of September, and one of those lovely autumnal days which are a last smile of the blue sky and the last caress of the sun.

There were races in the Bois de Boulogne; and the equipages were five and six abreast on the avenue. The side-alleys were crowded with idlers. Maxence, from the inside of his cab, never lost sight of Mlle. Lucienne.

She was evidently creating a sensation. The men stopped to look at her with gaping admiration: the women leaned out of their carriages to see her better.

" Where can she be going?" Maxence wondered.

She was going to the Bois; and soon her carriage joined the interminable line of equipages which were following the grand drive at a walk. It became easier now to follow on foot. Maxence sent off his cab to wait for him at a particular spot, and took the pedestrians' road, that follows the edge of the lakes. He had not gone fifty steps, however, before he heard some one call him. He turned around, and, within two lengths of his cane, saw M. Saint Pavin and M. Costeclar. Maxence hardly knew M. Saint Pavin, whom he had only seen two or three times in the Rue St. Gilles, and execrated M. Costeclar. Still he advanced towards them.

Mlle. Lucienne's carriage was now caught in the file; and he was sure of joining it whenever he thought proper.

"It is a miracle to see you here, my dear Maxence!" exclaimed M. Costeclar, loud enough to attract the attention of several persons.

To occupy the attention of others, anyhow and at any cost, was M. Costeclar's leading object in life. That was evident from the style of his dress, the shape of his hat, the bright stripes of his shirt, his ridiculous shirt-collar, his cuffs, his boots, his gloves, his cane, every thing, in fact.

"If you see us on foot," he added, "it is because we wanted to walk a little. The doctor's prescription, my dear. My carriage is yonder, behind those trees. Do you recognize my dapple-grays?" And he extended his cane in that direction, as if he were addressing himself, not to Maxence alone, but to all those who were passing by.

"Very well, very well! everybody knows you have a carriage," interrupted M. Saint Pavin.

The editor of "The Financial Pilot" was the living contrast of his companion. More slovenly still than M. Costeclar was careful of his dress, he exhibited cynically a loose cravat rolled over a shirt worn two or three days, a coat white with lint and plush, muddy boots, though it had not rained for a week, and large red hands, surprisingly filthy.

He was but the more proud; and he wore, cocked up to one side, a hat that had not known a brush since the day it had left the hatter's.

"That fellow Costeclar," he went on, "he won't believe that there are in France a number of people who live and die without ever having owned a horse or a *coupé;* which is a fact, nevertheless. Those fellows who were born with fifty or sixty thousand francs' income in their baby-clothes are all alike."

The unpleasant intention was evident; but M. Costeclar was not the man to get angry for such a trifle.

"You are in bad humor to-day, old fellow," he said.

The editor of " The Financial Pilot " made a threatening gesture.

"Well, yes," he answered, " I am in bad humor, like a man who for ten years past has been beating the drum in front of your d——d financial shops, and who does not pay expenses. Yes, for ten years I have shouted myself hoarse for your benefit: ' Walk in, ladies and gentlemen, and, for every twenty-cent-piece you deposit with us, we will return you a five-franc-piece. Walk in, follow the crowd, step up to the office: this is the time.' They go in. You receive mountains of twenty-cent-pieces: you never return anything, neither a five-franc-piece, nor even a centime. The trick is done, the public is sold. You drive your own carriage; you suspend diamonds to your mistress' ears; and I, the organizer of success, whose puffs open the tightest closed pockets, and start up the old louis from the bottom of the old woolen stocking,—I am driven to have my boots half-soled. You stint me my existence; you kick as soon as I ask you to pay for the big drums bursted in your behalf."

He spoke so loud, that three or four idlers had stopped. Without being very shrewd, Maxence understood readily that he had happened in in the midst of an acrimonious discussion. Closely pressed, and desirous of gaining time, M. Costeclar had called him in the hopes of effecting a diversion.

Bowing, therefore, politely,—

"Excuse me, gentlemen," he said: "I fear I have interrupted you."

But M. Costeclar detained him.

"Don't go," he declared; "you must come down and take a class of Madeira with us, down at the Cascade."

And, turning to the editor of "The Pilot"—

"Come, now, shut up," he said: "you shall have what you want."

"Really?"

"Upon my word."

"I'd rather have two or three lines in black and white."

"I'll give them to you to-night."

"All right, then! Forward the big guns! Look out for next Sunday's number!"

Peace being made, the gentlemen continued their walk in the most friendly manner, M. Costeclar pointing out to Maxence all the celebrities who were passing by them in their carriages.

He had just designated to his attention Mme. and Mlle. de Thaller, accompanied by two gigantic footmen, when, suddenly interrupting himself, and rising on tiptoe,—

"*Sacre bleu!*" he exclaimed: "what a handsome woman!"

Without too much affectation, Maxence fell back a step or two. He felt himself blushing to his very ears, and trembled lest his sudden emotion were noticed, and he were questioned; for it was Mlle. Lucienne who thus excited M. Costeclar's noisy enthusiasm. Once already she had been around the lake; and she was continuing her circular drive.

"Positively," approved the editor of "The Financial

Pilot," " she is somewhat better than the rest of those ladies we have just seen going by."

M. Costeclar was on the point of pulling out what little hair he had left.

" And I don't know her! " he went on. " A lovely woman rides in the Bois, and I don't know who she is! That is ridiculous and prodigious! Who can post us? "

A little ways off stood a group of gentlemen, who had also just left their carriages, and were looking on this interminable procession of equipages and this amazing display of toilets.

" They are friends of mine," said M. Costeclar: " let us join them."

They did so; and, after the usual greetings,—

" Who is that? " inquired M. Costeclar,—" that dark person, whose carriage follows Mme. de Thaller's? "

An old young man, with scanty hair, dyed beard, and a most impudent smile, answered him,—

" That's just what we are trying to find out. None of us have ever seen her."

" I must and shall find out," interrupted M. Costeclar. " I have a very intelligent servant "—

Already he was starting in the direction of the spot where his carriage was waiting for him. The old beau stopped him.

" Don't bother yourself, my dear friend," he said. " I have also a servant who is no fool; and he has had my orders for over fifteen minutes."

The others burst out laughing.

" Distanced, Costeclar! " exclaimed M. Saint Pavin, who, notwithstanding his slovenly dress and cynic manners, seemed perfectly well received.

No one was now paying any attention to Maxence; and he slipped off without the slightest care as to what

M. Costeclar might think. Reaching the spot where his cab awaited him,—

" Which way, boss? " inquired the driver.

Maxence hesitated. What better had he to do than to go home? And yet—

" We'll wait for that same carriage," he answered; " and we'll follow it on the return."

But he learned nothing further. Mlle. Lucienne drove straight to the Boulevard du Temple, and, as before, immediately resumed her eternal black dress; and Maxence saw, her go to the little restaurant for her modest dinner.

But he saw something else too.

Almost on the heels of the girl, a servant in livery entered the hotel corridor, and only went off after remaining a full quarter of an hour in busy conference with Mme. Fortin.

" It's all over," thought the poor fellow. " Lucienne will not be much longer my neighbor."

He was mistaken. A month went by without bringing about any change. As in the past, she went out early, came home late, and on Sundays remained alone all day in her room. Once or twice a week, when the weather was fine, the carriage came for her at about three o'clock, and brought her home at nightfall. Maxence had exhausted all conjectures, when one evening, it was the 31st of October, as he was coming in to go to bed, he heard a loud sound of voices in the office of the hotel. Led by an instinctive curiosity, he approached on tiptoe, so as to see and hear every thing. The Fortins and Mlle. Lucienne were having a great discussion.

" That's all nonsense," shrieked the worthy landlady; " and I mean to be paid."

Mlle. Lucienne was quite calm.

" Well," she replied: " don't I pay you? Here are forty francs,—thirty in advance for my room, and ten on the old account."

" I don't want your ten francs ! "

" What do you want, then? "

" All,—the hundred and fifty francs which you owe me still."

The girl shrugged her shoulders.

" You forget our agreement," she uttered.

" Our agreement? "

" Yes. After the Commune, it was understood that I would give you ten francs a month on the old account; as long as I give them to you, you have nothing to ask."

Crimson with rage, Mme. Fortin had risen from her seat.

" Formerly," she interrupted, " I presumed I had to deal with a poor working-girl, an honest girl."

Mlle. Lucienne took no notice of the insult.

" I have not the amount you ask," she said coldly.

" Well, then," vociferated the other, " you must go and ask it of those who pay for your carriages and your dresses."

Still impassible, the girl, instead of answering, stretched her hand towards her key; but M. Fortin stopped her arm.

" No, no ! " he said with a giggle. " People who don't pay their hotel-bill sleep out, my darling."

Maxence, that very morning, had received his month's pay, and he felt, as it were, his two hundred francs trembling in his pockets.

Yielding to a sudden inspiration, he threw open the

office-door, and, throwing down one hundred and fifty francs upon the table,—

"Here is your money, wretch!" he exclaimed.

And he withdrew at once.

XXVII.

MAXENCE had not spoken to Mlle. Lucienne for nearly a month. He tried to persuade himself that she despised him because he was poor. He kept watching for her, for he could not help it; but as much as possible he avoided her.

"I shall be miserable," he thought, "the day when she does not come home; and yet it would be the very best thing that could happen for me."

Nevertheless, he spent all his time trying to find some explanations for the conduct of this strange girl, who, beneath her woolen dress, had the haughty manners of a great lady. Then he delighted to imagine between her and himself some of those subjects of confidence, some of those facilities which chance never fails to supply to attentive passion, or some event which would enable him to emerge from his obscurity, and to acquire some rights by virtue of some great service rendered.

But never had he dared to hope for an occasion as propitious as the one he had just seized. And yet, after he had returned to his room, he hardly dared to congratulate himself upon the promptitude of his decision. He knew too well Mlle. Lucienne's excessive pride and sensitive nature.

"I should not be surprised if she were angry with me for what I've done," he thought.

The evening being quite chilly, he had lighted a few
sticks; and, sitting by the fireside, he was waiting, his
mind filled with vague hopes. It seemed to him that
his neighbor could not absolve herself from coming to
thank him; and he was listening intently to all the noises
of the house, starting at the sound of footsteps on the
stairs, and at the slamming of doors. Ten times, at
least, he went out on tiptoe to lean out of the window
on the landing, to make sure that there was no light in
Mlle. Lucienne's room. At eleven o'clock she had not
yet come home; and he was deliberating whether he
would not start out in quest of information, when there
was a knock at the door.

"Come in!" he cried, in a voice choked with emotion.

Mlle. Lucienne came in. She was somewhat paler
than usual, but calm and perfectly self-possessed. Having bowed without the slightest shade of embarrassment,
she laid upon the mantel-piece the thirty five-franc-notes
which Maxence had thrown down to the Fortins; and,
in her most natural tone,—

"Here are your hundred and fifty francs, sir," she
uttered. "I am more grateful than I can express for
your prompt kindness in lending them to me; but I did
not need them."

Maxence had risen from his seat, and was making
every effort to control his own feelings.

"Still," he began, "after what I heard"—

"Yes," she interrupted, "Mme. Fortin and her husband were trying to frighten me. But they were losing
their time. When, after the Commune, I settled with
them the manner in which I would discharge my debt
towards them, having a just estimate of their worth, I
made them write out and sign our agreement. Being in
the right, I could resist them, and was resisting them

when you threw them those hundred and fifty francs.
Having laid hands upon them, they had the pretension to
keep them. That's what I could not suffer. Not being
able to recover them by main force, I went at once to the
commissary of police. He was luckily at his office. He
is an honest man, who already, once before, helped me
out of a scrape. He listened to me kindly, and was
moved by my explanations. Notwithstanding the late-
ness of the hour, he put on his overcoat, and came with
me to see our landlord. After compelling them to return
me your money, he signified to them to observe strictly
our agreement, under penalty of incurring his utmost
severity."

Maxence was wonderstruck.

" How could you dare? " he said.

" Wasn't I in the right? "

" Oh, a thousand times yes! Still "—

" What? Should my right be less respected because I
am but a woman? And, because I have no one to protect me, am I outside the law, and condemned in advance to suffer the iniquitous fancies of every scoundrel? No, thank Heaven! Henceforth I shall feel easy.
People like the Fortins, who live of I know not what
shameful traffic, have too much to fear from the police
to dare to molest me further."

The resentment of the insult could be read in her
great black eyes; and a bitter disgust contracted her lips.

" Besides," she added, " the commissary had no need
of my explanations to understand what abject inspirations the Fortins were following. The wretches had in
their pocket the wages of their infamy. In refusing me
my key, in throwing me out in the street at ten o'clock
at night, they hoped to drive me to seek the assistance
of the base coward who paid their odious treason. And

we know the price which men demand for the slightest
service they render to a woman."

Maxênce turned pale. The idea flashed upon his mind
that it was to him, perhaps, that these last words were
addressed.

" Ah, I swear it! " he exclaimed, " it is without after-
thought that I tried to help you. You do not owe me
any thanks even."

" I do not thank you any the less, though," she said
gently, " and from the bottom of my heart "—

" It was so little! "

" Intention alone makes the value of a service, neighbor. And, besides, do not say that a hundred and fifty
francs are nothing to you: perhaps you do not earn
much more each month."

" I confess it," he said, blushing a little.

" You see, then? No, it was not to you that my words
were addressed, but to the man who has paid the Fortins.
He was waiting on the Boulevard, the result of the manœuvre, which, they thought, was about to place me at
his mercy. He ran quickly to me when I went out, and
followed me all the way to the office of the commissary
of police, as he follows me everywhere for the past
month, with his sickening gallantries and his degrading
propositions."

The eye flashing with anger,—

" Ah, if I had known! " exclaimed Maxence. " If
you had told me but a word! "

She smiled at his vehemence.

" What would you have done? " she said. " You cannot impart intelligence to a fool, heart to a coward, or
delicacy of feeling to a boor."

" I could have chastised the miserable insulter."

She had a superb gesture of indifference.

" Bash ! " she interrupted. " What are insults to me ?
I am so accustomed to them, that they no longer have
any effect upon me. I am eighteen : I have neither family, relatives, friends, nor any one in the world who even
knows my existence ; and I live by my labor. Can't you
see what must be the humiliations of each day ? Since I
was eight years old, I have been earning the bread I eat,
the dress I wear, and the rent of the den where I sleep.
Can you understand what I have endured, to what ig-
nominies I have been exposed, what traps have been set
for me, and how it has happened to me sometimes to
owe my safety to mere physical force ? And yet I do not
complain, since through it all I have been able to retain
the respect of myself, and to remain virtuous in spite
of all."

She was laughing a laugh that had something wild in
it.

And, as Maxence was looking at her with immense
surprise,—

" That seems strange to you, doesn't it ? " she resumed. " A girl of eighteen, without a sou, free as air,
very pretty, and yet virtuous in the midst of Paris.
Probably you don't believe it, or, if you do, you just
think, ' What on earth does she make by it ? '

" And really you are right ; for, after all, who cares,
and who thinks any the more of me, if I work sixteen
hours a day to remain virtuous ? But it's a fancy of my
own ; and don't imagine for a moment that I am deterred
by any scruples, or by timidity, or ignorance. No, no !
I believe in nothing. I fear nothing ; and I know as
much as the oldest libertines, the most vicious, and the
most depraved. And I don't say that I have not been
tempted sometimes, when, coming home from work, I'd
see some of them coming out of the restaurants, splen-

didly dressed, on their lover's arm, and getting into carriages to go to the theatre. There were moments when
I was cold and hungry, and when, not knowing where
to sleep, I wandered all night through the streets like
a lost dog. There were hours when I felt sick of all
this misery, and when I said to myself, that, since it was
my fate to end in the hospital, I might as well make the
trip gayly. But what! I should have had to traffic my
person, to sell myself! "

She shuddered, and in a hoarse voice,—

" I would rather die," she said.

It was difficult to reconcile words such as these with
certain circumstances of Mlle. Lucienne's existence,—
her rides around the lake, for instance, in that carriage
that came for her two or three times a week; her ever
renewed costumes, each time more eccentric and more
showy. But Maxence was not thinking of that. What
she told him he accepted as absolutely true and indis-
putable. And he felt penetrated with an almost religious
admiration for this young and beautiful girl, possessed
of so much vivid energy, who alone, through the
hazards, the perils, and the temptations of Paris, had
succeeded in protecting and defending herself.

" And yet," he said, " without suspecting it, you had
a friend near you."

She shuddered; and a pale smile flitted upon her lips.
She knew well enough what friendship means between
a youth of twenty-five and a girl of eighteen.

" A friend! " she murmured.

Maxence guessed her thought; and, in all the sincerity of his soul,—

" Yes, a friend," he repeated, " a comrade, a brother."

And thinking to touch her, and gain her confidence,—

" I could understand you," he added; " for I, to
have been very unhappy."

But he was singularly mistaken. She looked at him
with an astonished air, and slowly,—

" You unhappy ! " she uttered,—" you who have a
family, relations, a mother who adores you, a sister."

Less excited, Maxence might have wondered how she
had found this out, and would have concluded that she
must feel some interest in him, since she had doubtless
taken the trouble of getting information.

" Besides, you are a man," she went on; " and I do
not understand how a man can complain. Have you not
the freedom, the strength, and the right to undertake
and to dare any thing? Isn't the world open to your
activity and to your ambition? Woman submits to her
fate : man makes his."

This was hurting the dearest pretensions of Maxence,
who seriously thought that he had exhausted the rigors
of adversity.

" There are circumstances," he began.

But she shrugged her shoulders gently, and, interrupting him,—

" Do not insist," she said, " or else I might think that
you lack energy. What are you talking of circumstances ? There are none so adverse but that can be
overcome. What would you like, then ? To be born with
a hundred thousand francs a year, and have nothing to
do but to live according to your whim of each day, idle,
satiated, a burden upon yourself, useless, or offensive to
others ? Ah ! If I were a man, I would dream of another fate. I should like to start from the Foundling
Asylum, without a name, and by my will, my intelligence, my daring, and my labor, make something and

somebody of myself. I would start from nothing, and become every thing ! "

With flashing eyes and quivering nostrils, she drew herself up proudly. But almost at once, dropping her head,—

" The misfortune is," she added, " that I am but a woman ; and you who complain, if you only knew "—

She sat down, and with her elbow on the little table, her head resting upon her hand, she remained lost in her meditations, her eyes fixed, as if following through space all the phases of the eighteen years of her life.

There is no energy but unbends at some given moment, no will but has its hour of weakness ; and, strong and energetic as was Mlle. Lucienne, she had been deeply touched by Maxence's act. Had she, then, found at last upon her path the companion of whom she had often dreamed in the despairing hours of solitude and wretchedness? After a few moments, she raised her head, and, looking into Maxence's eyes with a gaze that made him quiver like the shock of an electric battery,—

" Doubtless," she said, in a tone of indifference somewhat forced, " you think you have in me a strange neighbor. Well, as between neighbors, it is well to know each other. Before you judge me, listen."

The recommendation was useless. Maxence was listening with all the powers of his attention.

" I was brought up," she began, " in a village of the neighborhood of Paris,—in Louveciennes. My mother had put me out to nurse with some honest gardeners, poor, and burdened with a large family. After two months, hearing nothing of my mother, they wrote to her : she made no answer. They then went to Paris, and called at the address she had given them. She had just moved out; and no one knew what had become of her. They could no longer, therefore, expect a single sou for the cares they would bestow upon me. They kept me, nevertheless, thinking that one child the more would not make much difference. I know nothing of my parents, therefore, except what I heard through these kind gardeners; and, as I was still quite young when I had the misfortune to lose them, I have but a very vague remembrance of what they told me. I remember very well, however, that according to their statements, my mother was a young working-woman of rare beauty, and that, very likely, she was not my father's wife. If I was ever told the name of my mother or my father, if I ever knew it, I have quite forgotten it. I had myself no name. My adopted parents called me the Parisian. I was happy, nevertheless, with these kind people, and treated exactly like their own children. In winter, they sent me to school; in summer, I helped weeding the garden. I drove a sheep or two along the road, or else I went to gather violets and strawberries through the woods.

" This was the happiest, indeed, the only happy time of my life, towards which my thoughts may turn when I feel despair and discouragement getting the better of me. Alas! I was but eight, when, within the same week, the gardener and his wife were both carried off by the same disease,—inflammation of the lungs.

" On a freezing December morning, in that house upon which the hand of death had just fallen, we found ourselves, six children, the oldest of whom was not eleven, crying with grief, fright, cold, and hunger.

" Neither the gardener nor his wife had any relatives; and they left nothing but a few wretched pieces of furniture, the sale of which barely sufficed to pay the expenses of their funeral. The two younger children were taken to an asylum: the others were taken charge of by the neighbors.

" It was a laundress of Marly who took me. I was quite tall and strong for my age. She made an apprentice of me. She was not unkind by nature; but she was violent and brutal in the extreme. She compelled me to do an excessive amount of work, and often of a kind above my strength.

" Fifty times a day, I had to go from the river to the house, carrying on my shoulders enormous bundles of wet napkins or sheets, wring them, spread them out, and then run to Rueil to get the soiled clothes from the customers. I did not complain (I was already too proud to complain) ; but, if I was ordered to do something that seemed to me too unjust, I refused obstinately to obey, and then I was unmercifully beaten. In spite of all, I might, perhaps, have become attached to the woman, had she not had the disgusting habit of drinking. Every week regularly, on the day when she took the clothes to Paris (it was on Wednesdays), she came home drunk. And then, according as, with the fumes of the wine, anger or gayety rose to her brain, there were atrocious scenes or obscene jests.

" When she was in that condition, she inspired me with horror. And one Wednesday, as I showed my feelings too plainly, she struck me so hard, that she broke my arm. I had been with her for twenty months. The injury she had done me sobered her at once. She became frightened, overpowered me with caresses, begging me to say nothing to any one. I promised, and kept faithfully my word.

" But a physician had to be called in. There had been witnesses who spoke. The story spread along the river,

as far as Bougival and Rueil. And one morning an officer of gendarmes called at the house; and I don't exactly know what would have happened, if I had not obstinately maintained that I had broken my arm in falling
down stairs."

What surprised Maxence most was Mlle. Lucienne's
simple and natural tone. No emphasis, scarcely an appearance of emotion. One might have thought it was
somebody's else life that she was narrating.

Meantime she was going on,—

" Thanks to my obstinate denials the woman was not
disturbed. But the truth was known; and her reputation,
which was not good before, became altogether bad. I
became an object of interest. The very same people who
had seen me twenty times staggering painfully under a
load of wet clothes, which was terrible, began to pity me
prodigiously because I had had an arm broken, which
was nothing.

" At last a number of our customers arranged to take
me out of a house, in which, they said, I must end by
perishing under bad treatment.

" And, after many fruitless efforts, they discovered,
at last, at La Jonchère, an old Jewess lady, very rich,
and a widow without children, who consented to take
charge of me.

" I hesitated at first to accept these offers; but noticing
that the laundress, since she had hurt me, had conceived
a still greater aversion for me, I made up my mind to
leave her.

" It was on the day when I was introduced to my new
mistress that I first discovered I had no name. After
examining me at length, turning me around and around,
making me walk, and sit down,—

" ' Now,' she inquired, ' what is your name? '

"I stared at her in surprise; for indeed I was then like a savage, not having the slightest notions of the things of life.

"'My name is the Parisian,' I replied.

"She burst out laughing, as also another old lady, a friend of hers, who assisted at my presentation; and I remember that my little pride was quite offended at their hilarity. I thought they were laughing at me.

"'That's not a name,' they said at last. 'That's a nickname.'

"'I have no other.'

"They seemed dumfounded, repeating over and over that such a thing was unheard of; and on the spot they began to look for a name for me.

"'Where were you born!' inquired my new mistress.

"'At Louveciennes.'

"'Very well,' said the other: 'let us call her Louvecienne.'

"A long discussion followed, which irritated me so much that I felt like running away; and it was agreed at last, that I should be called, not Louvecienne, but Lucienne; and Lucienne I have remained.

"There was nothing said about baptism, since my new mistress was a Jewess.

"She was an excellent woman, although the grief she had felt at the loss of her husband had somewhat deranged her faculties.

"As soon as it was decided that I was to remain, she desired to inspect my trousseau. I had none to show her, possessing nothing in the world but the rags on my back. As long as I had remained with the laundress, I had finished wearing out her old dresses; and I had never worn any other under-clothing save that which I

borrowed, 'by authority,' from the clients,—an economical system adopted by many laundresses.

" Dismayed at my state of destitution, my new mistress sent for a seamstress, and at once ordered wherewith to dress and change me.

" Since the death of the poor gardeners, this was the
first time that any one paid any attention to me, except to exact some service of me. I was moved to
tears ; and, in the excess of my gratitude, I would gladly
have died for that kind old lady.

" This feeling gave me the courage and the constancy required to bear with her whimsical nature. She
had singular manias, disconcerting fancies, ridiculous
and often exorbitant exactions. I lent myself to it all as
best I could.

" As she already had two servants, a cook and a
chambermaid, I had myself no special duties in the
house. I accompanied her when she went out riding. I
helped to wait on her at table, and to dress her. I picked
up her handkerchief when she dropped it; and, above
all, I looked for her snuff-box, which she was continually mislaying.

" She was pleased with my docility, took much interest in me, and, that I might read to her, she made
me learn to read, for I hardly knew my letters. And the
old man whom she gave me for a teacher, finding me intelligent, taught me all he knew, I imagine, of French,
of geography, and of history.

" The chambermaid, on the other hand, had been
commissioned to teach me to sew, to embroider, and to
execute all sorts of fancy-work; and she took the more
interest in her lessons, that little by little she shifted
upon me the most tedious part of her work.

" I would have been happy in that pretty house at La Jonchère, if I had only had some society better suited to my age than the old women with whom I was compelled to live, and who scolded me for a loud word or a somewhat abrupt gesture. What would I not have given to have been allowed to play with the young girls whom I saw on Sundays passing in crowds along the road!

" As time went on, my old mistress became more and more attached to me, and endeavored in every way to give me proofs of her affection. I sat at table with her, instead of waiting on her, as at first. She had given me clothes, so that she could take me and introduce me anywhere.

" She went about repeating everywhere that she was as fond of me as of a daughter; that she intended to set me up in life; and that certainly she would leave a part of her fortune to me.

" Alas! She said it too loud, for my misfortune,—so loud, that the news reached at last the ears of some nephews of hers in Paris, who came once in a while to La Jonchère.

" They had never paid much attention to me up to this time. Those speeches opened their eyes: they noticed what progress I had made in the heart of their relative; and their cupidity became alarmed.

" Trembling lest they should lose an inheritance which they considered as theirs, they united against me, determined to put a stop to their aunt's generous intentions by having me sent off.

" But it was in vain, that, for nearly a year, their hatred exhausted itself in skilful manœuvres.

" The instinct of preservation stimulating my perspicacity I had penetrated their intentions, and I was struggling with all my might. Every day, to make myself more indispensable, I invented some novel attention.

"They only came once a week to La Jonchère: I was there all the time. I had the advantage. I struggled successfully, and was probably approaching the end of my troubles, when my poor old mistress was taken sick. After forty-eight hours, she was very low. She was fully conscious, but for that very reason she could appreciate the danger; and the fear of death made her crazy.

"Her nieces had come to sit by her bedside; and I was expressly forbidden to enter the room. They had understood that this was an excellent opportunity to get rid of me forever.

"Evidently gained in advance, the physicians declared to my poor benefactress that the air of La Jonchère was fatal to her, and that her only chance of recovery was to establish herself in Paris. One of her nephews offered to have her taken to his house in a litter. She would soon get well, they said; and she could then go to finish her convalescence in some southern city.

"Her first word was for me. She did not wish to be separated from me, she protested, and insisted absolutely upon taking me with her. Her nephews represented gravely to her that this was an impossibility; that she must not think of burdening herself with me; that the simplest thing was to leave me at La Jonchère; and that, moreover, they would see that I should get a good situation.

"The sick woman struggled for a long time, and with an energy of which I would not have thought her capable.

"But the others were pressing. The physicians kept

repeating that they could not answer for any thing, if she did not follow their advice. She was afraid of death. She yielded, weeping.

" The very next morning, a sort of litter, carried by eight men, stopped in front of the door. My poor mistress was laid into it; and they carried her off, without even permitting me to kiss her for the last time.

" Two hours later, the cook and the chambermaid were dismissed. As to myself, the nephew who had promised to look after me put a twenty-franc-piece in my hand saying, ' Here are your eight days in advance. Pack up your things immediately, and clear out! ' "

It was impossible that Mlle. Lucienne should not be deeply moved whilst thus stirring the ashes of her past. She showed no evidence of it, however, except, now and then, a slight alteration in her voice.

As to Maxence, he would vainly have tried to conceal the passionate interest with which he was listening to these unexpected confidences.

" Have you, then, never seen your benefactress again? " he asked.

" Never," replied Mlle. Lucienne. " All my efforts to reach her have proved fruitless. She does not live in Paris now. I have written to her: my letters have remained without answer. Did she ever get them? I think not. Something tells me that she has not forgotten me."

She remained silent for a few moments, as if collecting herself before resuming the thread of her narrative. And then,—

" It was thus brutally," she resumed, " that I was sent off. It would have been useless to beg, I knew; and, moreover, I have never known how to beg. I piled

up hurriedly in two trunks and in some bandboxes all I
had in the world,—all I had received from the generosity of my poor mistress; and, before the stated hour,
I was ready. The cook and the chambermaid had already gone. The man who was treating me so cruelly
was waiting for me. He helped me carry out my boxes
and trunks, after which he locked the door, put the key
in his pocket; and, as the American omnibus was passing, he beckoned to it to stop.. And then, before entering
it,—

"'Good luck, my pretty girl!' he said with a laugh.

"This was in the month of January, 1866. I was just
thirteen. I have had since more terrible trials, and I
have found myself in much more desperate situations:
but I do not remember ever feeling such intense discouragement as I did that day, when I found myself
alone upon that road, not knowing which way to go.
I sat down on one of my trunks. The weather was cold
and gloomy: there were few persons on the road. They
looked at me, doubtless wondering what I was doing
there. I wept. I had a vague feeling that the well-meant
kindness of my poor benefactress, in bestowing upon
me the blessings of education, would in reality prove a
serious impediment in the life-struggle which I was
about to begin again. I thought of what I suffered with
the laundress; and, at the idea of the tortures which the
future still held in store for me, I desired death. The
Seine was near: why not put an end at once to the miserable existence which I foresaw?

"Such were my reflections, when a woman from
Rueil, a vegetable-vender, whom I knew by sight, happened to pass, pushing her hand-cart before her over
the muddy pavement. She stopped when she saw me;
and, in the softest voice she could command,

" ' What are you doing there, my darling?' she asked.

" In a few words I explained to her my situation. She seemed more surprised than moved.

" ' Such is life,' she remarked,—' sometimes up, sometimes down.'

" And, stepping up nearer,—

" ' What do you expect to do now?' she interrogated in a tone of voice so different from that in which she had spoken at first, that I felt more keenly the horror of my altered situation.

" ' I have no idea,' I replied.

" After thinking for a moment,—

" ' You can't stay there,' she resumed: 'the gend-armes would arrest you. Come with me. We will talk things over at the house; and I'll give you my advice.'

" I was so completely crushed, that I had neither strength nor will. Besides, what was the use of think-ing? Had I any choice of resolutions? Finally, the woman's offer seemed to me a last favor of destiny.

" ' I shall do as you say, madame,' I replied.

" She proceeded at once to load up my little baggage on her cart. We started; and soon we arrived ' home.'

" What she called thus was a sort of cellar, at least twelve inches lower than the street, receiving its only light through the glass door, in which several broken panes had been replaced by sheets of paper. It was re-voltingly filthy, and filled with a sickening odor. On all sides were heaps of vegetables,—cabbages, potatoes, onions. In one corner a nameless heap of decaying rags, which she called her bed; in the centre, a small cast-iron stove, the worn-out pipe of which allowed the smoke to escape in the room.

" ' Anyway,' she said to me, ' you have a home now!'

" I helped her to unload the cart. She filled the stove with coal, and at once declared that she wanted to inspect my things.

" My trunks were opened; and it was with exclamations of surprise that the woman handled my dresses, my skirts, my stockings.

" ' The mischief!' she exclaimed, ' you dressed well, didn't you?'

" Her eyes sparkled so, that a strong feeling of mistrust arose in my mind. She seemed to consider all my property as an unexpected godsend to herself. Her hands trembled as she handled some piece of jewelry; and she took me to the light that she might better estimate the value of my ear-rings.

" And so, when she asked me if I had any money, determined to hide at least my twenty-franc-piece, which was my sole fortune, I replied boldly, ' No.'

" ' That's a pity,' she grumbled.

" But she wished to know my history, and I was compelled to tell it to her. One thing only surprised her,— my age; and in fact, though only thirteen, I looked fully sixteen.

" When I had done,—

" ' Never mind!' she said. ' It was lucky for you that you met me. You are at least certain now of eating every day; for I am going to take charge of you. I am getting old: you'll help me to drag my cart. If you are as smart as you are pretty, we'll make money.'

" Nothing could suit me less. But how could I resist? She threw a few rags upon the floor; and on them I had to sleep. The next day, wearing my meanest dress, and a pair of wooden shoes which she had bought for me, and which bruised my feet horribly, I had to harness myself to the cart by means of a leather strap, which cut

my shoulders and my chest. She was an abominable
creature, that woman; and I soon found out that her
repulsive features indicated but too well her ignoble instincts. After leading a life of vice and shame, she had,
with the approach of old age, fallen into the most abject
poverty, and had adopted the trade of vegetable-vender,
which she carried on just enough to escape absolute
starvation. Enraged at her fate, she found a detestable
pleasure in ill-treating me, or in endeavoring to stain
my imagination by the foulest speeches.

" Ah, if I had only known where to fly, and where
to take refuge! But, abusing my ignorance, that execrable woman had persuaded me, that, if I attempted to go
out alone, I would be arrested. And I knew no one to
whom I could apply for protection and advice. And
then I began to learn that beauty, to a poor girl, is a
fatal gift. One by one, the woman had sold every thing
I had,—dresses, underclothes, jewels; and I was now reduced to rags almost as mean as when I was with the
laundress.

" Every morning, rain or shine, hot or cold, we
started, wheeling our cart from village to village, all
along the Seine, from Courbevoie to Pont-Marly. I
could see no end to this wretched existence, when one
evening the commissary of police presented himself at
our hovel, and ordered us to follow him.

"We were taken to prison; and there I found myself
thrown among some hundred women, whose faces,
words, and gestures frightened me. The vegetable-
woman had committed a theft; and I was accused of
complicity. Fortunately I was easily able to demonstrate
my innocence; and, at the end of two weeks, a jailer
opened the door to me, saying, ' Go: you are free!' "

Maxence understood now the gently ironical smile

with which Mlle. Lucienne had heard him assert that he, too, had been very unhappy. What a life hers had been! And how could such things be within a step of Paris, in the midst of a society which deems its organization too perfect to consent to modify it!

Mlle. Lucienne went on, speaking somewhat faster,—

" I was indeed free; but of what use could my freedom be to me? I knew not which way to go. A mechanical instinct took me back to Rueil. I fancied I would be safer among people who all knew me, and that I might find shelter in our old lodgings. But this last hope was disappointed. Immediately after our arrest, the owner of the building had thrown out every thing it contained, and had rented it to a hideous beggar, who offered me, with a giggle, to become his housekeeper. I ran off as fast as I could.

" The situation was certainly more horrible now than the day when I had been turned out of my benefactress' house. But the eight months I had just spent with the horrible woman had taught me anew how to bear misery, and had nerved up my energy.

" I took out from a fold of my dress, where I had kept it constantly hid, the twenty-franc-piece I had received; and, as I was hungry, I entered a sort of eating and lodging house, where I had occasionally taken a meal. The proprietor was a kind-hearted man. When I had told him my situation, he invited me to remain with him until I could find something better. On Sundays and Mondays the customers were plenty; and he was obliged to take an extra servant. He offered me that work to do, promising, in exchange, my lodging and one meal a day. I accepted. The next day being Sunday, I commenced the arduous duties of a bar-maid in a low drinking house. My *pourboires* amounted sometimes to five or ten francs; I had my board and lodging free; and at the end of three months I had been able to provide myself with some decent clothing, and was commencing to accumulate a little reserve, when the lodging-house keeper, whose business had unexpectedly developed itself to a considerable extent, concluded to engage a man-waiter, and urged me to look elsewhere for work. I did so. An old neighbor of ours told me of a situation at Bougival, where she said I would be very comfortable. Overcoming my repugnance, I applied, and was accepted. I was to get thirty francs a month.

" The place might have been a good one. There were only three in the family,—the gentleman and his wife, and a son of twenty-five. Every morning, father and son left for Paris by the first train, and only came home to dinner at about six o'clock. I was therefore alone all day with the woman. Unfortunately, she was a cross and disagreeable person, who, never having had a servant before, felt an insatiable desire of showing and exercising her authority. She was, moreover, extremely suspicious, and found some pretext to visit regularly my trunks once or twice a week, to see if I had not concealed some of her napkins or silver spoons. Having told her that I had once been a laundress, she made me wash and iron all the clothes in the house, and was forever accusing me of using too much soap and too much coal. Still I liked the place well enough; and I had a little room in the attic, which I thought charming, and where I spent delightful evenings reading or sewing.

" But luck was against me. The young gentleman of the house took a fancy to me, and determined to make me his mistress. I discouraged him in a way; but he persisted in his loathsome attention, until one night he broke into my room, and I was compelled to shout for help with all my might, before I could get rid of him.

"The next day I left that house; but I tried in vain to find another situation in Bougival. I resolved then to seek a place in Paris. I had a big trunk full of good clothes, and about a hundred francs of savings; and I felt no anxiety.

"When I arrived in Paris, I went straight to an intelligence-office. I was extremely well received by a very affable old woman who promised to get me a good place, and, in the mean time, solicited me to board with her. She kept a sort of boarding-house for servants out of place; and there were there some fifty or sixty of us, who slept at night in long dormitories.

"Time went by, and still I did not find that famous place. The board was expensive, too, for my scanty means; and I determined to leave. I started in quest of new lodgings, followed by a porter, carrying my trunk; but as I was crossing the Boulevard, not getting quick enough out of the way of a handsome private carriage which was coming at full trot, I was knocked down, and trampled under the horses's feet."

Without allowing Maxence to interrupt her,—

"I had lost consciousness," went on Mlle. Lucienne. "When I came to my senses, I was sitting in a drug-store; and three or four persons were busy around me. I had no fracture, but only some severe contusions, and a deep cut on the head.

"The physician who had attended me requested me to try and walk; but I could not even stand on my feet. Then he asked me where I lived, that I might be taken there; and I was compelled to own that I was a poor servant out of place, without a home or a friend to care for me.

" ' In that case,' said the doctor to the druggist, ' we must send her to the hospital.'

" And they sent for a cab.

" In the mean time, quite a crowd had gathered outside, and the conduct of the person who was in the carriage that had run over me was being indignantly criticised. It was a woman; and I had caught a glimpse of her at the very moment I was falling under the horses' feet. She had not even condescended to get out of her carriage; but, calling a policeman, she had given him her name and address, adding, loud enough to be heard by the crowd, ' I am in too great a hurry to stop. My coachman is an awkward fellow, whom I shall dismiss as soon as I get home. I am ready to pay any thing that may be asked.'

" She had also sent one of her cards for me. A policeman handed it to me; and I read the name, Baronne de Thaller.

" ' That's lucky for you,' said the doctor. ' That lady is the wife of a very rich banker; and she will be able to help you when you get well.'

" The cab had now come. I was carried into it; and, an hour later, I was admitted at the hospital, and laid on a clean, comfortable bed.

" But my trunk!—my trunk, which contained all my things, all I had in the world, and, worse still, all the money I had left. I asked for it, my heart filled with anxiety. No one had either seen or heard of it. Had the porter missed me in the crowd? or had he basely availed himself of the accident to rob me? This was hard to decide.

" The good sisters promised that they would have it looked after, and that the police would certainly be able to find that man whom I had engaged near the intelligence-office. But all these assurances failed to console me. This blow was the finishing one. I was taken with fever; and for more than two weeks my life was despaired of. I was saved at last: but my convalescence was long and tedious; and for over two months I lingered with alternations of better and of worse.

" Yet such had been my misery for the past two years, that this gloomy stay in a hospital was for me like an oasis in the desert. The good sisters were very kind to me; and, when I was able, I helped them with their lighter work, or went to the chapel with them. I shuddered at the thought that I must leave them as soon as I was entirely well; and then what would become of me? For my trunk had not been found, and I was destitute of all.

" And yet I had, at the hospital, more than one subject for gloomy reflections. Twice a week, on Thursdays and Sundays, visitors were admitted; and there was not on those days a single patient who did not receive a relative or a friend. But I, no one, nothing, never!

" But I am mistaken. I was commencing to get well, when one Sunday I saw by my bedside an old man, dressed all in black, of alarming appearance, wearing blue spectacles, and holding under his arm an enormous portfolio, crammed full of papers.

" ' You are Mlle. Lucienne, I believe,' he asked.

" ' Yes,' I replied, quite surprised.

" ' You are the person who was knocked down by a carriage on the corner of the Boulevard and the Faubourg St. Martin?'

" ' Yes sir.'

" ' Do you know whose equipage that was?'

" ' The Baronne de Thaller's, I was told.'

" He seemed a little surprised, but at once,—

" ' Have you seen that lady, or caused her to be seen in your behalf ? '

" ' No.'

" ' Have you heard from her in any manner ? '

" ' No.'

" A smile came back upon his lips.

" ' Luckily for you I am here,' he said. ' Several times already I have called; but you were too unwell to hear me. Now that you are better, listen.'

" And thereupon, taking a chair, he commenced to explain his profession to me.

" He was a sort of broker; and accidents were his specialty. As soon as one took place, he was notified by some friends of his at police headquarters. At once he started in quest of the victim, overtook her at home or at the hospital, and offered his services. For a moderate commission he undertook, if needs be, to recover damages. He commenced suit when necessary; and, if he thought the case tolerably safe, he made advances. He stated, for instance, that my case was a plain one, and that he would undertake to obtain four or five thousand francs, at least, from Mme. de Thaller. All he wanted was my power of attorney. But, in spite of his pressing instances, I declined his offers; and he withdrew, very much displeased, assuring me that I would soon repent.

" Upon second thought, indeed, I regretted to have followed the first inspiration of my pride, and the more so, that the good sisters whom I consulted on the subject told me that I was wrong, and that my reclamation would be perfectly proper. At their suggestion, I then adopted another line of conduct, which, they thought, would as surely bring about the same result.

" As briefly as possible, I wrote out the history of

my life from the day I had been left with the gardeners
at Louveciennes. I added to it a faithful account of my
present situation; and I addressed the whole to Mme.
de Thaller.

"'You'll see if she don't come before a day or two,'
said the sisters.

"They were mistaken. Mme. de Thaller came neither
the next nor the following days; and I was still awaiting
her answer, when, one morning, the doctor announced
that I was well enough to leave the hospital.

"I cannot say that I was very sorry. I had lately
made the acquaintance of a young workwoman, who had
been sent to the hospital in consequence of a fall, and
who occupied the bed next to mine. She was a girl of
about twenty, very gentle, very obliging, and whose
amiable countenance had attracted me from the first.

"Like myself, she had no parents. But she was rich,
very rich. She owned the furniture of the room, a
sewing-machine, which had cost her three hundred
francs, and, like a true child of Paris, she understood
five or six trades, the least lucrative of which yielded
her twenty-five or thirty cents a day. In less than a
week, we had become good friends; and, when she left
the hospital,—

"'Believe me,' she said: 'when you come out yourself, don't waste your time looking for a place. Come
to me: I can accommodate you. I'll teach you what I
know; and, if you are industrious, you'll make your
living, and you'll be free.'

"It was to her room that I went straight from the
hospital, carrying, tied in a handkerchief, my entire baggage,—one dress, and a few undergarments that the
good sisters had given me.

"She received me like a sister, and after showing

me her lodging, two little attic-rooms shining with cleanliness,—

"'You'll see,' she said, kissing me, 'how happy we'll
be here.'"

It was getting late. M. Fortin had long ago come
up and put out the gas on the stairs. One by one, every
noise had died away in the hotel. Nothing now disturbed the silence of the night save the distant sound of
some belated cab on the Boulevard. But neither Maxence nor Mlle. Lucienne were noticing the flight of
time, so interested were they, one in telling, and the other
in listening to, this story of a wonderful existence.
However, Mlle. Lucienne's voice had become hoarse
with fatigue. She poured herself a glass of water,
which she emptied at a draught, and then at once,—

"Never yet," she resumed, "had I been agitated by
such a sweet sensation. My eyes were full of tears;
but they were tears of gratitude and joy. After so
many years of isolation, to meet with such a friend, so
generous, and so devoted: it was like finding a family.
For a few weeks, I thought that fate had relented at
last. My friend was an excellent workwoman; but
with some intelligence, and the will to learn, I soon knew
as much as she did.

"There was plenty of work. By working twelve
hours, with the help of the thrice-blessed sewing-machine, we succeeded in making six, seven, and even
eight francs a day. It was a fortune.

"Thus several months elapsed in comparative comfort.

"Once more I was afloat, and I had more clothes than
I had lost in my trunk. I liked the life I was leading;
and I would be leading it still, if my friend had not one
day fallen desperately in love with a young man she had

met at a ball. I disliked him very much, and took no trouble to conceal my feelings : nevertheless, my friend imagined that I had designs upon him, and became fiercely jealous of me. Jealousy does not reason ; and I soon understood that we would no longer be able to live in common, and that I must look elsewhere for shelter. But my friend gave me no time to do so.

"Coming home one Monday night at about eleven, she notified me to clear out at once. I attempted to expostulate : she replied with abuse. Rather than enter upon a degrading struggle, I yielded, and went out.

"That night I spent on a chair in a neighbor's room. But the next day, when I went for my things, my former friend refused to give them, and presumed to keep every thing. I was compelled, though reluctantly, to resort to the intervention of the commissary of police.

"I gained my point. But the good days had gone. Luck did not follow me to the wretched furnished house where I hired a room. I had no sewing-machine, and but few acquaintances. By working fifteen or sixteen hours a day, I made thirty or forty cents. That was not enough to live on. Then work failed me altogether, and, piece by piece, every thing I had went to the pawn-broker's. On a gloomy December morning, I was turned out of my room, and left on the pavement with a ten-cent-piece for my fortune.

"Never had I been so low ; and I know not to what extremities I might have come at last, when I happened to think of that wealthy lady whose horses had upset me on the Boulevard. I had kept her card. Without hesitation, I went into a grocery, and calling for some paper and a pen, I wrote, overcoming the last struggle of my pride,—

"'Do you remember, madame, a poor girl whom

your carriage came near crushing to death? Once before she applied to you, and received no answer. She
is to-day without shelter and without bread; and you are
her supreme hope.'

"I placed these few lines in an envelope, and ran to
the address indicated on the card. It was a magnificent
residence, with a vast court-yard in front. In the porter's lodge, five or six servants were talking as I came
in, and looked at me impudently, from head to foot,
when I requested them to take my letter to Mme. de
Thaller. One of them, however, took pity on me,—

"'Come with me,' he said, 'come along!'

"He made me cross the yard, and enter the vestibule;
and then,—

"'Give me your letter,' he said, 'and wait here for
me.'"

Maxence was about to express the thoughts which
Mme. de Thaller's name naturally suggested to his
mind, but Mlle. Lucienne interrupted him,—

"In all my life," she went on, "I had never seen any
thing so magnificent as that vestibule with its tall columns, its tessellated floor, its large bronze vases filled
with the rarest flowers, and its red velvet benches, upon
which tall footmen in brilliant livery were lounging.

"I was, I confess, somewhat intimidated by all of
this splendor; and I remained awkwardly standing,
when suddenly the servants stood up respectfully.

"A door had just opened, through which appeared
a man already past middle age, tall, thin, dressed in the
extreme of fashion, and wearing long red whiskers falling over his chest."

"The Baron de Thaller," murmured Maxence.

Mlle. Lucienne took no notice of the interruption.

"The attitude of the servants," she went on, "had

made me easily guess that he was the master. I was bowing to him, blushing and embarrassed, when, noticing me, he stopped short, shuddering from head to foot.

" ' Who are you? ' he asked me roughly.

" I attributed his manner to the sad condition of my dress, which appeared more miserable and more dilapidated still amid the surrounding splendors; and, in a scarcely intelligible voice, I began,—

" ' I am a poor girl, sir '—

" But he interrupted me.

" ' To the point! What do you want? '

" ' I am awaiting an answer, sir, to a request which I have just forwarded to the baroness.'

" ' What about? '

" ' Once sir, I was run over in the street by the baroness's carriage: I was severely wounded, and had to be taken to the hospital.'

" I fancied there was something like terror in the man's look.

" ' It is you, then, who once before sent a long letter to my wife, in which you told the story of your life? '

" ' Yes, sir, it was I. '

" ' You stated in that letter that you had no parents, having been left by your mother with some gardeners at Louveciennes? '

" ' That is the truth.'

" ' What has become of these gardeners? '

" ' They are dead.'

" ' What was your mother's name? '

" ' I never knew.'

" To M. de Thaller's first surprise had succeeded a feeling of evident irritation; but, the more haughty and brutal his manners, the cooler and the more self-possessed I became.

" ' And you are soliciting assistance ? ' he said.

" I drew myself up, and, looking at him straight in the eyes,—

" ' I beg your pardon,' I replied: ' it is a legitimate indemnity which I claim.'

" Indeed, it seemed to me that my firmness alarmed him. With a feverish haste, he began to feel in his pockets. He took out their contents of gold and bank-notes all in a heap, and, thusting it into my hands without counting,—

" ' Here,' he said, ' take this. Are you satisfied ? '

" I observed to him, that, having sent a letter to Mme. de Thaller, it would perhaps be proper to await her answer. But he replied that it was not necessary, and, pushing me towards the door,—

" ' You may depend upon it,' he said, ' I shall tell my wife that I saw you.'

" I started to go out; but I had not gone ten steps across the yard, when I heard him crying excitedly to his servants,—

" ' You see that beggar, don't you? Well, the first one who allows her to cross the threshold of my door shall be turned out on the instant.'

" A beggar, I! Ah the wretch! I turned round to cast his alms into his face; but already he had disappeared, and I only found before me the footman, chuckling stupidly.

" I went out; and, as my anger gradually passed off, I felt thankful that I had been unable to follow the dictates of my wounded pride.

" ' Poor girl,' I thought to myself, ' where would you be at this hour? You would only have to select between suicide and the vilest existence; whereas now you are above want.'

" I was passing before a small restaurant. I went
in; for I was very hungry, having, so to speak, eaten
nothing for several days past. Besides, I felt anxious
to count my treasure. The Baron de Thaller had given
me nine hundred and thirty francs.

" This sum, which exceeded the utmost limits of my
ambition, seemed inexhaustible to me: I was dazzled
by its possession.

" ' And yet,' I thought, ' had M. de Thaller happened
to have ten thousand francs in his pockets he would
have given them to me all the same.'

" I was at a loss to explain this strange generosity.
Why his surprise when he first saw me, then his anger,
and his haste to get rid of me? How was it that a man
whose mind must be filled with the gravest cares had
so distinctly remembered me, and the letter I had written to his wife? Why, after showing himself so generous, had he so strictly excluded me from his house?

" After vainly trying for some time to solve this rid-
dle, I concluded that I must be the victim of my own imagination; and I turned my attention to making the
best possible use of my sudden fortune. On the same
day, I took a little room in the Faubourg St. Denis; and
I bought myself a sewing-machine. Before the week
was over, I had work before me for several months. Ah!
this time it seemed indeed that I had nothing more to
apprehend from destiny; and I looked forward, without fear, to the future. At the end of a month, I was
earning four to five francs a day, when, one afternoon,
a stout man, very well dressed, looking honest and good-
natured, and speaking French with some difficulty,
made his appearance at my room. He was an American,
he stated, and had been sent to me by the woman for
whom I worked. Having need of a skilled Parisian

work-woman, he came to propose to me to follow him to New York, where he would insure me a brilliant position.

" But I knew several poor girls, who, on the faith of dazzling promises, had expatriated themselves. Once abroad, they had been shamefully abandoned, and had been driven, to escape starvation, to resort to the vilest expedients. I refused, therefore, and frankly gave him my reasons for doing so.

" My visitor at once protested indignantly. Whom did I take him for? It was a fortune that I was refusing. He guaranteed me in New York board, lodging, and two hundred francs a month. He would pay all travelling and moving expenses. And, to prove to me the fairness of his intentions, he was ready, he said, to sign an agreement, and pay me a thousand down.

" These offers were so brilliant, that I was staggered in my resolution.

" ' Well,' I said, ' give me twenty-four hours to decide. I wish to see my employer.'

" He seemed very much annoyed; but, as I remained firm in my purpose, he left, promising to return the next day to receive my final answer.

" I ran at once to my employer. She did not know what I was talking about. She had sent no one, and was not acquainted with any American.

" Of course, I never saw him again; and I couldn't help thinking of this singular adventure, when, one evening during the following week, as I was coming home at about eleven o'clock, two policemen arrested me, and, in spite of my earnest protestations, took me to the station-house, where I was locked up with a dozen unfortunates who had just been taken up on the Boulevards. I spent the night crying with shame and anger; and I don't know what would have become of me, if the justice of the peace, who examined me the next morning, had not happened to be a just and kind man. As soon as I had explained to him that I was the victim of a most humiliating error, he sent an agent in quest of information, and having satisfied himself that I was an honest girl, working for my living, he discharged me. But, before permitting me to go,—

" ' Beware, my child,' he said to me : ' it is upon a formal and well-authenticated declaration that you were arrested. Therefore you must have enemies. People have an interest in getting rid of you ' "

Mademoiselle Lucienne was evidently almost exhausted with fatigue : her voice was failing her. But it was in vain that Maxence begged her to take a few moments of rest.

" No," she answered, " I'd rather get through as quick as possible."

And, making an effort, she resumed her narrative, hurrying more and more.

" I returned home, my mind all disturbed by the judge's warnings. I am no coward ; but it is a terrible thing to feel one's self incessantly threatened by an unknown and mysterious danger, against which nothing can be done.

" In vain did I search my past life : I could think of no one who could have any interest in effecting my ruin. Those alone have enemies who have had friends. I had never had but one friend, the kind-hearted girl who had turned me out of her home in a fit of absurd jealousy. But I knew her well enough to knew that she was incapable of malice, and that she must long since have forgotten the unlucky cause of our rupture.

" Weeks after weeks.passed without any new incident.

I had plenty of work and was earning enough money to begin saving. So I felt comfortable, laughed at my former fears, and neglected the precautions which I had taken at first; when, one evening, my employer, having a very important and pressing order, sent for me. We did not get through our work until long after midnight.

"She wished me to spend the rest of the night with her; but it would have been necessary to make up a bed for me, and disturb the whole household.

"'Bash!' I said, 'this will not be the first time I cross Paris in the middle of the night.'

"I started; and I was going along, walking as fast as I could, when, from the angle of a dark, narrow street, a man sprang upon me, threw me down, struck me, and would doubtless have killed me, but for two brave gentlemen who heard my screams and rushed to my assistance. The man ran off; and I was able to walk the rest of the way home, having received but a very slight wound.

"But the very next morning I ran to see my friend, the justice of the peace. He listened to me gravely, and, when I had concluded,—

"'How were you dressed?' he inquired.

"'All in black,' I replied, 'very modestly, like a workwoman.'

"'Had you nothing on your person that could tempt a thief?'

"'Nothing. No watch-chain, no jewelry, no earrings even.'

"'Then,' he uttered, knitting his brows, 'it is not a fortuitous crime: it is another attempt on the part of your enemies.'

"Such was also my opinion. And yet—

"'But, sir,' I exclaimed, 'who can have any interest

to destroy me,—a poor obscure girl as I am? I have
thought carefully and well, and I have not a single enemy that I can think of.' And, as I had full confidence in
his kindness, I went on telling him the story of my life.

" ' You are a natural child,' he said as soon as I had
done, ' and you have been basely abandoned. That
fact alone would be sufficient to justify every supposi-
tion. You do not know your parents; but it is quite
possible that *they* may know you, and that they may
never have lost sight of you. Your mother was a working-girl, you think? That may be. But your father?
Do you know what interests your existence may
threaten? Do you know what elaborate edifice of falsehood and infamy your sudden appearance might tumble
to the ground?'

" I was listening dumfounded.

" Never had such conjectures crossed my mind; and,
whilst I doubted their probability, I had, at least, to admit their possibility.

" ' What must I do, then?' I inquired.

The peace-officer shook his head.

" ' Indeed, my poor child, I hardly know what to
advise. The police is not omnipotent. It can do nothing to anticipate a crime conceived in the brain of an
unknown scoundrel.'

" I was terrified. He saw it, and took pity on me.

" ' In your place,' he added, ' I would change my
domicile. You might, perhaps, thus make them lose
your track. And, above all, do not fail to give me your
new address. Whatever I can do to protect you, and insure your safety, I shall do.'

" That excellent man has kept his word; and once
again I owed my safety to him. 'Tis he who is now commissary of police in this district, and who protected me

against Mme. Fortin. I hastened to follow his advice, and two days later I had hired the room in this house in which I am still living. In order to avoid every chance of discovery, I left my employer, and requested her to say, if any one came to inquire after me, that I had gone to America.

" I soon found work again in a very fashionable dress-making establishment, the name of which you must have heard,—Van Klopen's. Unfortunately, war had just been declared. Every day announced a new defeat. The Prussians were coming; then the siege began. Van Klopen had closed his shop, and left Paris. I had a few savings, thank heaven; and I husbanded them as carefully as shipwrecked mariners do their last ration of food, when I unexpectedly found some work.

" It was one Sunday, and I had gone out to see some battalions of National Guards passing along the Boulevard, when suddenly I saw one of the *vivandières,* who was marching behind the band, stop, and run towards me with open arms. It was my old friend from the Batignolles, who had recognized me. She threw her arms around my neck, and, as we had at once become the centre of a group of at least five hundred idlers,—

" ' I must speak to you,' she said. ' If you live in the neighborhood, let's go to your room. The service can wait.'

" I brought her here; and at once she commenced to excuse herself for her past conduct, begging me to restore her my friendship. As I expected, she had long since forgotten the young man, cause of our rupture. But she was now in love, and seriously this time, she declared, with a furniture-maker, who was a captain in the National Guards. It was through him that she had become a *vivandière* ; and she offered me a similar position, if I wished it. But I did not wish it; and, as I was complaining that I could find no work, she swore that she would get me some through her captain, who was a very influential man.

"Through him, I did in fact obtain a few dozen jackets to make. This work was very poorly paid; but the little I earned was that much less to take from my humble resources. In that way I managed to get through the siege without suffering too much.

"After the armistice, unfortunately, M. Van Klopen had not yet returned. I was unable to procure any work; my resources were exhausted; and I would have starved during the Commune, but for my old friend, who several times brought me a little money, and some provisions. Her captain was now a colonel, and was about to become a member of the government; at least, so she assured me. The entrance of the troops into Paris put an end to her dream. One night she came to me livid with fright. She supposed herself gravely compromised, and begged me to hide her. For four days she remained with me. On the fifth, just as we were sitting down to dinner, my room was invaded by a number of police-agents, who showed us an order of arrest, and commanded us to follow them.

"My friend sank down upon a chair, stupid with fright. But I retained my presence of mind, and persuaded one of the agents to go and notify my friend the justice. He happened luckily to be at home, and at once hastened to my assistance. He could do nothing, however, for the moment; the agents having positive orders to take us straight to Versailles.

"'Well,' said he, 'I shall accompany you.'

"From the very first steps he took the next morning, he discovered that my position was indeed grave.

But he also and very clearly recognized a new device of the enemy to bring about my destruction. The information filed against me stated that I had remained in the service of the Commune to the last moment; that I had been seen behind the barricades with a gun in my hand; and that I had formed one of a band of vile incendiaries. This infamous scheme had evidently been suggested by my relations with my friend from the Batignolles, who was still more terribly compromised than she thought, the poor girl; her colonel having been captured, and convicted of pillage and murder, and herself charged with complicity.

"Isolated as I was, without resources, and without relatives, I would certainly have perished, but for the devoted efforts of my friend the justice, whose official position gave him access everywhere, and enabled him to reach my judges. He succeeded in demonstrating my entire innocence; and after forty-eight hours' detention, which seemed an age to me, I was set at liberty.

"At the door, I found the man who had just saved me. He was waiting for me, but would not suffer me to express the gratitude with which my heart overflowed.

"'You will thank me,' he said, 'when I have deserved it better. I have done nothing as yet that any honest man wouldn't have done in my place. What I wish is to discover what interests you are threatening without knowing it, and which must be considerable, if I may judge by the passion and the tenacity of those who are pursuing you. What I desire to do is to lay hands upon the cowardly rascals in whose way you seem to stand.'

"I shook my head.

"'You will not succeed,' I said to him.

" ' Who knows? I've done harder things than that in my life.'

" And taking a large envelope from his pocket,—

" ' This,' he said, ' is the letter which caused your arrest. I have examined it attentively; and I am certain that the handwriting is not disguised. That's something to start with, and may enable me to verify my suspicions, should any occur to my mind. In the mean time, return quietly to Paris, resume your ordinary occupations, answer vaguely any questions that may be asked about this matter, and above all, never mention my name. Remain at the Hôtel des Folies: it is in my district, in my legitimate sphere of action; besides, the proprietors are in a position where they dare not disobey my orders. Never come to my office, unless something grave and unforeseen should occur. Our chances of success would be seriously compromised, if they could suspect the interest I take in your welfare. Keep your eyes open on every thing that is going on around you, and, if you notice any thing suspicious, write to me. I will myself organize a secret surveillance around you. If I can bag one of the rascals who are watching you, that's all I want.

" ' And now,' added this good man, ' good-by. Patience and courage.'

" Unfortunately he had not thought of offering me a little money: I had not dared to ask him for any, and I had but eight sous left. It was on foot, therefore, that I was compelled to return to Paris.

" Mme. Fortin received me with open arms. With me returned the hope of recovering the hundred and odd francs which I owed her, and which she had given up for lost. Moreover, she had excellent news for me. M.

Van Klopen had sent for me during my absence, requesting me to call at his shop. Tired as I was, I went
to see him at once. I found him very much downcast
by the poor prospects of business. Still he was determined to go on, and offered to employ me, not as workwoman, as heretofore, but to try on garments for customers, at a salary of one hundred and twenty francs a
month. I was not in a position to be very particular.
I accepted; and there I am still.

"Every morning, when I get to the shop, I take off
this simple costume, and I put on a sort of livery that
belongs to M. Van Klopen,—wide skirts, and a black
silk dress.

"Then whenever a customer comes who wants a
cloak, a mantle, or some other ' wrapping,' I step up,
and put on the garment, that the purchaser may see how
it looks. I have to walk, to turn around, sit down, etc.
It is absurdly ridiculous, often humiliating; and many a
time, during the first days, I felt tempted to give back
to M. Van Klopen his black silk dress.

"But the conjectures of my friend the peace-officer
were constantly agitating my brain. Since I thought I
had discovered a mystery in my existence, I indulged in
all sorts of fancies, and was momentarily expecting
some extraordinary occurrence, some compensation of
destiny. And I remained.

"But I was not yet at the end of my troubles."

Since she had been speaking of M. Van Klopen, Mlle.
Lucienne seemed to have lost her tone of haughty assurance and imperturbable coolness; and it was with a look
of mingled confusion and sadness that she went on.

"What I was doing at Van Klopen's was exceedingly
painful to me; and yet he very soon asked me to do
something more painful still. Gradually Paris was fill-

ing up again. The hotels had re-opened; foreigners
were pouring in; and the Bois Boulogne was resuming
its wonted animation. Still but few orders came in, and
those for dresses of the utmost simplicity, of dark color
and plain material, on which it was hard to make twenty-
five per cent profit. Van Klopen was disconsolate. He
kept speaking to me of the good old days, when some
of his customers spent as much as thirty thousand francs
a month for dresses and trifles, until one day,—

" ' You are the only one,' he told me, ' who can help
me out just now. You are really good looking; and I
am sure that in full dress, spread over the cushions of
a handsome carriage, you would create quite a sensation,
and that all the rest of the women would be jealous of
you, and would wish to look like you. There needs but
one, you know, to give the good example.' "

Maxence started up suddenly, and, striking his head
with hand,—

" Ah, I understand now ! " he exclaimed.

" I thought that Van Klopen was jesting." went on
the young girl. " But he had never been more in earnest; and, to prove it, he commenced explaining to me
what he wanted. He proposed to get up for me some of
those costumes which are sure to attract attention; and
two or three times a week he would send me a fine carriage, and I would go and show myself in the Bois.

" I felt disgusted at the proposition.

" ' Never ! ' I said.

" ' Why not ? '

" ' Because I respect myself too much to make a living advertisement of myself.'

" He shrugged his shoulders.

" ' You are wrong,' he said. ' You are not rich, and
I would give you twenty francs for each ride. At the

rate of eight rides a month, it would be one hundred and sixty francs added to your wages. Besides,' he added with a wink, ' it would be an excellent opportunity to make your fortune. Pretty as you are, who knows but what some millionaire might take a fancy to you!'

" I felt indignant.

" ' For that reason alone, if for no other,' I exclaimed, ' I refuse.'

" ' You are a little fool,' he replied. ' If you do not accept, you cease being in my employment. Reflect!'

" My mind was already made up, and I was thinking of looking out for some other occupation, when I received a note from my friend the peace-officer, requesting me to call at his office.

" I did so, and, after kindly inviting me to a seat,—

" ' Well,' he said, ' what is there new?'

" ' Nothing. I have noticed no one watching me.'

" He looked annoyed.

" ' My agents have not detected any thing, either,' he grumbled. ' And yet it is evident that your enemies cannot have given it up so. They are sharp ones: if they keep quiet, it is because they are preparing some good trick. What it is I must and shall find out. Already I have an idea which would be an excellent one, if I could discover some way of throwing you among what is called good society.'

" I explained to him, that, being employed at Van Klopen's, I had an opportunity to see there many ladies of the best society.

" ' That is not enough,' he said.

" Then M. Van Klopen's propositions came back to my mind, and I stated them to him.

" ' Just the thing!' he exclaimed, starting upon his

chair: ' a manifest proof that luck is with us. You must accept.'

"I felt bound to tell him my objections, which reflection had much increased.

"'I know but too well,' I said, 'what must happen if I accept this odious duty. Before I have been four times to the Bois, I shall be noticed, and every one will imagine that they know for what purpose I come there. I shall be assailed with vile offers. True, I have no fears for myself. I shall always be better guarded by my pride than by the most watchful of parents. But my reputation will be lost.'

"I failed to convince him.

"'I know very well that you are an honest girl,' he said to me; 'but, for that very reason, what do you care what all these people will think, whom you do not know? Your future is at stake. I repeat it, you must accept.'

"'If you command me to do so,' I said.

"'Yes, I command you; and I'll explain to you why.'"

For the first time, Mlle. Lucienne manifested some reticence, and omitted to repeat the explanations of the peace-officer. And, after a few moments' pause,—

"You know the rest, neighbor," she said, "since you have seen me yourself in that inept and ridiculous *rôle* of living advertisement, of fashionable lay-figure; and the result has been just as I expected. Can you find any one who believes in my honesty of purpose? You have heard Mme. Fortin to-night? Yourself, neighbor—what did you take me for? And yet you should have noticed something of my suffering and my humiliation the day that you were watching me so closely in the Bois de Boulogne."

"What!" exclaimed Maxence with a start, "you know?"

"Have I not just told you that I always fear being watched and followed, and that I am always on the look-out? Yes, I know that you tried to discover the secret of my rides."

Maxence tried to excuse himself.

"That will do for the present," she uttered. "You wish to be my friend, you say? Now that you know my whole life almost as well as I do myself, reflect, and to-morrow you will tell me the result of your thoughts."

Whereupon she went out.

XXVIII.

FOR about a minute Maxence remained stupefied at this sudden *dénouement;* and, when he had recovered his presence of mind and his voice, Mlle. Lucienne had disappeared, and he could hear her bolting her door, and striking a match against the wall.

He might also have thought that he was awaking from a dream, had he not had, to attest the reality, the vague perfume which filled his room, and the light shawl, which Mlle. Lucienne wore as she came in, and which she had forgotten, on a chair.

The night was almost ended: six o'clock had just struck. Still he did not feel in the least sleepy. His head was heavy, his temples throbbing, his eyes smarting. Opening his window, he leaned out to breathe the morning air. The day was dawning pale and cold. A furtive and livid light glanced along the damp walls of the narrow court of the Hôtel des Folies, as at the bottom of a well. Already arose those confused noises

which announce the waking of Paris, and above which
can be heard the sonorous rolling of the milkmen's carts,
the loud slamming of doors, and the sharp sound of
hurrying steps on the hard pavement.

But soon Maxence felt a chill coming over him. He
closed the window, threw some wood in the chimney,
and stretched himself on his chair, his feet towards the
fire. It was a most serious event which had just occurred in his existence; and, as much as he could, he
endeavored to measure its bearings, and to calculate its
consequences in the future.

He kept thinking of the story of that strange girl, her
haughty frankness when unrolling certain phases of her
life, of her wonderful impassibility, and of the implacable contempt for humanity which her every word betrayed. Where had she learned that dignity, so simple
and so noble, that measured speech, that admirable respect of herself, which had enabled her to pass through
so much filth without receiving a stain?

"What a woman!" he thought.

Before knowing her, he loved her. Now he was convulsed by one of those exclusive passions which master
the whole being. Already he felt himself so much under
the charm, subjugated, dominated, fascinated; he understood so well that he was going to cease being his own
master; that his free will was about escaping from him;
that he would be in Mlle. Lucienne's hands like wax
under the modeller's fingers; he saw himself so thoroughly at the discretion of an energy superior to his
own, that he was almost frightened.

"It's my whole future that I am going to risk," he
thought.

And there was no middle path. Either he must fly at
once, without waiting for Mlle. Lucienne to awake, fly

without looking behind, or else stay, and then accept all the chances of an incurable passion for a woman who, perhaps, might never care for him. And he remained wavering, like the traveller who finds himself at the intersection of two roads, and, knowing that one leads to the goal, and the other to an abyss, hesitates which to take.

With this difference, however, that if the traveller errs, and discovers his error, he is always free to retrace his steps; whereas man, in life, can never return to his starting-point. Every step he takes is final; and if he has erred, if he has taken the fatal road, there is no remedy.

"Well, no matter!" exclaimed Maxence. "It shall not be said that through cowardice I have allowed that happiness to escape which passes within my reach. I shall stay." And at once he began to examine what reasonably he might expect; for there was no mistaking Mlle. Lucienne's intentions. When she had said, "Do you wish to be friends?" she had meant exactly that, and nothing else,—friends, and only friends.

"And yet," thought Maxence, "if I had not inspired her with a real interest, would she have so wholly confided unto me? She is not ignorant of the fact that I love her; and she knows life too well to suppose that I will cease to love her when she has allowed me a certain amount of intimacy."

His heart filled with hope at the idea.

"My mistress," he thought, "never, evidently, but my wife. Why not?"

But the very next moment he became a prey to the bitterest discouragement. He thought that perhaps Mlle. Lucienne might have some capital interest in thus making a confidant of him. She had not told him the explanation given her by the peace-officer. Had she not, perhaps, succeeded in lifting a corner of the veil which covered the secret of her birth? Was she on the track of her enemies? and had she discovered the motive of their animosity?

"Is it possible," thought Maxence, "that I should be but one of the powers in the game she is playing? How do I know, that, if she wins, she will not cast me off?"

In the midst of these thoughts, he had gradually fallen asleep, murmuring to the last the name of Lucienne.

The creaking of his opening door woke him up suddenly. He started to his feet, and met Mlle. Lucienne coming in.

"How is this?" said she. "You did not go to bed?"

"You recommended me to reflect," he replied. "I've been reflecting."

He looked at his watch: it was twelve o'clock.

"Which, however," he added, "did not keep me from going to sleep."

All the doubts that besieged him at the moment when he had been overcome by sleep now came back to his mind with painful vividness.

"And not only have I been sleeping," he went on, "but I have been dreaming too."

Mlle. Lucienne fixed upon him her great black eyes.

"Can you tell me your dream?" she asked.

He hesitated. Had he had but one minute to reflect, perhaps he would not have spoken; but he was taken unawares.

"I dreamed," he replied, "that we were friends in the noblest and purest acceptance of that word. Intelligence, heart, will, all that I am, and all that I can,— I laid every thing at your feet. You accepted the most entire devotion the most respectful and the most tender

that man is capable of. Yes, we were friends indeed;
and upon a glimpse of love, never expressed, I planned
a whole future of love." He stopped.

" Well? " she asked.

" Well, when my hopes seemed on the point of being
realized, it happened that the mystery of your birth was
suddenly revealed to you. You found a noble, powerful,
and wealthy family. You resumed the illustrious name
of which you had been robbed; your enemies were
crushed; and your rights were restored to you. It was
no longer Van Klopen's hired carriage that stopped in
front of the Hôtel des Folies, but a carriage bearing
a gorgeous coat of arms. That carriage was yours;
and it came to take you to your own residence in the
Faubourg St. Germain, or to your ancestral manor."

" And yourself? " inquired the girl.

Maxence repressed one of those nervous spasms which
frequently break out in tears, and, with a gloomy look,—

" I," he answered, " standing on the edge of the pavement, I waited for a word or a look from you. You had
forgotten my very existence. Your coachman whipped
his horses; they started at a gallop; and soon I lost sight
of you. And then a voice, the inexorable voice of fate,
cried to me, ' Never more shalt thou see her! ' "

With a superb gesture Mlle. Lucienne drew herself
up.

" It is not with your heart, I trust, that you judge
me, M. Maxence Favoral," she uttered.

He trembled lest he had offended her.

" I beseech you," he began.

But she went on in a voice vibrating with emotion,—

" I am not of those who basely deny their past. Your
dream will never be realized. Those things are only

seen on the stage. If it did realize itself, however, if the carriage with the coat-of-arms did come to the door, the companion of the evil days, the friend who offered me his month's salary to pay my debt, would have a seat by my side."

That was more happiness than Maxence would have dared to hope for. He tried, in order to express his gratitude, to find some of those words which always seem to be lacking at the most critical moments. But he was suffocating; and the tears, accumulated by so many successive emotions, were rising to his eyes.

With a passionate impulse, he seized Mlle. Lucienne's hand, and, taking it to his lips, he covered it with kisses.

Gently but resolutely she withdrew her hand, and, fixing upon him her beautiful clear gaze,—

" Friends," she uttered.

Her accent alone would have been sufficient to dissipate the presumptuous illusions of Maxence, had he had any. But he had none.

" Friends only," he replied, " until the day when you shall be my wife. You cannot forbid me to hope. You love no one? "

" No one."

" Well since we are going to tread the path of life, let me think that we may find love at some turn of the road."

She made no answer. And thus was sealed between them a treaty of friendship, to which they were to remain so strictly faithful, that the word " love " never once rose to their lips.

In appearance there was no change in their mode of life.

Every morning, at seven o'clock, Mlle. Lucienne went

to M. Van Klopen's, and an hour later Maxence started
for his office. They returned home at night, and spent
their evenings together by the fireside.

But what was easy to foresee now took place.

Weak and undecided by nature, Maxence began very
soon to feel the influence of the obstinate and energetic
character of the girl. She infused, as it were, in his
veins, a warmer and more generous blood. Gradually
she imbued him with her ideas, and from her own will
gave him one.

He had told her in all sincerity his history, the mis-
eries of his home, M. Favoral's parsimony and exaggerated severity, his mother's resigned timidity, and Mlle.
Gilberte's resolute nature.

He had concealed nothing of his past life, of his er-
rors and his follies, confessing even the worst of his actions; as, for instance, having abused his mother's and
sister's affection to extort from them all the money they
earned.

He had admitted to her that it was only with great
reluctance and under pressure of necessity, that he
worked at all; that he was far from being rich; that although he took his dinner with his parents, his salary
barely sufficed for his wants; and that he had debts.

He hoped, however, he added, that it would not be
always thus, and that, sooner or later, he would see the
termination of all this misery and privation; for his
father had at least fifty thousand francs a year and some
day he must be rich.

Far from smiling, Mlle. Lucienne frowned at such a
prospect.

" Ah! your father is a millionaire, is he? " she interrupted. " Well, I understand now how, at twenty-five,
after refusing all the positions which have been offered

to you, you have no position. You relied on your father, instead of relying on yourself. Judging that he worked hard enough for two, you bravely folded your arms, waiting for the fortune which he is amassing, and which you seem to consider yours."

Such morality seemed a little steep to Maxence.

" I think," he began, " that, if one is the son of a rich man "—

" One has the right to be useless, I suppose? " added the girl.

" I do not mean that; but "—

" There is no but about it. And the proof that your views are wrong, is that they have brought you where you are, and deprived you of your own free will. To place one's self at the mercy of another, be that other your own father, is always silly; and one is always at the mercy of the man from whom he expects money that he has not earned. Your father would never have been so harsh, had he not believed that you could not do without him."

He wanted to discuss: she stopped him.

" Do you wish the proof that you are at M. Favoral's mercy? " she said. " Very well. You spoke of marrying me."

" Ah, if you were willing! "

" Very well. Go and speak of it to your father."

" I suppose "—

" You don't suppose any thing at all: you are absolutely certain that he will refuse you his consent."

" I could do without it."

" I admit that you could. But do you know what he would do then? He would arrange things in such a way that you would never get a centime of his fortune."

Maxence had never thought of that.

" Therefore," the young girl went on gayly, " though
there is as yet no question of marriage, learn to secure
your independence ; that is, the means of living. And to
that effect let us work."

It was from that moment, that Mme. Favoral had noticed in her son the change that had surprised her so
much.

Under the inspiration, under the impulsion, of Mlle.
Lucienne, Maxence had been suddenly taken with a
zeal for work, and a desire to earn money, of which he
could not have been suspected.

He was no longer late at his office, and had not, at
the end of each month, ten or fifteen francs' fines to pay.

Every morning, as soon as she was up, Mlle. Lucienne
came to knock at his door. " Come, get up ! " she cried
to him.

And quick he jumped out of bed and dressed, so that
he might bid her good-morning before she left.

In the evening, the last mouthful of his dinner was
hardly swallowed, before he began copying the documents which he procured from M. Chapelain's successor.

And often he worked quite late in the night whilst by
his side Mlle. Lucienne applied herself to some work of
embroidery.

The girl was the cashier of the association ; and she
administered the common capital with such skilful and
such scrupulous economy, that Maxence soon succeeded
in paying off his creditors.

" Do you know," she was saying at the end of December, " that, between us, we have earned over six
hundred francs this month ? "

On Sundays only, after a week of which not a minute
had been lost, they indulged in some little recreation.

If the weather was not too bad, they went out to-gether, dined in some modest restaurant, and finished the day at the theatre.

Having thus a common existence, both young, free, and having their rooms divided only by a narrow pas-sage it was difficult that people should believe in the in-nocence of their intercourse. The proprietors of the Hôtel des Folies believed nothing of the kind; and they were not alone in that opinion.

Mlle. Lucienne having continued to show herself in the Bois on the afternoons when the weather was fine, the number of fools who annoyed her with their atten-tions had greatly increased. Among the most obstinate could be numbered M. Costeclar, who was pleased to declare, upon his word of honor, that he had lost his sleep, and his taste for business, since the day when, together with M. Saint Pavin, he had first seen Mlle. Lucienne.

The efforts of his valet, and the letters which he had written, having proved useless, M. Costeclar had made up his mind to act in person; and gallantly he had come to put himself on guard in front of the Hôtel des Folies.

Great was his surprise, when he saw Mlle. Lucienne coming out arm in arm with Maxence; and greater still was his spite.

"That girl is a fool," he thought, "to prefer to me a fellow who has not two hundred francs a month to spend. But never mind! He laughs best who laughs last."

And, as he was a man fertile in expedients, he went the next day to take a walk in the neighborhood of the Mutual Credit; and, having met M. Favoral by chance, he told him how his son Maxence was ruining himself for a young lady whose toilets were a scandal, insinuating delicately that it was his duty, as the head of the family, to put a stop to such a thing.

This was precisely the time when Maxence was endeavoring to obtain a situation in the office of the Mutual Credit.

It is true that the idea was not original with him, and that he had even vehemently rejected it, when, for the first time, Mlle. Lucienne had suggested it.

" What! " had he exclaimed, " be employed in the same establishment as my father? Suffer at the office the same intolerable despotism as at home? I'd rather break stones on the roads."

But Mlle. Lucienne was not the girl to give up so easily a project conceived and carefully matured by herself.

She returned to the charge with that infinite art of women, who understand so marvellously well how to turn a position which they cannot carry in front. She kept the matter so well before him, she spoke of it so often and so much, on every occasion, and under all pretexts, that he ended by persuading himself that it was the only reasonable and practical thing he could do, the only way in which he had any chance of making his fortune; and so, one evening overcoming his last hesitations,—

" I am going to speak about it to my father," he said to Mlle. Lucienne.

But whether he had been influenced by M. Costeclar's insinuations, or for some other reason, M. Favoral had rejected indignantly his son's request, saying that it was impossible to trust a young man who was ruining himself for the sake of a miserable creature.

Maxence had become crimson with rage on hearing

the woman spoken of thus, whom he loved to madness, and who, far from ruining him, was making him.

He returned to the Hôtel des Folies in an indescribable state of exasperation.

" There's the result," he said to Mlle. Lucienne, " of the step which you have urged me so strongly to take."

She seemed neither surprised nor irritated.

" Very well," she replied simply.

But Maxence could not resign himself so quietly to such a cruel disappointment; and, not having the slightest suspicion of Costeclar's doings,—

" And such is," he added, " the result of all the gossip of these stupid shop-keepers who run to see you every time you go out in the carriage."

The girl shrugged her shoulders contemptuously.

" I expected it," she said, " the day when I accepted M. Van Klopen's offers."

" Everybody believes that you are my mistress."

" What matters it, since it is not so? "

Maxence did not dare to confess that this was precisely what made him doubly angry; and he shuddered at the thought of the ridicule that would certainly be heaped upon him, if the true state of the case was known.

" We ought to move," he suggested.

" What's the use? Wherever we should go, it would be the same thing. Besides, I don't want to leave this neighborhood."

" And I am too much your friend not to tell you, that your reputation in it is absolutely lost."

" I have no accounts to render to any one."

" Except to your friend the commissary of police, however."

A pale smile flitted upon her lips.

" Ah ! " she uttered, " he knows the truth."

" You have seen him again, then ? "

" Several times."

" Since we have known each other ? "

" Yes."

" And you never told me anything about it ? "

" I did not think it necessary."

Maxence insisted no more; but, by the sharp pang that he felt, he realized how dear Mlle. Lucienne had become to him.

" She has secrets from me," thought he,—" from me who would deem it a crime to have any from her."

What secrets ? Had she concealed from him that she was pursuing an object which had become, as it were, that of her whole life. Had she not told him, that with the assistance of her friend the peace-officer, who had now become commissary of police of the district, she hoped to penetrate the mystery of her birth, and to revenge herself on the villains, who, three times, had attempted to do away with her?

She had never mentioned her projects again; but it was evident that she had not abandoned them, for she would at the same time have given up her rides to the *bois*, which were to her an abominable torment.

But passion can neither reason nor discuss.

" She mistrusts me, who would give my life for her," repeated Maxence.

And the idea was so painful to him, that he resolved to clear his doubts at any cost, preferring the worst misery to the anxiety which was gnawing at his heart.

And as soon as he found himself alone with Mlle. Lucienne, arming himself with all his courage, and looking her straight in the eyes,—

" You never speak to me any more of your enemies? "
he said.

She doubtless understood what was passing within
him.

" It's because I don't hear any thing of them myself,"
she answered gently.

" Then you have given up your purpose? "

" Not at all."

" What are your hopes, then, and what are your prospects? "

" Extraordinary as it may seem to you, I must confess
that I know nothing about it. My friend the commissary has his plan, I am certain; and he is following it
with an indefatigable obstinacy. I am but an instrument in his hands. I never do any thing without consulting him; and what he advises me to do I do."

Maxence started upon his chair.

" Was it he, then," he said in a tone of bitter irony,
" who suggested to you the idea of our fraternal association? "

A frown appeared upon the girl's countenance. She
evidently felt hurt by the tone of this species of interrogatory.

" At least he did not disapprove of it," she replied.

But that answer was just evasive enough to excite
Maxence's anxiety.

" Was it from him too," he went on, " that came the
lovely idea of having me enter the Mutual Credit? "

" Yes, it was from him."

" For what purpose? "

" He did not explain."

" Why did you not tell me? "

" Because he requested me not to do so."

From being red at the start, Maxence had now become very pale.

"And so," he resumed, "it is that man, that police-agent, who is the real arbiter of my fate; and if to-morrow he commanded you to break off with me "—

Mlle. Lucienne drew herself up.

"Enough!" she interrupted in a brief tone, "enough! There is not in my whole existence a single act which would give to my bitterest enemy the right to suspect my loyalty; and now you accuse me of the basest treason. What have you to reproach me with? Have I not been faithful to the pact sworn between us. Have I not always been for you the best of comrades and the most devoted of friends? I remained silent, because the man in whom I have the fullest confidence requested me to do so; but he knew, that, if you questioned me, I would speak. Did you question me? And now what more do you want? That I should stoop to quiet the suspicions of your morbid mind? That I do not mean to do."

She was not, perhaps, entirely right; but Maxence was certainly wrong. He acknowledged it, wept, implored her pardon, which was granted; and this explanation only served to rivet more closely the fetters that bound him.

It is true, that, availing himself of the permission that had been granted him, he kept himself constantly informed of Mlle. Lucienne's doings. He learnt from her that her friend the commissary had held a most minute investigation at Louveciennes, and that the footman who went to the *bois* with her was now, in reality, a detective. And at last, one day,—

"My friend the commissary," she said, "thinks he is on the right track now."

XXIX.

SUCH was the exact situation of Maxence and Mlle. Lucienne on that eventful Saturday evening in the month of April, 1872, when the police came to arrest M. Vincent Favoral, on the charge of embezzlement and forgery.

It will be remembered, how, at his mother's request, Maxence had spent that night in the Rue St. Gilles, and how, the next morning, unable any longer to resist his eager desire to see Mlle. Lucienne, he had started for the Hôtel des Folies, leaving his sister alone at home.

He retired to his room, as she had requested him, and, sinking upon his old arm-chair in a fit of the deepest distress,—

" She is singing," he murmured: " Mme. Fortin has not told her any thing."

And at the same moment Mlle. Lucienne had resumed her song, the words of which reached him like a bitter raillery,—

> " Hope ! O sweet, deceiving word !
>   Mad indeed is he,
>   Who does think he can trust thee,
>   And take thy coin can afford.
>   Over his door every one
>   Will hang thee to his sorrow,
>   Then saying of days begone,
>   ' Cash to-day, credit to-morrow ! '
>   'Tis very nice to run;
>   But to have is better fun ! "

" What will she say," thought Maxence, " when she learns the horrible truth ? "

And he felt a cold perspiration starting on his temples when he remembered Mlle. Lucienne's pride, and that honor has her only faith, the safety-plank to which she had desperately clung in the midst of the storms of her life. What if she should leave him, now that the name he bore was disgraced!

A rapid and light step on the landing drew him from his gloomy thoughts. Almost immediately, the door opened, and Mlle. Lucienne came in.

She must have dressed in haste; for she was just finishing hooking her dress, the simplicity of which seemed studied, so marvellously did it set off the elegance of her figure, the splendors of her waist, and the rare perfections of her shoulders and of her neck.

A look of intense dissatisfaction could be read upon her lovely features; but, as soon as she had seen Maxence, her countenance changed.

And, in fact, his look of utter distress, the disorder of his garments, his livid paleness, and the sinister look of his eyes, showed plainly enough that a great misfortune had befallen him. In a voice whose agitation betrayed something more than the anxiety and the sympathy of a friend,—

"What is the matter? What has happened?" inquired the girl.

"A terrible misfortune," he replied.

He was hesitating: he wished to tell every thing at once, and knew not how to begin.

"I have told you," he said, "that my family was very rich."

"Yes."

"Well, we have nothing left, absolutely nothing."

She seemed to breathe more freely, and, in a tone of friendly irony,—

"And it is the loss of your fortune," she said, "that distresses you thus?"

He raised himself painfully to his feet, and, in a low hoarse voice,—

" Honor is lost too," he uttered.

" Honor? "

" Yes. My father has stolen: my father has forged! "

She had become whiter than her collar.

" Your father! " she stammered.

" Yes. For years he has been using the money that was intrusted to him, until the deficit now amounts to twelve millions."

" Great heavens! "

" And, notwithstanding the enormity of that sum, he was reduced, during the latter months, to the most miserable expedients,—going from door to door in the neighborhood, soliciting deposits, until he actually basely swindled a poor newspaper-vender out of five hundred francs."

" Why, this is madness! And how did you find out? "

" Last night they came to arrest him. Fortunately we had been notified; and I helped him to escape through a window of my sister's room, which opens on the yard of an adjoining house."

" And where is he now? "

" Who knows? "

" Had he any money? "

" Everybody thinks that he carries off millions. I do not believe it. He even refused to take the few thousand francs which M. de Thaller had brought him to facilitate his flight."

Mlle. Lucienne shuddered.

" Did you see M. de Thaller? " she asked.

" He got to the house a few moment in advance of the commissary of police; and a terrible scene took place between him and my father."

" What was he saying? "

" That my father had ruined him."

" And your father? "

" He stammered incoherent phrases. He was like a man who has received a stunning blow. But we have discovered incredible things. My father, so austere and so parsimonious at home, led a merry life elsewhere, spending money without stint. It was for a woman that he robbed."

" And—do you know who that woman is? "

" No. But I can find out from the writer of the article in this paper, who says that he knows her. See! "

Mlle. Lucienne took the paper which Maxence was holding out to her: but she hardly condescended to look at it.

" But what's your idea now? "

" I do not believe that my father is innocent; but I believe that there are people more guilty than he,—skilful and prudent knaves, who have made use of him as a man of straw,—villains who will quietly digest their share of the millions (the biggest one, of course), while he will be sent to prison."

A fugitive blush colored Mlle. Lucienne's cheeks.

" That being the case," she interrupted, " what do you expect to do? "

" Avenge my father, if possible, and discover his accomplices, if he has any."

She held out her hand to him.

" That's right," she said. " But how will you go about it? "

" I don't know yet. At any rate, I must first of all run to the newspaper office, and get that woman's address."

But Mlle. Lucienne stopped him.

"No," she uttered: "it isn't there that you must go. You must come with me to see my friend the commissary."

Maxence received this suggestion with a gesture of surprise, almost of terror.

"Why, how can you think of such a thing?" he exclaimed. "My father is fleeing from justice; and you want me to take for my confidant a commissary of police,—the very man whose duty it is to arrest him, if he can find him!"

But he interrupted himself for a moment, staring and gaping, as if the truth had suddenly flashed upon his mind in dazzling evidence.

"For my father has not gone abroad," he went on. "It is in Paris that he is hiding: I am sure of it. You have seen him?"

Mlle. Lucienne really thought that Maxence was losing his mind.

"I have seen your father—I?" she said.

"Yes, last evening. How could I have forgotten it? While you were waiting for me down stairs, between eleven and half-past eleven a middle-aged man, thin, wearing a long overcoat, came and asked for me."

"Yes, I remember."

"He spoke to you in the yard."

"That's a fact."

"What did he tell you?"

She hesitated for a moment, evidently trying to tax her memory; then,—

"Nothing," she replied, "that he had not already said before the Fortins; that he wanted to see you on important business, and was sorry not to find you in. What surprised me, though, is, that he was speaking as if he knew me, and knew that I was a friend of yours."

Then, striking her forehead,—

" Perhaps you are right," she went on. " Perhaps that man was indeed your father. Wait a minute. Yes, he seemed quite excited, and at every moment he looked around towards the door. He said it would be impossible for him to return, but that he would write to you, and that probably he would require your assistance and your services."

" You see," exclaimed Maxence, almost crazy with subdued excitement, " it was my father. He is going to write, to return, perhaps; and, under the circumstances, to apply to a commissary of police would be sheer folly, almost treason."

She shook her head.

" So much the more reason," she uttered, " why you should follow my advice. Have you ever had occasion to repent doing so ? "

" No, but you may be mistaken."

" I am not mistaken."

She expressed herself in a tone of such absolute certainty, that Maxence, in the disorder of his mind, was at a loss to know what to imagine, what to believe.

" You must have some reason to urge me thus," he said.

" I have."

" Why not tell it to me then ? "

" Because I should have no proofs to furnish you of my assertions. Because I should have to go into details which you would not understand. Because, above all, I am following one of those inexplicable presentiments which never deceive."

It was evident that she was not willing to unveil her whole mind; and yet Maxence felt himself terribly staggered.

"Think of my agony," he said, "if I were to cause my father's arrest."

"Would my own be less? Can any misfortune strike you without reaching me? Let us reason a little. What were you saying a moment since? That certainly your father is not as guilty as people think; at any rate, that he is not alone guilty; that he has been but the instrument of rascals more skilful and more powerful than himself; and that he has had but a small share of the twelve millions?"

"Such is my absolute conviction."

"And that you would like to deliver up to justice the villains who have benefited by your father's crime, and who think themselves sure of impunity?"

Tears of anger fell from Maxence's eyes.

"Do you wish to take away all my courage?" he murmured.

"No; but I wish to demonstrate to you the necessity of the step which I advise you to take. The end justifies the means; and we have not the choice of means. Come, 'tis to an honest man and a tried friend that I shall take you. Fear nothing. If he remembers that he is commissary of police, it will be to serve us, not to injure you. You hesitate? Perhaps at this moment he already knows more than we do ourselves."

Maxence took a sudden resolution.

"Very well," he said: "let us go."

In less than five minutes they were off; and, as they went out, they had to disturb Mme. Fortin, who stood at the door, gossiping with two or three of the neighboring shop-keepers.

As soon as Maxence and Mlle. Lucienne were out of hearing,—

"You see that young man," said the honorable pro-

prietress of the Hôtel des Folies to her interlocutors.
" Well, he is the son of that famous cashier who has
just run off with twelve millions, after ruining a thousand families. It don't seem to trouble him, either; for
there he is, going out to spend a pleasant day with his
mistress, and to treat her to a fine dinner with the old
man's money."

Meantime, Maxence and Lucienne reached the commissary's house. He was at home; they walked in. And,
as soon as they appeared,—

" I expected you," he said.

He was a man already past middle age, but active and
vigorous still. With his white cravat and long frock-
coat, he looked like a notary. Benign was the expression
of his countenance; but the lustre of his little gray eyes,
and the mobility of his nostrils, showed that it should
not be trusted too far.

" Yes, I expected you," he repeated, addressing himself as much to Maxence as to Mlle. Lucienne. " It is
the Mutual Credit matter which brings you here? "

Maxence stepped forward,—

" I am Vincent Favoral's son, sir," he replied. " I
have still my mother and a sister. Our situation is horrible. Mlle. Lucienne suggested that you might be
willing to give me some advice; and here we are."

The commissary rang, and, on the bell being answered,—

" I am at home for no one," he said.

And then turning to Maxence,—

" Mlle. Lucienne did well to bring you," he said;
" for it may be, that, whilst rendering her an important
service, I may also render you one. But I have no time
to lose. Sit down, and tell me all about it."

With the most scrupulous exactness Maxence told the

history of his family, and the events of the past twenty-four hours.

Not once did the commissary interrupt him; but, when he had done,—

" Tell me your father's interview with M. de Thaller all over again," he requested, " and, especially, do not omit any thing that you have heard or seen, not a word, not a gesture, not a look."

And, Maxence having complied,—

" Now," said the commissary, " repeat every thing your father said at the moment of going."

He did so. The commissary took a few notes, and then,—

" What were," he inquired, " the relations of your family with the Thaller family ? "

" There were none."

" What ! Neither Mme. nor Mlle. de Thaller ever visited you ? "

" Never."

" Do you know the Marquis de Trégars ? "

Maxence stared in surprise.

" Trégars ! " he repeated. " It's the first time that I hear that name."

The usual clients of the commissary would have hesitated to recognize him, so completely had he set aside his professional stiffness, so much had his freezing reserve given way to the most encouraging kindness.

" Now, then," he resumed, " never mind M. de Trégars : let us talk of the woman, who, you seem to think, has been the cause of M. Favoral's ruin.

On the table before him lay the paper in which Maxence had read in the morning the terrible article headed, " Another Financial Disaster."

" I know nothing of that woman," he replied; " but

it must be easy to find out, since the writer of this ar‹
ticle pretends to know."

The commissary smiled, not having quite as much
faith in newspapers as Maxence seemed to have.

"Yes, I read that," he said.

"We might send to the office of that paper," suggested Mlle. Lucienne.

"I have already sent, my child."

And, without noticing the surprise of Maxence and
of the young girl, he rang the bell, and asked whether
his secretary had returned. The secretary answered by
appearing in person.

"Well?" inquired the commissary.

"I have attended to the matter, sir," he replied. "I
saw the reporter who wrote the article in question; and,
after beating about the bush for some time, he finally
confessed that he knew nothing more than had been published, and that he had obtained his information from
two intimate friends of the cashier, M. Costeclar and M.
Saint Pavin."

"You should have gone to see those gentlemen."

"I did."

"Very well. What then?"

"Unfortunately, M. Costeclar had just gone out. As
to M. Saint Pavin, I found him at the office of his paper,
'The Financial Pilot.' He is a coarse and vulgar personage, and received me like a pickpocket. I had even a
notion to "—

"Never mind that! Go on."

"He was closeted with another gentleman, a banker,
named Jottras, of the house of Jottras and Brother. They
were both in a terrible rage, swearing like troopers, and
saying that the Favoral defalcation would ruin them;
that they had been taken in like fools, but that they were

not going to take things so easy, and they were preparing a crushing article."

But he stopped, winking, and pointing to Maxence
and Mlle. Lucienne, who were listening as attentively as
they could.

" Speak, speak ! " said the commissary.   " Fear nothing."

" Well," he went on, " M. Saint Pavin and M. Jottras
were saying that M. Favoral was only a poor dupe, but
that they would know how to find the others."

" What others ? "

" Ah ! they didn't say."

The commissary shrugged his shoulders.

" What ! " he exclaimed, " you find yourself in presence of two men furious to have been duped, who swear
and threaten, and you can't get from them a name that
you want ? You are not very smart, my dear ! "

And as the poor secretary, somewhat put out of countenance, looked down, and said nothing,—

" Did you at least ask them," he resumed, " who the
woman is to whom the article refers, and whose existence they have revealed to the reporter ? "

" Of course I did, sir."

" And what did they answer ? "

" That they were not spies, and had nothing to say.
M. Saint Pavin added, however, that he had said it
without much thought, and only because he had once
seen M. Favoral buying a three thousand francs bracelet, and also because it seemed impossible to him that a
man should do away with millions without the aid of a
woman."

The commissary could not conceal his ill humor.

" Of course ! " he grumbled. " Since Solomon said,
' Look for the woman ' (for it was King Solomon who

first said it), every fool thinks it smart to repeat with a cunning look that most obvious of truths. What next? "

" M. Saint Pavin politely invited me to go to—well, not here."

The commissary wrote rapidly a few lines, put them in an envelope, which he sealed with his private seal, and handed it to his secretary, saying,—

· " That will do. Take this to the prefecture yourself."

And, after the secretary had gone out,—

" Well, M. Maxence," he said, " you have heard? "

Of course he had. Only Maxence was thinking much less of what he had just heard than of the strange interest this commissary had taken in his affairs, even before he had seen him.

" I think," he stammered, " that it is very unfortunate the woman cannot be found."

With a gesture full of confidence,—

" Be easy," said the commissary: " she shall be found. A woman cannot swallow millions at that rate, without attracting attention. Believe me, we shall find her, unless "—

He paused for a moment, and, speaking slowly and emphatically,—

" Unless," he added, " she should have behind her a very skilful and very prudent man. Or else that she should be in a situation where her extravagance could not have created any scandal."

Mlle. Lucienne started. She fancied she understood the commissary's idea, and could catch a glimpse of the truth.

" Good heavens ! " she murmured.

But Maxence didn't notice any thing, his mind being

wholly bent upon following the commissary's deductions.

" Or unless," he said, " my father should have received almost nothing for his share of the enormous sums subtracted from the Mutual Credit, in which case he could have given relatively but little to that woman. M. Saint Pavin himself acknowledges that my father has been egregiously taken in."

" By whom? "

" Maxence hesitated for a moment.

" I think," he said at last, " and several friends of my family (among whom M. Chapelain, an old lawyer) think as I do, that it is very strange that my father should have drawn millions from the Mutual Credit without any knowledge of the fact on the part of the manager."

" Then, according to you, M. de Thaller must be an accomplice."

Maxence made no answer.

" Be it so," insisted the commissary. " I admit M. de Thaller's complicity ; but then we must suppose that he had over your father some powerful means of action."

" An employer always has a great deal of influence over his subordinates."

" An influence sufficiently powerful to make them run the risk of the galleys for his benefit ! That is not likely. We must try and imagine something else."

" I am trying ; but I don't find any thing."

" And yet it is not all. How do you explain your father's silence when M. de Thaller was heaping upon him the most outrageous insults ? "

" My father was stunned, as it were."

" And at the moment of escaping, if he did have any

accomplices, how is it that he did not mention their names to you, to your mother, or to your sister? "

" Because, doubtless, he had no proofs of their complicity to offer."

" Would you have asked him for any? "

" O sir! "

" Therefore such is not evidently the motive of his silence; and it might better be attributed to some secret hope that he still had left."

The commissary now had all the information, which, voluntarily or otherwise, Maxence was able to give him. He rose, and in the kindest tone,—

" You have come," he said to him, " to ask me for advice. Here it is: say nothing, and wait. Allow justice and the police to pursue their work. Whatever may be your suspicions, hide them. I shall do for you as I would for Lucienne, whom I love as if she were my own child; for it so happens, that, in helping you, I shall help her."

He could not help laughing at the astonishment, which at those words depicted itself upon Maxence's face; and gayly,—

" You don't understand," he added. " Well, never mind. It is not necessary that you should."

XXX.

Two o'clock struck as Mlle. Lucienne and Maxence left the office of the commissary of police, she pensive and agitated, he gloomy and irritated. They reached the Hôtel des Folies without exchanging a word. Mme. Fortin was again at the door, speechifying in the midst of a group with indefatigable volubility. Indeed, it was a perfect godsend for her, the fact of lodging the son of that cashier who had stolen twelve millions, and had thus suddenly become a celebrity. Seeing Maxence and Mlle. Lucienne coming, she stepped toward them, and, with her most obsequious smile,—

"Back already?" she said.

But they made no answer; and, entering the narrow corridor, they hurried to their fourth story. As he entered his room, Maxence threw his hat upon his bed with a gesture of impatience; and, after walking up and down for a moment, he returned to plant himself in front of Mlle. Lucienne.

"Well," he said, "are you satisfied now?"

She looked at him with an air of profound commiseration, knowing his weakness too well to be angry at his injustice.

"Of what should I be satisfied?" she asked gently.

"I have done what you wished me to."

"You did what reason dictated, my friend."

"Very well: we won't quarrel about words. I have seen your friend the commissary. Am I any better off?"

She shrugged her shoulders almost imperceptibly.

"What did you expect of him, then?" she asked. "Did you think that he could undo what is done? Did you suppose, that, by the sole power of his will, he would make up the deficit in the Mutual Credit's cash, and rehabilitate your father?"

"No, I am not quite mad yet."

"Well, then, could he do more than promise you his most ardent and devoted co-operation?"

But he did not allow her to proceed.

"And how do I know," he exclaimed, "that he is not trifling with me? If he was sincere, why his reticence and his enigmas? He pretends that I may rely on him, because to serve me is to serve you. What does that mean? What connection is there between your situation and mine, between your enemies and those of my father? And I—I replied to all his questions like a simpleton. Poor fool! But the man who drowns catches at straws; and I am drowning, I am sinking, I am foundering."

He sank upon a chair, and, hiding his face in his hands,—

"Ah, how I do suffer!" he groaned.

Mlle. Lucienne approached him, and in a severe tone, despite her emotion,—

"Are you, then, such a coward?" she uttered. "What! at the first misfortune that strikes you,—and this is the first real misfortune of your life, Maxence,— you despair. An obstacle rises, and, instead of gathering all your energy to overcome it, you sit down and weep like a woman. Who, then, is to inspire courage in your mother and in your sister, if you give up so?"

At the sound of these words, uttered by that voice which was all-powerful over his soul, Maxence looked up.

"I thank you, my friend," he said. "I thank you for reminding me of what I owe to my mother and sister. Poor women! They are wondering, doubtless, what has become of me."

"You must return to them," interrupted the girl.

He got up resolutely.

"I will," he replied. "I should be unworthy of you if I could not raise my own energy to the level of yours."

And, having pressed her hand, he left. But it was not by the usual route that he reached the Rue St. Gilles.

He made a long *détour*, so as not to meet any of his acquaintances.

"Here you are at last," said the servant as she opened the door. "Madame was getting very uneasy, I can tell you. She is in the parlor, with Mlle. Gilberte and M. Chapelain."

It was so. After his fruitless attempt to reach M. de Thaller, M. Chapelain had breakfasted there, and had remained, wishing, he said, to see Maxence. And so, as soon as the young man appeared, availing himself of the privileges of his age and his old intimacy,—

"How," said he, "dare you leave your mother and sister alone in a house where some brutal creditor may come in at any moment?"

"I was wrong," said Maxence, who preferred to plead guilty rather than attempt an explanation.

"Don't do it again then," resumed M. Chapelain. "I was waiting for you to say that I was unable to see M. de Thaller, and that I do not care to face once more the impudence of his valets. You will, therefore, have to take back the fifteen thousand francs he had brought to your father. Place them in his own hands; and don't give them up without a receipt."

After some further recommendations, he went off, leaving Mme. Favoral alone at last with her children. She was about to call Maxence to account for his absence, when Mlle. Gilberte interrupted her.

"I have to speak to you, mother," she said with a singular precipitation, "and to you also, brother."

And at once she began telling them of M. Costeclar's strange visit, his inconceivable audacity, and his offensive declarations.

Maxence was fairly stamping with rage.

" And I was not here," he exclaimed, " to put him
out of the house ! "

But another was there; and this was just what Mlle.
Gilberte wished to come to. But the avowal was difficult, painful even; and it was not without some degree
of confusion that she resumed at last,—

" You have suspected for a long time, mother, that I
was hiding something from you. When you questioned
me, I lied; not that I had any thing to blush for, but
because I feared for you my father's anger."

Her mother and her brother were gazing at her with
a look of blank amazement.

" Yes, I had a secret," she continued. " Boldly, without consulting any one, trusting the sole inspirations of
my heart, I had engaged my life to a stranger: I had
selected the man whose wife I wished to be."

Mme. Favoral raised her hands to heaven.

" But this is sheer madness ! " she said.

" Unfortunately," went on the girl, " between that
man, my affianced husband before God, and myself, rose
a terrible obstacle. He was poor: he thought my father
very rich; and he had asked me a delay of three years
to conquer a fortune which might enable him to aspire
to my hand."

She stopped : all the blood in her veins was rushing to
her face.

" This morning," she said, " at the news of our disaster, he came "—

" Here ? " interrupted Maxence.

" Yes, brother, here. He arrived at the very moment,
when, basely insulted by M. Costeclar, I commanded
him to withdraw, and, instead of going, he was walking
towards me with outstretched arms."

"He dared to penetrate here!" murmured Mme. Favoral.

"Yes, mother: he came in just in time to seize M. Costeclar by his coat-collar, and to throw him at my feet, livid with fear, and begging for mercy. He came, notwithstanding the terrible calamity that has befallen us. Notwithstanding ruin, and notwithstanding shame, he came to offer me his name, and to tell me, that, in the course of the day, he would send a friend of his family to apprise you of his intentions."

Here she was interrupted by the servant, who, throwing open the parlor-door, announced,—

"The Count de Villegré."

If it had occurred to the mind of Mme. Favoral or Maxence that Mlle. Gilberte might have been the victim of some base intrigue, the mere appearance of the man who now walked in must have been enough to disabuse them.

He was of a rather formidable aspect, with his military bearing, his bluff manners, his huge white mustache, and the deep scar across his forehead.

But in order to be re-assured, and to feel confident, it was enough to look at his broad face, at once energetic and debonair, his clear eye, in which shone the loyalty of his soul, and his thick red lips, which had never opened to utter an untruth.

At this moment, however, he was hardly in possession of all his faculties.

That valiant man, that old soldier, was timid; and he would have felt much more at ease under the fire of a battery than in that humble parlor in the Rue St. Gilles, under the uneasy glance of Maxence and Mme. Favoral.

Having bowed, having made a little friendly sign to Mlle. Gilberte, he had stopped short, two steps from the door, his hat in his hand.

Eloquence was not his forte. He had prepared himself well in advance; but though he kept coughing: hum! broum! though he kept running his finger around his shirt-collar to facilitate his delivery, the beginning of his speech stuck in his throat.

Seeing how urgent it was to come to his assistance,—

" I was expecting you, sir," said Mlle. Gilberte.

With this encouragement, he advanced towards Mme. Favoral, and, bowing low,—

" I see that my presence surprises you, madame," he began; " and I must confess that—hum!—it does not surprise me less than it does you. But extraordinary circumstances require exceptional action. On any other occasion, I would not fall upon you like a bombshell. But we had no time to waste in ceremonious formalities. I will, therefore, ask your leave to introduce myself: I am General Count de Villegré."

Maxence had brought him a chair.

" I am ready to hear you, sir," said Mme. Favoral.

He sat down, and, with a further effort,—

" I suppose, madame," he resumed, " that your daughter has explained to you our singular situation, which, as I had the honor of telling you—hum!—is not strictly in accordance with social usage."

Mlle. Gilberte interrupted him.

" When you came in, general, I was only just beginning to explain the facts to my mother and brother."

The old soldier made a gesture, and a face which showed plainly that he did not much relish the prospect of a somewhat difficult explanation—broum! Nevertheless, making up his mind bravely,—

"It is very simple," he said: "I come in behalf of M. de Trégars."

Maxence fairly bounced upon his chair. That was the very name which he had just heard mentioned by the commissary of police.

"Trégars!" he repeated in a tone of immense surprise.

"Yes," said M. de Villegré. "Do you know him, by chance?"

"No, sir, no!"

"Marius de Trégars is the son of the most honest man I ever knew, of the best friend I ever had,—of the Marquis de Trégars, in a word, who died of grief a few years ago, after—hum!—some quite inexplicable—broum!—reverses of fortune. Marius could not be dearer to me, if he were my own son. He has lost his parents: I have no relatives; and I have transferred to him all the feelings of affection which still remained at the bottom of my old heart.

"And I can say that never was a man more worthy of affection. I know him. To the most legitimate pride and the most scrupulous integrity, he unites a keen and supple mind, and wit enough to get the better of the toughest rascal. He has no fortune for the reason that —hum!—he gave up all he had to certain pretended creditors of his father. But whenever he wishes to be rich, he shall be; and—broum!—he may be so before long. I know his projects, his hopes, his resources."

But, as if feeling that he was treading on dangerous ground, the Count de Villegré stopped short, and, after taking breath for a moment,—

"In short," he went on, "Marius has been unable to see Mlle. Gilberte, and to appreciate the rare qualities of her heart, without falling desperately in love with her."

Mme. Favoral made a gesture of protest,—

"Allow me, sir," she began.

But he interrupted her.

"I understand you, madame," he resumed. "You wonder how M. de Trégars can have seen your daughter, have known her, and have appreciated her, without your seeing or hearing any thing of it. Nothing is more simple, and, if I may venture to say—hum!—more natural."

And the worthy old soldier began to explain to Mme. Favoral the meetings in the Place-Royale, his conversations with Marius, intended really for Mlle. Gilberte, and the part he had consented to play in this little comedy. But he became embarrassed in his sentences, he multiplied his hum! and his broum! in the most alarming manner; and his explanations explained nothing.

Mlle. Gilberte took pity on him; and, kindly interrupting him, she herself told her story, and that of Marius.

She told the pledge they had exchanged, how they had seen each other twice, and how they constantly heard of each other through the very innocent and very unconscious Signor Gismondo Pulei.

Maxence and Mme. Favoral were dumbfounded. They would have absolutely refused to believe such a story, had it not been told by Mlle. Gilberte herself.

"Ah, my dear sister!" thought Maxence, "who could have suspected such a thing, seeing you always so calm and so meek!"

"Is it possible," Mme. Favoral was saying to herself, "that I can have been so blind and so deaf?"

As to the Count de Villegré, he would have tried in

vain to express the gratitude he felt towards Mlle. Gilberte for having spared him these difficult explanations.

" I could not have done half as well myself, by the eternal ! " he thought, like a man who has no illusions on his own account.

But, as soon as she had done, addressing himself to Mme. Favoral,—

" Now, madame," he said, " you know all; and you will understand that the irreparable disaster that strikes you has removed the only obstacle which had hitherto stood in the way of Marius."

He rose, and in a solemn tone, without any hum or broum, this time,—

" I have the honor, madame," he uttered, " to solicit the hand of Mlle. Gilberte, your daughter, for my friend Yves-Marius de Genost, Marquis de Trégars."

A profound silence followed this speech. But this silence the Count de Villegré doubtless interpreted in his own favor; for, stepping to the parlor-door, he opened it, and called, " Marius ! "

Marius de Trégars had foreseen all that had just taken place, and had so informed the Count de Villegré in advance.

Being given Mme. Favoral's disposition, he knew what could be expected of her; and he had his own reasons to fear nothing from Maxence. And, if he mistrusted somewhat the diplomatic talents of his ambassador, he relied absolutely upon Mlle. Gilberte's energy.

And so confident was he of the correctness of his calculations, that he had insisted upon accompanying his old friend, so as to be on hand at the critical moment.

When the servant had opened the door to them, he had ordered her to introduce M. de Villegré, stating that he would himself wait in the dining-room. This arrangement had not seemed entirely natural to the girl; but so many strange things had happened in the house for the past twenty-four hours, that she was prepared for any thing.

Besides recognizing Marius as the gentleman who had had a violent altercation in the morning with M. Costeclar, she did as he requested, and, leaving him alone in the dining-room, went to attend to her duties.

He had taken a seat, impassive in appearance, but in reality agitated by that internal trepidation of which the strongest men cannot free themselves in the decisive moments of their life.

To a certain extent, the prospects of his whole life were to be decided on the other side of that door which had just closed behind the Count de Villegré. To the success of his love, other interests were united, which required immediate success.

And, counting the seconds by the beatings of his heart,—

" How very slow they are! " he thought.

And so, when the door opened at last, and his old friend called him, he jumped to his feet, and collecting all his coolness and self-possession, he walked in.

Maxence had risen to receive him; but, when he saw him, he stepped back, his eyes glaring in utter surprise.

" Ah, great heavens! " he muttered in a smothered voice.

But M. de Trégars seemed not to notice his stupor. Quite self-possessed, notwithstanding his emotion, he cast a rapid glance over the Count de Villegré, Mme. Favoral and Mlle. Gilberte. At their attitude, and at the expression of their countenance, he easily guessed the point to which things had come.

And, advancing towards Mme. Favoral, he bowed with an amount of respect which was certainly not put on.

" You have heard the Count de Villegré, madame," he said in a slightly altered tone of voice. " I am awaiting my fate."

The poor woman had never before in all her life been so fearfully perplexed. All these events, which succeeded each other so rapidly, had broken the feeble springs of her soul. She was utterly incapable of collecting her thoughts, or of taking a determination.

" At this moment, sir," she stammered, taken unwares, " it would be impossible for me to answer you. Grant me a few days for reflection. We have some old friends whom I ought to consult."

But Maxence, who had got over his stupor, interrupted her.

" Friends mother ! " he exclaimed. "And who are they? People in our position have no friends. What! when we are perishing, a man of heart holds out his hand to us, and you ask to reflect? To my sister, who bears a name henceforth disgraced, the Marquis de Trégare offers his name, and you think of consulting "—

The poor woman was shaking her head.

" I am not the mistress, my son," she murmured; " and your father "—

" My father ! " interrupted the young man,—" my father ! What rights can he have over us hereafter? "

And without further discussion, without awaiting an answer, he took his sister's hand, and, placing it in M. de Trégar's hand,—

" Ah! take her, sir," he uttered. " Never, whatever she may do, will she acquit the debt of eternal gratitude which we this day contract towards you."

A tremor that shook their frames, a long look which they exchanged, betrayed alone the feelings of Marius and Mlle. Gilberte. They had of life a too cruel experience not to mistrust their joy.

Returning to Mme. Favoral,—

"You do not understand, madame," he went on, "why I should have selected for such a step the very moment when an irreparable calamity befalls you. One word will explain all. Being in a position to serve you, I wished to acquire the right of doing so."

Fixing upon him a look in which the gloomiest despair could be read,—

"Alas!" stammered the poor woman, "what can you do for me, sir? My life is ended. I have but one wish left,—that of knowing where my husband is hid. It is not for me to judge him. He has not given me the happiness which I had, perhaps, the right to expect; but he is my husband, he is unhappy: my duty is to join him wherever he may be, and to share his sufferings."

She was interrupted by the servant, who was calling her at the parlor-door, "Madame, madame!"

"What is the matter?" inquired Maxence.

"I must speak to madame at once."

Making an effort to rise and walk, Mme. Favoral went out. She was gone but a minute; and, when she returned, her agitation had further increased.

"It is the hand of Providence, perhaps," she said.

The others were all looking at her anxiously. She took a seat, and, addressing herself more especially to M. de Trégars,—

"This is what happens," she said in a feeble voice. "M. Favoral was in the habit of always changing his coat as soon as he came home. As usual, he did so last evening. When they came to arrest him, he forgot to change again, and went off with the coat he had on. The other remained hanging in the room, where the girl took it just now to brush it, and put it away; and this portfolio, which my husband always carries with him, fell from its pocket."

It was an old Russia leather portfolio, which had once been red, but which time and use had turned black. It was full of papers.

"Perhaps, indeed," exclaimed Maxence, "we may find some information there."

He opened it, and had already taken out three-fourths of its contents without finding any thing of any consequence, when suddenly he uttered an exclamation.

He had just opened an anonymous note, evidently written in a disguised hand, and at one glance had read,—

"I cannot understand your negligence. You should get through that Van Klopen matter. There is the danger."

"What is that note?" inquired M. de Trégars.

Maxence handed it to him.

"See!" said he, "but you will not understand the immense interest it has for me."

But having read it,—

"You are mistaken," said Marius. "I understand perfectly; and I'll prove it to you."

The next moment, Maxence took out of the portfolio, and read aloud, the following bill, dated two days before.

"Sold to —— two leather trunks with safety locks at 220 francs each; say, francs 440."

M. de Trégars started.

"At last," he said, "here is doubtless one end of the

thread which will guide us to the truth through this labyrinth of iniquities."

And, tapping gently on Maxence's shoulders,—

" We must talk," he said, " and at length. To-morrow, before you go to M. de Thaller's with his fifteen thousand francs, call and see me: I shall expect you. We are now engaged upon a common work; and something tells me, that, before long, we shall know what has become of the Mutual Credit's millions."

PART II.

FISHING IN TROUBLED WATERS.

I.

" When I think," said Coleridge, " that every morning, in Paris alone, thirty thousand fellows wake up,
and rise with the fixed and settled idea of appropriating
other people's money, it is with renewed wonder that
every night, when I go home, I find my purse still in
my pocket."

And yet it is not those who simply aim to steal your
portemonnaie who are either the most dishonest or the
most formidable.

To stand at the corner of some dark street, and rush
upon the first man that comes along, demanding, " Your
money or your life," is but a poor business, devoid of all
prestige, and long since given up to chivalrous natures.

A man must be something worse than a simpleton
to still ply his trade on the high-roads, exposed to all
sorts of annoyances on the part of the *gensdarmes*, when
manufacturing and financial enterprises offer such a
magnificently fertile field to the activity of imaginative
people.

And, in order to thoroughly understand the mode of
proceeding in this particular field, it is sufficient to open
from time to time a copy of " The Police Gazette," and
to read some trial, like that, for instance, of one Lefur-

teux, ex-president of the *Company for the Drainage and Improvement of the Orne Swamps.*

This took place less than a month ago in one of the police-courts.

The Judge to the Accused.—Your profession?

M. Lefurteux.—President of the company.

Question.—Before that what were you doing?

Answer.—I speculated at the *bourse.*

Q.—You had no means?

A.—I beg your pardon: I was making money.

Q.—And it was under such circumstances that you had the audacity to organize a company with a capital stock of three million of francs, divided in shares of five hundred francs?

A.—Having discovered an idea, I did not suppose that I was forbidden to work it up.

Q.—What do you call an idea?

A.—The idea of draining swamps, and making them productive.

Q.—What swamps? Yours never had any existence, except in your prospectus.

A.—I expected to buy them as soon as my capital was paid in.

Q.—And in the mean time you promised ten per cent to your stockholders.

A—That's the least that draining operations ever pay.

Q.—You have advertised?

A.—Of course.

Q.—To what extent?

A.—To the extent of about sixty thousand francs.

Q.—Where did you get the money?

A.—I commenced with ten thousand francs, which a friend of mine had lent me; then I used the funds as they came in.

Q.—In other words, you made use of the money of your first dupes to attract others?

A.—Many people thought it was a good thing.

Q.—Who? Those to whom you sent your prospectus with a plan of your pretended swamps?

A.—Excuse me. Others too.

Q.—How much money did you ever receive?

A.—About six hundred thousand francs, as the expert has stated.

Q.—And you have spent the whole of the money?

A.—Permit me? I have never applied to my personal wants any thing beyond the salary which was allowed me by the By-laws.

Q.—How is it, then, that, when you were arrested, there were only twelve hundred and fifty francs found in your safe, and that amount had been sent you through the post-office that very morning? What has become of the rest?

A.—The rest has been spent for the good of the company.

Q.—Of course! You had a carriage?

A.—It was allowed to me by Article 27 of the By-laws.

Q.—For the good of the company too, I suppose.

A.—Certainly. I was compelled to make a certain display. The head of an important company must endeavor to inspire confidence.

The Judge, with an Ironical Look.—Was it also to inspire confidence that you had a mistress, for whom you spent considerable sums of money?

The Accused, in a Tone of Perfect Candor.—Yes, sir.

After a pause of a few moments, the judge resumes,—

Q.—Your offices were magnificent. They must have cost you a great deal to furnish.

A.—On the contrary, sir, almost nothing. The furniture was all hired. You can examine the upholsterer.

The upholsterer is sent for, and in answer to the judge's questions,—

"What M. Lefurteux has stated," he says, "is true. My specialty is to hire office-fixtures for financial and other companies. I furnish every thing, from the book-keepers' desks to the furniture for the president's private room: from the iron safe to the servant's livery. In twenty-four hours, every thing is ready, and the subscribers can come. As soon as a company is organized like the one in question, the officers call on me, and, according to the magnitude of the capital required, I furnish a more or less costly establishment. I have a good deal of experience, and I know just what's wanted. When M. Lefurteux came to see me, I gauged his operation at a glance. Three millions of capital, swamps in the Orne, shares of five hundred francs, small subscribers, anxious and noisy.

" ' Very well,' I said to him, ' it's a six-months' job. Don't go into useless expenses. Take reps for your private office: that's good enough.' "

The Judge, in a tone of Profound Surprise.—You told him that?

The Upholsterer, in the Simple Accent of an Honest Man.—Exactly as I am telling your Honor. He followed my advice; and I sent him red hot the furniture and fixtures which had been used by the River Fishery Company, whose president had just been sent to prison for three years.

When, after such revelations, renewed from week to week, with instructive variations, purchasers may still be found for the shares of the Tiffla Mines, the Bretoneche Lands, and the Forests of Formanoid, is it to be wondered that the Mutual Credit Company found numerous subscribers?

It had been admirably started at that propitious hour of the December *coup d'état*, when the first ideas of mutuality were beginning to penetrate the financial world.

It had lacked neither capital nor powerful patronage at the start, and had been at once admitted to the honor of being quoted at the *bourse*.

Beginning business ostensibly as an accommodation bank for manufacturers and merchants, the Mutual Credit had had, for a number of years, a well-determined specialty.

But gradually it had enlarged the circle of its operations, altered its by-laws, changed its board of directors;

and at the end the original subscribers would have been not a little embarrassed to tell what was the nature of its business, and from what sources it drew its profits.

All they knew was, that it always paid respectable dividends; that their manager, M. de Thaller, was personally very rich; and that they were willing to trust him to steer clear of the code.

There were some, of course, who did not view things in quite so favorable a light; who suggested that the dividends were suspiciously large; that M. de Thaller spent too much money on his house, his wife, his daughter, and his mistress.

One thing is certain, that the shares of the Mutual Credit Society were much above par, and were quoted at 580 francs on that Saturday, when, after the closing of the *bourse*, the rumor had spread that the cashier, Vincent Favoral, had run off with twelve millions.

" What a haul! " thought, not without a feeling of envy, more than one broker, who, for merely one-twelfth of that amount would have gayly crossed the frontier.

It was almost an event in Paris.

Although such adventures are frequent enough, and not taken much notice of, in the present instance, the magnitude of the amount more than made up for the vulgarity of the act.

Favoral was generally pronounced a very smart man; and some persons declared, that to take twelve millions could hardly be called stealing.

The first question asked was,—

" Is Thaller in the operation? Was he in collusion with his cashier? "

" That's the whole question."

" If he was, then the Mutual Credit is better off than ever: otherwise, it is gone under."

" Thaller is pretty smart."

" That Favoral was perhaps more so still."

This uncertainty kept up the price for about half an hour. But soon the most disastrous news began to spread, brought, no one knew whence or by whom; and there was an irresistible panic.

From 425, at which price it had maintained itself for a time, the Mutual Credit fell suddenly to 300, then 200, and finally to 150 francs.

Some friends of M. de Thaller, M. Costeclar, for instance, had endeavored to keep up the market; but they had soon recognized the futility of their efforts, and then they had bravely commenced doing like the rest.

The next day was Sunday. From the early morning, it was reported, with the most circumstantial details, that the Baron de Thaller had been arrested.

But in the evening this had been contradicted by people who had gone to the races, and who had met there Mme. de Thaller and her daughter, more brilliant than ever, very lively, and very talkative.

To the persons who went to speak to them,—

" My husband was unable to come," said the baroness. " He is busy with two of his clerks, looking over that poor Favoral's accounts. It seems that they are in the most inconceivable confusion. Who would ever have thought such a thing of a man who lived on bread and nuts? But he operated at the *bourse;* and he had organized, under a false name, a sort of bank, in which he has very foolishly sunk large sums of money."

And with a smile, as if all danger had been luckily averted,—

" Fortunately," she added, " the damage is not as great as has been reported, and this time, again, we shall get off with a good fright."

But the speeches of the baroness were hardly sufficient to quiet the anxiety of the people who felt in their
coat-pockets the worthless certificates of Mutual Credit
stock.

And the next day, Monday, as early as eight o'clock,
they began to arrive in crowds to demand of M. de
Thaller some sort of an explanation.

They were there, at least a hundred, huddled together
in the vestibule, on the stairs, and on the first landing,
a prey to the most painful emotion and the most violent
excitement; for they had been refused admittance.

To all those who insisted upon going in, a tall servant in livery, standing before the door, replied invariably, " The office is not open, M. de Thaller has not
yet come."

Whereupon they uttered such terrible threats and
such loud imprecations, that the frightened *concierge*
had run, and hid himself at the very bottom of his lodge.

No one can imagine to what epileptic contortions the
loss of money can drive an assemblage of men, who
has not seen a meeting of shareholders on the morrow
of a great disaster, with their clinched fists, their convulsed faces, their glaring eyes, and foaming lips.

They felt indignant at what had once been their delight. They laid the blame of their ruin upon the splendor of the house, the sumptuousness of the stairs, the
candelabras of the vestibule, the carpets, the chairs every
thing.

" And it is our money too," they cried, " that has paid
for all that ! "

Standing upon a bench, a little short man was exciting
transports of indignation by describing the magnificence
of the Baron de Thaller's residence, where he had once
had some dealings.

He had counted five carriages in the carriage-house, fifteen horses in the stables, and Heaven knows how many servants.

He had never been inside the apartments, but he had visited the kitchen; and he declared that he had been dazzled by the number and brightness of the saucepans, ranged in order of size over the furnace.

Gathered in a group under the vestibule, the most sensible deplored their rash confidence.

" That's the way," concluded one, " with all these ad-venturous affairs."

" That's a fact. There's nothing, after all, like government bonds."

" Or a first mortgage on good property, with subrogation of the wife's rights."

But what exasperated them all was not to be admitted to the presence of M. de Thaller, and to see that servant mounting guard before the door.

" What impudence," they growled, " to leave us on the stairs!—we who are the masters, after all."

" Who knows where M. de Thaller may be? "

" He is hiding, of course."

" No matter: I will see him," clamored a big fat man, with a brick-colored face, " if I shouldn't stir from here for a week."

" You'll see nothing at all," giggled his neighbor. " Do you suppose they don't have back-stairs and private entrances in this infernal shop? "

" Ah! if I believed any thing of the kind," exclaimed the big man in a voice trembling with passion. "I'd soon break in some of these doors: it isn't so hard, after all."

Already he was gazing at the servant with an alarming air, when an old gentleman with a discreet look, stepped up to him, and inquired,—

" Excuse me, sir: how many shares have you? "

" Three," answered the man with the brick-colored face.

The other sighed.

" I have two hundred and fifty," he said. " That's why, being at least as interested as yourself in not losing every thing, I beg of you to indulge in no violent proceedings."

There was no need of further speaking.

The door which the servant was guarding flew open. A clerk appeared, and made sign that he wished to speak.

" Gentlemen," he began, " M. de Thaller has just come; but he is just now engaged with the examining judge."

Shouts having drowned his voice, he withdrew precipitately.

" If the law gets its finger in," murmured the discreet gentleman, " good-by! "

" That's a fact," said another. " But we will have the precious advantage of hearing that dear baron condemned to one year's imprisonment, and a fine of fifty francs. That's the regular rate. He wouldn't get off so cheap, if he had stolen a loaf of bread from a baker."

" Do you believe that story about the judge? " interrupted rudely the big man.

They had to believe it, when they saw him appear, followed by a commissary of police and a porter, carrying on his back a load of books and papers.

They stood aside to let them pass; but there was no time to make any comments, as another clerk appeared immediately who said,—

" M. de Thaller is at your command, gentlemen. Please walk in."

There was then a terrible jamming and pushing to see who would get first into the directors' room, which stood wide open.

M. de Thaller was standing against the mantel-piece, neither paler nor more excited than usual, but like a man who feels sure of himself and of his means of action.

As soon as silence was restored,—

'First of all, gentlemen," he began, " I must tell you that the board of directors is about to meet, and that a general meeting of the stockholders will be called."

Not a murmur. As at the touch of a magician's wand, the dispositions of the shareholders seemed to have changed.

" I have nothing new to inform you of," he went on. " What happens is a misfortune, but not a disaster. The thing to do was to save the company ; and I had first thought of calling for funds."

" Well," said two or three timid voices, " If it was absolutely necessary "—

" But there is no need of it."

" Ah, ah ! "

" And I can manage to carry every thing through by adding to our reserve fund my own personal fortune."

This time the hurrahs and the bravos drowned the voice.

M. de Thaller received them like a man who deserves them, and, more slowly,—

" Honor commanded it," he continued. " I confess it, gentlemen, the wretch who has so basely deceived us had my entire confidence. You will understand my apparent blindness when you know with what infernal skill he managed."

Loud imprecations burst on all sides against Vincent

Favorai.   But the president of the Mutual Credit proceeded,—

"For the present, all I have to ask of you is to keep cool, and continue to give me your confidence."

"Yes, yes!"

"The panic of night before last was but a stock-gambling manœuvre, organized by rival establishments, who were in hopes of taking our clients away from us. They will be disappointed, gentlemen.   We will triumphantly demonstrate our soundness; and we shall come out of this trial more powerful than ever."

It was all over.   M. de Thaller understood his business.   They offered him a vote of thanks.   A smile was beaming upon the same faces that were a moment before contracted with rage.

One stockholder alone did not seem to share the general enthusiasm: he was no other than our old friend, M. Chapelain, the ex-lawyer.

"That fellow, Thaller, is just capable of getting himself out of the scrape," he grumbled.   "I must tell Maxence."

II.

WE have every species of courage in France, and to a superior degree, except that of braving public opinion. Few men would have dared, like Marius de Trégars, to offer their name to the daughter of a wretch charged with embezzlement and forgery, and that at the very moment when the scandal of the crime was at its height. But, when Marius judged a thing good and just, he did it without troubling himself in the least about what others would think.   And so his mere presence in the

Rue. St. Gilles had brought back hope to its inmates. Of his designs he had said but a word,—" I have the means of helping you : I mean, by marrying Gilberte, to acquire the right of doing so."

But that word had been enough. Mme. Favoral and Maxence had understood that the man who spoke thus was one of those cool and resolute men whom nothing disconcerts or discourages, and who know how to make the best of the most perilous situations.

And, when he had retired with the Count de Ville-gré,—

" I don't know what he will do," said Mlle. Gilberte to her mother and her brother: " but he will certainly do something; and, if it is humanly possible to succeed, he will succeed."

And how proudly she spoke thus ! The assistance of Marius was the justification of her conduct. She trembled with joy at the thought that it would, perhaps, be to the man whom she had alone and boldly selected, that her family would owe their salvation. Shaking his head, and making allusion to events of which he kept the secret,—

" I really believe," approved Maxence, " that, to reach the enemies of our father, M. de Trégars possesses some powerful means; and what they are we will doubtless soon know, since I have an appointment with him for to-morrow morning."

It came at last, that morrow, which he had awaited with an impatience that neither his mother nor his sister could suspect. And towards half-past nine he was ready to go out, when M. Chapelain came in. Still ir-ritated by the scenes he had just witnessed at the Mu-tual Credit office, the old lawyer had a most lugubrious countenance.

"I bring bad news," he began. "I have just seen the Baron de Thaller."

He had said so much the day before about having nothing more to do with it, that Maxence could not repress a gesture of surprise.

"Oh! it isn't alone that I saw him," added M. Chapelain, "but together with at least a hundred stockholders of the Mutual Credit."

"They are going to do something, then?"

"No: they only came near doing something. You should have seen them this morning! They were furious; they threatened to break every thing; they wanted M. de Thaller's blood. It was terrible. But M. de Thaller condescended to receive them; and they became at once as meek as lambs. It is perfectly simple. What do you suppose stockholders can do, no matter how exasperated they may be, when their manager tells them?—

"'Well, yes, it's a fact you have been robbed, and your money is in great jeopardy; but if you make any fuss, if you complain thus, all is sure to be lost.' Of course, the stockholders keep quiet. It is a well-known fact that a business which has to be liquidated through the courts is gone; and swindled stockholders fear the law almost as much as the swindling manager. A single fact will make the situation clearer to you. Less than an hour ago, M. de Thaller's stockholders offered him money to make up the loss."

And, after a moment of silence,—

"But this is not all. Justice has interfered; and M. de Thaller spent the morning with an examining-magistrate."

"Well?"

"Well, I have enough experience to affirm that you

must not rely any more upon justice than upon the
stockholders. Unless there are proofs so evident that
they are not likely to exist, M. de Thaller will not be
disturbed."

" Oh ! "

" Why? Because, my dear, in all those big financial
operations, justice, as much as possible, remains blind.
Not through corruption or any guilty connivance, but
through considerations of public interest. If the manager was prosecuted he would be condemned to a few
years' imprisonment; but his stockholders would at the
same time be condemned to lose what they have left; so
that the victims would be more severely punished than
the swindler. And so, powerless, justice does not interfere. And that's what accounts for the impudence and
impunity of all these high-flown rascals who go about
with their heads high, their pockets filled with other
people's money, and half a dozen decorations at their
button-hole."

" And what then? " asked Maxence.

" Then it is evident that your father is lost. Whether
or not he have accomplices, he will be alone sacrificed.
A scapegoat is needed to be slaughtered on the altar of
credit. Well, they will give that much satisfaction to
the swindled stockholders. The twelve millions will be
lost; but the shares of the Mutual Credit will go up,
and public morality will be safe."

Somewhat moved by the old lawyer's tone,—

" What do you advise me to do, then? " inquired
Maxence.

" The very reverse of what, on the first impulse, I advised you to do. That's why I have come. I told you
yesterday, ' Make a row, act, scream. It is impossible
that your father be alone guilty; attack M. de Thaller.'

To-day, after mature deliberation, I say, ' Keep quiet, hide yourself, let the scandal drop.' "

A bitter smile contracted Maxence's lips.

" It is not very brave advice you are giving me there," he said.

" It is a friend's advice,—the advice of a man who knows life better than yourself. Poor young man, you are not aware of the peril of certain struggles. All knaves are in league and sustain each other. To attack one is to attack them all. You have no idea of the occult influences of which a man can dispose who handles millions, and who, in exchange for a favor, has always a bonus to offer, or a good operation to propose. If at least I could see any chance of success! But you have not one. You never can reach M. de Thaller, henceforth backed by his stockholders. You will only succeed in making an enemy whose hostility will weigh upon your whole life."

" What does it matter?"

M. Chapelain shrugged his shoulders.

" If you were alone," he went on, " I would say as you do, ' What does it matter?' But you are no longer alone : you have your mother and sister to take care of. You must think of food before thinking of vengeance. How much a month do you earn? Two hundred francs! It is not much for three persons. I would never suggest that you should solicit M. de Thaller's protection; but it would be well, perhaps, to let him know that he has nothing to fear from you. Why shouldn't you do so when you take his fifteen thousand francs back to him? If, as every thing indicates, he has been your father's accomplice, he will certainly be touched by the distress of your family, and, if he has any heart left, he will manage to make you find, without appearing to have any thing to do with it, a situation better suited to your wants. I know that such a step must be very painful; but I repeat it, my dear child, you can no longer think of yourself alone; and what one would not do for himself, one does for a mother and a sister."

Maxence said nothing. Not that he was in any way affected by the worthy old lawyer's speech; but he was asking himself whether or not he should confide to him the events which in the past twenty-four hours had so suddenly modified the situation. He did not feel authorized to do so.

Marius de Trégars had not bound him to secrecy; but an indiscretion might have fatal consequences.

And, after a moment of thought,—

"I am obliged to you, sir," he replied evasively, "for the interest you have manifested in our welfare; and we shall always greatly prize your advice. But for the present you must allow me to leave you with my mother and sister. I have an appointment with—a friend."

And, without waiting for an answer, he slipped M. de Thaller's fifteen thousand francs in his pocket, and hurried out. It was not to M. de Trégars that he went first, however, but to the Hôtel des Folies.

"Mlle. Lucienne has just come home with a big bundle," said Mme. Fortin to Maxence, with her pleasantest smile, as soon as she had seen him emerge from the shades of the corridor.

For the past twenty-four hours, the worthy hostess had been watching for her guest, in the hopes of obtaining some information which she might communicate to the neighbors. Without even condescending to answer, a piece of rudeness at which she felt much hurt, he crossed the narrow court of the hotel at a bound, and started up stairs.

Mlle. Lucienne's room was open. He walked in, and, still out of breath from his rapid ascension,—

"I am glad to find you in," he exclaimed.

The young girl was busy, arranging upon her bed a dress of very light colored silk, trimmed with ruches and lace, an overdress to match, and a bonnet of wonderful shape, loaded with the most brilliant feathers and flowers.

"You see what brings me here," she replied. "I came home to dress. At two o'clock the carriage is coming to take me to the *bois*, where I am to exhibit this costume, certainly the most ridiculous that Van Klopen has yet made me wear."

A smile flitted upon Maxence's lips.

"Who knows," said he, "if this is not the last time you will have to perform this odious task? Ah, my friend! what events have taken place since I last saw you!"

"Fortunate ones?"

"You will judge for yourself."

He closed the door carefully, and, returning to Mlle. Lucienne,—

"Do you know the Marquis de Trégars?" he asked.

"No more than you do. It was yesterday, at the commissary of police, that I first heard his name."

"Well, before a month, M. de Trégars will be Mlle. Gilberte Favoral's husband."

"Is it possible?" exclaimed Mlle. Lucienne with a look of extreme surprise.

But, instead of answering,—

"You told me," resumed Maxence, "that once, in a day of supreme distress, you had applied to Mme. de Thaller for assistance, whereas you were actually entitled to an indemnity for having been run over and seriously hurt by her carriage."

" That is true."

" Whilst you were in the vestibule, waiting for an answer to your letter, which a servant had taken up stairs, M. de Thaller came in; and, when he saw you, he could not repress a gesture of surprise, almost of terror."

" That is true too."

" This behavior of M. de Thaller always remained an enigma to you."

" An inexplicable one."

" Well, I think that I can explain it to you now."

" You? "

Lowering his voice; for he knew that at the Hôtel des Folies there was always to fear some indiscreet ear,—

" Yes, I," he answered; " and for the reason that yesterday, when M. de Trégars appeared in my mother's parlor, I could not suppress an exclamation of surprise, for the reason, Lucienne, that, between Marius de Trégars and yourself, there is a resemblance with which it is impossible not to be struck."

Mlle. Lucienne had become very pale.

" What do you suppose, then? " she asked.

" I believe, my friend, that we are very near penetrating at once the mystery of your birth and the secret of the hatred that has pursued you since the day when you first set your foot in M. de Thaller's house."

Admirably self-possessed as Mlle. Lucienne usually was, the quivering of her lips betrayed at this moment the intensity of her emotion.

After more than a minute of profound meditation,—

"The commissary of police," she said, "has never told me his hopes, except in vague terms. He has told me enough, however, to make me think that he has already had suspicions similar to yours."

"Of course! Would he otherwise have questioned me on the subject of M. de Trégars?"

Mlle. Lucienne shook her head.

"And yet," she said, "even after your explanation, it is in vain that I seek why and how I can so far disturb M. de Thaller's security that he wishes to do away with me."

Maxence made a gesture of superb indifference.

"I confess," he said, "that I don't see it either. But what matters it? Without being able to explain why, I feel that the Baron de Thaller is the common enemy,— yours, mine, my father's, and M. de Trégars'. And something tells me, that, with M. de Trégars' help, we shall triumph. You would share my confidence, Lucienne, if you knew him. There is a man! and my sister has made no vulgar choice. If he has told my mother that he has the means of serving her, it is because he certainly has."

He stopped, and, after a moment of silence,—

"Perhaps," he went on, "the commissary of police might readily understand what I only dimly suspect; but, until further orders, we are forbidden to have recourse to him. It is not my own secret that I have just told you; and, if I have confided it to you, it is because I feel that it is a great piece of good fortune for us; and there is no joy for me, that you do not share."

Mlle. Lucienne wanted to ask many more particulars.

But, looking at his watch,—

"Half-past ten!" he exclaimed, "and M. de Trégars waiting for me."

And he started off, repeating once more to the young girl,—

" I will see you to-night: until then, good hope and good courage."

In the court, two ill-looking men were talking. with the Fortins. But it happened often to the Fortins to talk with ill-looking men: so he took no notice of them, ran out to the Boulevard, and jumping into a cab,—

" Rue Lafitte 70," he cried to the driver, " I pay the trip,—three francs."

When Marius de Trégars had finally determined to compel the bold rascals who had swindled his father to disgorge, he had taken in the Rue Lafitte a small, plainly-furnished apartment on the *entresol*, a fit dwelling for the man of action, the tent in which he takes shelter on the eve of battle ; and he had to wait upon him an old family servant, whom he had found out of place, and who had for him that unquestioning and obstinate devotion peculiar to Breton servants.

It was this excellent man who came at the first stroke of the bell to open the door. And, as soon as Maxence had told him his name,—

" Ah ! " he exclaimed, " my master has been expecting you with a terrible impatience."

It was so true, that M. de Trégars himself appeared at the same moment, and, leading Maxence into the little room which he used as a study,—

" Do you know," he said whilst shaking him cordially by the hand, " that you are almost an hour behind time ? "

Maxence had, among others the detestable fault, sure indication of a weak nature, of being never willing to be in the wrong, and of having always an excuse ready. On this occasion, the excuse was too tempting to al-

low it to escape; and quick he began telling how he had
been detained by M. Chapelain, and how he had heard
from the old lawyer what had taken place at the Mutual
Credit office.

" I know the scene already," said M. de Trégars.

And, fixing upon Maxence a look of friendly raillery,—

" Only," he added, " I attributed your want of punctuality to another reason, a very pretty one this time,
a brunette."

A purple cloud spread over Maxence's cheeks.

" What! " he stammered, " you know? "

" I thought you must have been in haste to go and
tell a person of your acquaintance why, when you saw
me yesterday, you uttered an exclamation of surprise."

This time Maxence lost all countenance.

" What," he said, " you know too? "

M. de Trégars smiled.

" I know a great many things, my dear M. Maxence,"
he replied; " and yet, as I do not wish to be suspected
of witchcraft, I will tell you where all my science comes
from. At the time when your house was closed to me,
after seeking for a long time some means of hearing
from your sister, I discovered at last that she had for
her music-teacher an old Italian, the Signor Gismondi
Pulei. I applied to him for lessons, and became his pupil. But, in the beginning, he kept looking at me with
singular persistence. I inquired the reason; and he told
me that he had once had for a neighbor, at the Batignolles, a young working-girl, who resembled me prodigiously. I paid no attention to this circumstance, and
had, in fact, completely forgotten it; when, quite lately,
Gismondo told me that he had just seen his former
neighbor again, and, what's more, arm in arm with you,

and that you both entered together the Hôtel des Folies.
As he insisted again upon that famous resemblance, I
determined to see for myself. I watched, and I stated,
de visa, that my old Italian was not quite wrong, and
that I had, perhaps, just found the weapon I was looking for."

His eyes staring, and his mouth gaping, Maxence
looked like a man fallen from the clouds.

" Ah, you did watch! " he said.

M. de Trégars snapped his fingers with a gesture of
indifference.

" It is certain," he replied, " that, for a month past,
I have been doing a singular business. But it is not
by remaining on my chair, preaching against the corruption of the age, that I can attain my object. The end
justifies the means. Honest men are very silly, I think,
to allow the rascals to get the better of them under the
sentimental pretext that they cannot condescend to make
use of their weapons."

But an honorable scruple was tormenting Maxence.

"And you think yourself well-informed, sir?" he
inquired. " You know Lucienne? "

" Enough to know that she is not what she seems
to be, and what almost any other would have been in her
place; enough to be certain, that, if she shows herself
two or three times a week riding around the lake, it is
not for her pleasure; enough, also, to be persuaded, that,
despite appearances, she is not your mistress, and that,
far from having disturbed your life, and compromised
your prospects, she set you back into the right road, at
the moment, perhaps, when you were about to branch
off into the wrong path."

Marius de Trégars was assuming fantastic proportions in the mind of Maxence.

"How did you manage," he stammered, "thus to find out the truth?"

"With time and money, every thing is possible."

"But you must have had grave reasons to take so much trouble about Lucienne."

"Very grave ones, indeed."

"You know that she was basely forsaken when quite a child?"

"Perfectly."

"And that she was brought up through charity"—

"By some poor gardeners at Louveciennes: yes, I know all that."

Maxence was trembling with joy. It seemed to him that his most dazzling hopes were about to be realized. Seizing the hands of Marius de Trégars,—

"Ah, you know Lucienne's family!" he exclaimed.

But M. de Trégars shook his head.

"I have suspicions," he answered; "but, up to this time, I have suspicions only, I assure you."

"But that family does exist; since they have already, at three different times, attempted to get rid of the poor girl."

"I think as you do; but we must have proofs: and we shall find some. You may rest assured of that."

Here he was interrupted by the noise of the opening door.

The old servant came in, and advancing to the centre of the room with a mysterious look,—

"Madame la Baronne de Thaller," he said in a low voice.

Marius de Trégars started violently.

" Where ? " he asked.

" She is down stairs in her carriage," replied the ser·
vant. " Her footman is here, asking whether monsieur
is at home, and whether she can come up."

" Can she possibly have heard any thing ? " murmured M. de Trégars with a deep frown.

And, after a moment of reflection,—

" So much the more reason to see her," he added
quickly. " Let her come. Request her to do me the
honor of coming up stairs."

This last incident completely upset all Maxence's
ideas. He no longer knew what to imagine.

" Quick," said M. de Trégars to him : " quick, disappear ; and, whatever you may hear, not a word ! "

And he pushed him into his bedroom, which was divided from the study by a mere tapestry curtain.

It was time ; for already in the next room could be
heard a great rustling of silk and starched petticoats.
Mme. de Thaller appeared.

She was still the same coarsely beautiful woman, who,
sixteen years before, had sat at Mme. Favoral's table.
Time had passed without scarcely touching her with the
tip of his wing. Her flesh had retained its dazzling
whiteness ; her hair, of a bluish black, its marvellous
opulence ; her lips, their carmine hue ; her eyes, their
lustre. Her figure only had become heavier, her features less delicate ; and her neck and throat had lost their
undulations, and the purity of their outlines.

But neither the years, nor the millions, nor the intimacy of the most fashionable women, had been able to
give her those qualities which cannot be acquired,—
grace, distinction, and taste.

If there was a woman accustomed to dress, it was she :
a splendid dry-goods store could have been set up with

the silks and the velvets, the satins and cashmeres, the muslins, the laces, and all the known tissues, that had passed over her shoulders.

Her elegance was quoted and copied. And yet there was about her always and under all circumstances, an indescribable flavor of the *parvenue*. Her gestures had remained trivial; her voice, common and vulgar.

Throwing herself into an arm-chair, and bursting into a loud laugh,—

" Confess, my dear marquis," she said, " that you are terribly astonished to see me thus drop upon you, without warning, at eleven o'clock in the morning."

" I feel, above all, terribly flattered," replied M. de Trégars, smiling.

With a rapid glance she was surveying the little study, the modest furniture, the papers piled on the desk, as if she had hoped that the dwelling would reveal to her something of the master's ideas and projects.

" I was just coming from Van Klopen's," she resumed; " and passing before your house, I took a fancy to come in and stir you up; and here I am."

M. de Trégars was too much a man of the world, and of the best world, to allow his features to betray the secret of his impressions; and yet, to any one who had known him well, a certain contraction of the eyelids would have revealed a serious annoyance and an intense anxiety.

" How is the baron?" he inquired.

" As sound as an oak," answered Mme. de Thaller, " notwithstanding all the cares and the troubles, which you can well imagine. By the way, you know what has happened to us?"

" I read in the papers that the cashier of the Mutual Credit had disappeared."

" And it is but too true. That wretch Favoral has gone off with an enormous amount of money."

" Twelve millions, I heard."

" Something like it. A man who had the reputation of a saint too; a puritan. Trust people's faces after that! I never liked him, I confess. But M. de Thaller had a perfect fancy for him; and, when he had spoken of his Favoral, there was nothing more to say. Any way, he has cleared out, leaving his family without means. A very interesting family, it seems, too,—a wife who is goodness itself, and a charming daughter: at least, so says Costeclar, who is very much in love with her."

M. de Trégars' countenance remained perfectly indifferent, like that of a man who is hearing about persons and things in which he does not take the slightest interest.

Mme. de Thaller noticed this.

" But it isn't to tell you all this," she went on, " that I came up. It is an interested motive brought me. We have, some of my friends and myself, organized a lottery —a work of charity, my dear marquis, and quite patriotic—for the benefit of the Alsatians. I have lots of tickets to dispose of; and I've thought of you to help me out."

More smiling than ever,—

" I am at your orders, madame," answered Marius, " but, in mercy, spare me."

She took out some tickets from a small shell pocketbook.

" Twenty, at ten francs," she said. " It isn't too much, is it ? "

" It is a great deal for my modest resources."

She pocketed the ten napoleons which he handed her, and, in a tone of ironical compassion,—

"Are you so very poor, then?" she asked.

"Why, I am neither banker nor broker, you know."

She had risen, and was smoothing the folds of her dress.

"Well, my dear marquis," she resumed, "it is certainly not me who will pity you. When a man of your age, and with your name, remains poor, it is his own fault. Are there no rich heiresses?"

"I confess that I haven't tried to find one yet."

She looked at him straight in the eyes, and then suddenly bursting out laughing,—

"Look around you," she said, "and I am sure you'll not be long discovering a beautiful young girl, very blonde, who would be delighted to become Marquise de Trégars, and who would bring in her apron a dowry of twelve or fifteen hundred thousand francs in good securities,—securities which the Favorals can't carry off. Think well, and then come to see us. You know that M. de Thaller is very fond of you; and, after all the trouble we have been having, you owe us a visit."

Whereupon she went out, M. de Trégars, going down to escort her to her carriage.

But as he came up,—

"Attention!" he cried to Maxence; "for it's very evident that the Thallers have wind of something."

III.

It was a revelation, that visit of Mme. de Thaller's; and there was no need of very much perspicacity to guess her anxiety beneath her bursts of laughter, and to understand that it was a bargain she had come to propose. It was evident, therefore, that Marius de Trégars held within his hands the principal threads of that complicated intrigue which had just culminated in that robbery of twelve millions. But would he be able to make use of them? What were his designs, and his means of action? That is what Maxence could not in any way conjecture.

He had no time to ask questions.

" Come," said M. Trégars, whose agitation was manifest,—" come, let us breakfast: we have not a moment to lose."

And, whilst his servant was bringing in his modest meal,—

" I am expecting M. d'Escajoul," he said. " Show him in as soon as he comes."

Retired as he had lived from the financial world, Maxence had yet heard the name of Octave d'Escajoul.

Who has not seen him, happy and smiling, his eye bright, and his lip ruddy, notwithstanding his fifty years, walking on the sunny side of the Boulevard, with his royal blue jacket and his eternal white vest? He is passionately fond of everything that tends to make life pleasant and easy; dines at Bignon's, or the Café Anglais; plays baccarat at the club with extraordinary luck; has the most comfortable apartment and the most elegant *coupé* in all Paris. With all this, he is pleased to declare that he is the happiest of men, and is certainly one of the most popular; for he cannot walk three blocks on the Boulevard without lifting his hat at least fifty times, and shaking hands twice as often.

And when any one asks, " What does he do? " the invariable answer is, " Why he operates."

To explain what sort of operations, would not be, perhaps, very easy. In the world of rogues, there are some rogues more formidable and more skilful than the rest, who always manage to escape the hand of the law. They are not such fools as to operate in person,—not they! They content themselves with watching their friends and comrades. If a good haul is made, at once they appear and claim their share. And, as they always threaten to inform, there is no help for it but to let them pocket the clearest of the profit.

Well, in a more elevated sphere, in the world of speculation, it is precisely that lucrative and honorable industry which M. d'Escajoul carries on. Thoroughly master of his ground, possessing a superior scent and an imperturbable patience, always awake, and continually on the watch, he never operates unless he is sure to win.

And the day when the manager of some company has violated his charter or stretched the law a little too far, he may be sure to see M. d'Escajoul appear, and ask for some little—advantages, and proffer, in exchange, the most thorough discretion, and even his kind offices.

Two or three of his friends have heard him say,—

" Who would dare to blame me? It's very moral, what I am doing."

Such is the man who came in, smiling, just as Maxence and Marius de Trégars had sat down at the table.

M. de Trégars rose to receive him.

' You will breakfast with us? " he said.

" Thank you," answered M. d'Escajoul. " I breakfasted precisely at eleven, as usual. Punctuality is a politeness which a man owes to his stomach. But I will accept with pleasure a drop of that old Cognac which you offered me the other evening."

He took a seat; and the valet brought him a glass, which he set on the edge of the table.   Then,—

"I have just seen our man," he said.

Maxence understood that he was referring to M. de Thaller.

"Well?" inquired M. de Trégars.

"Impossible to get any thing out of him.   I turned him over and over, every way.   Nothing!"

"Indeed!"

"It's so; and you know if I understand the business. But what can you say to a man who answers you all the time, 'The matter is in the hands of the law; experts have been named; I have nothing to fear from the most minute investigations'?"

By the look which Marius de Trégars kept riveted upon M. d'Escajoul, it was easy to see that his confidence in him was not without limits.   He felt it, and, with an air of injured innocence,—

"Do you suspect me, by chance," he said, "to have allowed myself to be hoodwinked by Thaller?"

And as M. de Trégars said nothing, which was the most eloquent of answers,—

"Upon my word," he insisted, "you are wrong to doubt me.   Was it you who came after me?   No.   It was I, who, hearing through Marcolet the history of your fortune, came to tell you, 'Do you want to know a way of swamping Thaller?'   And the reasons I had to wish that Thaller might be swamped: I have them still.   He trifled with me, he 'sold' me, and he must suffer for it; for, if it came to be known that I could be taken in with impunity, it would be all over with my credit."

After a moment of silence,—

" Do you believe, then," asked M. de Trégars, " that
M. de Thaller is innocent?"

" Perhaps."

" That would be curious."

" Or else his measures are so well taken that he has
absolutely nothing to fear. If Favoral takes everything
upon himself, what can they say to the other? If they
have acted in collusion, the thing has been prepared
for a long time; and, before commencing to fish, they
must have troubled the water so well, that justice will
be unable to see anything in it."

" And you see no one who could help us?"

" Favoral "—

To Maxence's great surprise, M. de Trégars shrugged
his shoulders.

" That one is gone," he said; " and, were he at hand,
it is quite evident that if he was in collusion with M.
de Thaller, he would not speak."

" Of course."

" That being the case, what can we do?"

" Wait."

M. de Trégars made a gesture of discouragement.

" I might as well give up the fight, then," he said,
" and try to compromise."

" Why so? We don't know what may happen. Keep
quiet, be patient; I am here, and I am looking out for
squalls."

He got up and prepared to leave.

" You have more experience than I have," said M. de
Trégars; " and, since that's your opinion "—

M. d'Escajoul had resumed all his good humor.

" Very well, then, it's understood," he said, pressing

M. de Trégars' hand. "I am watching for both of us; and if I see a chance, I come at once, and you act."

But the outer door had hardly closed, when suddenly the countenance of Marius de Trégars changed. Shaking the hand which M. d'Escajoul had just touched,—

"Pouah!" he said with a look of thorough disgust,— "pouah!"

And noticing Maxence's look of utter surprise,—

"Don't you understand," he said, "that this old rascal has been sent to me by Thaller to feel my intentions, and mislead me by false information? I had scented him, fortunately; and, if either one of us is dupe of the other, I have every reason to believe that it will not be me."

They had finished their breakfast. M. de Trégars called his servant.

"Have you been for a carriage?" he asked.

"It is at the door, sir."

"Well, then, come along."

Maxence had the good sense not to over-estimate himself. Perfectly convinced that he could accomplish nothing alone, he was firmly resolved to trust blindly to Marius de Trégars.

He followed him, therefore; and it was only after the carriage had started, that he ventured to ask,—

"Where are we going?"

"Didn't you hear me," replied M. de Trégars, "order the driver to take us to the court-house?"

"I beg your pardon; but what I wish to know is, what we are going to do there?"

"You are going, my dear friend, to ask an audience of the judge who has your father's case in charge, and deposit into his hands the fifteen thousand francs you have in your pocket."

" What! You wish me to "—

" I think it better to place that money into the hands of justice, which will appreciate the step, than into those of M. de Thaller, who would not breathe a word about it. We are in a position where nothing should be neglected; and that money may prove an indication."

But they had arrived. M. de Trégars guided Maxence through the labyrinth of corridors of the building, until he came to a long gallery, at the entrance of which an usher was seated reading a newspaper.

" M. Barban d'Avranchel?" inquired M. de Trégars.

" He is in his office." replied the usher.

" Please ask him if he would receive an important deposition in the Favoral case."

The usher rose somewhat reluctantly, and, while he was gone,—

" You will go in alone," said M. de Trégars to Maxence. " I shall not appear; and it is important that my name should not even be pronounced. But, above all, try and remember even the most insignificant words of the judge; for, upon what he tells you, I shall regulate my conduct."

The usher returned.

" M. d'Avranchel will receive you," he said.

And, leading Maxence to the extremity of the gallery, he opened a small door, and pushed him in, saying at the same time,—

" That is it, sir: walk in."

It was a small room, with a low ceiling, and poorly furnished. The faded curtains and threadbare carpet showed plainly that more than one judge had occupied it, and that legions of accused criminals had passed through it. In front of a table, two men—one old,

the judge; the other young, the clerk—were signing
and classifying papers. These papers related to the
Favoral case, and were all indorsed in large letters:
Mutual Credit Company.

As soon as Maxence appeared, the judge rose, and,
after measuring him with a clear and cold look:—

"Who are you?" he interrogated.

In a somewhat husky voice, Maxence stated his name
and surname.

"Ah! you are Vincent Favoral's son," interrupted
the judge. "And it was you who helped him escape
through the window? I was going to send you a summons this very day; but, since you are here, so much
the better. You have something important to communicate, I have been told."

Very few people, even among the most strictly honest, can overcome a certain unpleasant feeling when,
having crossed the threshold of the palace of justice,
they find themselves in presence of a judge. More
than almost any one else, Maxence was likely to be
accessible to that vague and inexplicable feeling; and
it was with an effort that he answered,—

"On Saturday evening, the Baron de Thaller called
at our house a few minutes before the commissary.
After loading my father with reproaches, he invited
him to leave the country; and, in order to facilitate his
flight, he handed him these fifteen thousand francs. My
father declined to accept them; and, at the moment of
parting, he recommended to me particularly to return
them to M. de Thaller. I thought it best to return them
to you, sir."

"Why?"

"Because I wished the fact known to you of the
money having been offered and refused."

M. Barban d'Avranchel was quietly stroking his whiskers, once of a bright red, but now almost entirely white.

"Is this an insinuation against the manager of the Mutual Credit?" he asked.

Maxence looked straight at him; and, in a tone which affirmed precisely the reverse,—

"I accuse no one," he said.

"I must tell you," resumed the judge, "that M. de Thaller has himself informed me of this circumstance. When he called at your house, he was ignorant, as yet, of the extent of the embezzlements, and was in hopes of being able to hush up the affair. That's why he wished his cashier to start for Belgium. This system of helping criminals to escape the just punishment of their crimes is to be bitterly deplored; but it is quite the habit of your financial magnates, who prefer sending some poor devil of an employé to hang himself abroad, than run the risk of compromising their credit by confessing that they have been robbed."

Maxence might have had a great deal to say; but M. de Trégars had recommended him the most extreme reserve. He remained silent.

"On the other hand," resumed the judge, "the refusal to accept the money so generously offered does not speak in favor of Vincent Favoral. He was well aware, when he left, that it would require a great deal of money to reach the frontier, escape pursuit, and hide himself abroad; and, if he refused the fifteen thousand francs, it must have been because he was well provided for already."

Tears of shame and rage started from Maxence's eyes.

"I am certain, sir," he exclaimed, "that my father went off without a sou."

" What has become of the millions, then ? " he asked coldly.

Maxence hesitated. Why not mention his suspicions? He dared not.

" My father speculated at the *bourse,*" he stammered.

" And he led a scandalous conduct, keeping up, away from home, a style of living which must have absorbed immense sums."

" We knew nothing of it, sir; and our first suspicions were aroused by what the commissary of police told us."

The judge insisted no more; and in a tone which indicated that his question was a mere matter of form, and he attached but little importance to the answer,—

" You have no news from your father? " he asked.

" None whatever."

" And you have no idea where he has gone? "

" None in the least."

M. d'Avranchel had already resumed his seat at the table, and was again busy with his papers.

" You may retire," he said. You will be notified if I need you."

Maxence felt much discouraged when he joined M. de Trégars at the entrance of the gallery.

" The judge is convinced of M. de Thaller's entire innocence," he said.

But as soon as he had narrated, with a fidelity that did honor to his memory, all that had just occurred,—

" Nothing is lost yet," declared M. de Trégars.

And, taking from his pocket the bill for two trunks, which had been found in M. Favoral's portfolio,—

" There," he said, " we shall know our fate."

IV.

M. DE TREGARS and Maxence were in luck. They had a good driver and a fair horse; and in twenty minutes they were at the trunk store. As soon as the cab stopped,—

"Well," exclaimed M. de Trégars, "I suppose it has to be done."

And, with the look of a man who has made up his mind to do something which is extremely repugnant to him, he jumped out, and, followed by Maxence, entered the shop.

"It was a modest establishment; and the people who kept it, husband and wife, seeing two customers coming in, rushed to meet them, with that welcoming smile which blossoms upon the lips of every Parisian shop-keeper.

"What will you have, gentlemen?"

And, with wonderful volubility, they went on enumerating every article which they had for sale in their shop,—from the "indispensable-necessary," containing seventy-seven pieces of solid silver, and costing four thousand francs, down to the humblest carpet-bag at thirty-nine cents.

But Marius de Trégars interrupted them as soon as he could get an opportunity, and, showing them their bill,—

"It was here, wasn't it," he inquired, "that the two trunks were bought which are charged in this bill?"

"Yes, sir," answered simultaneously both husband and wife.

"When were they delivered?"

"Our porter went to deliver them, less than two hours after they were bought."

" Where ? "

By this time the shopkeepers were beginning to exchange uneasy looks.

" Why do you ask ? " inquired the woman in a tone which indicated that she had the settled intention not to answer, unless for good and valid reason.

To obtain the simplest information is not always as easy as might be supposed. The suspicion of the Parisian tradesman is easily aroused; and, as his head is stuffed with stories of spies and robbers, as soon as he is questioned he becomes as dumb as an oyster.

But M. de Trégars had foreseen the difficulty.

" I beg you to believe, madame," he went on, " that my questions are not dictated by an idle curiosity. Here are the facts. A relative of ours, a man of a certain age, of whom we are very fond, and whose head is a little weak, left his home some forty-eight hours since. We are looking for him, and we are in hopes, if we find these trunks, to find him at the same time."

With furtive glances, the husband and wife were tacitly consulting each other.

" The fact is," they said, " we wouldn't like, under any consideration, to commit an indiscretion which might result to the prejudice of a customer."

" Fear nothing," said M. de Trégars with a reassuring gesture. " If we have not had recourse to the police, it's because, you know, it isn't pleasant to have the police interfere in one's affairs. If you have any objections to answer me, however, I must, of course, apply to the commissary."

The argument proved decisive.

" If that's the case," replied the woman, " I am ready to tell all I know."

" Well, then, madame, what do you know ? "

" These two trunks were bought on Friday afternoon
last, by a man of a certain age, tall, very thin, with a
stern countenance, and wearing a long frock coat."

" No more doubt," murmured Maxence. " It was
he."

" And now," the woman went on, " that you have just
told me that your relative was a little weak in the head,
I remember that this gentleman had a strange sort of
way about him, and that he kept walking about the
store as if he had fleas on his legs. And awful particular he was too! Nothing was handsome enough and
strong enough for him; and he was anxious about the
safety-locks, as he had, he said, many objects of value,
papers, and securities, to put away."

" And where did he tell you to send the two trunks? "

" Rue du Cirque, to Mme. ——wait a minute, I have
the name at the end of my tongue."

" You must have it on your books, too," remarked
M. de Trégars.

The husband was already looking over his blotter.

" April 26, 1872," he said. " 26, here it is: ' Two
leather trunks, patent safety-locks : Mme. Zélie Cadelle,
49 Rue du Cirque.' "

Without too much affectation, M. de Trégars had
drawn near to the shopkeeper, and was looking over his
shoulder.

" What is that," he asked, " written there, below the
address? "

" That, sir, is the direction left by the customer
' Mark on each end of the trunks, in large letters, " Rio
de Janeiro." ' "

Maxence could not suppress an exclamation. " Oh! "

But the tradesman mistook him; and, seizing this
magnificent opportunity to display his knowledge,—

" Rio de Janeiro is the capital of Brazil," he said in a tone of importance. " And your relative evidently intended to go there; and, if he has not changed his mind, I doubt whether you can overtake him; for the Brazilian steamer was to have sailed yesterday from Havre."

Whatever may have been his intentions, M. de Trégars remained perfectly calm.

" If that's the case," he said to the shopkeepers, " I think I had better give up the chase. I am much obliged to you, however, for your information."

But, once out again,—

" Do you really believe," inquired Maxence, " that my father has left France? "

M. de Trégars shook his head.

" I will give you my opinion," he uttered, " after I have investigated matters in the Rue du Cirque."

They drove there in a few minutes; and, the cab having stopped at the entrance of the street, they walked on foot in front of No. 49. It was a small cottage, only one story in height, built between a sanded court-yard and a garden, whose tall trees showed above the roof. At the windows could be seen curtains of light-colored silk,—a sure indication of the presence of a young and pretty woman.

For a few minutes Marius de Trégars remained in observation; but, as nothing stirred,—

" We must find out something, somehow," he exclaimed impatiently.

And noticing a large grocery store bearing No. 62, he directed his steps towards it, still accompanied by Maxence.

It was the hour of the day when customers are rare. Standing in the centre of the shop, the grocer, a big fat man with an air of importance, was overseeing his men, who were busy putting things in order.

M. de Trégars took him aside, and with an accent of mystery,—

" I am," he said, " a clerk with M. Drayton, the jeweller in the Rue de la Paix; and I come to ask you one of those little favors which tradespeople owe to each other."

A frown appeared on the fat man's countenance. He thought, perhaps, that M. Drayton's clerks were rather too stylish-looking; or else, perhaps, he felt apprehensive of one of those numerous petty swindles of which shopkeepers are constantly the victims.

" What is it? " said he. " Speak! "

" I am on my way," spoke M. de Trégars, " to deliver a ring which a lady purchased of us yesterday. She is not a regular customer, and has given us no references. If she doesn't pay, shall I leave the ring? My employer told me, ' Consult some prominent tradesman of the neighborhood, and follow his advice.' "

Prominent tradesman! Delicately tickled vanity was dancing in the grocer's eyes.

" What is the name of the lady? " he inquired.

" Mme. Zélie Cadelle."

The grocer burst out laughing.

" In that case, my boy," he said, tapping familiarly the shoulder of the so-called clerk, " whether she pays or not, you can deliver the article."

The familiarity was not, perhaps, very much to the taste of the Marquis de Trégars. No matter.

" She is rich, then, that lady? " he said.

" Personally no. But she is protected by an old fool, who allows her all her fancies."

" Indeed! "

"It is scandalous; and you cannot form an idea of the amount of money that is spent in that house. Horses, carriages, servants, dresses, balls, dinners, card-playing all night, a perpetual carnival: it must be ruinous!"

M. de Trégars never winced.

"And the old man who pays?" he asked; "do you know him?"

"I have seen him pass,—a tall, lean, old fellow, who doesn't look very rich, either. But excuse me: here is a customer I must wait upon."

Having walked out into the street,—

"We must separate now," declared M. de Trégars to Maxence.

"What! You wish to"—

"Go and wait for me in that *café* yonder, at the corner of the street. I must see that Zélie Cadelle and speak to her."

And without suffering an objection on the part of Maxence, he walked resolutely up to the cottage-gate, and rang vigorously.

At the sound of the bell, one of those servants stepped out into the yard, who seem manufactured on purpose, heaven knows where, for the special service of young ladies who keep house,—a tall rascal with sallow complexion and straight hair, a cynical eye, and a low, impudent smile.

"What do you wish, sir?" he inquired through the grating.

"That you should open the door, first," uttered M. de Trégars, with such a look and such an accent, that the other obeyed at once.

"And now," he added, "go and announce me to Mme. Zélie Cadelle."

"Madame is out," replied the valet.

And noticing that M. de Trégars shrugged his shoulders,—

"Upon my word," he said, "she has gone to the *bois* with one of her friends. If you won't believe me, ask my comrades there."

And he pointed out two other servants of the same pattern as himself, who were sitting at a table in the carriage-house, playing cards, and drinking.

But M. de Trégars did not mean to be imposed upon. He felt certain that the man was lying. Instead, therefore, of discussing,—

"I want you to take me to your mistress," he ordered, in a tone that admitted of no objection; "or else I'll find my way to her alone."

It was evident that he would do just as he said, by force if needs be. The valet saw this, and, after hesitating a moment longer,—

"Come along, then," he said, "since you insist so much. We'll talk to the chambermaid."

And, having led M. de Trégars into the vestibule, he called out, "Mam'selle Amanda!"

A woman at once made her appearance who was a worthy mate for the valet. She must have been about forty, and the most alarming duplicity could be read upon her features, deeply pitted by the small-pox. She wore a pretentious dress, an apron like a stage-servant, and a cap profusely decorated with flowers and ribbons.

"Here is a gentleman," said the valet, "who insists upon seeing madame. You fix it with him."

Better than her fellow servant, Mlle. Amanda could judge with whom she had to deal. A single glance at this obstinate visitor convinced her that he was not one who can be easily turned off.

Putting on, therefore, her pleasantest smile, thus displaying at the same time her decayed teeth,—

"The fact is that monsieur will very much disturb madame," she observed.

"I shall excuse myself."

"But I'll be scolded."

Instead of answering, M. de Trégars took a couple of twenty-franc-notes out of his pocket, and slipped them into her hand.

"Please follow me to the parlor, then," she said with a heavy sigh.

M. de Trégars did so, whilst observing everything around him with the attentive perspicacity of a deputy sheriff preparing to make out an inventory.

Being double, the house was much more spacious than could have been thought from the street, and arranged with that science of comfort which is the genius of modern architects.

The most lavish luxury was displayed on all sides; not that solid, quiet, and harmonious luxury which is the result of long years of opulence, but the coarse, loud, and superficial luxury of the *parvenu*, who is eager to enjoy quick, and to possess all that he has craved from others.

The vestibule was a folly, with its exotic plants climbing along crystal trellises, and its Sèvres and China *jardinières* filled with gigantic azaleas. And along the gilt railing of the stairs marble and bronze statuary was intermingled with masses of growing flowers.

"It must take twenty thousand francs a year to keep up this conservatory alone," thought M. de Trégars.

Meantime the old chambermaid opened a satinwood door with silver lock.

" That's the parlor," she said. " Take a seat whilst
I go and tell madame."

In this parlor everything had been combined to daz-
zle. Furniture, carpets, hangings, every thing, was
rich, too rich, furiously, incontestably, obviously rich.
The chandelier was a masterpiece, the clock an original and unique piece of work. The pictures hanging
upon the wall were all signed with the most famous
names.

" To judge of the rest by what I have seen," thought
M. de Trégars, " there must have been at least four or
five hundred thousand francs spent on this house."

And, although he was shocked by a quantity of details which betrayed the most absolute lack of taste, he
could hardly persuade himself that the cashier of the
Mutual Credit could be the master of this sumptuous
dwelling; and he was asking himself whether he had not
followed the wrong scent, when a circumstance came to
put an end to all his doubts.

Upon the mantlepiece, in a small velvet frame, was
Vincent Favoral's portrait.

M. de Trégars had been seated for a few minutes,
and was collecting his somewhat scattered thoughts,
when a slight grating sound, and a rustling noise, made
him turn around.

Mme. Zélie Cadelle was coming in.

She was a woman of some twenty-five or six, rather
tall, lithe, and well made. Her face was pale and worn;
and her heavy dark hair was scattered over her neck
and shoulders. She looked at once sarcastic and good-
natured, impudent and *naive*, with her sparkling eyes,
her turned-up nose, and wide mouth furnished with
teeth, sound and white, like those of a young dog. She
had wasted no time upon her dress; for she wore a

plain blue cashmere wrapper, fastened at the waist with a sort of silk scarf of similar color.

From the very threshold,—

"Dear me!" she exclaimed, "how very singular!"

M. de Trégars stepped forward.

"What?" he inquired.

"Oh, nothing!" she replied,—"nothing at all!"

And without ceasing to look at him with a wondering eye, but suddenly changing her tone of voice,—

"And so, sir," she said, "my servants have been unable to keep you from forcing yourself into my house!"

"I hope, madame," said M. de Trégars with a polite bow, "that you will excuse my persistence. I come for a matter which can suffer no delay."

She was still looking at him obstinately.

"Who are you?" she asked.

"My name will not afford you any information. I am the Marquis de Trégars."

"Trégars!" she repeated, looking up at the ceiling, as if in search of an inspiration. "Trégars! Never heard of it!"

And throwing herself into an arm chair,—

"Well, sir, what do you wish with me, then? Speak!"

He had taken a seat near her, and kept his eyes riveted upon hers.

"I have come, madame," he replied, "to ask you to put me in the way to see and speak to the man whose photograph is there on the mantlepiece."

He expected to take her by surprise, and that by a shudder, a cry, a gesture, she might betray her secret. Not at all.

"Are you, then, one of M. Vincent's friends?" she asked quietly.

M. de Trégars understood, and this was subsequently confirmed, that it was under his Christian name of Vincent alone, that the cashier of the Mutual Credit was known in the Rue du Cirque.

"Yes, I am a friend of his," he replied; "and if I could see him, I could probably render him an important service."

"Well, you are too late."

"Why?"

"Because M. Vincent put off more than twenty-four hours since?"

"Are you sure of that?"

"As sure as a person can be who went to the railway station yesterday with him and all his baggage."

"You saw him leave?"

"As I see you."

"Where was he going?"

"To Havre, to take the steamer for Brazil, which was to sail on the same day; so that, by this time, he must be awfully seasick."

"And you really think that it was his intention to go to Brazil?"

"He said so. It was written on his thirty-six trunks in letters half a foot high. Besides, he showed me his ticket."

"Have you any idea what could have induced him to expatriate himself thus, at his age?"

"He told me he had spent all his money, and also some of other people's; that he was afraid of being arrested; and that he was going yonder to be quiet, and try to make another fortune."

Was Mme. Zélie speaking in good faith? To ask the question would have been rather *naive;* but an effort might be made to find out.

Carefully concealing his own impressions, and the importance he attached to this conversation,—

"I pity you sincerely, madame," resumed M. de Trégars; "for you must be sorely grieved by this sud' den departure."

"Me!" she said in a voice that came from the heart. "I don't care a straw."

Marquis de Trégars knew well enough the ladies of the class to which he supposed that Mme. Zélie Cadelle must belong, not to be surprised at this frank declaration.

"And yet," he said, "you are indebted to him for the princely magnificence that surrounds you here."

"Of course."

"He being gone, as you say, will you be able to keep up your style of living?"

Half raising herself from her seat,—

"I haven't the slightest idea of doing so," she exclaimed. "Never in the whole world have I had such a stupid time as for the last five months that I have spent in this gilded cage. What a bore, my beloved brethren! I am yawning still at the mere thought of the number of times I have yawned in it."

M. de Trégars' gesture of surprise was the more natural, that his surprise was immense.

"You are tired being here?" he said.

"To death."

"And you have only been here five months?"

"Dear me, yes! and by the merest chance, too, you'll see. One day at the beginning of last December, I was coming from—but no matter where I was coming from.

At any rate, I hadn't a cent in my pocket, and nothing but an old calico dress on my back; and I was going along, not in the best of humor, as you may imagine, when I feel that some one is following me. Without looking around, and from the corner of my eye, I look over my shoulder, and I see a respectable-looking old gentleman, wearing a long frock-coat."

" M. Vincent? "

" In his own natural person, and who was walking, walking. I quietly begin to walk slower; and, as soon as we come to a place where there was hardly any one, he comes up alongside of me."

Something comical must have happened at this moment, which Mme. Zélie Cadelle said nothing about; for she was laughing most heartily,—a frank and sonorous laughter.

" Then," she resumed, " he begins at once to explain that I remind him of a person whom he loved tenderly, and whom he has just had the misfortune to lose, adding, that he would deem himself the happiest of men if I would allow him to take care of me, and insure me a brilliant position."

" You see! That rascally Vincent! " said M. de Trégars, just to be saying something.

Mme. Zélie shook her head.

" You know him," she resumed. " He is not young; he is not handsome; he is not funny. I did not fancy him one bit; and, if I had only known where to find shelter for the night, I'd soon have sent him to the old Nick,—him and his brilliant position. But, not having enough money to buy myself a penny-loaf, it wasn't the time to put on any airs. So I tell him that I accept. He goes for a cab; we get into it; and he brings me right straight here."

Positively M. de Trégars required his entire self-control to conceal the intensity of his curiosity.

"Was this house, then, already as it is now?" he interrogated.

"Precisely, except that there were no servants in it, except the chambermaid Amanda, who is M. Favoral's confidante. All the others had been dismissed; and it was a hostler from a stable near by who came to take care of the horses."

"And what then?"

"Then you may imagine what I looked like in the midst of all this magnificence, with my old shoes and my fourpenny skirt. Something like a grease-spot on a satin dress. M. Vincent seemed delighted, nevertheless. He had sent Amanda out to get me some under-clothing and a ready-made wrapper; and, whilst waiting, he took me all through the house, from the cellar to the garret, saying that everything was at my command, and that the next day I would have a battalion of servants to wait on me."

It was evidently with perfect frankness that she was speaking, and with the pleasure one feels in telling an extraordinary adventure. But suddenly she stopped short, as if discovering that she was forgetting herself, and going farther than was proper.

And it was only after a moment of reflection that she went on,—

"It was like fairyland to me. I had never tasted the opulence of the great, you see, and I had never had any money except that which I earned. So, during the first days, I did nothing but run up and down stairs, admiring everything, feeling everything with my own hands, and looking at myself in the glass to make sure that I was not dreaming. I rang the bell just to make the servants come up; I spent hours trying dresses; then I'd have the horses put to the carriage, and either ride to the *bois,* or go out shopping. M. Vincent gave me as much money as I wanted; and it seemed as though I never spent enough. I shout, I was like a mad woman."

A cloud appeared upon Mme. Zélie's countenance, and, changing suddenly her tone and her manner,—

"Unfortunately," she went on, "one gets tired of every thing. At the end of two weeks I knew the house from top to bottom, and after a month I was sick of the whole thing; so that one night I began dressing. 'Where do you want to go?' Amanda asked me. 'Why, to Mabille, to dance a quadrille, or two.'—'Impossible!'—'Why?'—'Because M. Vincent does not wish you to go out at night.'—'We'll see about that!' The next day, I tell all this to M. Vincent; and he says that Amanda is right; that it is not proper for a woman in my position to frequent balls; and that, if I want to go out at night, I can stay. Get out! I tell you what, if it hadn't been for the fine carriage, and all that, I would have cleared out that minute. Any way, I became disgusted from that moment, and have been more and more ever since; and, if M. Vincent had not himself left, I certainly would."

"To go where?"

"Anywhere. Look here, now! do you suppose I need a man to support me! No, thank Heaven! Little Zélie, here present, has only to apply to any dressmaker, and she'll be glad to give her four francs a day to run the machine. And she'll be free, at least; and she can laugh and dance as much as she likes."

M. de Trégars had made a mistake: he had just discovered it.

Mme. Zélie Cadelle was certainly not particularly virtuous; but she was far from being the woman he expected to meet.

"At any rate," he said, "you did well to wait patiently."

"I do not regret it."

"If you can keep this house "—

She interrupted him with a great burst of laughter.

"This house!" she exclaimed. "Why, it was sold long ago, with every thing in it,—furniture, horses, carriages, every thing except me. A young gentleman, very well dressed, bought it for a tall girl, who looks like a goose, and has far over a thousand francs of red hair on her head."

"Are you sure of that?"

"Sure as I live, having seen with my own eyes the young swell and his red-headed friend counting heaps of bank-notes to M. Vincent. They are to move in day after to-morrow; and they have invited me to the housewarming. But no more of it for me, I thank you! I am sick and tired of all these people. And the proof of it is, I am busy packing my things; and lots of them I have too,—dresses, underclothes, jewelry. He was a good-natured fellow, old Vincent was, anyhow. He gave me money enough to buy some furniture. I have hired a small apartment; and I am going to set up dressmaking on my own hook. And won't we laugh then! and won't we have some fun to make up for lost time! Come, my children, take your places for a quadrille. Forward two!"

And, bouncing out of her chair, she began sketching out one of those bold cancan steps which astound the policemen on duty in the ball-rooms.

"Bravo!" said M. de Trégars, forcing himself to smile,—"bravo!"

He saw clearly now what sort of woman was Mme. Zélie Cadelle; how he should speak to her, and what cords he might yet cause to vibrate within her. He recognized the true daughter of Paris, wayward and nervous, who in the midst of her disorders preserves an instinctive pride; who places her independence far above all the money in the world; who gives, rather than sells, herself; who knows no law but her caprice, no morality but the policeman, no religion but pleasure.

As soon as she had returned to her seat,—

"There you are dancing gayly," he said, "and poor Vincent is doubtless groaning at this moment over his separation from you."

"Ah! I'd pity him if I had time," she said.

"He was fond of you?"

"Don't speak of it."

"If he had not been fond of you, he would not have put you here."

Mme. Zélie made a little face of equivocal meaning.

"What proof is that?" she murmured.

"He would not have spent so much money for you."

"For me!" she interrupted,—"for me! What have I cost him of any consequence? Is it for me that he bought, furnished, and fitted out this house? No, no! He had the cage; and he put in the bird,—the first he happened to find. He brought me here as he might have brought any other woman, young or old, pretty or ugly, blonde or brunette. As to what I spent here, it was a mere bagatelle compared with what the other did,—the one before me. Amanda kept telling me all the time I was a fool. You may believe me, then, when I tell you that M. Vincent will not wet many handkerchiefs with the tears he'll shed over me."

"But do you know what became of the one before

you, as you call her,—whether she is alive or dead, and owing to what circumstances the cage became empty? "

But, instead of answering, Mme. Zélie was fixing upon Marius de Trégars a suspicious glance. And, after a moment only,—

" Why do you ask me that? " she said.

" I would like to know."

She did not permit him to proceed. Rising from her seat, and stepping briskly up to him,—

" Do you belong to the police, by chance? " she asked in a tone of mistrust.

If she was anxious, it was evidently because she had motives of anxiety which she had concealed. If, two or three times she had interrupted herself, it was because, manifestly, she had a secret to keep. If the idea of police had come into her mind, it is because, very probably, they had recommended her to be on her guard.

M. de Trégars understood all this, and, also, that he had tried to go too fast.

" Do I look like a secret police-agent? " he asked.

She was examining him with all her power of penetration.

" Not at all, I confess," she replied. " But, if you are not one, how is it that you come to my house, without knowing me from this side of sole leather, to ask me a whole lot of questions, which I am fool enough to answer? "

" I told you I was a friend of M. Favoral."

" Who's that Favoral? "

" That's M. Vincent's real name, madame."

She opened her eyes wide.

" You must be mistaken. I never heard him called any thing but Vincent."

" It is because he had especial motives for concealing

his personality. The money he spent here did not belong to him: he took it, he stole it, from the Mutual Credit Company where he was cashier, and where he left a deficit of twelve millions."

Mme. Zélie stepped back as though she had trodden on a snake.

" It's impossible! " she cried.

" It is the exact truth. Haven't you seen in the papers the case of Vincent Favoral, cashier of the Mutual Credit? "

And, taking a paper from his pocket, he handed it to the young woman, saying, " Read."

But she pushed it back, not without a slight blush.

" Oh, I believe you! " she said.

The fact is, and Marius understood it, she did not read very fluently.

" The worst of M. Vincent Favoral's conduct," he resumed, " is, that, while he was throwing away money here by the handful, he subjected his family to the most cruel privations."

" Oh! "

" He refused the necessaries of life to his wife, the best and the worthiest of women; he never gave a cent to his son; and he deprived his daughter of every thing."

" Ah, if I could have suspected such a thing! " murmured Mme. Zélie.

" Finally, and to cap the climax, he has gone, leaving his wife and children literally without bread."

Transported with indignation,—

" Why, that man must have been a horrible old scoundrel " exclaimed the young woman.

This is just the point to which M. de Trégars wished to bring her.

"And now," he resumed, "you must understand the enormous interest we have in knowing what has become of him."

"I have already told you."

M. de Trégars had risen, in his turn. Taking Mme. Zélie's hands, and fixing upon her one of those acute looks, which search for the truth down to the innermost recesses of the conscience,—

"Come, my dear child," he began in a penetrating voice, "you are a worthy and honest girl. Will you leave in the most frightful despair a family who appeal to your heart? Be sure that no harm will ever happen through us to Vincent Favoral."

She raised her hand, as they do to take an oath in a court of justice, and, in a solemn tone,—

"I swear," she uttered, "that I went to the station with M. Vincent; that he assured me that he was going to Brazil; that he had his passage-ticket; and that all his baggage was marked, 'Rio de Janeiro.'"

The disappointment was great: and M. de Trégars manifested it by a gesture.

"At least," he insisted, "tell me who the woman was whose place you took here."

But already had the young woman returned to her feeling of mistrust.

"How in the world do you expect me to know?" she replied. "Go and ask Amanda. I have no accounts to give you. Besides, I have to go and finish packing my trunks. So good-by, and enjoy yourself."

And she went out so quick, that she caught Amanda, the chambermaid, kneeling behind the door.

"So that woman was listening," thought M. de Trégars, anxious and dissatisfied.

But it was in vain that he begged Mme. Zélie to return, and to hear a single word more. She disappeared; and he had to resign himself to leave the house without learning any thing more for the present.

He had remained there very long; and he was wondering, as he walked out, whether Maxence had not got tired waiting for him in the little *café* where he had sent him.

But Maxence had remained faithfully at his post. And when Marius de Trégars came to sit by him, whilst exclaiming, " Here you are at last! " he called his attention at the same time with a gesture, and a wink from the corner of his eye, to two men sitting at the adjoining table before a bowl of punch.

Certain, now, that M. de Trégars would remain on the lookout, Maxence was knocking on the table with his fist, to call the waiter, who was busy playing billiards with a customer.

And when he came at last, justly annoyed at being disturbed,—

" Give us two mugs of beer," Maxence ordered, " and bring us a pack of cards."

M. de Trégars understood very well that something extraordinary had happened; but, unable to guess what, he leaned over towards his companion.

" What is it? " he whispered.

" We must hear what these two men are saying; and we'll play a game of piquet for a subterfuge."

The waiter returned, bringing two glasses of a muddy liquid, a piece of cloth, the color of which was concealed under a layer of dirt, and a pack of cards horribly soft and greasy.

" My deal," said Maxence.

And he began shuffling, and giving the cards, whilst
M. de Trégars was examining the punch-drinkers at the
next table.

In one of the two, a man still young, wearing a striped
vest with alpaca sleeves, he thought he recognized one
of the rascally-looking fellows he had caught a glimpse
of in Mme. Zélie Cadelle's carriage-house.

The other, an old man, whose inflamed complexion
and blossoming nose betrayed old habits of drunken-
ness, looked very much like a coachman out of place.
Baseness and duplicity bloomed upon his countenance;
and the brightness of his small eyes rendered still more
alarming the slyly obsequious smile that was stereotyped
upon his thin and pale lips.

They were so completely absorbed in their conversation, that they paid no attention whatever to what was
going on around them.

" Then," the old one was saying, " it's all over."

" Entirely. The house is sold."

" And the boss ? "

" Gone to America."

" What ! Suddenly, that way ? "

" No. We supposed he was going on some journey,
because, every day since the beginning of the week, they
were bringing in trunks and boxes ; but no one knew exactly when he would go. Now, in the night of Saturday
to Sunday, he drops in the house like a bombshell, wakes
up everybody, and says he must leave immediately. At
once we harness up, we load the baggage up, we drive
him to the Western Railway Station, and good-by, Vincent ! "

" And the young lady ? "

" She's got to get out in the next twenty-four hours ;

but she don't seem to mind it one bit. The fact is we are
the ones who grieve the most, after all."

" Is it possible? "

" It is so. She was a good girl; and we won't soon
find one like her."

The old man seemed distressed.

" Bad luck! " he growled. " I would have liked that
house myself."

" Oh, I dare say you would! "

" And there is no way to get in? "

" Can't tell. It will be well to see the others, those who
have bought. But I mistrust them: they look too stupid
not to be mean."

Listening intently to the conversation of these two
men, it was mechanically and at random that M. de Trégars and Maxence threw their cards on the table, and
uttered the common terms of the game of piquet,—

" Five cards! Tierce, major! Three aces."

Meantime the old man was going on,—

" Who knows but what M. Vincent may come back? "

" No danger of that! "

" Why? "

The other looked carefully around, and, seeing only
two players absorbed in their game,—

" Because," he replied, " M. Vincent is completely
ruined, it seems. He spent all his money, and a good
deal of other people's money besides. Amanda, the
chambermaid, told me; and I guess she knows."

" You thought he was so rich! "

" He was. But no matter how big a bag is: if you
keep taking out of it, you must get to the bottom."

" Then he spent a great deal? "

" It's incredible! I have been in extravagant houses;

but nowhere have I ever seen money fly as it has during the five months that I have been in that house. A regular pillage! Everybody helped themselves; and what was not in the house, they could get from the tradespeople, have it charged on the bill; and it was all paid without a word."

" Then, yes, indeed, the money must have gone pretty lively," said the old one in a convinced tone.

" Well," replied the other, " that was nothing yet. Amanda the chambermaid, who has been in the house fifteen years, told us some stories that would make you jump. She was not much for spending, Zélie; but some of the others, it seems "—

It required the greatest effort on the part of Maxence and M. de Trégars not to play, but only to pretend to play, and to continue to count imaginary points, —" One, two, three, four."

Fortunately the coachman with the red nose seemed much interested.

" What others? " he asked.

" That I don't know any thing about," replied the younger valet. " But you may imagine that there must have been more than one in that little house during the many years that M. Vincent owned it,—a man who hadn't his equal for women, and who was worth millions."

" And what was his business? "

" Don't know that, either."

" What! there were ten of you in the house, and you didn't know the profession of the man who paid you all? "

" We were all new."

" The chambermaid, Amanda, must have known."

" When she was asked, she said that he was a merchant. One thing is sure, he was a queer old chap."

So interested was the old coachman, that, seeing the punch-bowl empty, he called for another. His comrade could not fail to show his appreciation of such politeness.

" Ah, yes ! " he went on, " old Vincent was an eccentric fellow; and never, to see him, could you have suspected that he cut up such capers, and that he threw money away by the handful."

" Indeed ! "

" Imagine a man about fifty years old, stiff as a post, with a face about as pleasant as a prison-gate. That's the boss ! Summer and winter, he wore laced shoes, blue stockings, gray pantaloons that were too short, a cotton necktie, and a frock-coat that came down to his ankles. In the street, you would have taken him for a hosier who had retired before his fortune was made."

" You don't say so ! "

" No, never have I seen a man look so much like an old miser. You think, perhaps, that he came in a carriage. Not a bit of it! He came in the omnibus, my boy, and outside too, for three sous; and when it rained he opened his umbrella. But the moment he had crossed the threshold of the house, presto, pass ! complete change of scene. The miser became pacha. He took off his old duds, put on a blue velvet robe; and then there was nothing handsome enough, nothing good enough, nothing expensive enough for him. And, when he had acted the *my lord* to his heart's content, he put on his old traps again, resumed his prison-gate face, climbed up on top of the omnibus, and went off as he came."

" And you were not surprised, all of you, at such a life? "

" Very much so."

" And you did not think that these singular whims must conceal something? "

" Oh, but we did! "

" And you didn't try to find out what that something was? "

" How could we? "

" Was it very difficult to follow your boss, and ascertain where he went, after leaving the house? "

" Certainly not; but what then? "

" Why," he replied, " you would have found out his secret in the end; and then you would have gone to him and told him, ' Give me so much, or I peach.' "

V.

THIS story of M. Vincent, as told by these two honest companions, was something like the vulgar legend of other people's money, so eagerly craved, and so madly dissipated. Easily-gotten wealth is easily gotten rid of. Stolen money has fatal tendencies, and turns irresistibly to gambling, horse-jockeys, fast women, all the ruinous fancies, all the unwholesome gratifications.

They are rare indeed, among the daring cut-throats of speculation, those to whom their ill-gotten gain proves of real service,—so rare, that they are pointed out, and are as easily numbered as the girls who leap some night from the street to a ten-thousand-franc apartment, and manage to remain there.

Seized with the intoxication of sudden wealth, they

lose all measure and all prudence. Whether they believe
their luck inexhaustible, or fear a sudden turn of fortune, they make haste to enjoy themselves, and they fill
the noted restaurants, the leading *cafés*, the theatres, the
clubs, the race-courses, with their impudent personality,
the clash of their voice, the extravagance of their mistresses, the noise of their expenses, and the absurdity of
their vanity. And they go on and on, lavishing other
people's money, until the fatal hour of one of those disastrous liquidations which terrify the courts and the exchange, and cause pallid faces and a gnashing of teeth
in the " street," until the moment when they have the
choice between a pistol-shot, which they never choose,
the criminal court, which they do their best to avoid,
and a trip abroad.

What becomes of them afterwards? To what gut-
ters do they tumble from fall to fall? Does any one
know what becomes of the women who disappear suddenly after two or three years of follies and of splendors?

But it happens sometimes, as you step out of a carriage in front of some theatre, that you wonder where
you have already seen the face of the wretched beggar
who opens the door for you, and in a husky voice claims
his two sous. You saw him at the Café Riche, during
the six months that he was a big financier.

Some other time you may catch, in the crowd,
snatches of a strange conversation between two crapu-
lous rascals.

" It was at the time," says one, " when I drove that
bright chestnut team that I had bought for twenty thousand francs of the eldest son of the Duke de Ser-
meuse."

" I remember," replies the other; " for at that mo-

ment I gave six thousand francs a month to little Cabri-
ole of the Varieties."

And, improbable as this may seem, it is the exact
truth; for one was manager of a manufacturing enterprise that sank ten millions; and the other was at the
head of a financial operation that ruined five hundred
families. They had a house like the one in the Rue du
Cirque, mistresses more expensive than Mme. Zélie
Cadelle, and servants like those who were now talking
within a step of Maxence and Marius de Trégars. The
latter had resumed their conversation; and the oldest
one, the coachman with the red nose, was saying to his
younger comrade,—

"This Vincent affair must be a lesson to you. If ever
you find yourself again in a house where so much
money is spent, remember that it hasn't cost much
trouble to make it, and manage somehow to get as big
a share of it as you can."

"That's what I've always done wherever I have
been."

"And, above all, make haste to fill your bag, because,
you see, in houses like that, one is never sure, one day,
whether, the next, the gentleman will not be at Mazas,
and the lady at St. Lazares."

They had done their second bowl of punch, and
finished their conversation. They paid, and left.

And Maxence and M. de Trégars were able, at last,
to throw down their cards.

Maxence was very pale; and big tears were rolling
down his cheeks.

"What disgrace!" he murmured. "This, then, is
the other side of my father's existence! This is the way
in which he spent the millions which he stole; whilst, in

the Rue St. Gilles, he deprived his family of the necessaries of life!"

And, in a tone of utter discouragement,—

"Now it is indeed all over, and it is useless to continue our search. My father is certainly guilty."

But M. de Trégars was not the man thus to give up
the game.

"Guilty? Yes," he said, "but dupe also."

"Whose dupe?"

"That's what we'll find out, you may depend upon
it."

"What! after what we have just heard?"

"I have more hope than ever."

"Did you learn any thing from Mme. Zélie Cadelle,
then?"

"Nothing more than you know by those two rascals'
conversation."

A dozen questions were pressing upon Maxence's
lips; but M. de Trégars interrupted him.

"In this case, my friend, less than ever must we trust
appearances. Let me speak. Was your father a simpleton? No! His ability to dissimulate, for years, his
double existence, proves, on the contrary, a wonderful
amount of duplicity. How is it, then, that latterly his
conduct has been so extraordinary and so absurd? But
you will doubtless say it was always such. In that case,
I answer you, No; for then his secret could not have
been kept for a year. We hear that other women lived
in that house before Mme. Zélie Cadelle. But who were
they? What has become of them? Is there any certainty
that they have ever existed? Nothing proves it.

"The servants having been all changed, Amanda, the
chambermaid, is the only one who knows the truth; and

she will be very careful to say nothing about it. Therefore, all our positive information goes back no farther than five months. And what do we hear? That your father seemed to try and make his extravagant expenditures as conspicuous as possible. That he did not even take the trouble to conceal the source of the money he spent so profusely; for he told Mme. Zélie that he was at the end of his tether, and that, after having spent his own fortune, he was spending other people's money. He had announced his intended departure; he had sold the house, and received its price. Finally, at the last moment, what does he do?

"Instead of going off quietly and secretly, like a man who is running away, and who knows that he is pursued, he tells every one where he intends to go; he writes it on all his trunks, in letters half a foot high; and then rides in great display to the railway station, with a woman, several carriages, servants, etc. What is the object of all this? To get caught? No, but to start a false scent. Therefore, in his mind, every thing must have been arranged in advance, and the catastrophe was far from taking him by surprise; therefore the scene with M. de Thaller must have been prepared; therefore, it must have been on purpose that he left his pocketbook behind, with the bill in it that was to lead us straight here; therefore all we have seen is but a transparent comedy, got up for our special benefit, and intended to cover up the truth, and mislead the law."

But Maxence was not entirely convinced.

"Still," he remarked, "those enormous expenses."

M. de Trégars shrugged his shoulders.

"Have you any idea," he said, "what display can be made with a million? Let us admit that your father was spent two, four millions even. The loss of the Mutual Credit is twelve millions. What has become of the other eight?"

And, as Maxence made no answer,—

"It is those eight millions," he added, "that I want, and that I shall have. It is in Paris that your father is hid, I feel certain. We must find him; and we must make him tell the truth, which I already more than suspect."

Whereupon, throwing on the table the pint of beer which he had not drunk, he walked out of the *café* with Maxence.

"Here you are at last!" exclaimed the coachman, who had been waiting at the corner for over three hours, a prey to the utmost anxiety.

But M. de Trégars had no time for explanations; and, pushing Maxence into the cab, he jumped in after him, crying to the coachman,—

"24 Rue Joquelet. Five francs extra for yourself."

A driver who expects an extra five francs, always has, for five minutes at least, a horse as fast as Gladiateur.

Whilst the cab was speeding on to its destination,—

"What is most important for us now," said M. de Trégars to Maxence, "is to ascertain how far the Mutual Credit crisis has progressed; and M. Latterman of the Rue Joquelet is the man in all Paris who can best inform us."

Whoever has made or lost five hundred francs at the *bourse* knows M. Latterman, who, since the war, calls himself an Alsatian and curses with a fearful accent those "parparous Broossians." This worthy speculator modestly calls himself a money-changer; but he would be a simpleton who should ask him for change: and it is certainly not that sort of business which gives him the three hundred thousand francs' profits which he pockets every year.

When a company has failed, when it has been wound up, and the defrauded stockholders have received two or three per cent in all on their original investment, there is a prevailing idea that the certificates of its stocks are no longer good for any thing, except to light the fire. That's a mistake. Long after the company has foundered, its shares float, like the shattered *débris* which the sea casts upon the beach months after the ship has been wrecked. These shares M. Latterman collects, and carefully stores away; and upon the shelves of his office you may see numberless shares and bonds of those numerous companies which have absorbed, in the past twenty years, according to some statistics, twelve hundred millions, and, according to others, two thousand millions, of the public fortune.

Say but a word, and his clerks will offer you some " Franco-American Company," some " Steam Navigation Company of Marseilles," some " Coal and Metal Company of the Asturias," some " Transcontinental Memphis and El Paso " (of the United States), some " Caumart Slate Works," and hundreds of others, which, for the general public, have no value, save that of old paper, that is from three to five cents a pound. And yet speculators are found who buy and sell these rags.

In an obscure corner of the *bourse* may be seen a miscellaneous population of old men with pointed beards, and overdressed young men, who deal in every thing salable, and other things besides. There are found foreign merchants, who will offer you stocks of merchandise, goods from auction, good claims to recover, and who at last will take out of their pockets an opera-glass, a Geneva watch (smuggled in), a revolver, or a bottle of patent hair-restorer.

Such is the market to which drift those shares which were once issued to represent millions, and which now represent nothing but a palpable proof of the audacity of swindlers, and the credulity of their dupes. And there are actually buyers for these shares, and they go up or down, according to the ordinary laws of supply and demand; for there is a demand for them, and here comes in the usefulness of M. Latterman's business.

Does a tradesman, on the eve of declaring himself bankrupt, wish to defraud his creditors of a part of his assets, to conceal excessive expenses, or cover up some embezzlement, at once he goes to the Rue Joquelet, pro-cures a select assortment of " Cantonal Credit," " Ross-dorff Mines," or " Maumusson Salt Works," and puts them carefully away in his safe.

And, when the receiver arrives,—

" There are my assets," he says. " I have there some twenty, fifty, or a hundred thousand francs of stocks, the whole of which is not worth five francs to-day; but it isn't my fault. I thought it a good investment; and I didn't sell, because I always thought the price would come up again."

And he gets his discharge, because it would really be too cruel to punish a man because he has made unfor-tunate investments.

Better than any one, M. Latterman knows for what purpose are purchased the valueless securities which he sells; and he actually advises his customers which to take in preference, in order that their purchase at the time of their issue may appear more natural, and more likely. Nevertheless, he claims to be a perfectly honest man, and declares that he is no more responsible for the swindles that are committed by means of his stocks than a gunsmith for a murder committed with a gun that he has sold.

"But he will surely be able to tell us all about the Mutual Credit," repeated Maxence to M. de Trégars.

Four o'clock struck when the carriage stopped in the Rue Joquelet. The *bourse* had just closed; and a few groups were still standing in the square, or along the railings.

"I hope we shall find this Latterman at home," said Maxence.

They started up the stairs (for it is up on the second floor that this worthy operator has his offices); and, having inquired,—

"M. Latterman is engaged with a customer," answered a clerk. "Please sit down and wait."

M. Latterman's office was like all other caverns of the same kind. A very narrow space was reserved to the public; and all around, behind a heavy wire screen, the clerks could be seen busy with figures, or handling coupons. On the right, over a small window, appeared the word, "CASHIER." A small door on the left led to the private office.

M. de Trégars and Maxence had patiently taken a seat on a hard leather bench, once red; and they were listening and looking on.

There was considerable animation about the place. Every few minutes, well-dressed young men came in with a hurried and important look, and, taking out of their pocket a memorandum-book, they would speak a few sentences of that peculiar dialect, bristling with figures, which is the language of the *bourse*. At the end of fifteen or twenty minutes,—

" Will M. Latterman be engaged much longer? " inquired M. de Trégars.

" I do not know," replied a clerk.

At that very moment, the little door on the left opened, and the customer came out who had detained M. Latterman so long. This customer was no other than M. Costeclar. Noticing M. de Trégars and Maxence, who had risen at the noise of the door, he appeared most disagreeably surprised. He even turned slightly pale, and took a step backwards, as if intending to return precipitately into the room that he was leaving; for M. Latterman's office, like that of all other large operators, had several doors, without counting the one that leads to the police-court. But M. de Trégars gave him no time to effect this retreat. Stepping suddenly forward,—

" Well? " he asked him in a tone that was almost threatening.

The brilliant financier had condescended to take off his hat, usually riveted upon his head, and, with the smile of a knave caught in the act,—

" I did not expect to meet you here, my lord-marquis," he said.

At the title of " marquis," everybody looked up.

" I believe you, indeed," said M. de Trégars. " But what I want to know is, how is the matter progressing? "

" The plot is thickening. Justice is acting."

" Indeed! "

" It is a fact. Jules Jottras, of the house of Jottras and Brother, was arrested this morning, just as he arrived at the *bourse*."

" Why? "

" Because, it seems, he was an accomplice of Favoral;

and it was he who sold the bonds stolen from the Mutual Credit."

Maxence had started at the mention of his father's name; but, with a significant glance, M. de Trégars bid him remain silent, and, in a sarcastic tone,—

"Famous capture!" he murmured. "And which proves the clear-sightedness of justice."

"But this is not all," resumed M. Costeclar. "Saint Pavin, the editor of 'The Financial Pilot,' you know, is thought to be seriously compromised. There was a rumor, at the close of the market, that a warrant either had been, or was about to be, issued against him."

"And the Baron de Thaller?"

The employés of the office could not help admiring M. Costeclar's extraordinary amount of patience.

"The baron," he replied, "made his appearance at the *bourse* this afternoon, and was the object of a veritable ovation."

"That is admirable! And what did he say?"

"That the damage was already repaired."

"Then the shares of the Mutual Credit must have advanced."

"Unfortunately, not. They did not go above one hundred and ten francs."

"Were you not astonished at that?"

"Not much, because, you see, I am a business-man, I am; and I know pretty well how things work. When they left M. de Thaller this morning, the stockholders of the Mutual Credit had a meeting; and they pledged themselves, upon honor, not to sell, so as not to break the market. As soon as they had separated, each one said to himself, 'Since the others are going to keep their stock, like fools, I am going to sell mine.' Now, as there were three or four hundred of them who argued in the same way, the market was flooded with shares."

Looking the brilliant financier straight in the eyes,—

" And yourself? " interrupted M. de Trégars.

" I! " stammered M. Costeclar, so visibly agitated, that the clerks could not help laughing.

" Yes. I wish to know if you have been more faithful to your word than the stockholders of whom you are speaking, and whether you have done as we had agreed."

" Certainly ; and, if you find me here "—

But M. de Trégars, placing his own hand over his shoulder, stopped him short.

" I think I know what brought you here," he uttered ; " and in a few moments I shall have ascertained."

" I swear to you."

" Don't swear. If I am mistaken, so much the better for you. If I am not mistaken, I'll prove to you that it is dangerous to try any sharp game on me, though I am not a business-man."

Meantime M. Latterman, seeing no customer coming to take the place of the one who had left, became impatient at last, and appeared upon the threshold of his private office.

He was a man still young, small, thick-set, and vulgar. At the first glance, nothing of him could be seen but his abdomen,—a big, great, and ponderous abdomen, seat of his thoughts, and tabernacle of his aspirations, over which dangled a double gold chain, loaded with trinkets. Above an apoplectic neck, red as that of a turkey-cock, stood his little head, covered with coarse red hair, cut very short. He wore a heavy beard, trimmed in the form of a fan. His large, full-moon face

was divided in two by a nose as flat as a Kalmuck's, and
illuminated by two small eyes, in which could be read the
most thorough duplicity.

Seeing M. de Trégars and M. Costeclar engaged in
conversation,—

"Why! you know each other?" he said.

M. de Trégars advanced a step,—

"We are even—intimate friends," he replied. "And
it is very lucky that we should have met. I am brought
here by the same matter as our dear Costeclar; and I
was just explaining to him that he has been too hasty,
and that it would be best to wait three or four days
longer."

"That's just what I told him," echoed the honorable
financier.

Maxence understood only one thing,—that M. de
Trégars had penetrated M. Costeclar's designs; and he
could not sufficiently admire his presence of mind, and
his skill in grasping an unexpected opportunity.

"Fortunately there is nothing done yet," added M.
Latterman.

"And it is yet time to alter what has been agreed on,"
said M. de Trégars. And, addressing himself to Costeclar,—

"Come," he added, "we'll fix things with M. Latterman."

But the other, who remembered the scene in the Rue
St. Gilles, and who had his own reasons to be alarmed,
would sooner have jumped out of the window.

"I am expected," he stammered. "Arrange matters
without me."

"Then you give me *carte blanche?*"

Ah, if the brilliant financier had dared! But he felt

riveted upon him such threatening eyes, that he dared not even make a gesture of denial.

"Whatever you do will be satisfactory," he said in the tone of a man who sees himself lost.

And, as he was going out of the door, M. de Trégars stepped into M. Latterman's private office. He remained only five minutes; and when he joined Maxence, whom he had begged to wait for him,—

"I think that we have got them," he said as they walked off.

Their next visit was to M. Saint Pavin, at the office of "The Financial Pilot." Every one must have seen at least one copy of that paper with, its ingenious vignette, representing a bold mariner steering a boat, filled with timid passengers, towards the harbor of Million, over a stormy sea, bristling with the rocks of failure and the shoals of ruin. The office of "The Pilot" is, in fact, less a newspaper office than a sort of general business agency.

As at M. Latterman's, there are clerks scribbling behind wire screens, small windows, a cashier, and an immense blackboard, on which the latest quotations of the Rente, and other French and foreign securities, are written in chalk.

As "The Pilot" spends some hundred thousand francs a year in advertising, in order to obtain subscribers; as, on the other hand, it only costs three francs a year,—it is clear that it is not on its subscriptions that it realizes any profits. It has other sources of income: its brokerages first; for it buys, sells, and executes, as the prospectus says, all orders for stocks, bonds, or other securities, for the best interests of the client. And it has plenty of business.

To the opulent brokerages, must be added advertising and puffing,—another mine. Six times out of ten, when a new enterprise is set on foot, the organizers send for Saint Pavin. Honest men, or knaves, they must all pass through his hands. They know it, and are resigned in advance.

"We rely upon you," they say to him.

"What advantages have you to offer?" he replies.

Then they discuss the operation, the expected profits of the new company, and M. Saint Pavin's demands. For a hundred thousand francs he promises bursts of lyrism; for fifty thousand he will be enthusiastic only. Twenty thousand francs will secure a moderate praise of the affair; ten thousand, a friendly neutrality.

And, if the said company refuses any advantages to "The Pilot"—

"Ah, you must beware!" says Saint Pavin.

And from the very next number he commences his campaign. He is moderate at first, and leaves a door open for his retreat. He puts forth doubts only. He does not know much about it. "It may be an excellent thing; it may be a wretched one: the safest is to wait and see."

That's the first hint. If it remains without result, he takes up his pen again, and makes his doubts more pointed.

He knows how to steer clear of libel suits, how to handle figures so as to demonstrate, according to the requirements of the case, that two and two make three, or make five. It is seldom, that, before the third article, the company does not surrender at discretion.

All Paris knows him; and he has many friends. When M. de Trégars and Maxence arrived, they found the office full of people—speculators, brokers, go-betweens—come there to discuss the fluctuations of the day and the probabilities of the evening market.

"M. Saint Pavin is engaged," one of the clerks told them.

Indeed, his coarse voice could be distinctly heard behind the screen. Soon he appeared, showing out an old gentleman, who seemed utterly confused at the scene, and to whom he was screaming,—

"No, sir, no! 'The Financial Pilot' does not take that sort of business; and I find you very bold to come and propose to me a twopenny rascality." But, noticing Maxence,—

"M. Favoral!" he said. "By Jove! it is your good star that has brought you here. Come into the private office, my dear sir: come, we'll have some fun now."

Many of the people who were in the office had a word to say to M. Saint Pavin, some advice to ask him, an order to transmit, or some news to communicate. They had all stepped forward, and were holding out their hands with a friendly smile. He set them aside with his usual rudeness.

"By and by. I am busy now: leave me alone."

And pushing Maxence towards the office-door, which he had just opened,—

"Come in, come in!" he said in a tone of extraordinary impatience.

But M. de Trégars was coming in too; and, as he did not know him,—

"What do you want, you?" he asked roughly.

"The gentleman is my best friend," said Maxence, turning to him; "and I have no secret from him."

"Let him walk in, then; but, by Heaven, let us hurry!"

Once very sumptuous, the private office of the editor

of " The Financial Pilot " had fallen into a state of sordid dilapidation.   If the janitor had received orders
never to use a broom or a duster there, he obeyed them
strictly. Disorder and dirt reigned supreme. Papers and
manuscripts lay in all directions ; and on the broad sofas
the mud from the boots of all those who had lounged
upon them had been drying for months. On the mantel-
piece, in the midst of some half-dozen dirty glasses,
stood a bottle of Madeira, half empty. Finally, before
the fireplace, on the carpet, and along the furniture,
cigar and cigarette stumps were heaped in profusion. ˙

As soon as he had bolted the door, coming straight to
Maxence,—

" What has become of your father? " inquired M.
Saint Pavin rudely.

Maxence started. That was the last question he expected to hear.

" I do not know," he replied.

The manager of " The Pilot " shrugged his shoulders.

" That you should say so to the commissary of police,
to the judges, and to all Favoral's enemies, I understand: it is your duty. That they should believe you, I
understand too ; for, after all, what do they care? But
to me, a friend, though you may not think so, and who
has reasons not to be credulous "—

" I swear to you that we have no idea where he has
taken refuge."

Maxence said this with such an accent of sincerity,
that doubt was no longer possible. M. Saint Pavin's
features expressed the utmost surprise.

" What ! " he exclaimed, " your father has gone without securing the means of hearing from his family? "

" Yes."

"Without saying a word of his intentions to your mother, or your sister, or yourself?"

"Without one word."

"Without leaving any money, perhaps?"

"We found only an insignificant sum after he left."

The editor of "The Pilot" made a gesture of ironical admiration. "Well, the thing is complete," he said; "and Vincent is a smarter fellow than I gave him credit for; or else he must have cared more for those infernal women of his than any one supposed."

M. de Trégars, who had remained hitherto silent, now stepped forward.

"What women?" he asked.

"How do I know?" he replied roughly. "How could any one ever find out any thing about a man who was more hermetically shut up in his coat than a Jesuit in his gown?"

"M. Costeclar"—

"That's another nice bird! Still he may possibly have discovered something of Vincent's life; for he led him a pretty dance. Wasn't he about to marry Mlle. Favoral once?"

"Yes, in spite of herself even."

"Then you are right: he had discovered something. But, if you rely on him to tell you anything whatever, you are reckoning without your host."

"Who knows?" murmured M. de Trégars.

But M. Saint Pavin heard him not. Prey to a violent agitation, he was pacing up and down the room.

"Ah, those men of cold appearance," he growled, "those men with discreet countenance, those close-shaving calculators, those moralists! What fools they do make of themselves when once started! Who can imagine to what insane extremities this one may have been driven under the spur of some mad passion!"

And stamping violently his foot upon the carpet, from which arose clouds of dust,—

"And yet," he swore, "I must find him. And, by thunder! wherever he may be hid, I shall find him."

M. de Trégars was watching M. Saint Pavin with a scrutinizing eye.

"You have a great interest in finding him, then?" he said.

The other stopped short.

"I have the interest," he replied, "of a man who thought himself shrewd, and who has been taken in like a child,—of a man to whom they had promised wonders, and who finds his situation imperilled,— of a man who is tired of working for a band of brigands who heap millions upon millions, and to whom, for all reward, they offer the police-court and a retreat in the State Prison for his old age,—in a word, the interests of a man who will and shall have revenge, by all that is holy!"

"On whom?"

"On the Baron de Thaller, sir! How, in the world, has he been able to compel Favoral to assume the responsibility of all, and to disappear? What enormous sum has he given to him?"

"Sir," interrupted Maxence, "my father went off without a sou."

M. Saint Pavin burst out in a loud laugh.

"And the twelve millions?" he asked. "What has become of them? Do you suppose they have been distributed in deeds of charity?"

And without waiting for any further objections,—

"And yet," he went on, "it is not with money alone

that a man can be induced to disgrace himself, to confess himself a thief and a forger, to brave the galleys,
to give up everything,—country, family, friends. Evidently the Baron de Thaller must have had other means
of action, some hold on Favoral "—

M. de Trégars interrupted him.

" You speak," he said, " as if you were absolutely certain of M. de Thaller's complicity."

" Of course."

" Why don't you inform on him, then? "

The editor of " The Pilot " started back.

" What ! " he exclaimed, " draw the fingers of the law
into my own business! You don't think of it ! Besides,
what good would that do me? I have no proofs of my
allegations. Do you suppose that Thaller has not taken
his precautions, and tied my hands? No, no! without
Favoral there is nothing to be done."

" Do you suppose, then, that you could induce him
to surrender himself? "

" No, but to furnish me the proofs I need, to send
Thaller where they have already sent that poor Jottras."

And, becoming more and more excited,—

" But it is not in a month that I should want those
proofs," he went on, " nor even in two weeks, but to-
morrow, but at this very moment. Before the end of the
week, Thaller will have wound up the operation, realized, Heaven knows how many millions, and put every
thing in such nice order, that justice, who in financial
matters is not of the first capacity, will discover nothing
wrong. If he can do that, he is safe, he is beyond reach,
and will be dubbed a first-class financier. Then to what
may he not aspire! Already he talks of having himself
elected deputy; and he says everywhere that he has

found, to marry his daughter, a gentleman who bears one of the oldest names in France,—the Marquis de Trégars."

" Why, this is the Marquis de Trégars!" exclaimed Maxence, pointing to Marius.

For the first time, M. Saint Pavin took the trouble to examine his visitor; and he, who knew life too well not to be a judge of men, he seemed surprised.

" Please excuse me, sir," he uttered with a politeness very different from his usual manner, " and permit me to ask you if you know the reasons why M. de Thaller is so prodigiously anxious to have you for a son-in-law."

" I think," replied M. de Trégars coldly, " that M. de Thaller would not be sorry to deprive me of the right to seek the causes of my father's ruin."

But he was interrupted by a great noise of voices in the adjoining room; and almost at once there was a loud knock at the door, and a voice called,—

" In the name of the law!"

The editor of " The Pilot" had become whiter than his shirt.

" That's what I was afraid of," he said. " Thaller has got ahead of me; and perhaps I may be lost."

Meantime he did not lose his wits. Quick as thought he took out of a drawer a package of letters, threw them into the fireplace, and set fire to them, saying, in a voice made hoarse by emotion and anger,—

" No one shall come in until they are burnt."

But it required an incredibly long time to make them catch fire; and M. Saint Pavin, kneeling before the hearth, was stirring them up, and scattering them, to make them burn faster.

" And now," said M. de Trégars, " will you hesitate to deliver up the Baron de Thaller into the hands of. justice?"

He turned around with flashing eyes.

" Now," he replied, " if I wish to save myself, I must save him too. Don't you understand that he holds me?"

And, seeing that the last sheets of his correspondence were consumed,—

" You may open now," he said to Maxence.

Maxence obeyed; and a commissary of police, wearing his scarf of office, rushed into the room; whilst his men, not without difficulty, kept back the crowd in the outer office,—

The commissary, who was an old hand, and had perhaps been on a hundred expeditions of this kind, had surveyed the scene at a glance. Noticing in the fireplace the carbonized *débris,* upon which still fluttered an expiring flame,—

" That's the reason, then," he said, " why you were so long opening the door?"

A sarcastic smile appeared upon the lips of the editor of " The Pilot."

" Private matters," he replied; " women's letters."

" This will be moral evidence against you, sir."

" I prefer it to material evidence."

Without condescending to notice the impertinence, the commissary was casting a suspicious glance on Maxence and M. de Trégars.

" Who are these gentlemen who were closeted with you?" he asked.

" Visitors, sir. This is M. Favoral."

" The son of the cashier of the Mutual Credit?"

" Exactly; and this gentleman is the Marquis de Trégars."

"You should have opened the door when you heard a knocking in the name of the law," grumbled the commissary.

But he did not insist. Taking a paper from his pocket, he opened it, and, handing it to M. Saint Pavin,—

"I have orders to arrest you," he said. "Here is the warrant."

With a careless gesture, the other pushed it back.

"What's the use of reading?" he said. "When I heard of the arrest of that poor Jottras, I guessed at once what was in store for me. It is about the Mutual Credit swindle, I imagine."

"Exactly."

"I have no more to do with it than yourself, sir; and I shall have very little trouble in proving it. But that is not your business. And you are going, I suppose, to put the seals on my papers?"

"Except on those that you have burnt."

M. Saint Pavin burst out laughing. He had recovered his coolness and his impudence, and seemed as much at ease as if it were the most natural thing in the world.

"Shall I be allowed to speak to my clerks," he asked, "and to give them my instructions?"

"Yes," replied the commissary, "but in my presence."

The clerks, being called, appeared, consternation depicted upon their countenances, but joy sparkling in their eyes. In reality they were delighted at the misfortune which befell their employer.

"You see what happens to me, my boys," he said. "But don't be uneasy. In less than forty-eight hours, the error of which I am the victim will be recognized, and I shall be liberated on bail. At any rate, I can rely upon you, can't I?"

They all swore that they would be more attentive and more zealous than ever.

And then addressing himself to his cashier, who was his confidential and right-hand man,—

" As to you, Bernard," he said, " you will run to M. de Thaller's, and advise him of what's going on. Let him have funds ready; for all our depositors will want to draw out their money at once. You will then call at the printing-office: have my article on the Mutual Credit kept out, and insert in its place some financial news cut out from other papers. Above all, don't mention my arrest, unless M. de Thaller should demand it.   Go ahead, and let ' The Pilot' appear as usual: that's important."

He had, whilst speaking, lighted a cigar. The honest man, victim of human iniquity, has not a firmer and more tranquil countenance.

" Justice does not know," he said to the commissary, who was fumbling in all the drawers of the desk, " what irreparable damage she may cause by arresting so hastily a man who has charge of immense interests like me. It is the fortune of ten or twelve small capitalists that is put in jeopardy."

Already the witnesses of the arrest had retired, one by one, to go and scatter the news along the Boulevard, and also to see what could be made out of it; for, at the *bourse,* news is money.

M. de Trégars and Maxence left also. As they passed the door,—

" Don't you say any thing about what I told you," M. Saint Pavin recommended to them.

M. de Trégars made no answer. He had the contracted features and tightly-drawn lips of a man who is maturing a grave determination, which, once taken will be irrevocable.

Once in the street, and when Maxence had opened the carriage-door,—

" We are going to separate here," he told him in that brief tone of voice which reveals a settled plan. " I know enough now to venture to call at M. de Thaller's. There only shall I be able to see how to strike the decisive blow. Return to the Rue St. Gilles, and relieve your mother's and sister's anxiety. You shall see me during the evening, I promise you."

And, without waiting for an answer, he jumped into the cab, which started off.

But it was not to the Rue St. Gilles that Maxence went. He was anxious, first, to see Mlle. Lucienne, to tell her the events of that day, the busiest of his existence; to tell her his discoveries, his surprises, his anxieties, and his hopes.

To his great surprise, he failed to find her at the Hôtel des Folies. She had gone riding at three o'clock, M. Fortin told him, and had not yet returned; but she could not be much longer, as it was already getting dark. Maxence went out again then, to see if he could not meet her. He had walked a little way along the Boulevard, when, at some distance off, on the Place du Château d'Eau, he thought he noticed an unusual bustle. Almost immediately he heard shouts of terror. Frightened people were running in all directions; and right before him a carriage, going at full gallop, passed like a flash.

But, quick as it had passed, he had time to recognize Mlle. Lucienne, pale, and clinging desperately to the seat. Wild with fear, he started after it as fast as he could run. It was clear that the driver had no control

over his horses. A policeman who tried to stop them was
knocked down. Ten steps farther, the hind-wheel of the
carriage, catching the wheel of a heavy wagon, broke to
splinters; and Mlle. Lucienne was thrown into the street,
whilst the driver fell over on the sidewalk.

VI.

THE Baron de Thaller was too practical a man to
live in the same house, or even in the same district,
where his offices were located. To dwell in the midst
of his business; to be constantly subjected to the contact of his employés, to the unkindly comments of a
crowd of subordinates; to expose himself to hourly annoyances, to sickening solicitations, to the reclamations
and eternal complaints of his stockholders and his clients! Pouah! He'd have given up the business first.
And so, on the very days when he had established the
offices of the Mutual Credit in the Rue de Quatre-Sep-
tembre, he had purchased a house in the Rue de la
Pépinière, within a step of the Faubourg St. Honoré.

It was a brand-new house, which had never yet been
occupied, and which had just been erected by a contractor who was almost celebrated, towards 1866, at the
moment of the great transformations of Paris, when
whole blocks were levelled to the ground, and rose again
so rapidly, that one might well wonder whether the ma-
sons, instead of a trowel, did not make use of a magician's wand.

This contractor, named Parcimieux, had come from
the Limousin in 1860, with his carpenter's tools for all
fortune, and, in less than six years, had accumulated,
at the lowest estimate, six millions of francs. Only he

was a modest man, and took as much pains to conceal his fortune, and offend no one, as most *parvenus* do to display their wealth, and insult the public.

Though he could hardly sign his name, yet he knew and practised the maxim of the Greek philosopher, which is, perhaps, the true secret of happiness,—hide thy life. And there were no expedients to which he did not resort to hide it. At the time of his greatest prosperity, for instance, having need of a carriage, he had applied to the manager of the Petites Voitures Company, and had had built for himself two cabs, outwardly similar in every respect to those used by the company, but within, most luxuriously upholstered, and drawn by horses of common appearance, but who could go their twenty-five miles in two hours any day. And these he had hired by the year.

Having his carriage, the worthy builder determined to have, also, his house, his own house, built by himself. But this required infinitely greater precautions still.

" For, as you may imagine," he explained to his friends, "a man does not make as much money as I have, without also making many cruel, bitter, and irreconcilable enemies. I have against me all the builders who have not succeeded, all the sub-contractors I employ, and who say that I speculate on their poverty, and the thousands of workmen who work for me, and swear that I grind them down to the dust. Already they call me brigand, slaver, thief, leech. What would it be, if they saw me living in a beautiful house of my own? They'd swear that I could not possibly have got so rich honestly, and that I must have committed some crimes. Besides, to build me a handsome house on the street would be, in case of a mob, setting up windows for the stones of all the rascals who have been in my employment."

Such were M. Parcimieux's thoughts, when, as he expressed it, he resolved to build.

A lot was for sale in the Rue de la Pépinière. He bought it, and at the same time purchased the adjoining house, which he immediately caused to be torn down. This operation placed in his possession a vast piece of ground, not very wide, but of great depth, stretching, as it did, back to the Rue Labaume. At once work was begun according to a plan which his architect and himself had spent six months in maturing. On the line of the street arose a house of the most modest appearance, two stories in height only, with a very high and very wide carriage-door for the passage of vehicles. This was to deceive the vulgar eye,—the outside of the cab, as it were. Behind this house, between a spacious court and a vast garden was built the residence of which M. Parcimieux had dreamed; and it really was an exceptional building both by the excellence of the materials used, and by the infinite care which presided over the minutest details. The marbles for the vestibule and the stairs were brought from Africa, Italy, and Corsica. He sent to Rome for workmen for the mosaics. The joiner and locksmithing work was intrusted to real artists.

Repeating to every one that he was working for a great foreign lord, whose orders he went to take every morning, he was free to indulge his most extravagant fancies, without fearing jests or unpleasant remarks.

Poor old man! The day when the last workman had driven in the last nail, an attack of apoplexy carried him off, without giving him time to say, "Oh!" Two days after, all his relatives from the Limousin were swooping

into Paris like a pack of wolves. Six millions to divide:
what a godsend! Litigation followed, as a matter of
course; and the house was offered for sale under a judgment.

M. de Thaller bought it for two hundred and seventy-
five thousand francs,—about one-third what it had cost
to build.

A month later he had moved into it; and the expenses
which he incurred to furnish it in a style worthy of the
building itself was the talk of the town. And yet he was
not fully satisfied with his purchase.

Unlike M. Parcimieux, he had no wish whatever to
conceal his wealth.

What! he owned one of those exquisite houses which
excite at once the wonder and the envy of passers-by,
and that house was hid behind such a common-looking
building!

" I must have that shanty pulled down," he said from
time to time.

And then he thought of something else; and the
" shanty " was still standing on that evening, when,
after leaving Maxence, M. de Trégars presented himself at M. de Thaller's.

The servants had, doubtless, received their instructions; for, as soon as Marius emerged from the porch
of the front-house, the porter advanced from his lodge,
bent double, his mouth open to his very ears by the most
obsequious smile.

Without waiting for a question,—

" The baron has not yet come home," he said. " But
he cannot be much longer away; and certainly the
baroness is at home for my lord-marquis. Please, then,
give yourself the trouble to pass."

And, standing aside, he struck upon the enormous

gong that stood near his lodge a single sharp blow, intended to wake up the footman on duty in the vestibule, and to announce a visitor of note. Slowly, but not without quietly observing every thing, M. de Trégars crossed the courtyard, covered with fine sand,—they would have powdered it with golden dust, if they had dared,—and surrounded on all sides with bronze baskets, in which beautiful rhododendrons were blossoming.

It was nearly six o'clock. The manager of the Mutual Credit dined at seven; and the preparations for this important event were everywhere apparent. Through the large windows of the dining-room the steward could be seen presiding over the setting of the table. The butler was coming up from the cellar, loaded with bottles. Finally, through the apertures of the basement arose the appetizing perfumes of the kitchen.

What enormous business it required to support such a style, to display this luxury, which would shame one of those German princelings, who exchanged the crown of their ancestors for a Prussian livery gilded with French gold!—other people's money.

Meantime, the blow struck by the porter on the gong had produced the desired effect; and the gates of the vestibule seemed to open of their own accord before M. de Trégars as he ascended the stoop.

This vestibule with the splendor of which Mlle. Lucienne had been so deeply impressed, would, indeed, have been worthy the attention of an artist, had it been allowed to retain the simple grandeur and the severe harmony which M. Parcimieux's architect had imparted to it.

But M. de Thaller, as he was proud of boasting, had a perfect horror of simplicity; and, wherever he discovered a vacant space as big as his hand, he hung a picture, a bronze, or a piece of china, any thing and anyhow.

The two footmen were standing when M. de Trégars came in. Without asking any question, " Will M. le Marquis please follow me? " said the youngest.

And, opening the broad glass doors, he began walking in front of M. de Trégars, along a staircase with marble railing, the elegant proportions of which were absolutely ruined by a ridiculous profusion of " objects of art " of all nature, and from all sources.   This staircase led to a vast semicircular landing, upon which, between columns of precious marble, opened three wide doors.   The footman opened the middle one, which led to M. de Thaller's picture-gallery, a celebrated one in the financial world, and which had acquired for him the reputation of an enlightened amateur.

But M. de Trégars had no time to examine this gallery, which, moreover, he already knew well enough. The footman showed him into the small drawing-room of the baroness, a *bijou* of a room, furnished in gilt and crimson satin.

" Will M. le Marquis be kind enough to take a seat? " he said. " I run to notify Mme. le Baronne of M. le Marquis's visit."

The footman uttered these titles of nobility with a singular pomp, and as if some of their lustre was reflected upon himself. Nevertheless, it was evident that " Marquis " jingled to his ear much more pleasantly than " Baronne."

Remaining alone, M. de Trégars threw himself upon a seat. Worn out by the emotions of the day, and by an extraordinary contention of mind, he felt thankful for this moment of respite, which permitted him, at the moment of a decisive step, to collect all his energy and all his presence of mind.

And after two minutes he was so deeply absorbed in his thoughts, that he started, like a man suddenly aroused from his sleep, at the sound of an opening door. At the same moment he heard a slight exclamation of surprise, " Ah ! "

Instead of the Baroness de Thaller, it was her daughter, Mlle. Césarine, who had come in.

Stepping forward to the centre of the room, and acknowledging by a familiar gesture M. de Trégars' most respectful bow,—

" You should warn people," she said. " I came here to look for my mother, and it is you I find. Why, you scared me to death. What a crack! Princess dear ! "

And taking the young man's hand, and pressing it to her breast,—

" Feel," she added, " how my heart beats."

Younger than Mlle. Gilberte, Mlle. Césarine de Thaller had a reputation for beauty so thoroughly established, that to call it in question would have seemed a crime to her numerous admirers. And really she was a handsome person. Rather tall and well made, she had broad hips, the waist round and supple as a steel rod, and a magnificent throat. Her neck was, perhaps, a little too thick and too short; but upon her robust shoulders was scattered in wild ringlets the rebellious hair that escaped from her comb. She was a blonde, but of that reddish blonde, almost as dark as mahogany, which Titian admired, and which the handsome Venetians obtained by means of rather repulsive practices, and by exposing themselves to the noonday sun on the terraces of their palaces. Her complexion had the gilded hues of amber. Her lips, red as blood, displayed as they opened,. teeth of dazzling whiteness. In her large prominent eyes, of a milky blue, like the Northern skies, laughed the eternal irony of a soul that no longer has faith in any thing. More anxious of her fame than of good taste, she wore a dress of doubtful shade, puffed up by means of an extravagant *pannier,* and buttoned obliquely across the chest, according to that ridiculous and ungraceful style invented by flat or humped women.

Throwing herself upon a chair, and placing cavalierly one foot upon another, so as to display her leg, which was admirable,—

" Do you know that it's perfectly stunning to see you here? " she said to M. de Trégars. " Just imagine, for a moment, what a face the Baron Three Francs Sixty-eight will make when he sees you! "

It was her father whom she called thus, since the day when she had discovered that there was a German coin called thaler, which represents three francs and sixty-eight centimes in French currency.

" You know, I suppose," she went on, " that papa has just been badly stuck? "

M. de Trégars was excusing himself in vague terms ; but it was one of Mlle. Césarine's habits never to listen to the answers which were made to her questions.

" Favoral," she continued, " papa's cashier, has just started on an international picnic. Did you know him? "

" Very little."

" An old fellow, always dressed like a country sexton, and with a face like an undertaker. And the Baron Three Francs Sixty-eight, an old bird, was fool enough to be taken in by him! For he was taken in. He had a face like a man whose chimney is on fire, when he came to tell us, mamma and myself, that Favoral had gone off with twelve millions."

"And has he really carried off that enormous sum?"

"Not entire, of course, because it was not since day before yesterday only that he began digging into the Mutual Credit's pile. There were years that this venerable old swell was leading a somewhat—variegated existence, in company with rather—funny ladies, you know. And as he was not exactly calculated to be adored at par, why, it cost papa's stockholders a pretty lively premium. But, anyhow, he must have carried off a handsome nugget."

And, bouncing to the piano, she began an accompaniment loud enough to crack the window-panes, singing at the same time the popular refrain of the "Young Ladies of Pautin:"—

> "Cashier, you've got the bag;
> Quick on your little nag,
> And then, ho, ho, for Belgium!"

Any one but Marius de Trégars would have been doubtless strangely surprised at Mlle. de Thaller's manners. But he had known her for some time already: he was familiar with her past life, her habits, her tastes, and her pretensions. Until the age of fifteen, Mlle. Césarine had remained shut up in one of those pleasant Parisian boarding-schools, where young ladies are initiated into the great art of the toilet, and from which they emerge armed with the gayest theories, knowing how to see without seeming to look, and to lie boldly without blushing; in a word, ripe for society. The directress of the boarding-school, a lady of the *ton*, who had met with reverses, and who was a good deal more of a dressmaker than a teacher, said of Mlle. Césarine, who paid her three thousand five hundred francs a year,—

" She gives the greatest hopes for the future; and I shall certainly make a superior woman of her."

But the opportunity was not allowed her. The Baroness de Thaller discovered, one morning, that it was impossible for her to live without her daughter, and that her maternal heart was lacerated by a separation which was against the sacred laws of nature. She took her home, therefore, declaring that nothing, henceforth, not even her marriage, should separate them, and that she should finish herself the education of the dear child. From that moment, in fact, whoever saw the Baroness de Thaller would also see Mlle. Césarine following in her wake.

A girl of fifteen, discreet and well-trained, is a convenient chaperon; a chaperon which enables a woman to show herself boldly where she might not have dared to venture alone. In presence of a mother followed by her daughter, disconcerted slander hesitates, and dares not speak.

Under the pretext that Césarine was still but a child, and of no consequence, Mme. de Thaller dragged her everywhere,—to the *bois* and to the races, visiting and shopping, to balls and parties, to the watering-places and the seashore, to the restaurant, and to all the " first nights " at the Palais Royal, the Bouffés, the Variétés, and the Délassements. It was, therefore, especially at the theatre, that the education of Mlle. de Thaller, so happily commenced, had received the finishing touch. At sixteen she was thoroughly familiar with the *répertoire* of the *genre* theatres, imitated Schneider far better than ever did Silly, and sang with surprising intonations and astonishing gestures Blanche d'Autigny's successful moods, and Theresa's most wanton verses.

Between times, she studied the fashion papers, and formed her style in reading the " Vie Parisienne," whose most enigmatic articles had no allusions sufficiently obscure to escape her penetration.

She learned to ride on horseback, to fence and to shoot, and distinguished herself at pigeon-matches. She kept a betting-book, played *Trente et Quarante* at Monaco; and *Baccarat* had no secrets for her. At Trouville she astonished the natives with the startling novelty of her bathing-costumes; and, when she found herself the centre of a reasonable circle of lookers-on, she threw herself in the water with a pluck that drew upon her the applause of the bathing-masters. She could smoke a cigarette, empty nearly a glass of champagne; and once her mother was obliged to bring her home, and put her quick to bed, because she had insisted upon trying absinthe, and her conversation had become somewhat too eccentric.

Leading such a life, it was difficult that public opinion should always spare Mme. and Mlle. de Thaller. There were sceptics who insinuated that this steadfast friendship between mother and daughter had very much the appearance of the association of two women bound together by the complicity of a common secret. A broker told how, one evening, or one night rather, for it was nearly two o'clock, happening to pass in front of the Moulin-Rouge, he had seen the Baroness and Mlle. Césarine coming out, accompanied by a gentleman, to him unknown, but who, he was quite sure, was not the Baron de Thaller.

A certain journey which mother and daughter had un-

dertaken in the heart of the winter, and which had lasted
not less than two months, had been generally attributed
to an imprudence, the consequences of which it had become impossible to conceal. They had been in Italy, they
said when they returned; but no one had seen them
there. Yet, as Mme. and Mlle. de Thaller's mode of life
was, after all, the same as that of a great many women
who passed for being perfectly proper, as there was no
positive or palpable fact brought against them, as no
name was mentioned, many people shrugged their shoulders, and replied,—

" Pure slanders."

And why not, since the Baron de Thaller, the most interested party, held himself satisfied?

To the ill-advised friends who ventured some allusions
to the public rumors, he replied, according to his humor,—

" My daughter can play the mischief generally, if she
sees fit. As I shall give a dowry of a million, she will always find a husband."

Or else, " And what of it? Do not American young
ladies enjoyed unlimited freedom? Are they not constantly seen going out with young gentlemen, or walking or travelling alone? Are they, for all that, less virtuous than our girls, who are kept under such close watch?
Do they make less faithful wives, or less excellent mothers? Hypocrisy is not virtue."

To a certain extent, the Manager of the Mutual
Credit was right.

Already Mlle. de Thaller had had to decide upon several quite suitable offers of marriage. She had squarely
refused them all.

" A husband! " she had answered each time. " Thank
you, none for me. I have good enough teeth to eat up

my dowry myself. Later, we'll see,—when I've cut my wisdom teeth, and I am tired of my bachelor life."

She did not seem near getting tired of it, though she pretended that she had no more illusions, was thoroughly *blasée,* had exhausted every sensation, and that life henceforth had no surprise in reserve for her. Her reception of M. de Trégars was, therefore, one of Mlle. Césarine's least eccentricities, as was also that sudden fancy to apply to the situation one of the most idiotic rondos of her *répertoires:*—

> " Cashier, you've got the bag;
> Quick on your little nag."

Neither did she spare him a single verse; and, when she stopped,—

" I see with pleasure," said M. de Trégars, " that the embezzlement of which your father has just been the victim does not in any way offend your good humor."

She shrugged her shoulders.

" Would you have me cry," she said, " because the stockholders of the Baron Three Francs Sixty-eight have been swindled? Console yourself: they are accustomed to it."

And, as M. de Trégars made no answer,—

" And in all that," she went on, " I see no one to pity except the wife and daughter of that old stick Favoral."

" They are, indeed, much to be pitied."

" They say that the mother is a good old thing."

" She is an excellent person."

" And the daughter? Costeclar was crazy about her once. He made eyes like a carp in love, as he told us, to mamma and myself, ' She is an angel, mesdames, an angel! And when I have given her a little *chic!* ' Now tell me, is she really as good looking as all that? "

" She is quite good looking."

" Better looking than me? "

" It is not the same style, mademoiselle."

Mlle. de Thaller had stopped singing; but she has not left the piano. Half turned towards M. de Trégars, she ran her fingers listlessly over the keys, striking a note here and there, as if to punctuate her sentences.

" Ah, how nice! " she exclaimed, " and, above all, how gallant! Really, if you venture often on such declarations, mothers would be very wrong to trust you alone with their daughters."

" You did not understand me right, mademoiselle."

" Perfectly right, on the contrary. I asked you if I was better looking than Mlle. Favoral; and you replied to me, that it was not the same style."

" It is because, mademoiselle, there is indeed no possible comparison between you, who are a wealthy heiress, and whose life is a perpetual enchantment, and a poor girl, very humble, and very modest, who rides in the omnibus, and who makes her dresses herself."

A contemptuous smile contracted Mlle. Césarine's lips.

" Why not? " she interrupted. " Men have such funny tastes! "

And, turning around suddenly, she began another rondo, no less famous than the first, and borrowed, this time, from the third act of the *Petites-Blanchisseuses:*—

> " What matters the quality?
> Beauty alone takes the prize:
> Women before man must rise,
> And claim perfect equality."

Very attentively M. de Trégars was observing her. He had not been the dupe of the great surprise she had manifested when she found him in the little parlor.

"She knew I was here," he thought; "and it is her mother who has sent her to me. But why? and for what purpose?"

"With all that," she resumed, "I see the sweet Mme. Favoral and her modest daughter in a terribly tight place. What a 'bust,' marquis!"

"They have a great deal of courage, mademoiselle."

"Naturally. But, what is better, the daughter has a splendid voice: at least, so her professor told Costeclar. Why should she not go on the stage? Actresses make lots of money, you know. Papa'll help her, if she wishes. He has a great deal of influence in the theatres, papa has."

"Mme. and Mlle. Favoral have friends."

"Ah, yes! Costeclar."

"Others besides."

"I beg your pardon; but it seems to me that this one will do to begin with. He is gallant, Costeclar, extremely gallant, and, moreover, generous as a lord. Why should he not offer to that youthful and timid damsel a nice little position in mahogany and rosewood? That way, we should have the pleasure of meeting her around the lake."

And she began singing again, with a slight variation:—

> "Manon, who, before the war,
>   Carried clothes for a living,
>   Now for her gains is trusting
>   To that insane Costeclar."

"Ah, that big red-headed girl is terribly provoking!" thought M. de Trégars.

But, as he did not as yet understand very clearly what she wished to come to, he kept on his guard, and remained cold as marble.

Already she had again turned towards him.

" What a face you are making ! " she said. " Are you jealous of the fiery Costeclar, by chance? "

" No, mademoiselle, no ! "

" Then, why don't you want him to succeed in his love? But he will, you'll see ! Five hundred francs on Costeclar ! Do you take it? No? I am sorry. It's twenty-five napoleons lost for me. I know very well that Mlle.—what's her name? "

" Gilberte."

" Halloo ! a nice name for a cashier's daughter ! I am aware that she once sent that poor Costeclar and his offer to—Chaillot. But she had resources then ; whilst now— It's stupid as it can be ; but people have to eat ! "

" There are still women, mademoiselle, capable of starving to death."

M. de Trégars now felt satisfied. It seemed evident to him that they had somehow got wind of his intentions ; that Mlle. de Thaller had been sent to feel the ground ; and that she only attacked Mlle. Gilberte in order to irritate him, and compel him, in a moment of anger, to declare himself.

" Bash ! " she said, " Mlle. Favoral is like all the others. If she had to select between the amiable Costeclar and a charcoal furnace, it is not the furnace she would take."

At all times, Marius de Trégars disliked Mlle. Césarine to a supreme degree ; but at this moment, without the pressing desire he had to see the Baron and Baroness de Thaller, he would have withdrawn.

" Believe me, mademoiselle," he uttered coldly.

" Spare a poor girl stricken by a most cruel misfortune. Worse might happen to you."

" To me! And what the mischief do you suppose can happen me? "

" Who knows? "

She started to her feet so violently, that she upset the piano-stool.

" Whatever it may be," she exclaimed, " I say in advance, I am glad! "

And as M. de Trégars turned his head in some surprise,—

" Yes, I am glad! " she repeated, " because it would be a change; and I am sick of the life I lead. Yes, sick to be eternally and invariably happy of that same dreary happiness. And to think that there are idiots who believe that I amuse myself, and who envy my fate! To think, that, when I ride through the streets, I hear girls exclaim, whilst looking at me, ' Isn't she lucky? ' Little fools! I'd like to see them in my place. They live, they do. Their pleasures are not all alike. They have anxieties and hopes, ups and downs, hours of rain and hours of sunshine; whilst I—always dead calm! the barometer always at ' Set fair.' What a bore! Do you know what I did to-day? Exactly the same thing as yesterday; and to-morrow I'll do the same thing as to-day.

" A good dinner is a good thing; but always the same dinner, without extras or additions—pouah! Too many truffles. I want some corned beef and cabbage. I know the bill of fare by heart, you see. In winter, theatres and balls; in summer, races and the seashore; summer and winter, shopping, rides to the *bois*, calls, trying dresses, perpetual adoration by mother's friends, all of them brilliant and gallant fellows to whom the mere thought of my dowry gives the jaundice. Excuse me, if I yawn: I am thinking of their conversations.

" And to think," she went on, " that such will be my existence until I make up my mind to take a husband ! For I'll have to come to it too. The Baron Three Sixty-eight will present to me some sort of a swell, attracted by my money. I'll answer, ' I'd just as soon have him as any other ; ' and he will be admitted to the honor of paying his attentions to me. Every morning he will send me a splendid bouquet : every evening, after bank-hours, he'll come along with fresh kid gloves and a white vest. During the afternoon, he and papa will pull each other's hair out on the subject of the dowry. At last the happy day will arrive. Can't you see it from here? Mass with music, dinner, ball. The Baron Three Sixty-eight will not spare me a single ceremony. The marriage of the manager of the Mutual Credit must certainly be an advertisement. The papers will publish the names of the bridesmaids and of the guests.

" To be sure, papa will have a face a yard long, because he will have been compelled to pay the dowry the day before. Mamma will be all upset at the idea of becoming a grandmother. The bridegroom will be in a wretched humor, because his boots will be too tight ; and I'll look like a goose, because I'll be dressed in white ; and white is a stupid color, which is not at all becoming to me. Charming family gathering, isn't it? Two weeks later, my husband will be sick of me, and I'll be disgusted with him. After a month, we'll be at daggers' points. He'll go back to his club and his mistresses ; and I—I shall have conquered the right to go out alone ; and I'll begin again going to the *bois,* to balls, to races, wherever my mother goes. I'll spend an enormous amount of money on my dress, and I'll make debts which papa will pay."

Though any thing might be expected of Mlle. César·

ine, still M. de Trégars seemed visibly astonished. And she, laughing at his surprise,—

"That's the invariable programme," she went on; "and that's why I say I'm glad at the idea of a change, whatever it may be. You find fault with me for not pitying Mlle. Gilberte. How could I, since I envy her? She is happy, because her future is not settled, laid out, fixed in advance. She is poor; but she is free. She is twenty; she is pretty; she has an admirable voice; she can go on the stage to-morrow, and be, before six months, one of the pet actresses of Paris. What a life then! Ah, that is the one I dream, the one I would have selected, had I been mistress of my destiny."

But she was interrupted by the noise of the opening door.

The Baroness de Thaller appeared. As she was, immediately after dinner, to go to the opera, and afterwards to a party given by the Viscountess de Bois d'Ardon, she was in full dress. She wore a dress, cut audaciously low in the neck, of very light gray satin, trimmed with bands of cherry-colored silk edged with lace. In her hair, worn high over her head, she had a bunch of fuchsias, the flexible stems of which, fastened by a large diamond star, trailed down to her very shoulders, white and smooth as marble.

But, though she forced herself to smile, her countenance was not that of festive days; and the glance which she cast upon her daughter and Marius de Trégars was laden with threats. In a voice of which she tried in vain to control the emotion,—

"How very kind of you, marquis," she began, "to respond so soon to my invitation of this morning! I am really distressed to have kept you waiting; but I was dressing. After what has happened to M de Thaller. it is absolutely indispensable that I should go out, show myself: otherwise our enemies will be going around to-morrow, saying everywhere that I am in Belgium, pre-paring lodgings for my husband."

And, suddenly changing her tone,—

"But what was that madcap Césarine telling you?" she asked.

It was with a profound surprise that M. de Trégars discovered that the *entente cordiale* which he suspected between the mother and daughter did not exist, at least at this moment.

Veiling under a jesting tone the strange conjectures which the unexpected discovery aroused within him,—

"Mlle. Césarine," he replied, "who is much to be pitied, was telling me all her troubles."

She interrupted him.

"Do not take the trouble to tell a story, M. le Mar-quis," she said. "Mamma knows it as well as yourself; for she was listening at the door."

"Césarine!" exclaimed Mme. de Thaller.

"And, if she came in so suddenly, it is because she thought it was fully time to cut short my confidences."

The face of the baroness became crimson.

"The child is mad!" she said.

The child burst out laughing.

"That's my way," she went on. "You should not have sent me here by chance, and against my wish. You made me do it: don't complain. You were sure that I had but to appear, and M. de Trégars would fall at my feet. I appeared, and—you saw the effect through the keyhole, didn't you?"

Her features contracted, her eyes flashing, twisting her lace handkerchief between her fingers loaded with rings,—

" It is unheard of," said Mme. de Thaller. " She has
certainly lost her head."

Dropping her mother an ironical courtesy,—

" Thanks for the compliment! " said the young lady.
" Unfortunately, I never was more completely in possession of all the good sense I may boast of than I am
now, dear mamma. What were you telling me a moment
since? ' Run, the Marquis de Trégars is coming to ask
your hand: it's all settled.' And what did I answer?
' No use to trouble myself: if, instead of one million,
papa were to give me two, four millions, indeed all the
millions paid by France to Prussia, M. de Trégars
would not have me for a wife.' "

And, looking Marius straight in the face,—

" Am I not right, M. le Marquis? " she asked. " And
isn't it a fact that you wouldn't have me at any price?
Come, now, your hand upon your heart, answer."

M. de Trégars' situation was somewhat embarrassing
between these two women, whose anger was equal,
though it manifested itself in a different way. Evidently it was a discussion begun before, which was now
continued in his presence.

" I think, madamoiselle," he began, " that you have
been slandering yourself gratuitously."

" Oh, no! I swear it to you," she replied; " and, if
mamma had not happened in, you would have heard
much more. But that was not an answer."

And, as M. de Trégars said nothing, she turned towards the baroness,—

" Ah, ah! you see," she said. " Who was crazy,—
you, or I? Ah! you imagine here that money is every
thing, that every thing is for sale, and that every thing
can be bought. Well, no! There are still men, who,
for all the gold in the world, would not give their name

to Césarine de Thaller. It is strange; but it is so, dear
mamma, and we must make up our mind to it."   ,

Then turning towards Marius, and bearing upon each
syllable, as if afraid that the allusion might escape
him,—

" The men of whom I speak," she added, " marry
the girls who can starve to death."

Knowing her daughter well enough to be aware that
she could not impose silence upon her, the Baroness de
Thaller had dropped upon a chair. She was trying
hard to appear indifferent to what her daughter was
saying; but at every moment a threatening gesture, or
a hoarse exclamation, betrayed the storm that raged
within her.

" Go, on, poor foolish child! " she said, —" go on! "

And she did go on.

" Finally, were M. de Trégars willing to have me, I
would refuse him myself, because, then "—

A fugitive blush colored her cheeks, her bold eyes
vacillated, and, dropping her voice,—

" Because, then," she added, " he would no longer be
what he is; because I feel that fatally I shall despise
the husband whom papa will buy for me. And, if I
came here to expose myself to an affront which I foresaw, it is because I wanted to make sure of a fact of
which a word of Costeclar, a few days ago, had given
me an idea,—of a fact which you do not, perhaps, suspect, dear mother, despite your astonishing perspicacity.
I wanted to find out M. de Trégars' secret; and I have
found it out."

M. de Trégars had come to the Thaller mansion with
a plan well settled in advance. He had pondered long
before deciding what he would do, and what he would
say, and how he would begin the decisive struggle. What

had taken place showed him the idleness of his conjectures, and, as a natural consequence, upset his plans.

To abandon himself to the chances of the hour, and to make the best possible use of them, was now the wisest thing to do.

"Give me credit, mademoiselle," he uttered, "for sufficient penetration to have perfectly well discerned your intentions. There was no need of artifice, because I have nothing to conceal. You had but to question me, I would have answered you frankly, ' Yes, it is true I love Mlle. Gilberte; and before a month she will be Marquise de Trégars.' "

Mme. de Thaller, at those words, had started to her feet, pushing back her arm-chair so violently, that it rolled all the way to the wall.

"What!" she exclaimed, "you marry Gilberte Favoral,—you!"

"I—yes."

"The daughter of a defaulting cashier, a dishonored man whom justice pursues and the galleys await!"

"Yes!" And in an accent that caused a shiver to run over the white shoulders of Mme. de Thaller,—

"Whatever may have been," he uttered, "Vincent Favoral's crime; whether he has or has not stolen, the twelve millions which are wanting from the funds of the Mutual Credit; whether he is alone guilty, or has accomplices; whether he be a knave, or a fool, an impostor, or a dupe,—Mlle. Gilberte is not responsible."

"You know the Favoral family, then?"

"Enough to make their cause henceforth my own."

The agitation of the baroness was so great, that she did not even attempt to conceal it.

"A nobody's daughter!" she said.

"I love her."

"Without a sou!"

Mlle. Césarine made a superb gesture.

"Why, that's the very reason why a man may marry her!" she exclaimed. And, holding out her hand to M. de Trégars,—

"What you do here is well," she added, "very well."

There was a wild look in the eyes of the baroness.

"Mad, unhappy child!" she exclaimed. "If your father should hear!"

"And who, then, would report our conversation to him? M. de Trégars? He would not do such a thing. You? You dare not."

Drawing herself up to her fullest height, her breast swelling with anger, her head thrown back, her eyes flashing,—

"Césarine," ordered Mme. de Thaller, her arm extended towards the door,—"Césarine, leave the room: I command you."

But, motionless in her place, the girl cast upon her mother a look of defiance.

"Come, calm yourself," she said in a tone of crushing irony, "or you'll spoil your complexion for the rest of the evening. Do I complain? do I get excited? And yet whose fault is it, if honor makes it a duty for me to cry 'Beware!' to an honest man who wishes to marry me? That Gilberte should get married; that she should be very happy, have many children, darn her husband's stockings, and skim her *pot-au-feu*,—that is her part in life. Ours, dear mother,—that which you have taught me,—is to laugh and have fun, all the time, night and day, till death."

A footman who came in interrupted her. Handing a card to Mme. de Thaller,—

" The gentleman who gave it to me," he said, " is in the large parlor."

The baroness had become very pale.

" Oh ! " she said turning the card between her fingers,—" oh ! "—

Then suddenly she ran out exclaiming,—

" I'll be back directly."

An embarrassing, painful silence followed, as it was inevitable that it would, the Baroness de Thaller's precipitate departure.

Mlle. Césarine had approached the mantel-piece. She was leaning her elbow upon it, her forehead on her hand, all palpitating and excited. Intimidated for, perhaps, the first time in her life, she turned away her great blue eyes, as if afraid that they should betray a reflex of her thoughts.

As to M. de Trégars, he remained at his place, not having one whit too much of that power of self-control, which is acquired by a long experience of the world, to conceal his impressions. If he had a fault, it was certainly not self-conceit; but Mlle. de Thaller had been too explicit and too clear to leave him a doubt. All she had said could be comprised in one sentence,—

" My parents were in hopes that I would become your wife : I had judged you well enough to understand their error. Precisely because I love you, I acknowledge myself unworthy of you ; and I wish you to know, that if you had asked my hand,—the hand of a girl who has a dowry of a million,—I would have ceased to esteem you."

That such a feeling should have budded and blossomed in Mlle. Césarine's soul, withered as it was by vanity, and blunted by pleasure, was almost a miracle. It was, at any rate, an astonishing proof of love which she gave; and Marius de Trégars would not have been a man, if he had not been deeply moved by it.

Suddenly,—

" What a miserable wretch I am! " she uttered.

" You mean unhappy," said M. de Trégars gently.

" What can you think of my sincerity? You must, doubtless, find it strange, impudent, grotesque."

He lifted his hand in protest; for she gave him no time to put in a word.

" And yet," she went on, " this is not the first time that I am assailed by sinister ideas, and that I feel ashamed of myself. I was convinced once that this mad existence of mine is the only enviable one, the only one that can give happiness. And now I discover that it is not the right path which I have taken, or, rather, which I have been made to take. And there is no possibility of retracing my steps."

She turned pale, and, in an accent of gloomy despair,—

" Every thing fails me," she said. " It seems as though I were rolling into a bottomless abyss, without a branch or a tuft of grass to cling to. Around me, emptiness, night, chaos. I am not yet twenty; and it seems to me that I have lived thousands of years, and exhausted every sensation. I have seen every thing, learned every thing, experienced every thing; and I am tired of every thing, and satiated and nauseated. You see me looking like a brainless hoyden. I sing, I jest, I talk slang. My gayety surprises everybody. In reality, I am literally tired to death. What I feel I could not express; there are no words to render absolute disgust. Sometimes I say to myself, ' It is stupid to be so sad. What do you need? Are you not young, handsome, rich?' But I must need something, or else

I would not be thus agitated, nervous, anxious, unable
to stay in one place, tormented by confused aspirations,
and by desires which I cannot formulate. What can I
do? Seek oblivion in pleasure and dissipation? I try,
and I succeed for an hour or so; but the re-action comes,
and the effect vanishes, like froth from champagne. The
lassitude returns; and, whilst outwardly I continue to
laugh, I shed within tears of blood which scald my
heart. What is to become of me, without a memory in
the past, or a hope in the future, upon which to rest my
thought?"

And bursting into tears,—

"Oh, I am wretchedly unhappy!" she exclaimed;
"and I wish I was dead."

M. de Trégars rose, feeling more deeply moved than
he would, perhaps, have liked to acknowledge.

"I was laughing at you only a moment since," he said
in his grave and vibrating voice. "Pardon me, mademoiselle. It is with the utmost sincerity, and from
the innermost depths of my soul, that I pity you."

She was looking at him with an air of timid doubt,
big tears trembling between her long eyelashes.

"Honest?" she asked.

"Upon my honor."

"And you will not go with too poor an opinion of
me?"

"I shall retain the firm belief that when you were
yet but a child, you were spoiled by insane theories."

Gently and sadly she was passing her hand over her
forehead.

"Yes, that's it," she murmured. "How could I resist examples coming from certain persons? How could
I help becoming intoxicated when I saw myself, as it
were, in a cloud of incense when I heard nothing but

praises and applause? And then there is the money, which depraves when it comes in a certain way."

She ceased to speak; but the silence was soon again broken by a slight noise, which came from the adjoining room.

Mechanically, M. de Trégars looked around him. The little parlor in which he found himself was divided from the main drawing-room of the house by a tall and broad door, closed only by heavy curtains, which had remained partially drawn. Now, such was the disposition of the mirrors in the two rooms, that M. de Trégars could see almost the whole of the large one reflected in the mirror over the mantelpiece of the little parlor. A man of suspicious appearance, and wearing wretched clothes, was standing in it.

And, the more M. de Trégars examined him, the more it seemed to him that he had already seen somewhere that uneasy countenance, that anxious glance, that wicked smile flitting upon flat and thin lips.

But suddenly the man bowed very low. It was probable that Mme. de Thaller, who had gone around through the hall to reach the grand parlor, must be coming in; and in fact she almost immediately appeared within the range of the glass. She seemed much agitated; and, with a finger upon her lips, she was recommending to the man to be prudent, and to speak low. It was therefore in a whisper, and such a low whisper that not even a vague murmur reached the little parlor, that the man uttered a few words.

They were such that the baroness started back as if she had seen a precipice yawning at her feet; and by this action it was easy to understand that she must have said,—

" Is it possible? "

With the voice which still could not be heard, but with a gesture which could be seen, the man evidently replied,—

" It is so, I assure you ! "

And leaning towards Mme. de Thaller, who seemed in no wise shocked to feel this repulsive personage's lips almost touching her ear, he began speaking to her.

The surprise which this species of vision caused to M. de Trégars was great, but did not keep him from reflecting what could be the meaning of this scene. How came this suspicious-looking man to have obtained access, without difficulty, into the grand parlor? Why had the baroness, on receiving his card, turned whiter than the laces on her dress? What news had he brought, which had made such a deep impression ? What was he saying that seemed at once to terrify and to delight Mme. de Thaller?

But soon she interrupted the man, beckoned to him to wait, disappeared for a minute; and, when she came in again, she held in her hand a package of bank-notes, which she began counting upon the parlor-table.

She counted twenty-five, which, so far as M. de Trégars could judge, must have been hundred-franc notes. The man took them, counted them over, slipped them into his pocket with a grin of satisfaction, and then seemed disposed to retire.

The baroness detained him, however; and it was she now, who, leaning towards him, commenced to explain to him, or rather, as far as her attitude showed, to ask him something. It must have been a serious matter; for he shook his head, and moved his arms, as if he meant to say, " The deuse, the deuse ! "

The strangest suspicions flashed across M. de Trégars' mind. What was that bargain to which the mirror made him, thus an accidental witness? For it was a bargain: there could be no mistake about it. The man, having received a mission, had fulfilled it, and had come to receive the price of it. And now a new commission was offered to him.

But M. de Trégars' attention was now called off by Mlle. Césarine. Shaking off the torpor which for a moment had overpowered her,—

" But why fret and worry? " she said, answering, rather, the objections of her own mind than addressing herself to M. de Trégars. " Things are just as they are, and I cannot undo them.

" Ah! if the mistakes of life were like soiled clothes, which are allowed to accumulate in a wardrobe, and which are all sent out at once to the wash. But nothing washes the past, not even repentance, whatever they may say. There are some ideas which should be set aside. A prisoner should not allow himself to think of freedom.

" And yet," she added, shrugging her shoulders, " a prisoner has always the hope of escaping; whereas I "—

Then, making a visible effort to resume her usual manner,—

" Bash! " she said, " that's enough sentiment for one day; and instead of staying here, boring you to death, I ought to go and dress; for I am going to the opera with my sweet mamma, and afterwards to the ball. You ought to come. I am going to wear a stunning dress. The ball is at Mme. de Bois d'Ardon's,— one of our friends, a progressive woman. She has a smoking-room for ladies. What do you think of that? Come, will you go? We'll drink champagne, and we'll laugh. No Zut then, and my compliments to your family."

But, at the moment of leaving the room, her heart failed her.

" This is doubtless the last time I shall ever see you, M. de Trégars," she said. " Farewell! You know now why I, who have a dowry of a million, I envy Gilberte Favoral. Once more farewell. And, whatever happiness may fall to your lot in life, remember that Césarine has wished it all to you."

And she went out at the very moment when the Baroness de Thaller returned.

VII.

" CÉSARINE! " Mme. de Thaller called, in a voice which sounded at once like a prayer and a threat.

" I am going to dress myself, mamma," she answered.

" Come back! "

" So that you can scold me if I am not ready when you want to go? Thank you, no."

" I command you to come back, Césarine."

No answer. She was far already.

Mme. de Thaller closed the door of the little parlor, and returning to take a seat by M. de Trégars,—

" What a singular girl! " she said.

Meantime he was watching in the glass what was going on in the other room. The suspicious-looking man was there still, and alone. A servant had brought him pen, ink and paper; and he was writing rapidly.

" How is it that they leave him there alone? " wondered Marius.

And he endeavored to find upon the features of the baroness an answer to the confused presentiments which

agitated his brain. But there was no longer any trace
of the emotion which she had manifested when taken
unawares. Having had time for reflection, she had
composed for herself an impenetrable countenance.
Somewhat surprised at M. de Trégars' silence,—

"I was saying," she repeated, "that Césarine is a
strange girl."

Still absorbed by the scene in the grand parlor,—

"Strange, indeed!" he answered.

"And such is," said the baroness with a sigh, "the
result of M. de Thaller's weakness, and above all of my
own."

"Ah!"

"We have no child but Césarine; and it was natural
that we should spoil her. Her fancy has been, and is
still, our only law. She has never had time to express
a wish: she is obeyed before she has spoken."

She sighed again, and deeper than the first time.

"You have just seen," she went on, "the results of
that insane education. And yet it would not do to trust
appearances. Césarine, believe me, is not as extravagant as she seems. She possesses solid qualities,—of
those which a man expects of the woman who is to be
his wife."

Without taking his eyes off the glass,—

"I believe you madame," said M. de Trégars.

"With her father, with me especially, she is capri-
cious, wilful, and violent; but, in the hands of the husband of her choice, she would be like wax in the hands
of the modeller."

The man in the parlor had finished his letter, and,
with an equivocal smile, was reading it over.

"Believe me, madame," replied M. de Trégars, "I

have perfectly understood how much *naive* boasting there was in all that Mlle. Césarine told me."

"Then, really, you do not judge her too severely?"

"Your heart has not more indulgence for her than my own."

"And yet it is from you that her first real sorrow comes."

"From me?"

The baroness shook her head in a melancholy way, to convey an idea of her maternal affection and anxiety.

"Yes, from you, my dear marquis," she replied,— "from you alone. On the very day you entered this house, Césarine's whole nature changed."

Having read his letter over, the man in the grand parlor had folded it, and slipped it into his pocket, and, having left his seat, seemed to be waiting for something. M. de Trégars was following, in the glass, his every motion, with the most eager curiosity. And nevertheless, as he felt the absolute necessity of saying something, were it only to avoid attracting the attention of the baroness,—

"What!" he said, "Mlle. Césarine's nature did change, then?"

"In one night. Had she not met the hero of whom every girl dreams?—a man of thirty, bearing one of the oldest names in France."

She stopped, expecting an answer, a word, an exclamation. But, as M. de Trégars said nothing,—

"Did you never notice any thing then?" she asked.

"Nothing."

"And suppose I were to tell you myself, that my poor Césarine, alas!—loves you?"

M. de Trégars started. Had he been less occupied with the personage in the grand parlor, he would certainly not have allowed the conversation to drift in this channel. He understood his mistake; and, in an icy tone,—

"Permit me, madame," he said, "to believe that you are jesting."

"And suppose it were the truth."

"It would make me unhappy in the extreme."

"Sir!"

"For the reason which I have already told you, that I love Mlle. Gilberte Favoral with the deepest and the purest love, and that for the past three years she has been, before God, my affianced bride."

Something like a flash of anger passed over Mme. de Thaller's eyes.

"And I," she exclaimed,—"I tell you that this marriage is senseless."

"I wish it were still more so, that I might the better show to Gilberte how dear she is to me."

Calm in appearance, the baroness was scratching with her nails the satin of the chair on which she was sitting.

"Then," she went on, "your resolution is settled."

"Irrevocably."

"Still, now, come, between us who are no longer children, suppose M. de Thaller were to double Césarine's dowry, to treble it?"

An expression of intense disgust contracted the manly features of Marius de Trégars.

"Ah! not another word, madame," he interrupted.

There was no hope left. Mme. de Thaller fully realized it by the tone in which he spoke. She remained pensive for over a minute, and suddenly, like a person who has finally made up her mind, she rang.

A footman appeared.

" Do what I told you! " she ordered.

And as soon as the footman had gone, turning to M. de Trégars,—

" Alas! " she said, " who would have thought that I would curse the day when you first entered our house? "

But, whilst she spoke, M. de Trégars noticed in the glass the result of the order she had just given.

The footman walked into the grand parlor, spoke a few words; and at once the man with the alarming countenance put on his hat and went out.

" This is very strange! " thought M. de Trégars.

Meantime, the baroness was going on,—

" If your intentions are to that point irrevocable, how is it that you are here? You have too much experience of the world not to have understood, this morning, the object of my visit and of my allusions."

Fortunately, M. de Trégars' attention was no longer drawn by the proceedings in the next room. The decisive moment had come: the success of the game he was playing would, perhaps, depend upon his coolness and self-command.

" It is because I did understand, madame, and even better than you suppose, that I am here."

" Indeed! "

" I came, expecting to deal with M. de Thaller alone. I have been compelled, by what has happened, to alter my intentions. It is to you that I must speak first."

Mme. de Thaller continued to manifest the same tranquil assurance; but she stood up. Feeling the approach of the storm, she wished to be up, and ready to meet it.

" You honor me," she said with an ironical smile.

There was, henceforth, no human power capable of

turning Marius de Trégars from the object he had in view.

"It is to you I shall speak," he repeated, "because, after you have heard me, you may perhaps judge that it is your interest to join me in endeavoring to obtain from your husband what I ask, what I demand, what I must have."

With an air of surprise marvellously well simulated, if it was not real, the baroness was looking at him.

"My father," he proceeded to say, "the Marquis de Trégars, was once rich: he had several millions. And yet when I had the misfortune of losing him, three years ago, he was so thoroughly ruined, that to relieve the scruples of his honor, and to make his death easier, I gave up to his creditors all I had in the world. What had become of my father's fortune? What filter had been administered to him to induce him to launch into hazardous speculations,—he, an old Breton gentleman, full, even to absurdity, of the most obstinate prejudices of the nobility? That's what I wished to ascertain."

"Ah!"

"And now, madame, I—have ascertained."

She was a strong-minded woman, the Baroness de Thaller. She had had so many adventures in her life, she had walked on the very edge of so many precipices, concealed so many anxieties, that danger was, as it were, her element, and that, at the decisive moment of an almost desperate game, she could remain smiling like those old gamblers whose face never betrays their terrible emotion at the moment when they risk their last stake. Not a muscle of her face moved; and it was with the most imperturbable calm that she said,—

"Go on, I am listening: it must be quite interesting."

That was not the way to propitiate M. de Trégars. He resumed, in a brief and harsh tone,—

"When my father died, I was young. I did not know then what I have learned since,—that to contribute to insure the impunity of knaves is almost to make one's self their accomplice. And the victim who says nothing and submits, does contribute to it. The honest man, on the contrary, should speak, and point out to others the trap into which he has fallen, that they may avoid it."

The baroness was listening with the air of a person who is compelled by politeness to hear a tiresome story.

"That is a rather gloomy preamble," she said.

M. de Trégars took no notice of the interruption.

"At all times," he went on, "my father seemed careless of his affairs: that affectation, he thought, was due to the name he bore. But his negligence was only apparent. I might mention things of him that would do honor to the most methodical tradesman. He had, for instance, the habit of preserving all the letters of any importance which he received. He left twelve or fifteen boxes full of such. They were carefully classified; and many bore upon their margin a few notes indicating what answer had been made to them."

Half suppressing a yawn,—

"That is order," said the baroness, "if I know any thing about it."

"At the first moment, determined not to stir up the past, I attached no importance to those letters; and they would certainly have been burnt, but for an old friend of the family, the Count de Villegré, who had them carried to his own house. But later, acting under the influence of circumstances which it would be too long to explain to you, I regretted my apathy; and I thought that I should, perhaps, find in that correspondence something to either dissipate or justify certain suspicions which had occurred to me."

" So that, like a respectful son, you read it?"

M. de Trégars bowed ceremoniously.

" I believe," he said, " that to avenge a father of the imposture of which he was the victim during his life, is to render homage to his memory. Yes, madame, I read the whole of that correspondence, and with an interest which you will readily understand. I had already, and without result, examined the contents of several boxes, when in the package marked 1852, a year which my father spent in Paris, certain letters attracted my attention. They were written upon coarse paper, in a very primitive handwriting and wretchedly spelt. They were signed sometimes Phrasie, sometimes Marquise de Javelle. Some gave the address, ' Rue des Bergers, No. 3, Paris-Grenelle.'

" Those letters left me no doubt upon what had taken place. My father had met a young working-girl of rare beauty: he had taken a fancy to her; and, as he was tormented by the fear of being loved for his money alone, he had passed himself off for a poor clerk in one of the departments."

" Quite a touching little love-romance," remarked the baroness.

But there was no impertinence that could affect Marius de Trégars' coolness.

" A romance, perhaps," he said, " but in that case a money-romance, not a love-romance. This Phrasie, or Marquise de Javelle, announces in one of her letters, that in February, 1853, she has given birth to a daughter, whom she has confided to some relatives of her in the south, near Toulouse. It was doubtless that event which induced my father to acknowledge who he was. He confesses that he is not a poor clerk, but the Marquis de Trégars, having an income of over a hundred thousand francs. At once the tone of the correspondence changes. The Marquise de Javelle has a stupid time where she lives; the neighbors reproach her with her fault; work spoils her pretty hands. Result: less than two weeks after the birth of her daughter, my father hires for his pretty mistress a lovely apartment, which she occupies under the name of Mme. Devil; she is allowed fifteen hundred francs a month, servants, horses, carriage."

Mme. de Thaller was giving signs of the utmost impatience. Without paying any attention to them, M. de Trégars proceeded,—

"Henceforth free to see each other daily, my father and his mistress cease to write. But Mme. Devil does not waste her time. During a space of less than eight months, from February to September, she induces my father to dispose—not in her favor, she is too disinterested for that, but in favor of her daughter—of a sum exceeding five hundred thousand francs. In September, the correspondence is resumed. Mme. Devil discovers that she is not happy, and acknowledges it in a letter, which shows, by its improved writing and more correct spelling, that she has been taking lessons.

"She complains of her precarious situation: the future frightens her: she longs for respectability. Such is, for three months, the constant burden of her correspondence. She regrets the time when she was a working-girl: why has she been so weak? Then, at last, in a note which betrays long debates and stormy discussions, she announces that she has an unexpected offer of marriage; a fine fellow, who, if she only had two hundred thousand francs, would give his name to herself and to her darling little daughter. For a long time my father hesitates; but she presses her point with such rare skill, she demonstrates so conclusively that this marriage will insure the happiness of their child, that my father yields at last, and resigns himself to the sacrifice. And in a memorandum on the margin of a last letter, he states that he has just given two hundred thousand francs to Mme. Devil; that he will never see her again; and that he returns to live in Brittany, where he wishes, by the most rigid economy, to repair the breach he has just made in his fortune."

"Thus end all these love-stories," said Mme. de Thaller in a jesting tone.

"I beg your pardon: this one is not ended yet. For many years, my father kept his word, and never left our homestead of Trégars. But at last he grew tired of his solitude, and returned to Paris. Did he seek to see his former mistress again? I think not. I suppose that chance brought them together; or else, that, being aware of his return, she managed to put herself in his way. He found her more fascinating than ever, and, according to what she wrote him, rich and respected; for her husband had become a personage. She would have been perfectly happy, she added, had it been possible for her to forget the man whom she had once loved so much, and to whom she owed her position.

"I have that letter. The elegant hand, the style, and the correct orthography, express better than any thing else the transformations of the Marquise de Javelle. Only it is not signed. The little working-girl has become prudent: she has much to lose, and fears to compromise herself.

"A week later, in a laconic note, apparently dictated

by an irresistible passion, she begs my father to come to see her at her own house. He does so, and finds there a little girl, whom he believes to be his own child, and whom he at once begins to idolize.

"And that's all. Again he falls under the charm. He ceases to belong to himself: his former mistress can dispose, at her pleasure, of his fortune and of his fate.

"But see now what bad luck! The husband takes a notion to become jealous of my father's visits. In a letter which is a masterpiece of diplomacy, the lady explains her anxiety. 'He has suspicions,' she writes; 'and to what extremities might he not resort, were he to discover the truth!' And with infinite art she insinuates that the best way to justify his constant presence is to associate himself with that jealous husband.

"It is with childish haste that my father jumps at the suggestion. But money is needed. He sells his lands, and everywhere announces that he has great financial ideas, and that he is going to increase his fortune tenfold.

"There he is now, partner of his former mistress's husband, engaged in speculations, director of a company. He thinks that he is doing an excellent business: he is convinced that he is making lots of money. Poor honest man! They prove to him, one morning, that he is ruined, and, what is more, compromised. And this is made to look so much like the truth, that I interfere myself, and pay the creditors. We were ruined; but honor was safe. A few weeks later, my father died broken-hearted."

Mme. de Thaller half rose from her seat with a gesture which indicated the joy of escaping at last a merciless bore. A glance from M. de Trégars riveted her to her seat, freezing upon her lips the jest she was about to utter.

" I have not done yet," he said rudely.

And, without suffering any interruption,—

" From this correspondence," he resumed, " resulted the flagrant, irrefutable proof of a shameful intrigue, long since suspected by my old friend, General Count de Villegré. It became evident to me that my poor father had been most shamefully imposed upon by that mistress, so handsome and so dearly loved, and, later, despoiled, by the husband of that mistress. But all this availed me nothing. Being ignorant of my father's life and connections, the letters giving neither a name nor a precise detail, I knew not whom to accuse. Besides, in order to accuse, it is necessary to have, at least, some material proof."

The baroness had resumed her seat ; and every thing about her—her attitude, her gestures, the motion of her lips—seemed to say,—

" You are my guest. Civility has its demands ; but really you abuse your privileges."

M. de Trégars went on,—

" At this moment I was still a sort of savage, wholly absorbed in my experiments, and scarcely ever setting foot outside my laboratory. I was indignant ; I ardently wished to find and to punish the villains who had robbed us : but I knew not how to go about it, nor in what direction to seek information. The wretches would, perhaps, have gone unpunished, but for a good and worthy man, now a commissary of police, to whom I once rendered a slight service, one night, in a riot, when he was close pressed by some half-dozen rascals. I explained the situation to him : he took much interest in it, promised his assistance, and marked out my line of conduct."

Mme. de Thaller seemed restless upon her seat.

" I must confess," she began, " that I am not wholly mistress of my time. I am dressed, as you see: I have to go out."

If she had preserved any hope of adjourning the explanation which she felt coming, she must have lost it when she heard the tone in which M. de Trégars interrupted her.

" You can go out to-morrow."

And, without hurrying,—

" Advised, as I have just told you," he continued, " and assisted by the experience of a professional man, I went first to No. 3, Rue des Bergers, in Grenelle. I found there some old people, the foreman of a neighboring factory and his wife, who had been living in the house for nearly twenty-five years. At my first question, they exchanged a glance, and commenced laughing. They remembered perfectly the Marquise de Javelle, which was but a nickname for a young and pretty laundress, whose real name was Euphrasie Taponnet. She had lived for eighteen months on the same landing as themselves: she had a lover, who passed himself off for a clerk, but who was, in fact, she had told them, a very wealthy nobleman. They added that she had given birth to a little girl, and that, two weeks later she had disappeared, and they had never heard a word from her. When I left them, they said to me, ' If you see Phrasie, ask her if she ever knew old Chandour and his wife. I am sure she'll remember us.' "

For the first time Mme. de Thaller shuddered slightly; but it was almost imperceptible.

" From Grenelle," continued M. de Trégars, " I went
to the house where my father's mistress had lived under
the name of Mme. Devil. I was in luck. I found there
the same *concierge* as in 1853. As soon as I mentioned
Mme. Devil, she answered me that she had not in the
least forgotten her, but, on the contrary, would know
her among a thousand. She was, she said, one of the
prettiest little women she had ever seen, and the most
generous tenant. I understood the hint, handed her a
couple of napoleons, and heard from her every thing
she knew on the subject. It seemed that this pretty
Mme. Devil had, not one lover, but two,—the acknowledged one, who was the master, and footed the bills ; and
the other an anonymous one, who went out through the
back-stairs, and who did not pay, on the contrary. The
first was called the Marquis de Trégars : of the second,
she had never known but the first name, Frederic. I
tried to ascertain what had become of Mme. Devil ; but
the worthy *concierge* swore to me that she did not know.

" One morning, like a person who is going abroad,
or who wishes to cover up her tracks, Mme. Devil had
sent for a furniture-dealer, and a dealer in second-hand
clothes, and had sold them every thing she had, going
away with nothing but a little leather satchel, in which
were her jewels and her money."

The Baroness de Thaller still kept a good countenance. After examining her for a moment, with a sort
of eager curiosity, Marius de Trégars went on,—

" When I communicated this information to my
friend, the commissary of police, he shook his head.
' Two years ago,' he told me, ' I would have said, That's
more than we want to find those people ; for the public
records would have given us at once the key of this enigma. But we have had the war and the Commune ; and

the books of record have been burnt up. Still we must
not give up. A last hope remains; and I know the man
who is capable of realizing it.'

"Two days after, he brought me an excellent fellow,
named Victor Chupin, in whom I could have entire confidence; for he was recommended to me by one of the
men whom I like and esteem the most, the Duke de
Champdoce. Giving up all idea of applying at the various mayors' offices, Victor Chupin, with the patience
and the tenacity of an Indian following a scent, began
beating about the districts of Grenelle, Vargirard, and
the Invalids. And not in vain; for, after a week of investigations he brought me a nurse, residing Rue de
l'Université, who remembered perfectly having once attended, on the occasion of her confinement, a remarkably
pretty young woman, living in the Rue des Bergers,
and nicknamed the Marquise de Javelle. And as she
was a very orderly woman, who at all times had kept
a very exact account of her receipts, she brought me a
little book in which I read this entry: ' For attending
Euphrasie Taponnet, *alias* the Marquise de Javelle (a
girl), one hundred francs.' And this is not all. This
woman informed me, moreover, that she had been requested to present the child at the mayor's office, and
that she had been duly registered there under the names
of Euphrasie Césarine Taponnet, born of Euphrasie
Taponnet, laundress, and an unknown father. Finally
she placed at my disposal her account-book and her testimony."

Taxed beyond measure, the energy of the baroness
was beginning to fail her; she was turning livid under
her rice-powder. Still in the same icy tone,—

"You can understand, madame," said Marius de
Trégars, "that this woman's testimony, together with

the letters which are in my possession, enables me to establish before the courts the exact date of the birth of a daughter whom my father had of his mistress. But that's nothing yet. With renewed zeal, Victor Chupin had resumed his investigations. He had undertaken the examination of the marriage-registers in all the parishes of Paris, and, as early as the following week, he discovered at Notre Dame des Lorettes the entry of the marriage of Euphrasie Taponnet with Frederic de Thaller."

Though she must have expected that name, the baroness started up violently and livid, and with a haggard look.

" It's false! " she began in a choking voice.

A smile of ironical pity passed over Marius' lips.

" Five minutes' reflection will prove to you that it is useless to deny," he interrupted. " But wait. In the books of that same church, Victor Chupin has found registered the baptism of a daughter of M. and Mme de Thaller, bearing the same names as the first one,—Euphrasie Césarine."

With a convulsive motion the baroness shrugged her shoulder.

" What does all that prove? " she said.

" That proves, madame, the well-settled intention of substituting one child for another; that proves that my father was imprudently deceived when he was made to believe that the second Césarine was his daughter, the daughter in whose favor he had formerly disposed of over five hundred thousand francs; that proves that there is somewhere in the world a poor girl who has been basely forsaken by her mother, the Marquise de Javelle, now become the Baroness de Thaller."

Beside herself with terror and anger,—

" That is an infamous lie ! " exclaimed the baroness.
M. de Trégars bowed.

" The evidence of the truth of my statements," he
said, " I shall find at Louveciennes, and at the Hôtel des
Folies, Boulevard du Temple, Paris."

Night had come. A footman came in carrying lamps,
which he placed upon the mantelpiece. He was not all
together one minute in the little parlor ; but that one
minute was enough to enable the Marquise de Thaller
to recover her coolness, and to collect her ideas. When
the footman retired, she had made up her mind, with
the resolute promptness of a person accustomed to perilous situations. She gave up the discussion, and, drawing near to M. de Trégars,—

" Enough allusions," she said : " let us speak frankly,
and face to face now. What do you want ? "

But the change was too sudden not to arouse Marius's
suspicions.

" I want a great many things," he replied.

" Still you must specify."

" Well, I claim first the five hundred thousand francs
which my father had settled upon his daughter,—the
daughter whom you cast off."

" And what next ? "

" I want besides, my own and my father's fortune,
of which we have been robbed by M. de Thaller, with
your assistance, madame."

" Is that all, at least ? "

M. de Trégars shook his head.

" That's nothing yet," he replied.

" Oh ! "

" We have now to say something of Vincent Favoral's
affairs."

An attorney who is defending the interests of a client

is neither calmer nor cooler than Mme. de Thaller at this moment.

" Do the affairs of my husband's cashier concern me, then? " she said with a shade of irony.

" Yes, madame, very much."

" I am glad to hear it."

" I know it from excellent sources, because, on my return from Louveciennes, I called in the Rue du Cirque, where I saw one Zélie Cadelle."

He thought that the baroness would at least start on hearing that name. Not at all. With a look of profound astonishment,—

" Rue du Cirque," she repeated, like a person who is making a prodigious effort of memory,—" Rue du Cirque! Zélie Cadelle! Really, I do not understand."

But, from the glance which M. de Trégars cast upon her, she must have understood that she would not easily draw from him the particulars which he had resolved not to tell.

" I believe, on the contrary," he uttered, " that you understand perfectly."

" Be it so, if you insist upon it. What do you ask for Favoral? "

" I demand, not for Favoral, but for the stockholders who have been impudently defrauded, the twelve millions which are missing from the funds of the Mutual Credit."

Mme. de Thaller burst out laughing.

" Only that? " she said.

" Yes, only that! "

" Well, then, it seems to me that you should present your reclamations to M. Favoral himself. You have the right to run after him."

"It is useless, for the reason that it is not he, the poor fool! who has carried off the twelve millions."

"Who is it, then?"

"M. le Baron de Thaller, no doubt."

With that accent of pity which one takes to reply to an absurd proposition,—"You are mad, my poor marquis," said Mme. de Thaller.

"You do not think so."

"But suppose I should refuse to do any thing more?"

He fixed upon her a glance in which she could read an irrevocable determination; and slowly,—

"I have a perfect horror of scandal," he replied, "and, as you perceive, I am trying to arrange every thing quietly between us. But, if I do not succeed thus, I must appeal to the courts"

"Where are your proofs?"

"Don't be afraid: I have proofs to sustain all my allegations."

The baroness had stretched herself comfortably in her arm-chair.

"May we know them?" she inquired.

Marius was getting somewhat uneasy in presence of Mme. de Thaller's imperturbable assurance. What hope had she? Could she see some means of escape from a situation apparently so desperate? Determined to prove to her that all was lost, and that she had nothing to do but to surrender,—

"Oh! I know, madame," he replied, "that you have taken your precautions. But, when Providence interferes, you see, human foresight does not amount to much. See, rather, what happens in regard to your first daughter,—the one you had when you were still only Marquise de Javelle."

And briefly he called to her mind the principal incidents of Mlle. Lucienne's life from the time that she had
left her with the poor gardeners at Louveciennes, without giving either her name or her address,— the injury
she had received by being run over by Mme. de Thaller's carriage; the long letter she had written from the
hospital, begging for assistance; her visit to the house,
and her meeting with the Baron de Thaller; the effort
to induce her to emigrate to America; her arrest by
means of false information, and her escape, thanks to the
kind peace-officer; the attempt upon her life as she was
going home late one night; and, finally, her imprisonment after the Commune, among the *petroleuses*, and
her release through the interference of the same honest
friend."

And, charging her with the responsibility of all these
infamous acts, he paused for an answer or a protest.

And, as Mme. de Thaller said nothing,—

" You are looking at me, madame, and wondering
how I have discovered all that. A single word will explain it all. The peace-officer who saved your daughter
is precisely the same to whom it was once my good fortune to render a service. By comparing notes, we have
gradually reached the truth,—reached you, madame.
Will you acknowledge now that I have more proofs
than are necessary to apply to the courts? "

Whether she acknowledged it or not, she did not condescend to discuss.

" What then? " she said coldly.

But M. de Trégars was too much on his guard to
expose himself, by continuing to speak thus, to reveal
the secret of his designs.

Besides, whilst he was thoroughly satisfied as to the

manœuvres used to defraud his father he had, as yet, but presumptions on what concerned Vincent Favoral.

"Permit me not to say another word, madame," he replied. "I have told you enough to enable you to judge of the value of my weapons."

She must have felt that she could not make him change his mind, for she rose to go.

"That is sufficient," she uttered. "I shall reflect; and to-morrow I shall give you an answer."

She started to go; but M. de Trégars threw himself quickly between her and the door.

"Excuse me," he said; "but it is not to-morrow that I want an answer: it is to-night, this instant!"

Ah, if she could have annihilated him with a look.

"Why, this is violence," she said in a voice which betrayed the incredible effort she was making to control herself.

"It is imposed upon me by circumstances, madame."

"You would be less exacting, if my husband were here."

He must have been within hearing; for suddenly the door opened, and he appeared upon the threshold.

There are people for whom the unforeseen does not exist, and whom no event can disconcert. Having ventured every thing, they expect every thing. Such was the Baron de Thaller. With a sagacious glance he examined his wife and M. de Trégars; and in a cordial tone,—

"We are quarreling here?" he said.

"I am glad you have come!" exclaimed the baroness.

"What is the matter?"

"The matter is, that M. de Trégars is endeavoring to

take an odious advantage of some incidents of our past life."

"There's woman's exaggeration for you!" he said laughing.

And, holding out his hand to Marius,—

"Let me make your peace for you, my dear marquis," he said: "that's within the province of the husband."

But, instead of taking his extended hand, M. de Trégars stepped back.

"There is no more peace possible, sir, I am an enemy."

"An enemy!" he repeated in a tone of surprise which was wonderfully well assumed, if it was not real.

"Yes," interrupted the baroness; "and I must speak to you at once, Frederic. Come: M. de Trégars will wait for you."

And she led her husband into the adjoining room, not without first casting upon Marius a look of burning and triumphant hatred.

Left alone, M. de Trégars sat down. Far from annoying him, this sudden intervention of the manager of the Mutual Credit seemed to him a stroke of fortune. It spared him an explanation more painful still than the first, and the unpleasant necessity of having to confound a villain by proving his infamy to him.

"And besides," he thought, "when the husband and the wife have consulted with each other, they will acknowledge that they cannot resist, and that it is best to surrender." The deliberation was brief. In less than ten minutes, M. de Thaller returned alone. He was pale; and his face expressed well the grief of an honest man who discovers too late that he has misplaced his confidence.

"My wife has told me all, sir," he began.

M. de Trégars had risen. " Well? " he asked.

" You see me distressed. Ah, M. le Marquis ! how could I ever expect such a thing from you ?—you, whom I thought I had the right to look upon as a friend. And it is you, who, when a great misfortune befalls me, attempts to give me the finishing stroke. It is you who would crush me under the weight of slanders gathered in the gutter."

M. de Trégars stopped him with a gesture.

" Mme. de Thaller cannot have correctly repeated my words to you, else you would not utter that word ' slander.' "

" She has repeated them to me without the least change."

" Then she cannot have told you the importance of the proofs I have in my hands."

But the Baron persisted, as Mlle. Césarine would have said, to " do it up in the tender style."

" There is scarcely a family," he resumed, " in which there is not some one of those painful secrets which they try to withhold from the wickedness of the world. There is one in mine. Yes, it is true, that before our marriage, my wife had had a child, whom poverty had compelled her to abandon. We have since done every thing that it was humanly possible to find that child, but without success. It is a great misfortune, which has weighed upon our life; but it is not a crime. If, however, you deem it your interest to divulge our secret, and to disgrace a woman, you are free to do so: I cannot prevent you. But I declare it to you, that fact is the only thing real in your accusations. You say that your father has been duped and defrauded. From whom did you get such an idea ?

" From Marcolet, doubtless, a man without character,

who has become my mortal enemy since the day when he tried a sharp game on me, and came out second best. Or from Costeclar, perhaps, who does not forgive me for having refused him my daughter's hand, and who hates me because I know that he committed forgery once, and that he would be in prison but for your father's extreme indulgence. Well, Costeclar and Marcolet have deceived you. If the Marquis de Trégars ruined himself, it is because he undertook a business that he knew nothing about, and speculated right and left. It does not take long to sink a fortune, even without the assistance of thieves.

" As to pretend that I have benefited by the embezzlements of my cashier that is simply stupid; and there can be no one to suggest such a thing, except Jottras and Saint Pavin, two scoundrels whom I have had ten times the opportunity to send to prison and who were the accomplices of Favoral. Besides, the matter is in the hands of justice; and I shall prove in the broad daylight of the court-room, as I have already done in the office of the examining judge, that, to save the Mutual Credit, I have sacrificed more than half my private fortune."

Tired of this speech, the evident object of which was to lead him to discuss, and to betray himself,—

" Conclude, sir," M. de Trégars interrupted harshly.

Still in the same placid tone,—

" To conclude is easy enough," replied the baron. " My wife has told me that you were about to marry the daughter of my old cashier,—a very handsome girl, but without a sou. She ought to have a dowry."

" Sir! "

" Let us show our hands. I am in a critical position: you know it, and you are trying to take advantage of it. Very well: we can still come to an understanding.

What would you say, if I were to give to Mlle. Gilberte the dowry I intended for my daughter?"

All M. de Trégars' blood rushed to his face.

"Ah, not another word!" he exclaimed with a gesture of unprecedented violence.

But, controlling himself almost at once,—

"I demand," he added, "my father's fortune. I demand that you should restore to the Mutual Credit Company the twelve millions which have been abstracted."

"And if not?"

"Then I shall apply to the courts."

They remained for a moment face to face, looking into each other's eyes. Then,—

"What have you decided?" asked M. de Trégars.

Without perhaps, suspecting that his offer was a new insult,—

"I will go as far as fifteen hundred thousand francs," replied M. de Thaller, "and I pay cash."

"Is that your last word?"

"It is."

"If I enter a complaint, with the proofs in my hands, you are lost."

"We'll see about that."

To insist further would have been puerile.

"Very well, we'll see, then," said M. de Trégars.

But as he walked out and got into his cab, which had been waiting for him at the door, he could not help wondering what gave the Baron de Thaller so much assurance, and whether he was not mistaken in his conjectures.

It was nearly eight o'clock, and Maxence, Mme. Favoral and Mlle. Gilberte must have been waiting for him with a feverish impatience; but he had eaten nothing since morning, and he stopped in front of one of the restaurants of the Boulevard.

He had just ordered his dinner, when a gentleman of a certain age, but active and vigorous still, of military bearing, wearing a mustache, and a vari-colored ribbon at his buttonhole, came to take a seat at the adjoining table.

In less than fifteen minutes M. de Trégars had despatched a bowl of soup and a slice of beef, and was hastening out, when his foot struck his neighbor's foot, without his being able to understand how it had happened.

Though fully convinced that it was not his fault, he hastened to excuse himself. But the other began to talk angrily, and so loud, that everybody turned around.

Vexed as he was, Marius renewed his apologies.

But the other, like those cowards who think they have found a greater coward than themselves, was pouring forth a torrent of the grossest insults.

M. de Trégars was lifting his hand to administer a well-deserved correction, when suddenly the scene in the grand parlor of the Thaller mansion came back vividly to his mind. He saw again, as in the glass, the ill-looking man listening, with an anxious look, to Mme. de Thaller's propositions, and afterwards sitting down to write.

" That's it! " he exclaimed, a multitude of circumstances occurring to his mind, which had escaped him at the moment.

And, without further reflection, seizing his adversary by the throat, he threw him over on the table, holding him down with his knee.

" I am sure he must have the letter about him," he said to the people who surrounded him.

And in fact he did take from the side-pocket of the villain a letter, which he unfolded, and commenced reading aloud,—

" I am waiting for you, my dear major, come quick, for the thing is pressing,—a troublesome gentleman who is to be made to keep quiet. It will be for you the matter of a sword-thrust, and for us the occasion to divide a round amount."

" And, that's why he picked a quarrel with me," added M. de Trégars.

Two waiters had taken hold of the villain, who was struggling furiously, and wanted to surrender him to the police.

" What's the use? " said Marius. " I have his letter: that's enough. The police will find him when they want him."

And, getting back into his cab,—

" Rue St. Gilles," he ordered, " and lively, if possible."

VIII.

IN the Rue St. Gilles the hours were dragging, slow and gloomy. After Maxence had left to go and meet M. de Trégars, Mme. Favoral and her daughter had remained alone with M. Chapelain, and had been compelled to bear the brunt of his wrath, and to hear his interminable complaints.

He was certainly an excellent man, that old lawyer, and too just to hold Mlle. Gilberte or her mother responsible for Vincent Favoral's acts. He spoke the truth when he assured them that he had for them a sincere affection, and that they might rely upon his devotion. But he was losing a hundred and sixty thousand francs;

and a man who loses such a large sum is naturally in bad humor, and not much disposed to optimism.

The cruellest enemies of the poor women would not have tortured them so mercilessly as this devoted friend.

He spared them not one sad detail of that meeting at the Mutual Credit office, from which he had just come. He exaggerated the proud assurance of the manager, and the confiding simplicity of the stockholders. " That Baron de Thaller," he said to them, " is certainly the most impudent scoundrel and the cleverest rascal I have ever seen. You'll see that he'll get out of it with clean hands and full pockets. Whether or not he has accomplices, Vincent will be the scapegoat. We must make up our mind to that."

His positive intention was to console Mme. Favoral and Gilberte. Had he sworn to drive them to distraction, he could not have succeeded better.

" Poor woman! " he said, " what is to become of you? Maxence is a good and honest fellow, I am sure, but so weak, so thoughtless, so fond of pleasure! He finds it difficult enough to get along by himself. Of what assistance will he be to you? "

Then came advice.

Mme. Favoral, he declared, should not hesitate to ask for a separation, which the tribunal would certainly grant. For want of this precaution, she would remain all her life under the burden of her husband's debts, and constantly exposed to the annoyances of the creditors.

And always he wound up by saying,—

" Who could ever have expected such a thing from Vincent,—a friend of twenty years' standing! A hundred and sixty thousand francs! Who in the world can be trusted hereafter? "

Big tears were rolling slowly down Mme. Favoral's withered cheeks. But Mlle. Gilberte was of those for whom the pity of others is the worst misfortune and the most acute suffering.

Twenty times she was on the point of exclaiming,—

"Keep your compassion, sir: we are neither so much to be pitied nor so much forsaken as you think. Our misfortune has revealed to us a true friend,—one who does not speak, but acts."

At last, as twelve o'clock struck, M. Chapelain withdrew, announcing that he would return the next day to get the news, and to bring further consolation.

"Thank Heaven, we are alone at last!" said Mlle. Gilberte.

But they had not much peace, for all that.

Great as had been the noise of Vincent Favoral's disaster, it had not reached at once all those who had intrusted their savings to him. All day long, the belated creditors kept coming in; and the scenes of the morning were renewed on a smaller scale. Then legal summonses began to pour in, three or four at a time. Mme. Favoral was losing all courage.

"What disgrace!" she groaned. "Will it always be so hereafter?"

And she exhausted herself in useless conjectures upon the causes of the catastrophe; and such was the disorder of her mind, that she knew not what to hope and what to fear, and that from one minute to another she wished for the most contradictory things.

She would have been glad to hear that her husband was safe out of the country, and yet she would have deemed herself less miserable, had she known that he was hid somewhere in Paris.

And obstinately the same questions returned to het lips,—

"Where is he now? What is he doing? What is he thinking about? How can he leave us without news? Is it possible that it is a woman who has driven him into the precipice? And, if so, who is that woman?"

Very different were Mlle. Gilberte's thoughts.

The great calamity that befell her family had brought about the sudden realization of her hopes. Her father's disaster had given her an opportunity to test the man she loved; and she had found him even superior to all that she could have dared to dream. The name of Favoral was forever disgraced; but she was going to be the wife of Marius, Marquise de Trégars.

And, in the candor of her loyal soul, she accused herself of not taking enough interest in her mother's grief, and reproached herself for the quivers of joy which she felt within her.

"Where is Maxence?" asked Mme. Favoral. "Where is M. de Trégars? Why have they told us nothing of their projects?"

"They will, no doubt, come home to dinner," replied Mlle. Gilberte.

So well was she convinced of this, that she had given orders to the servant to have a somewhat better dinner than usual; and her heart was beating at the thought of being seated near Marius, between her mother and her brother.

At about six o'clock, the bell rang violently.

"There he is!" said the young girl, rising to her feet.

But no: it was only the porter, bringing up a summons ordering Mme. Favoral, under penalty of the law, to appear the next day, at one o'clock precisely, before the examining judge, Barban d'Avranchel, at his office in the Palace of Justice.

The poor woman came near fainting.

"What can this judge want with me? It ought to be forbidden to call a wife to testify against her husband," she said.

"M. de Trégars will tell you what to answer, mamma," said Mlle. Gilberte.

Meantime, seven o'clock came, then eight, and still neither Maxence nor M. de Trégars had come.

Both mother and daughter were becoming anxious, when at last, a little before nine, they heard steps in the hall.

Marius de Trégars appeared almost immediately.

He was pale; and his face bore the trace of the crushing fatigues of the day, of the cares which oppressed him, of the reflections which had been suggested to his mind by the quarrel of which he had nearly been the victim a few moments since.

"Maxence is not here?" he asked at once.

"We have not seen him," answered Mlle. Gilberte.

He seemed so much surprised, that Mme. Favoral was frightened.

"What is the matter again, good God!" she exclaimed.

"Nothing, madame," said M. de Trégars,—"nothing that should alarm you. Compelled, about two hours ago, to part from Maxence, I was to have met him here. Since he has not come, he must have been detained. I know where; and I will ask your permission to run and join him."

He went out; but Mlle. Gilberte followed him in the hall, and, taking his hand,—

"How kind of you!" she began, "and how can we ever sufficiently thank you?"

He interrupted her.

"You owe me no thanks, my beloved; for, in what I am doing, there is more selfishness than you think. It is my own cause, more than yours, that I am defending. Any way, every thing is going on well."

And, without giving any more explanations, he started again. He had no doubt that Maxence, after leaving him, had run to the Hôtel des Folies to give to Mlle. Lucienne an account of the day's work. And, though somewhat annoyed that he had tarried so long, on second thought, he was not surprised.

It was, therefore, to the Hôtel des Folies that he was going. Now that he had unmasked his batteries and begun the struggle, he was not sorry to meet Mlle Lucienne.

In less than five minutes he had reached the Boulevard du Temple. In front of the Fortins' narrow corridor a dozen idlers were standing, talking.

M. de Trégars was listening as he went along.

"It is a frightful accident," said one,—"such a pretty girl, and so young too!"

"As to me," said another, "it is the driver that I pity the most; for after all, if that pretty miss was in that carriage, it was for her own pleasure; whereas, the poor coachman was only attending to his business."

A confused presentiment oppressed M. de Trégars' heart. Addressing himself to one of those worthy citizens,—

"Have you heard any particulars?" he inquired.

Flattered by the confidence,—

"Certainly I have," he replied. "I didn't see the thing with my own proper eyes; but my wife did. It was terrible. The carriage, a magnificent private carriage too, came from the direction of the Madeleine. The horses had run away; and already there had been an accident in the Place du Château d'Eau, where an old woman had been knocked down. Suddenly, here, over there, opposite the toy-shop, which is mine, by the way, the wheel of the carriage catches into the wheel of an enormous truck; and at once, *patata!* the coachman is thrown down, and so is the lady, who was inside,—a very pretty girl, who lives in this hotel."

Leaving there the obliging narrator, M. de Trégars rushed through the narrow corridor of the Hôtel des Folies. At the moment when he reached the yard, he found himself in presence of Maxence.

Pale, his head bare, his eyes wild, shaking with a nervous chill, the poor fellow looked like a madman. Noticing M. de Trégars,—

" Ah, my friend ! " he exclaimed, " what misfortune ! "

" Lucienne ? "

" Dead, perhaps. The doctor will not answer for her recovery. I am going to the druggist's to get a prescription."

He was interrupted by the commissary of police, whose kind protection had hitherto preserved Mlle. Lucienne. He was coming out of the little room on the ground-floor, which the Fortins used for an office, bedroom, and dining-room.

He had recognized Marius de Trégars, and, coming up to him, he pressed his hand, saying, " Well, you know ? "

" Yes."

" It is my fault, M. le Marquis; for we were fully notified. I knew so well that Mlle. Lucienne's existence was threatened, I was so fully expecting a new attempt upon her life, that, whenever she went out riding, it was one of my men, wearing a footman's livery, who took his seat by the side of the coachman. To-day my man was so busy, that I said to myself, ' Bash, for once! ' And behold the consequences! "

It was with inexpressible astonishment that Maxence was listening. It was with a profound stupor that he discovered between Marius and the commissary that serious intimacy which is the result of long intercourse, real esteem, and common hopes.

" It is not an accident, then," remarked M. de Trégars.

" No."

" The coachman has spoken, doubtless? "

" No : the wretch was killed on the spot."

And, without waiting for another question,—

" But don't let us stay here," said the commissary. " Whilst Maxence runs to the drug-store, let us go into the Fortins' office."

The husband was alone there, the wife being at that moment with Mlle. Lucienne.

" Do me the favor to go and take a walk for about fifteen minutes," said the commissary to him. "We have to talk, this gentleman and myself."

Humbly, without a word, and like a man who does himself justice, M. Fortin slipped off.

And at once,—" It is clear, M. le Marquis, it is manifest, that a crime has been committed. Listen, and judge for yourself. I was just rising from dinner, when I was notified of what was called our poor Lucienne's accident. Without even changing my clothes, I ran. The carriage was lying in the street, broken to pieces. Two policemen were holding the horses, which had been stopped.

I inquire. I learn that Lucienne, picked up by Maxence, has been able to drag herself as far as the Hôtel des Folies, and that the driver has been taken to the nearest drug-store. Furious at my own negligence, and tormented by vague suspicions, it is to the druggist's that I go first, and in all haste. The driver was in a back-room, stretched on a mattress.

" His head having struck the angle of the curbstone, his skull was broken; and he had just breathed his last. It was, apparently, the annihilation of the hope which I had, of enlightening myself by questioning this man. Nevertheless, I give orders to have him searched. No paper is discovered upon him to establish his identity; but, in one of the pockets of his pantaloons, do you know what they find? Two bank-notes of a thousand francs each, carefully wrapped up in a fragment of newspaper."

M. de Trégars had shuddered.

" What a revelation ! " he murmured.

It was not to the present circumstance that he applied that word. But the commissary naturally mistook him.

" Yes," he went on, " it was a revelation. To me these two thousand francs were worth a confession: they could only be the wages of a crime. So, without losing a moment, I jump into a cab, and drive to Brion's. Everybody was upside down, because the horses had just been brought back. I question; and, from the very first words, the correctness of my presumption is demonstrated to me. The wretch who had just died was not one of Brion's coachmen. This is what had happened. At two o'clock, when the carriage ordered by M. Van Klopen was ready to go for Mlle. Lucienne, they had been compelled to send for the driver and the footman, who had forgotten themselves drinking in a neighboring wine-shop, with a man who had called to see them in the morning. They were slightly under the influence of wine, but not enough so to make it imprudent to trust them with horses; and it was even probable that the fresh air would sober them completely. They had then started; but they had not gone very far, for one of their comrades had seen them stop the carriage in front of a wine-shop, and join there the same individual with whom they had been drinking all the morning "—

"And who was no other than the man who was killed?"

"Wait. Having obtained this information, I get some one to take me to the wine-shop; and I ask for the coachman and the footman from Brion's. They were there still; and they are shown to me in a private room, lying on the floor, fast asleep. I try to wake them up, but in vain. I order to water them freely; but a pitcher of water thrown on their faces has no effect, save to make them utter an inarticulate groan. I guess at once what they have taken. I send for a physician, and I call on the wine-merchant for explanations. It is his wife and his barkeeper who answer me. They tell me, that, at about two o'clock, a man came in the shop, who stated that he was employed at Brion's, and who ordered three glasses for himself and two comrades, whom he was expecting.

"A few moments later, a carriage stops at the door; and the driver and the footman leave it to come in. They were in a great hurry, they said, and only wished to take one glass. They do take three, one after another; then they order a bottle. They were evidently forgetting their horses, which they had given to hold to a commissionaire. Soon the man proposes a game. The others accept; and here they are, settled in the back-room, knocking on the table for sealed wine. The game must have lasted at least twenty minutes. At the end of that time, the man who had come in first appeared, looking very much annoyed, saying that it was very unpleasant, that his comrades were dead drunk, that they will miss their work, and that the boss, who is anxious to please his customers, will certainly dismiss them. Although he had taken as much, and more than the rest, he was perfectly steady; and, after reflecting for a moment,—

" ' I have an idea,' he says. ' Friends should help each other, shouldn't they? I am going to take the coachman's livery, and drive in his stead. I happen to know the customer they were going after. She is a very kind old lady, and I'll tell her a story to explain the absence of the footman.'

" Convinced that the man is in Brion's employment, they have no objection to offer to this fine project.

" The brigand puts on the livery of the sleeping coachman, gets up on the box, and starts off, after stating that he will return for his comrades as soon as he has got through the job, and that doubtless they will be sober by that time."

M. de Trégars knew well enough the *savoir-faire* of the commissary not to be surprised at his promptness in obtaining precise information.

Already he was going on,—

" Just as I was closing my examination, the doctor arrived. I show him my drunkards; and at once he recognizes that I have guessed correctly, and that these men have been put asleep by means of one of those narcotics of which certain thieves make use to rob their victims. A potion, which he administers to them by forcing their teeth open with a knife, draws them from this lethargy. They open their eyes, and soon are in condition to reply to my questions. They are furious at the trick that has been played upon them; but they do not know the man. They saw him, they swear to me, for the first time that very morning; and they are ignorant even of his name."

There was no doubt possible after such complete explanations. The commissary had seen correctly, and he proved it.

It was not of a vulgar accident that Mlle. Lucienne had just been the victim, but of a crime laboriously conceived, and executed with unheard-of audacity,—of one of those crimes such as too many are committed, whose combinations, nine times out of ten, set aside even a suspicion, and foil all the efforts of human justice.

M. de Trégars knew now what had taken place, as clearly as if he had himself received the confession of the guilty parties.

A man had been found to execute that perilous programme,—to make the horses run away, and then to run into some heavy wagon. The wretch was staking his life on that game; it being evident that the light carriage must be smashed in a thousand pieces. But he must have relied upon his skill and his presence of mind, to avoid the shock, to jump off safe and sound; whilst Mlle. Lucienne, thrown upon the pavement, would probably be killed on the spot. The event had deceived his expectations, and he had been the victim of his rascality; but his death was a misfortune.

"Because now," resumed the commissary, "the thread is broken in our hands which would infallibly have led us to the truth. Who is it that ordered the crime, and paid for it? We know it, since we know who benefits by the crime. But that is not sufficient. Justice requires something more than moral proofs. Living, this bandit would have spoken. His death insures the impunity of the wretches of whom he was but the instrument."

"Perhaps," said M. Trégars.

And at the same time he took out of his pocket, and showed the note found in Vincent Favoral's pocket-book,—that note, so obscure the day before, now so terribly clear:—

"I cannot understand your negligence. You should get through with that Van Klopen affair: there is the danger."

The commissary of police cast but a glance upon it, and, replying to the objections of his old experience rather more than addressing himself to M. de Trégars,—

"There can be no doubt about it," he murmured. "It is to the crime committed to-day that these pressing recommendations relate; and, directed as they are to Vincent Favoral, they attest his complicity. It was he who had charge of finishing the Van Klopen affair; in other words, to get rid of Lucienne. It was he, I'd wager my head, who had treated with the false coachman."

He remained for over a minute absorbed in his own thoughts, then,—

"But who is the author of these recommendations to Vincent Favoral? Do you know that, M. le Marquis?" he said.

They looked at each other; and the same name rose to their lips,—

"The Baroness de Thaller!"

This name, however, they did not utter.

The commissary had placed himself under the gas-burner which gave light to the Fortin's office; and, adjusting his glasses, he was scrutinizing the note with the most minute attention, studying the grain and the transparency of the paper, the ink, and the handwriting. And at last,—

" This note," he declared, " cannot constitute a proof against its author: I mean an evident, material proof, such as we require to obtain from a judge an order of arrest."

And, as Marius was protesting,—

" This note," he insisted, " is written with the left hand, with common ink, on ordinary foolscap paper, such as is found everywhere. Now all left-hand writings look alike. Draw your own conclusions."

But M. de Trégars did not give it up yet.

" Wait a moment," he interrupted.

And briefly, though with the utmost exactness, he began telling his visit to the Thaller mansion, his conversation with Mlle. Césarine, then with the baroness, and finally with the baron himself.

He described in the most graphic manner the scene which had taken place in the grand parlor between Mme. de Thaller and a worse than suspicious-looking man,—that scene, the secret of which had been revealed to him in its minutest details by the looking-glass. Its meaning was now as clear as day.

This suspicious-looking man had been one of the agents in arranging the intended murder: hence the agitation of the baroness when she had received his card, and her haste to join him. If she had started when he first spoke to her, it was because he was telling her of the successful execution of the crime. If she had afterwards made a gesture of joy, it was because he had just informed her that the coachman had been killed at the same time, and that she found herself thus rid of a dangerous accomplice.

The commissary of police shook his head.

" All this is quite probable," he murmured; " but that's all."

Again M. de Trégars stopped him.

" I have not done yet," he said.

And he went on saying how he had been suddenly and brutally assaulted by an unknown man in a restaurant; how he had collared this abject scoundrel, and taken out of his pocket a crushing letter, which left no doubt as to the nature of his mission.

The commissary's eyes were sparkling,—

" That letter! " he exclaimed, " that letter! "

And, as soon as he had looked over it,—

" Ah! This time," he resumed, " I think that we have something tangible. 'A troublesome gentleman to keep quiet,'—the Marquis de Trégars, of course, who is on the right track. ' It will be for you the matter of a sword-thrust.' Naturally, dead men tell no tales. ' It will be for us the occasion of dividing a round amount.' An honest trade, indeed! "

The good man was rubbing his hand with all his might.

" At last we have a positive fact," he went on,—" a foundation upon which to base our accusations. Don't be uneasy. That letter is going to place into our hands the scoundrel who assaulted you,—who will make known the go-between, who himself will not fail to surrender the Baroness de Thaller. Lucienne shall be avenged. If we could only now lay our hands on Vincent Favoral! But we'll find him yet. I set two fellows after him this afternoon, who have a superior scent, and understand their business."

He was here interrupted by Maxence, who was returning all out of breath, holding in his hand the medi-
cines which he had gone after.

" I thought that druggist would never get through,"
he said.

And regretting to have remained away so long, feeling uneasy, and anxious to return up stairs,—

" Don't you wish to see Lucienne? " he added, addressing himself to M. de Trégars rather more than to
the commissary.

For all answer, they followed him at once.

A cheerless-looking place was Mlle. Lucienne's room,
without any furniture but a narrow iron bedstead, a dilapidated bureau, four straw-bottomed chairs, and a
small table. Over the bed, and at the windows, were
white muslin curtains, with an edging that had once
been blue, but had become yellow from repeated wash-
ings.

Often Maxence had begged his friend to take a more
comfortable lodging, and always she had refused.

" We must economize," she would say. " This room
does well enough for me; and, besides, I am accustomed
to it."

When M. de Trègars and the commissary walked in,
the estimable hostess of the Hôtel des Folies was kneeling in front of the fire, preparing some medicine.

Hearing the footsteps, she got up, and, with a finger
upon her lips,—

" Hush ! " she said. " Take care not to wake her up ! "

The precaution was useless.

" I am not asleep," said Mlle. Lucienne in a feeble
voice. " Who is there? "

" I," replied Maxence, advancing towards the bed.

It was only necessary to see the poor girl in order to

understand Maxence's frightful anxiety. She was whiter than the sheet; and fever, that horrible fever which follows severe wounds, gave to her eyes a sinister lustre.

" But you are not alone," she said again.

" I am with him, my child," replied the commissary. " I come to beg your pardon for having so badly protected you."

She shook her head with a sad and gentle motion.

" It was myself who lacked prudence," she said; " for to-day, while out, I thought I noticed something wrong; but it looked so foolish to be afraid! If it had not happened to-day, it would have happened some other day. The villains who have been pursuing me for years must be satisfied now. They will soon be rid of me."

" Lucienne," said Maxence in a sorrowful tone

M. de Trégars now stepped forward.

" You shall live, mademoiselle," he uttered in a grave voice. " You shall live to learn to love life."

And, as she was looking at him in surprise,—

" You do not know me," he added.

Timidly, and as if doubting the reality,—

" You," she said, " the Marquis de Trégars ! "

" Yes, mademoiselle, your brother."

Had he had the control of events, Marius de Trégars would probably not have been in such haste to reveal this fact.

But how could he control himself in presence of that bed where a poor girl was, perhaps, about to die, sacrificed to the terrors and to the cravings of the miserable woman who was her mother,—to die at twenty, victim of the basest and most odious of crimes? How could he help feeling an intense pity at the sight of this unfortunate young woman who had endured every thing that a

human being can suffer, whose life had been but a long
and painful struggle, whose courage had risen above
all the woes of adversity, and who had been able to pass
without a stain through the mud and mire of Paris.

Besides, Marius was not one of those men who mistrust their first impulse, who manifest their emotion only
for a purpose, who reflect and calculate before giving
themselves up to the inspirations of their heart.

Lucienne was the daughter of the Marquis de Trégars : of that he was absolutely certain. He knew that
the same blood flowed in his veins and in hers ; and he
told her so.

He told her so, above all, because he believed her in
danger ; and he wished, were she to die, that she should
have, at least, that supreme joy.

Poor Lucienne ! Never had she dared to dream of
such happiness. All her blood rushed to her cheeks ; and,
in a voice vibrating with the most intense emotion,—

" Ah ! now, yes," she uttered, " I would like to live."

The commissary of police, also, felt moved.

" Do not be alarmed, my child," he said in his kindest
tone. " Before two weeks you will be up. M. de Trégars is a great physician."

In the mean time, she had attempted to raise herself
on her pillow ; and that simple effort had wrung from
her a cry of anguish.

" Dear me ! How I do suffer ! "

" That's because you won't keep quiet, my darling,"
said Mme. Fortin in a tone of gentle scolding. " Have
you forgotten that the doctor has expressly forbidden
you to stir ? "

Then taking aside the commissary, Maxence, and M.
de Trégars, she explained to them how imprudent it was
to disturb Mlle. Lucienne's rest. She was very ill,

affirmed the worthy hostess; and her advice was, that they should send for a sick-nurse as soon as possible.

She would have been extremely happy, of course, to spend the night by the side of her dear lodger; but, unfortunately, she could not think of it, the hotel requiring all her time and attention. Fortunately, however, she knew in the neighborhood a widow, a very honest woman, and without her equal in taking care of the sick.

With an anxious and beseeching look, Maxence was consulting M. de Trégars. In his eyes could be read the proposition that was burning upon his lips,—

" Shall I not go for Gilberte? "

But that proposition he had no time to express. Though they had been speaking very low, Mlle. Lucienne had heard.

" I have a friend," she said, " who would certainly be willing to sit up with me."

They all went up to her.

" What friend," inquired the commissary of police.

" You know her very well, sir. It is that poor girl who had taken me home with her at Batignolles when I left the hospital, who came to my assistance during the Commune, and whom you helped to get out of the Versailles prisons."

" Do you know what has become of her? "

" Only since yesterday, when I received a letter from her, a very friendly letter. She writes that she has found money to set up a dressmaking establishment, and that she is relying upon me to be her forewoman. She is going to open in the Rue St. Lazare; but, in the mean time, she is stopping in the Rue du Cirque."

M. de Trégars and Maxence had started slightly.

" What is your friend's name? " they inquired at once.
" Zélie Cadelle."

Not being aware of the particulars of the two young
men's visit to the Rue du Cirque, the commissary of police could not understand the cause of their agitation.

" I think," he said, " that it would hardly be proper
now to send for that girl."

" It is to her alone, on the contrary, that we must resort," interrupted M. de Trégars.

And, as he had good reasons to mistrust Mme. Fortin, he took the commissary outside the room, on the
landing; and there, in a few words, he explained to him
that this Zélie was precisely the same woman whom
they had found in the Rue du Cirque, in that sumptuous
mansion where Vincent Favoral, under the simple name
of Vincent, had been living, according to the neighbors,
in such a princely style.

The commissary of police was astounded. Why had
he not known all this sooner? Better late than never,
however.

" Ah! you are right, M. le Marquis, a hundred times
right! " he declared. " This girl must evidently know
Vincent Favoral's secret, the key of the enigma that
we are vainly trying to solve. What she would not tell
to you, a stranger, she will tell to Lucienne, her friend."

Maxence offered to go himself for Zélie Cadelle.

" No," answered Marius. " If she should happen to
know you, she would mistrust you, and would refuse
to come."

It was, therefore, M. Fortin who was despatched to
the Rue du Cirque, and who went off muttering, though
he had received five francs to take a carriage, and five
francs for his trouble.

" And now," said the commissary of police to Maxence, " we must both of us get out of the way. I, because the fact of my being a commissary would frighten Mme. Cadelle; you because, being Vincent Favoral's son, your presence would certainly prove embarrassing to her."

And so they went out; but M. de Trégars did not remain long alone with Mlle. Lucienne. M. Fortin had had the delicacy not to tarry on the way.

Eleven o'clock struck as Zélie Cadelle rushed like a whirlwind into her friend's room.

Such had been his haste, that she had given no thought whatever to her dress. She had stuck upon her uncombed hair the first bonnet she had laid her hand upon, and thrown an old shawl over the wrapper in which she had received Marius in the afternoon.

" What, my poor Lucienne! " she exclaimed. " Are you so sick as all that? "

But she stopped short as she recognized M. de Trégars; and, in a suspicious tone,—

" What a singular meeting! " she said.

Marius bowed.

" You know Lucienne? "

What she meant by that he understood perfectly.

" Lucienne is my sister, madame," he said coldly.

She shrugged her shoulders. " What humbug! "

" It's the truth," affirmed Mlle. Lucienne; " and you know that I never lie."

Mme. Zélie was dumbfounded.

" If you say so," she muttered. " But no matter, that's queer."

M. de Trégars interrupted her with a gesture,—

" And, what's more, it is because Lucienne is my sister that you see her there lying upon that bed. They attempted to murder her to-day! "

" Oh ! "

" It was her mother who tried to get rid of her, so as to possess herself of the fortune which my father had left her; and there is every reason to believe that the snare was contrived by Vincent Favoral."

Mme. Zélie did not understand very well; but, when Marius and Mlle. Lucienne had informed her of all that it was useful for her to know,—

" Why," she exclaimed, " what a horrid rascal that old Vincent must be ! "

And, as M. de Trégars remained dumb,—

" This afternoon," she went on, " I didn't tell you any stories; but I didn't tell you every thing, either."

She stopped; and, after a moment of deliberation,—

" Well, I don't care for old Vincent," she said. " Ah ! he tried to have Lucienne killed, did he? Well, then, I am going to tell every thing I know. First of all, he wasn't any thing to me. It isn't very flattering; but it is so. He has never kissed so much as the end of my finger. He used to say that he loved me, but that he respected me still more, because I looked so much like a daughter he had lost. Old humbug ! And I believed him too ! I did, upon my word, at least in the beginning. But I am not such a fool as I look. I found out very soon that he was making fun of me; and that he was only using me as a blind to keep suspicion away from another woman."

" From what woman ? "

" Ah ! now, I do not know ! All I know is that she is married, that he is crazy about her, and that they are to run away together "

" Hasn't he gone, then ? "

Mme. Cadelle's face had become somewhat anxious, and for over a minute she seemed to hesitate.

"Do you know," she said at last, " that my answer is going to cost me a lot? They have promised me a pile of money; but I haven't got it yet. And, if I say any thing, good-by! I sha'n't have any thing."

M. de Trégars was opening his lips to tell her that she might rest easy on that score; but she cut him short.

" Well, no," she said: " Old Vincent hasn't gone. He got up a comedy, so he told me, to throw the lady's husband off the track. He sent off a whole lot of baggage by the railroad; but he staid in Paris."

" And do you know where he is hid?"

" In the Rue St. Lazare, of course: in the apartment that I hired two weeks ago."

In a voice trembling with the excitement of almost certain success, " Would you consent to take me there?" asked M. de Trégars.

" Whenever you like,—to-morrow."

IX.

As he left Mlle. Lucienne's room,—

" There is nothing more to keep me at the Hôtel des Folies," said the commissary of police to Maxence. " Every thing possible will be done, and well done, by M. de Trégars. I am going home, therefore; and I am going to take you with me. I have a great deal to do; and you'll help me."

That was not exactly true; but he feared, on the part of Maxence, some imprudence which might compromise the success of M. de Trégars' mission.

He was trying to think of every thing to leave as little as possible to chance; like a man who has seen the best combined plans fail for want of a trifling precaution.

Once in the yard, he opened the door of the lodge where the honorable Fortins, man and wife, were deliberating, and exchanging their conjectures, instead of going to bed. For they were wonderfully puzzled by all those events that succeeded each other, and anxious about all these goings and comings.

"I am going home," the commissary said to them; "but, before that, listen to my instructions. You will allow no one, you understand,—no one who is not known to you, to go up to Mlle. Lucienne's room. And remember that I will admit of no excuse, and that you must not come and tell me afterwards, ' It isn't our fault, we can't see everybody that comes in,' and all that sort of nonsense."

He was speaking in that harsh and imperious tone of which police-agents have the secret, when they are addressing people who have, by their conduct, placed themselves under their dependence.

"We are going to close our front-door," replied the estimable hotel-keepers. "We will comply strictly with your orders."

"I trust so; because, if you should disobey me, I should hear it, and the result would be a serious trouble to you. Besides your hotel being unmercifully closed up, you would find yourselves implicated in a very bad piece of business."

The most ardent curiosity could be read in Mme. Fortin's little eyes.

"I understood at once," she began, "that something extraordinary was going on."

But the commissary interrupted her,—

"I have not done yet. It may be that to-night or to-morrow some one will call and inquire how Mlle. Lucienne is."

" And then ? "

" You will answer that she is as bad as possible; and that she has neither spoken a word, nor recovered her senses, since the accident; and that she will certainly not live through the day."

The effort which Mme. Fortin made to remain silent gave, better than any thing else, an idea of the terror with which the commissary inspired her.

" That is not all," he went on. " As soon as the person in question has started off, you will follow him, without affectation, as far as the street-door, and you will point him out with your finger, here, like that, to one of my agents, who will happen to be on the Boulevard."

" And suppose he should not be there? "

" He shall be there. You can make yourself easy on that score."

The looks of distress which the honorable hotel-keepers were exchanging did not announce a very tranquil conscience.

" In other words, here we are under surveillance," said M. Fortin with a groan. " What have we done to be thus mistrusted? "

To reply to him would have been a task more long than difficult.

" Do as I tell you," insisted the commissary harshly, " and don't mind the rest, and, meantime, good-night."

He was right in trusting implicitly to his agent's punctuality; for, as soon as he came out of the Hôtel des Folies, a man passed by him, and without seeming to address him, or even to recognize him, said in a whisper,—

" What news? "

" Nothing," he replied, " except that the Fortins are notified. The trap is well set. Keep your eyes open now, and spot any one who comes to ask about Mlle. Lucienne."

And he hurried on, still followed by Maxence, who walked along like a body without soul, tortured by the most frightful anguish.

As he had been away the whole evening, four or five persons were waiting for him at his office on matters of current business. He despatched them in less than no time; after which, addressing himself to an agent on duty,—

" This evening," he said, " at about nine o'clock, in a restaurant on the Boulevard, a quarrel took place. A person tried to pick a quarrel with another.

" You will proceed at once to that restaurant; you will get the particulars of what took place; and you will ascertain exactly who this man is, his name, his profession, and his residence."

Like a man accustomed to such errands,—

" Can I have a description of him? " inquired the agent.

" Yes. He is a man past middle age, military bearing, heavy mustache, ribbons in his buttonhole."

" Yes, I see: one of your regular fighting fellows."

" Very well. Go then. I shall not retire before your return. Ah, I forgot; find out what they thought tonight on the ' street ' about the Mutual Credit affair, and what they said of the arrest of one Saint Pavin, editor of ' The Financial Pilot,' and of a banker named Jottras."

" Can I take a carriage? "

" Do so."

The agent started; and he was not fairly out of the

house, when the commissary, opening a door which gave into a small study, called, " Felix! "

It was his secretary, a man of about thirty, blonde, with a gentle and timid countenance, having, with his long coat, somewhat the appearance of a theological student. He appeared immediately.

" You call me, sir? "

" My dear Felix," replied the commissary, " I have seen you, sometimes, imitate very nicely all sorts of hand-writings."

The secretary blushed very much, no doubt on account of Maxence, who was sitting by the side of his employer. He was a very honest fellow; but there are certain little talents of which people do not like to boast; and the talent of imitating the writing of others is of the number, for the reason, that, fatally and at once, it suggests the idea of forgery.

" It was only for fun that I used to do that, sir," he stammered.

" Would you be here if it had been otherwise? " said the commissary. " Only this time it is not for fun, but to do me a favor that I wish you to try again."

And, taking out of his pocket the letter taken by M. de Trégars from the man in the restaurant,—

" Examine this writing," he said. " and see whether you feel capable of imitating it tolerably well."

Spreading the letter under the full light of the lamp, the secretary spent at least two minutes examining it with the minute attention of an expert. And at the same time he was muttering,—

" Not at all convenient, this. Hard writing to imitate. Not a salient feature, not a characteristic sign! Nothing to strike the eye, or attract attention. It must be some old lawyer's clerk who wrote this."

In spite of his anxiety of mind, the commissary smiled.

" I shouldn't be surprised if you had guessed right."

Thus encouraged,—

" At any rate." Felix declared, " I am going to try."
He took a pen, and, after trying a dozen times,—

" How is this?" he asked, holding out a sheet of paper.

The commissary carefully compared the original with the copy.

" It is not perfect," he murmured ; " but at night, with the imagination excited by a great peril— Besides, we must risk something."

" If I had a few hours to practise! "

" But you have not. Come, take up your pen, and write as well as you can, in that same hand, what I am going to tell you."

And after a moment's thought, he dictated as follows :—

" All goes well. T., drawn into a quarrel, is to fight in the morning with swords. But our man, whom I cannot leave, refuses to go ahead, unless he is paid two thousand francs before the duel. I have not the amount, Please hand it to the bearer, who has orders to wait for you."

The commissary, leaning over his secretary's shoulder, was following his hand, and, the last word being written,—

" Perfect! " he exclaimed. " Now quick, the address: Mme. le Baronne de Thaller, Rue de le Pépinière."

There are professions which extinguish, in those who exercise them, all curiosity. It is with the most complete indifference, and without asking a question, that the secretary had done what he had been requested.

"Now, my dear Felix," resumed the commissary, "you will please get yourself up as near as possible like a restaurant-waiter, and take this letter to its address."

"At this hour!"

"Yes. The Baroness de Thaller is out to a ball. You will tell the servants that you are bringing her an answer concerning an important matter. They know nothing about it; but they will allow you to wait for their mistress in the porter's lodge. As soon as she comes in, you will hand her the letter, stating that two gentlemen who are taking supper in your restaurant are waiting for the answer. It may be that she will exclaim that you are a scoundrel, that she does not know what it means: in that case, we shall have been anticipated, and you must get away as fast as you can. But the chances are, that she will give you two thousand francs; and then you must so manage, that she will be seen plainly when she does it. Is it all understood?"

"Perfectly."

"Go ahead, then, and do not lose a minute. I shall wait."

Away from Mlle. Lucienne, Maxence had gradually been recalled to the strangeness of the situation; and it was with a mingled feeling of curiosity and surprise that he observed the commissary acting and bustling about.

The good man had found again all the activity of his youth, together with that fever of hope and that impatience of success, which usually disappear with age.

He was going over the whole of the case again,—his first meeting with Mlle. Lucienne, the various attempts upon her life; and he had just taken out of the file the letter of information which had been intrusted to him, in order to compare the writing with that of the letter taken from his adversary by M. de Trégars, when the latter came in all out of breath.

" Zélie has spoken ! " he said.

And, at once addressing Maxence,—

" You, my dear friend," he resumed, " you must run to the Hôtel des Folies."

" Is Lucienne worse ? "

" No. Lucienne is getting on well enough. Zélie has spoken ; but there is no certainty, that, after due reflection, she will not repent, and go and give the alarm. You will return, therefore, and you will not lose sight of her until I call for her in the morning. If she wishes to go out, you must prevent her."

The commissary had understood the importance of the precaution.

" You must prevent her," he added, " even by force ; and I authorize you, if need be, to call upon the agent whom I have placed on duty, watching the Hôtel des Folies, and to whom I am going to send word immediately."

Maxence started off on a run.

" Poor fellow ! " murmured Marius, " I know where your father is. What are we going to learn now ? "

He had scarcely had time to communicate the information he had received from Mme. Cadelle, when the first of the commissary's emissaries made his appearance.

" The commission is done," he said, in that confident tone of a man who thinks he has successfully accomplished a difficult task.

" You know the name of the individual who sought a quarrel with M. de Trégars ? "

" His name is Corvi. He is well known in all the

tables d'hôte, where there are women, and where they deal a healthy little game after dinner. I know him well too. He is a bad fellow, who passes himself off for a former superior officer in the Italian army."

" His address? "

" He lives at Rue de la Michodiere, in a furnished house. I went there. The porter told me that my man had just gone out with an ill-looking individual, and that they must be in a little *café* on the corner of the next street. I ran there, and found my two fellows drinking beer."

" Won't they give us the slip? "

" No danger of that: I have got them fixed."

" How is that? "

" It is an idea of mine. I just thought, ' Suppose they put off? ' And at once I went to notify some policemen, and I returned to station myself near the *café*. It was just closing up. My two fellows came out: I picked a quarrel with them; and now they are in the station-house, well recommended."

The commissary knit his brows.

" That's almost too much zeal," he murmured. " Well, what's done is done. Did you make any inquiries about the Saint Pavin and Jottras matter? "

" I had no time, it was too late. You forget, perhaps, sir, that it is nearly two o'clock."

Just as he got through, the secretary who had been sent to the Rue de la Pépinière came in.

" Well? " inquired the commissary, not without evident anxiety.

" I waited for Mme. de Thaller over an hour," he said. " When she came home, I gave her the letter. She read it; and, in presence of a number of her servants, she handed me these two thousand francs."

At the sight of the bank notes, the commissary jumped to his feet.

"Now we have it!" he exclaimed. "Here is the proof that we wanted."

X.

It was after four o'clock when M. de Trégars was at last permitted to return home. He had minutely, and at length, arranged every thing with the commissary: he had endeavored to anticipate every eventuality. His line of conduct was perfectly well marked out, and he carried with him the certainty that on the day which was about to dawn the strange game that he was playing must be finally won or lost. When he reached home,—

"At last, here you are, sir!" exclaimed his faithful servant.

It was doubtless anxiety that had kept up the old man all night; but so absorbed was Marius's mind, that he scarcely noticed the fact.

"Did any one call in my absence?" he asked.

"Yes, sir. A gentleman called during the evening, M. Costeclar, who appeared very much vexed not to find you in. He stated that he came on a very important matter that you would know all about: and he requested me to ask you to wait for him to-morrow, that is to-day, by twelve o'clock."

Was M. Costeclar sent by M. de Thaller? Had the manager of the Mutual Credit changed his mind? and had he decided to accept the conditions which he had at first rejected? In that case, it was too late. It was no longer in the power of any human being to suspend

the action of justice.   Without giving any further
thought to that visit,—

" I am worn out with fatigue," said M. de Trégars,
" and I am going to lie down.   At eight o'clock precisely
you will call me."

But it was in vain that he tried to find a short respite
in sleep.   For forty-eight hours his mind had been taxed
beyond measure, his nerves had been wrought up to an
almost intolerable degree of exaltation.

As soon as he closed his eyes, it was with a merciless
precision that his imagination presented to him all the
events which had taken place since that afternoon in
the Place-Royale when he had ventured to declare his
love to Mlle. Gilberte.   Who could have told him then,
that he would engage in that struggle, the issue of which
must certainly be some abominable scandal in which
his name would be mixed?   Who could have told him,
that gradually, and by the very force of circumstances,
he would be led to overcome his repugnance, and to
rival the ruses and the tortuous combinations of the
wretches he was trying to reach?

But he was not of those who, once engaged, regret,
hesitate, and draw back.   His conscience reproached him
for nothing.   It was for justice and right that he was
battling; and Mlle. Gilberte was the prize that would
reward him.

Eight o'clock struck; and his servant came in.

" Run for a cab," he said: " I'll be ready in a moment."

He was ready, in fact, when the old servant returned;
and, as he had in his pocket some of those arguments
that lend wings to the poorest cab-horses, in less than
ten minutes he had reached the Hôtel des Folies.

" How is Mlle. Lucienne?" he inquired first of all of the worthy hostess.

The intervention of the commissary of police had made M. Fortin and his wife more supple than gloves, and more gentle than doves.

" The poor dear child is much better," answered Mme. Fortin; " and the doctor, who has just left, now feels sure of her recovery. But there is a row up there."

" A row? "

" Yes. That lady whom my husband went after last night insists upon going out; and M. Maxence won't let her: so that they are quarreling up there. Just listen."

The loud noise of a violent altercation could be heard distinctly. M. de Trégars started up stairs, and on the second-story landing he found Maxence holding on obstinately to the railing, whilst Mme. Zélie Cadelle, redder than a peony, was trying to induce him to let her pass, treating him at the same time to some of the choicest epithets of her well-stocked repertory. Catching sight of Marius,—

" Is it you," she cried, " who gave orders to keep me here against my wishes? By what right? Am I your prisoner? "

To irritate her would have been imprudent.

" Why did you wish to leave," said M. de Trégars gently, " at the very moment when you knew that I was to call for you? "

But she interrupted him, and, shrugging her shoulders,—

" Why don't you tell the truth? " she said. " You were afraid to trust me."

" Oh! "

" You are wrong! What I promise to do I do. I

only wanted to go home to dress. Can I go in the street in this costume?"

And she was spreading out her wrapper, all faded and stained.

"I have a carriage below," said Marius. "No one will see us."

Doubtless she understood that it was useless to hesitate.

"As you please," she said.

M. de Trégars took Maxence aside, and in a hurried whisper,—

"You must," said he, "go at once to the Rue St. Gilles, and in my name request your sister to accompany you. You will take a closed carriage, and you'll go and wait in the Rue St. Lazare, opposite No. 25. It may be that Mlle. Gilberte's assistance will become indispensable to me. And, as Lucienne must not be left alone, you will request Mme. Fortin to go and stay with her."

And, without waiting for an answer,—

"Let us go," he said to Mme. Cadelle.

They started; but the young woman was far from being in her usual spirits. It was clear that she was regretting bitterly having gone so far, and not having been able to get away at the last moment. As the carriage went on, she became paler and a frown appeared upon her face.

"No matter," she began: "it's a nasty thing I am doing there."

"Do you repent then, assisting me to punish your friend's assassins?" said M. de Trégars.

She shook her head.

"I know very well that old Vincent is a scoundrel,"

she said; " but he had trusted me, and I am betraying
him."

" You are mistaken, madame. To furnish me the
means of speaking to M. Favoral is not to betray him;
and I shall do every thing in my power to enable him
to escape the police, and make his way abroad."

" What a joke ! "

" It is the exact truth : I give you my word of honor."

She seemed to feel easier; and, when the carriage
turned into the Rue St. Lazare, " Let us stop a moment," she said.

" Why ? "

" So that I can buy old Vincent's breakfast. He
can't go out to eat, of course; and so I have to take all
his meals to him."

Marius's mistrust was far from being dissipated; and
yet he did not think it prudent to refuse, promising himself, however, not to lose sight of Mme. Zélie. He followed her, therefore, to the baker's and the butcher's;
and when she had done her marketing, he entered with
her the house of modest appearance where she had her
apartment.

They were already going up stairs, when the porter
ran out of his lodge.

" Madame ! " he said, " madame ! "

Mme. Cadelle stopped.

" What is the matter ? "

" A letter for you."

" For me ? "

" Here it is. A lady brought it less than five minutes ago. Really, she looked annoyed not to find you in.
But she is going to come back. She knew you were
to be here this morning."

M. de Trégars had· also stopped.

"What kind of a looking person was this lady?" he asked.

"Dressed all in black, with a thick veil on her face."

"All right. I thank you."

The porter returned to his lodge. Mme. Zélie broke the seal. The first envelope contained another, upon which she spelt, for she did not read very fluently,—

"*To be handed to M. Vincent.*"

"Some one knows that he is hiding here," she said in a tone of utter surprise. "Who can it be?"

"Who? Why, the woman whose reputation M. Favoral was so anxious to spare when he put you in the Rue du Cirque house."

There was nothing that irritated the young woman so much as this idea.

"You are right," she said. "What a fool he made of me, the old rascal! But never mind. I am going to pay him for it now."

Nevertheless when she reached her story, the third, and at the moment of slipping the key into the keyhole, she again seemed perplexed.

"If some misfortune should happen," she sighed.

"What are you afraid of?"

"Old Vincent has got all sorts of arms in there. He has sworn to me that the first person who forced his way into the apartments, he would kill him like a dog. Suppose he should fire at us?"

She was afraid, terribly afraid: she was livid, and her teeth chattered.

"Let me go first," suggested M. de Trégars.

"No. Only, if you were a good fellow, you would do what I am going to ask you. Say, will you?"

"If it can be done."

"Oh, certainly! Here is the thing. We'll go in together; but you must not make any noise. There is a large closet with glass doors, from which every thing can be heard and seen that goes on in the large room. You'll get in there. I'll go ahead, and draw out old Vincent into the parlor, and at the right moment, *v'lan!* you appear."

It was after all, quite reasonable.

"Agreed!" said Marius.

"Then," she said, "every thing will go on right. The entrance of the closet with the glass doors is on the right as you go in. Come along now, and walk easy."

And she opened the door.

XI.

THE apartment was exactly as described by Mme. Cadelle. In the dark and narrow ante-chamber, three doors opened,—on the left, that of the dining-room; in the centre, that of a parlor and bedroom which communicated; on the right, that of the closet. M. de Trégars slipped in noiselessly through the latter, and at once recognized that Mme. Zélie had not deceived him, and that he would see and hear every thing that went on in the parlor. He saw the young woman walk into it. She laid her provisions down upon the table, and called,—

"Vincent!"

The former cashier of the Mutual Credit appeared at once, coming out of the bedroom.

He was so changed, that his wife and children would have hesitated in recognizing him. He had cut off his beard, pulled out almost the whole of his thick eyebrows, and covered his rough and straight hair under a

brown curly wig, He wore patent-leather boots, wide
pantaloons, and one of those short jackets of rough
material, and with broad sleeves which French elegance
has borrowed from English stable-boys. He tried to
appear calm, careless, and playful; but the contraction
of his lips betrayed a horrible anguish, and his look had
the strange mobility of the wild beasts' eye, when, almost at bay, they stop for a moment, listening to the
barking of the hounds.

"I was beginning to fear that you would disappoint
me," he said to Mme. Zélie.

"It took me some time to buy your breakfast."

"And is that all that kept you?"

"The porter detained me too, to hand me a letter, in
which I found one for you. Here it is."

"A letter!" exclaimed Vincent Favoral.

And, snatching it from her, he tore off the envelope.
But he had scarcely looked over it, when he crushed
it in his hand, exclaiming,—

"It is monstrous! It is a mean, infamous treason!"

He was interrupted by a violent ringing of the door-
bell.

"Who can it be?" stammered Mme. Cadelle.

"I know who it is," replied the former cashier.
"Open, open quick."

She obeyed; and almost at once a woman walked into
the parlor, wearing a cheap, black woolen dress. With
a sudden gesture, she threw off her veil; and M. de Trégars recognized the Baroness de Thaller.

"Leave us!" she said to Mme. Zélie, in a tone which
one would hardly dare to assume towards a bar-maid.

The other felt indignant.

"What, what!" she began. "I am in my own house
here."

" Leave us ! " repeated M. Favoral with a threatening gesture. " Go, go ! "

She went out but only to take refuge by the side of
M. de Trégars.

" You hear how they treat me," she said in a hoarse
voice.

He made no answer. All his attention was centred
upon the parlor. The Baroness de Thaller and the former cashier were standing opposite each other, like two
adversaries about to fight a duel.

" I have just read your letter," began Vincent Favoral.

Coldly the baroness said, " Ah ! "

" It is a joke, I suppose."

" Not at all."

" You refuse to go with me? "

" Positively."

" And yet it was all agreed upon. I have acted wholly
under your urgent, pressing advice. How many times
have you repeated to me that to live with your husband
had become an intolerable torment to you ! How many
times have you sworn to me that you wished to be mine
alone, begging me to procure a large sum of money,
and to fly with you ! "

" I was in earnest at the time. I have discovered, at
the last moment, that it would be impossible for me thus
to abandon my country, my daughter, my friends."

" We can take Césarine with us."

" Do not insist."

He was looking at her with a stupid, gloomy gaze.

" Then," he stammered, " those tears, those prayers,
those oaths ! "

" I have reflected."

"It is not possible! If you spoke the truth, you would not be here."

"I am here to make you understand that we must give up projects which cannot be realized. There are some social conventionalities which cannot be torn up."

As if he scarcely understood what she said, he repeated,—

"Social conventionalities!"

And suddenly falling at Mme. de Thaller's feet, his head thrown back, and his hands clasped together,—

"You lie!" he said. "Confess that you lie, and that it is a final trial which you are imposing upon me. Or else have you, then, never loved me? That's impossible! I would not believe you if you were to say so. A woman who does not love a man cannot be to him what you have been to me: she does not give herself up thus so joyously and so completely. Have you, then, forgotten every thing? Is it possible that you do not remember those divine evenings in the Rue de Cirque?—those nights, the mere thought of which fires my brain, and consumes my blood."

He was horrible to look at, horrible and ridiculous at the same time. As he wished to take Mme. de Thaller's hands, she stepped back, and he followed her, dragging himself on his knees.

"Where could you find," he continued, "a man to worship you like me, with an ardent, absolute, blind, mad passion? With what can you reproach me? Have I not sacrificed to you without a murmur every thing that a man can sacrifice here below,—fortune, family, honor,—to supply your extravagance, to anticipate your slightest fancies, to give you gold to scatter by the handful. Did I not leave my own family struggling with poverty. I would have snatched bread from my children's mouths in order to purchase roses to scatter under your footsteps. And for years did ever a word from me betray the secret of our love? What have I not endured? You deceived me. I knew it, and I said nothing. Upon a word from you I stepped aside before him whom your caprice made happy for a day. You told me, ' Steal! ' and I stole. You told me, ' Kill! ' and I tried to kill."

" Fly. A man who has twelve hundred thousand francs in gold, bank-notes, and good securities, can always get along."

" And my wife and children? "

" Maxence is old enough to help his mother. Gilberte will find a husband: depend upon it. Besides, what's to prevent you from sending them money? "

" They would refuse it."

" You will always be a fool, my dear! "

To Vincent Favoral's first stupor and miserable weakness now succeeded a terrible passion. All the blood had left his face: his eyes was flashing.

" Then," he resumed, " all is really over? "

" Of course."

" Then I have been duped like the rest,—like that poor Marquis de Trégars, whom you had made mad also. But he, at least saved his honor; whereas I— And I have no excuse; for I should have known. I knew that you were but the bait which the Baron de Thaller held out to his victims."

He waited for an answer; but she maintained a contemptuous silence.

" Then you think," he said with a threatening laugh, " that it will all end that way? "

" What can you do? "

" There is such a thing as justice, I imagine, and judges too. I can give myself up, and reveal every thing."

She shrugged her shoulders.

" That would be throwing yourself into the wolf's mouth for nothing," she said. " You know better than any one else that my precautions are well enough taken to defy any thing you can do or say. I have nothing to fear."

" Are you quite sure of that? "

" Trust to me," she said with a smile of perfect se- curity.

The former cashier of the Mutual Credit made a ter- rible gesture; but, checking himself at once, he seized one of the baroness's hands. She withdrew it quickly, however, and, in an accent of insurmountable disgust,—

" Enough, enough! " she said.

In the adjoining closet Marius de Trégars could feel Mme. Zélie Cadelle shuddering by his side.

" What a wretch that woman is! " she murmured; " and he—what a base coward! "

The former cashier remained prostrated, striking the floor with his head.

" And you would forsake me," he groaned, " when we are united by a past such as ours! How could you replace me? Where would you find a slave so devoted to your every wish? "

The baroness was getting impatient.

" Stop! " she interrupted,—" stop these demonstra- tions as useless as ridiculous."

This time he did start up, as if lashed with a whip, and, double locking the door which communicated with the ante-chamber, he put the key in his pocket; and, with a step as stiff and mechanical as that of an automaton, he disappeared in the sleeping-room.

" He is going for a weapon," whispered Mme. Cadelle.

It was also what Marius thought.

" Run down quick," he said to Mme. Zélie. " In a cab standing opposite No. 25, you will find Mlle. Gilberte Favoral waiting. Let her come at once."

And, rushing into the parlor,—

" Fly ! " he said to Mme. Thaller.

But she was as petrified by this apparition.

" M. de Trégars ! "

" Yes, yes, me. But hurry and go ! "

And he pushed her into the closet.

It was but time. Vincent Favoral reappeared upon the threshold of the bedroom. But, if it was a weapon he had gone for, it was not for the one which Marius and Mme. Cadelle supposed. It was a bundle of papers which he held in his hand. Seeing M. de Trégars there, instead of Mme. de Thaller, an exclamation of terror and surprise rose to his lips. He understood vaguely what must have taken place; that the man who stood there must have been concealed in the glass closet, and that he had assisted the baroness to escape.

" Ah the miserable wretch ! " he stammered with a tongue made thick by passion, " the infamous wretch ! She has betrayed me ; she has surrendered me. I am lost ! "

Mastering the most terrible emotion he had ever felt,—

" No, no ! you shall not be surrendered," uttered M. de Trégars.

Collecting all the energy that the devouring passion

which had blasted his existence had left him, the former cashier of the Mutual Credit took one or two steps forward.

"Who are you, then?" he asked.

"Do you not know me? I am the son of that unfortunate Marquis de Trégars of whom you spoke a moment since. I am Lucienne's brother."

Like a man who has received a stunning blow, Vincent Favoral sank heavily upon a chair.

"He knows all," he groaned.

"Yes, all!"

"You must hate me mortally."

"I pity you."

The old cashier had reached that point when all the faculties, after being strained to their utmost limits, suddenly break down, when the strongest man gives up, and weeps like a child.

"Ah, I am the most wretched of villains!" he exclaimed.

He had hid his face in his hands; and in one second, —as it happens, they say, to the dying on the threshold of eternity,—he reviewed his entire existence.

"And yet," he said, "I had not the soul of a villain. I wanted to get rich, but honestly, by labor, and by rigid economy. And I should have succeeded. I had a hundred and fifty thousand francs of my own when I met the Baron de Thaller. Alas! why did I meet him? 'Twas he who first gave me to understand that it was stupid to work and save, when, at the *bourse*, with moderate luck, one might become a millionaire in six months."

He stopped, shook his head, and suddenly,—

"Do you know the Baron de Thaller?" he asked.

And, without giving Marius time to answer,—

"He is a German," he went on, "a Prussian. His father was a cab-driver in Berlin, and his mother waiting-maid in a brewery. At the age of eighteen, he was compelled to leave his country, owing to some petty swindle, and came to take up his residence in Paris. He found employment in the office of a stock-broker, and was living very poorly, when he made the acquaintance of a young laundress named Euphrasie, who had for a lover a very wealthy gentleman, the Marquis de Trégars, whose weakness was to pass himself off for a poor clerk. Euphrasie and Thaller were well calculated to agree. They did agree, and formed an association,—she contributing her beauty; he, his genius for intrigue; both, their corruption and their vices. Soon after they met, she gave birth to a child, a daughter, whom she intrusted to some poor gardeners at Louveciennes, with the firm and settled intention to leave her there forever. And yet it was upon this daughter, whom they firmly hoped never to see again, that the two accomplices were building their fortune.

"It was in the name of that daughter that Euphrasie wrung considerable sums from the Marquis de Trégars. As soon as Thaller and she found themselves in possession of six hundred thousand francs, they dismissed the marquis, and got married. Already, at that time, Thaller had taken the title of baron, and lived in some style. But his first speculations were not successful. The revolution of 1848 finished his ruin, and he was about being expelled from the *bourse*, when he found me on his way,—I, poor fool, who was going about everywhere, asking how I could advantageously invest my hundred and fifty thousand francs."

He was speaking in a hoarse voice, shaking his

clinched fist in the air, doubtless at the Baron de Thaller.

"Unfortunately," he resumed, "it was only much later that I discovered all this. At the moment, M. de Thaller dazzled me. His friends, Saint Pavin and the bankers Jottras, proclaimed him the smartest and the most honest man in France. Still I would not have given my money, if it had not been for the baroness. The first time that I was introduced to her, and that she fixed upon me her great black eyes, I felt myself moved to the deepest recesses of my soul. In order to see her again, I invited her, together with her husband and her husband's friends, to dine with me, by the side of my wife and children. She came. Her husband made me sign every thing he pleased; but, as she went off, she pressed my hand."

He was still shuddering at the recollection of it, the poor fellow!

"The next day," he went on, "I handed to Thaller all I had in the world; and, in exchange, he gave me the position of cashier in the Mutual Credit, which he had just founded. He treated me like an inferior, and did not admit me to visit his family. But I didn't care: the baroness had permitted me to see her again, and almost every afternoon I met her at the Tuileries; and I had made bold to tell her that I loved her to desperation. At last, one evening, she consented to make an appointment with me for the second following day, in an apartment which I had rented.

"The day before I was to meet her, and whilst I was beside myself with joy, the Baron de Thaller requested me to assist him, by means of certain irregular entries, to conceal a deficit arising from unsuccessful specula-

tions. How could I refuse a man, whom, as I thought,
I was about to deceive grossly! I did as he wished. The
next day Mme. de Thaller became my mistress; and I
was a lost man."

Was he trying to exculpate himself? Was he merely
yielding to that imperious sentiment, more powerful
than the will or the reason, which impels the criminal
to reveal the secret which oppresses him?

" From that day," he went on, " began for me the torment of that double existence which I underwent for
years. I had given to my mistress all I had in the world;
and she was insatiable. She wanted money always, any
way, and in heaps. She made me buy the house in the
Rue du Cirque for our meetings; and, between the demands of the husband and those of the wife, I was almost insane. I drew from the funds of the Mutual
Credit as from an inexhaustible mine; and, as I foresaw
that some day must come when all would be discovered,
I always carried about me a loaded revolver, with which
to blow out my brains when they came to arrest me."

And he showed to Marius the handle of a revolver
protruding from his pocket.

" And if only she had been faithful to me!" he continued, becoming more and more animated. " But what
have I not endured! When the Marquis de Trégars
returned to Paris, and they set about defrauding him of
his fortune, she did not hesitate a moment to become his
mistress again. She used to tell me, ' What a fool you
are! all I want is his money. I love no one but you.'
But after his death she took others. She made use of
our house in the Rue du Cirque for purposes of dissipation for herself and her daughter Césarine. And I—
miserable coward that I was!—I suffered all, so much
did I tremble to lose her, so much did I fear to be weaned

from the semblance of love with which she paid my fearful sacrifices. And now she would betray me, forsake me! For every thing that has taken place was suggested by her in order to procure a sum wherewith to fly to America. It was she who imagined the wretched comedy which I played, so as to throw upon myself the whole responsibility. M. de Thaller has had millions for his share: I have only had twelve hundred thousand francs."

Violent nervous shudders shook his frame: his face became purple. He drew himself up, and, brandishing the letters which he held in his hand,—

"But all is not over!" he exclaimed. "There are proofs which neither the baron nor his wife know that I have. I have the proof of the infamous swindle of which the Marquis de Trégars was the victim. I have the proof of the farce got up by M. de Thaller and myself to defraud the stockholders of the Mutual Credit!"

"What do you hope for?"

He was laughing a stupid laugh.

"I? I shall go and hide myself in some suburb of Paris, and write to Euphrasie to come. She knows that I have twelve hundred thousand francs. She will come; and she will keep coming as long as I have any money. And when I have no more "—

He stopped short, starting back, his arms outstretched as if to repel a terrifying apparition. Mlle. Gilberte had just appeared at the door.

"My daughter!" stammered the wretch. "Gilberte!"

"The Marquise de Trégars," uttered Marius.

An inexpressible look of terror and anguish convulsed the features of Vincent Favoral: he guessed that it was the end.

"What do you want with me?" he stammered.

" The money that you have stolen, father," replied the girl in an inexorable tone of voice,—" the twelve hundred thousand francs which you have here, then the proofs which are in your hands, and, finally your weapons."

He was trembling from head to foot.

" Take away my money! " he said. " Why, that would be compelling me to give myself up! Do you wish to see me in prison? "

" The disgrace would fall back upon your children, sir," said M. de Trégars. " We shall, on the contrary, do every thing in the world to enable you to evade the pursuit of the police."

" Well, yes, then. But to-morrow I must write to Euphrasie: I must see her! "

" You have lost your mind, father," said Mlle. Gilberte. " Come, do as I ask you."

He drew himself up to his full height.

" And suppose I refuse? "

But it was the last effort of his will. He yielded, though not without an agonizing struggle and gave up to his daughter the money, the proofs and the arms. And as she was walking away, leaning on M. de Trégars' arm,—

" But send me your mother, at least," he begged. " She will understand me: she will not be without pity. She is my wife: let her come quick. I will not, I can not remain alone."

XII.

IT was with convulsive haste that the Baroness de Thaller went over the distance that separated the Rue St. Lazare from the Rue de la Pépinière. The sudden

intervention of M. de Trégars had upset all her ideas.
The most sinister presentiments agitated her mind.   In
the courtyard of her residence, all the servants, gathered
in a group, were talking.   They did not take the trouble
to stand aside to let her pass; and she even noticed some
smiles and ironical gigglings.   This was a terrible blow
to her.   What was the matter?   What had they heard?
In the magnificent vestibule, a man was sitting as she
came in.   It was the same suspicious character that
Marius de Trégars had seen in the grand parlor, in close
conference with the baroness.

"Bad news." he said with a sheepish look.

"What?"

"That little Lucienne must have her soul riveted to
her body.   She is only wounded; and she'll get over it."

"Never mind Lucienne.   What about M. de Trègars?"

"Oh! he is another sharp one.   Instead of taking up
our man's provocation, he collared him, and took away
from him the note I had sent him."

Mme. de Thaller started violently.

"What is the meaning, then," she asked, "of your
letter of last night, in which you requested me to hand
two thousand francs to the bearer?"

The man became pale as death.

"You received a letter from me," he stammered,
"last night?"

"Yes, from you; and I gave the money."

The man struck his forehead.

"I understand it all!" he exclaimed.

"What?"

"They wanted proofs.   They imitated my handwriting, and you swallowed the bait.   That's the reason
why I spent the night in the station-house; and, if they

let me go this morning, it was to find out where I'd go.
I have been followed, they are shadowing me. We are
gone up, Mme. le Baronne. *Sauve qui peut!*"

And he ran out.

More agitated than ever Mme. de Thaller went up
stairs. In the little red-and-gold parlor, the Baron de
Thaller and Mlle. Césarine were waiting for her.
Stretched upon an arm-chair, her legs crossed, the tip
of her boot on a level with her eye, Mlle. Césarine, with
a look of ironical curiosity, was watching her father,
who, livid and trembling with nervous excitement, was
walking up and down, like a wild beast in his cage. As
soon as the baroness appeared,—

" Things are going badly," said her husband, " very
badly. Our game is devilishly compromised."

" You think so? "

" I am but too sure of it. Such a well-combined
stroke too! But every thing is against us. In presence
of the examining magistrate, Jottras held out well; but
Saint Pavin spoke. That dirty rascal was not satisfied
with the share allotted to him. On the information furnished by him, Costeclar was arrested this morning.
And Costeclar knows all, since he has been your confidant, Vincent Favoral's, and my own. When a man has,
like him, two or three forgeries in his record, he is sure
to speak. He will speak. Perhaps he has already done
so, since the police has taken possession of Latterman's
office, with whom I had organized the panic and the
tumble in the Mutual Credit stock. What can we do to
ward off this blow? "

With a surer glance than her husband, Mme. de
Thaller had measured the situation.

" Do not try to ward it off," she replied: " It would be
useless."

" Because? "

" Because M. de Trégars has found Vincent Favoral; because, at this very moment, they are together, arranging their plans."

The baron made a terrible gesture.

" Ah, thunder and lightning! " he exclaimed. " I always told you that this stupid fool, Favoral, would cause our ruin. It was so easy for you to find an occasion for him to blow his brains out."

" Was it so difficult for you to accept, M. de Trégars' offers? "

" It was you who made me refuse."

" Was it me, too, who was so anxious to get rid of Lucienne? "

For years, Mlle. Césarine had not seemed so amused; and, in a half whisper, she was humming the famous tune, from " The Pearl of Poutoise,"—

" Happy accord! Happy couple! "

M. de Thaller, beside himself, was advancing to seize the baroness: she was drawing back, knowing him, perhaps to be capable of any thing, when suddenly there was a violent knocking at the door.

" In the name of the law! "

It was a commissary of police.

And, whilst surrounded by agents, they were taken to a cab.—

" Orphan on both sides! " exclaimed Mlle. Césarine, " I am free, then. Now we'll have some fun! "

At that very moment, M. de Trégars and Mlle. Gilberte reached the Rue St. Gilles.

Hearing that her husband had been found,—

" I must see him! " exclaimed Mme. Favoral.

And, in spite of any thing they could tell her, she threw a shawl over her shoulders, and started with Mlle. Gilberte.

When they had entered Mme. Zélie's apartment, of which they had a key, they found in the parlor, with his back towards them, Vincent Favoral sitting at the table, leaning forward, and apparently writing. Mme. Favoral approached on tiptoe, and over her husband's shoulder she read what he had just written,—

"Euphrasie, my beloved, eternally-adored mistress, will you forgive me? The money that I was keeping for you, my darling, the proofs which will crush your husband—they have taken every thing from me, basely, by force. And it is my daughter—"

He had stopped there. Surprised at his immobility, Mme. Favoral called,—

"Vincent!"

He made no answer. She pushed him with her finger. He rolled to the ground. He was dead.

Three months later the great Mutual Credit suit was tried before the Sixth Court. The scandal was great; but public curiosity was strangely disappointed. As in most of these financial affairs, justice, whilst exposing the most audacious frauds, was not able to unravel the true secret.

She managed, at least, to lay hands upon every thing that the Baron de Thaller had hoped to save. That worthy was condemned to five years' prison; M. Costeclar got off with three years; and M. Jottras with two. M. Saint Pavin was acquitted.

Arrested for subornation of murder, the former Marquise de Javelle the Baroness de Thaller, was released for want of proper proof. But, implicated in the suit against her husband, she lost three-fourths of her fortune, and is now living with her daughter, whose *debut* is announced at the *Bouffes-Parisiens,* or at the *Délassements-Comiques.*

Already, before that time, Mlle. Lucienne, completely restored, had married Maxence Favoral.

Of the five hundred thousand francs which were returned to her, she applied three hundred thousand to discharge the debts of her father-in-law, and with the rest she induced her husband to emigrate to America.

Paris had become odious to both.

Marius and Mlle. Gilberte, who has now become Marquise de Trégars, have taken up their residence at the Château de Trégars, three leagues from Quimper. They have been followed in their retreat by Mme. Favoral and by General Count de Villegré.

The greater portion of his father's fortune, Marius had applied to pay off all the personal creditors of the former cashier of the Mutual Credit, all the trades-people, and also M. Chapelain, old man Désormeaux, and M. and Mme. Desclavettes.

All that is left to the Marquis and Marquise de Trégars is some twenty thousand francs a year, and if they ever lose them, it will not be at the *bourse.*

The Mutual Credit is quoted at 467.25!

THE END.

www.ingramcontent.com/pod-product-compliance
Lightning Source LLC
Chambersburg PA
CBHW032256020726
47495CB00001B/136